AF572760

THE STORY OF THE

DALLAS MAVERICKS

CREATIVE EDUCATION

Published by Creative Education
123 South Broad Street
Mankato, Minnesota 56001
Creative Education is an imprint of The Creative Company.

DESIGN AND PRODUCTION BY **EVANSDAY DESIGN**

PHOTOGRAPHS BY Getty Images (Andrew D. Bernstein / NBAE, Nathaniel S. Butler, Jerry Driendl, Stephen Dunn, Sam Forencich / NBAE, Barry Gossage, Otto Greule Jr., Andy Hayt / NBAE, Glenn James / NBAE, Mike Powell, Jeff Reinking / NBAE, Rick Stewart / ALLSPORT, Rocky Widner / NBAE), SportsChrome (Jim Jackson)

Printed in the United States of America

LIBRARY OF CONGRESS CATALOGING-IN-PUBLICATION DATA

Frisch, Aaron.
The story of the Dallas Mavericks / by Aaron Frisch.
p. cm. — (The NBA—a history of hoops)
ISBN-13: 978-1-58341-404-0
1. Dallas Mavericks (Basketball team)—History—Juvenile literature. I. Title. II. Series.

GV885.52.D34F75 2006
796.323.'64'097642812—dc22 2005051204

9 8 7 6 5 4 3

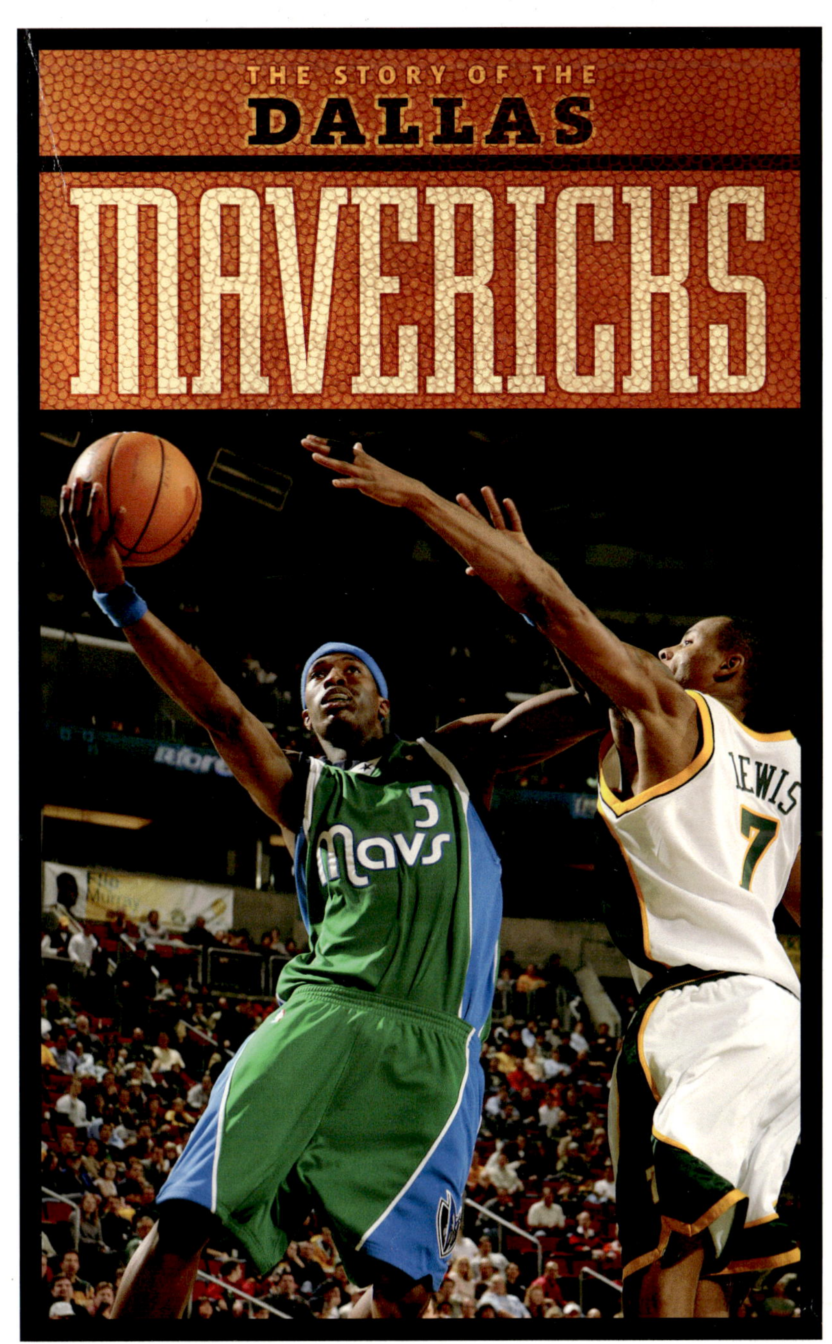

AARON FRISCH

CREATIVE EDUCATION

MAVS WIN!
MAVS WIN!
MAVS WIN!
AMERICAN AIRLINES CENTER
NBA.COM
MAVS
MAVS

What a difference a decade makes.

IN THE EARLY 1990S, DALLAS'S REUNION ARENA WAS A GHOST TOWN, INHABITED BY SPARSE CROWDS AND THE NBA'S WORST TEAM. FLASH FORWARD 10 YEARS. AMERICAN AIRLINES CENTER IS THE PLACE TO BE IN DALLAS, AND EVERY MAVERICKS GAME IS A PARTY. THROBBING MUSIC MERGES WITH THE ROAR OF 20,000 FANS AS REPLAYS ROLL ACROSS AN ENORMOUS SCREEN. ON IT, JOSH HOWARD IS SOARING FOR A DUNK, OR DIRK NOWITZKI IS SWISHING A LONG THREE-POINTER IN ANOTHER BIG PLAYOFF GAME. IT IS A NEW DECADE, AND THE MAVS ARE MOVING.

DALLAS MAVERICKS
Dallas Texas

"BIG D" BEGINNINGS

1

DALLAS IS A LARGE CITY LOCATED ON THE ROLLING prairie of northern Texas. Known today as "Big D," Dallas started out as a lonely frontier town. A trader named John Neely Bryan founded the settlement in 1841 and soon named it after George M. Dallas, the vice president of the United States in the late 1840s. As the city grew, it became a major center for banking and cotton production.

DALLAS

MAVERICKS

Dallas went from a 15–67 record to a 55–27 mark in seven seasons under original coach Dick Motta

Brad Davis gave the Mavericks 12 years of hustle, great passes, and smart leadership on the court

Ranching was also big business on the prairie surrounding Dallas. In the 1800s, cowboys often drove huge herds of horses or cattle across the vast Texas landscape. Common among these herds were mavericks—wild, headstrong animals that refused to stay with the rest of the herd. Today, Dallas is the home of a professional basketball team named the Mavericks, which joined the National Basketball Association (NBA) in 1980.

The Mavericks were optimistic heading into their first season. Their head coach was Dick Motta, who just two years earlier had led the Washington Bullets to the NBA championship. Motta was known as a demanding leader who got the most out of his players. About the only player with much to offer, though, was point guard Brad Davis, and the first-year Mavericks went just 15–67.

Dallas then selected three talented rookies in the 1981 NBA Draft: guard Rolando Blackman and forwards Mark Aguirre and Jay Vincent. Aguirre and Vincent gave the team plenty of inside muscle, while Blackman proved to be a fierce defender and a great outside shooter. These young stars led the Mavericks slowly but surely up the standings in the early '80s.

FIRST-DRAFT FIASCO

In 1980, the Mavericks used their very first NBA Draft pick on Kiki Vandeweghe, a sweet-shooting forward from the University of California at Los Angeles (UCLA). But Vandeweghe then seemed to wreck Dallas's building plans by refusing to sign with the Mavs. Although Vandeweghe's refusal upset much of Texas, the story had a happy ending for Dallas. The Mavs eventually traded him to the Denver Nuggets for two draft picks used to add standout guard Rolando Blackman (1981) and forward Sam Perkins (1984). Still, fans in the Dallas area never missed an opportunity to boo Vandeweghe when he came to town wearing a Nuggets, Trail Blazers, Knicks, or Clippers jersey over the next 13 years. "Somehow," said Greg Williams, a Dallas sports radio host, "booing Kiki has been passed down through a generation."

Although the Mavericks' steady improvement was a team effort, Aguirre emerged as Dallas's first true star. With a soft shooting touch and an assortment of spinning low-post moves, the powerful forward was almost unstoppable at times. In 1983–84, Aguirre would finish second in the NBA in scoring with 29.5 points per game.

In 1983 and 1984, the Mavericks continued to have great success in the NBA Draft, adding guard Derek Harper and forward Sam Perkins. Harper had incredibly quick hands, which made him one of the league's best defenders. After spending his first few NBA seasons backing up Davis, he became a permanent part of Dallas's starting lineup. "Derek is always ready to play at the end of a basketball game," said Blackman. "He's willing to be a hero. He's willing to be a goat—he doesn't care. You've got to get the basketball to guys like that."

In 1985–86, the Mavs traded for center James Donaldson. At a massive 7-foot-2, Donaldson gave Dallas intimidating size and strength in the middle. With his addition, the Mavs went 44–38, then whipped the Utah Jazz in the first round of the playoffs before falling to the mighty Los Angeles Lakers in round two. The Mavs were starting to run.

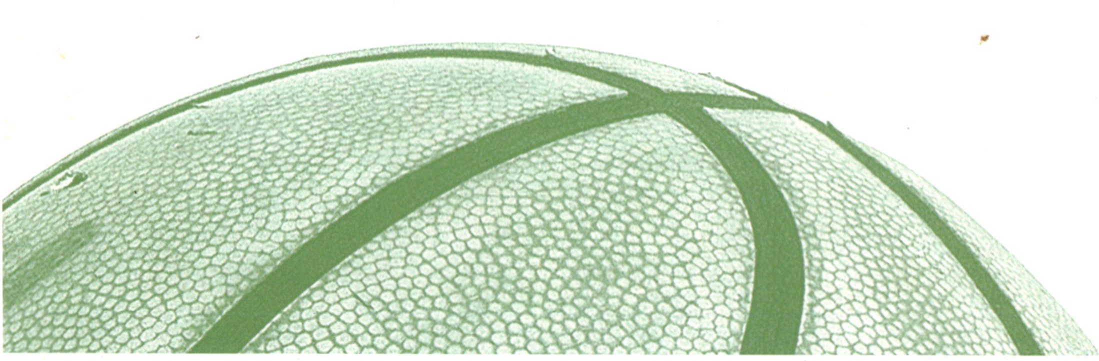

DALLAS MAVERICKS

Although short for a forward at 6-foot-6, Mark Aguirre emerged as a devastating scorer in the early '80s

A PLAYOFF STAMPEDE

BY 1986, MAVERICKS FANS HAD GROWN ACCUSTOMED to watching their team win during the regular season but get bounced from the playoffs. When the Mavs drafted towering forward Roy Tarpley, though, an NBA championship seemed within reach. The Mavs' loaded lineup went 55–27 in 1986–87. Among those wins was Dick Motta's 800th pro coaching victory—the third-highest total in NBA history. The excitement came to a halt, though, as the Mavs lost to the Seattle SuperSonics in a first-round playoff upset.

Big center Roy Tarpley astonished fans and opponents alike with his remarkable speed and agility

Longtime guard and fan favorite Rolando Blackman represented the Mavericks in four All-Star Games

Motta stepped down as coach after the bitter defeat. Dallas then hired coach John MacLeod to lead the Mavs to the next level. Coach MacLeod did that more quickly than anyone expected, partly by making Tarpley the team's sixth man. By coming off the bench late in the game, Tarpley often dominated his tired opponents. "With Roy on the floor, we talk NBA championship," said Blackman. "He brings us that little piece of magic... you see in a player who is superior to everyone he plays against."

In 1988, Tarpley and the Mavs earned playoff victories over the Houston Rockets and Denver Nuggets. The only team standing between them and the NBA Finals was their old nemesis, the Lakers. In a titanic battle, the two teams split the first six games of the Western Conference Finals, but the more experienced Lakers won Game 7 easily. Los Angeles went on to win the NBA championship, while the Mavs again went home empty-handed.

Still, Dallas fans were as enthusiastic as ever heading into the 1988–89 season. Their team had made the playoffs five straight years, inching closer to the NBA title every time. But everything then fell apart. First,

TARPLEY'S TRAGIC TALE

The story of Roy Tarpley is one of brilliant talent wasted. A 7-footer with rare quickness and a great shooting touch, Tarpley averaged 13 points and 12 rebounds a game in his second NBA season (1987–88) and was named Sixth Man of the Year. But in 1990, he was banned from the NBA for repeated drug abuse. Tarpley was allowed back into the league in 1994 and rejoined the Mavs, but alcohol abuse got him banned for good just a year later. As Tarpley went on to play basketball in Russia, China, and other distant parts of the world, Dallas fans were left to wonder what might have been. "He could have been one of the great ones," said Richie Adubato, who coached the Mavericks in the early 1990s. "No question."

Tarpley was suspended for drug abuse. Then Aguirre demanded to be traded and was dealt to the Detroit Pistons for a player—forward Adrian Dantley—who at first refused to play for Dallas. To top it all off, Donaldson went down with a serious knee injury.

In just a few weeks, the team chemistry that Dallas had worked so long to build was almost totally destroyed. Even though Dantley eventually signed and Tarpley returned from his suspension, the damage was done. The Mavericks missed the 1989 playoffs, made a brief comeback the next season, and then became the worst team in the NBA. Despite the best efforts of such players as rugged rebounder Terry Davis, Dallas went 11–71 and 13–69 in 1992–93 and 1993–94. Only late-season victories each year kept the Mavericks from setting a new NBA record for fewest wins in a season.

MULTINATIONAL MAVS By the start of the 21st century, the NBA had become popular globally, with more and more countries sending talented players to America to play. No team embraced this multicultural blending more than the Mavericks. During the 2001–02 season, Dallas featured perhaps the most nationally diverse roster in NBA history. This included Canadian point guard Steve Nash (who was born in South Africa), German forward Dirk Nowitzki, Chinese center Wang Zhizhi, Mexican forward Eduardo Najera, and French guard Tariq Abdul-Wahad. "Having players that are national heroes adds quite a bit to the team," Mavericks owner Mark Cuban said of his players from foreign lands. "Having a whole country counting on you to represent them and win is a whole lot more pressure than an NBA playoff game."

DALLAS

MAVERICKS

A controversial figure, Adrian Dantley contributed 20 points a game in the first of his two Dallas seasons

THE THREE J'S EXPERIMENT

THE ONLY SILVER LINING TO THE MAVS' HORRIBLE seasons of the early '90s was that the team consistently had high picks in the annual NBA Draft. Dallas used these picks to stockpile some of the nation's best college players. From 1992 to 1994, the Mavs drafted three outstanding young players: guard Jim Jackson, forward Jamal Mashburn, and point guard Jason Kidd.

In just his second NBA season, Jamal Mashburn set a Mavericks record with 50 points in a single game

Jim Jackson led the Mavs in scoring for three straight seasons, averaging more than 21 points a game

In 1994–95, the Mavs at last showed signs of life by assembling a respectable 36–46 record. Part of the credit went to such players as big forward Popeye Jones. The driving force behind this improvement, however, was the team's "Three J's"—Jim, Jamal, and Jason. Jackson and Mashburn combined to score nearly 50 points a game, while Kidd dished out almost 8 assists per game and was named NBA Co-Rookie of the Year (along with Detroit Pistons forward Grant Hill).

Jackson and Mashburn were talented, but Kidd was the brightest star of them all. At 6-foot-4 and 210 pounds, Kidd could do it all: run the fast break, score, rebound, and shut down opposing guards on the defensive end of the court. Even Chicago Bulls star Michael Jordan called Kidd "the future" of the NBA. In 1995–96, Kidd backed up the hype by averaging 16 points and almost 10 assists—many of them in alley-oop, behind-the-back, or "no-look" fashion—per game.

Sadly, this great collection of talent would go to waste. Mashburn suffered a serious knee injury in 1995, and feuding among players began to tear the team apart. In 1996, Dallas hired a new coach, Jim Cleamons, and installed a new half-court offense. Kidd, who preferred a faster-paced offense that allowed him to create plays in the open court, did not adapt well to the change. All of these problems triggered a major house-cleaning in Dallas. In a rapid series of stunning moves, the Mavericks traded away Kidd, Mashburn, and Jackson.

A fierce defender, brilliant passer, tough rebounder, and clutch scorer, Jason Kidd could do it all

MAVERICK MARK

Mavericks owner Mark Cuban is not a typical NBA owner. Quite possibly his team's biggest and most vocal fan, Cuban watches his Mavs from a seat near their bench, often dressed in jeans and a Dallas jersey, and frequently exchanges high-fives with his players. He also is strongly committed to fan interaction and personally responds to thousands of fan e-mails. With a net worth of almost $2 billion, made through computer, Internet, and television businesses, Cuban has proved willing to spend big money on players and accommodations to make his team a success and Dallas an exciting basketball city. "He's always there at practice, and he flies with us to every game," said forward Dirk Nowitzki. "He's just in there with his whole heart. It's great to have an owner like that."

THE NEW-LOOK MAVS

4

WHEN THE DUST FINALLY SETTLED IN 1997 AFTER ALL of the trades, Dallas had an almost entirely new team. Among the new faces in town were 7-foot-6 center Shawn Bradley, speedy point guard Robert Pack, and high-scoring swingman Michael Finley. The changes did little to improve the Mavs' fortunes, however. In 1999–00, Dallas put together a losing record for the 10th straight season.

The year 2000 signaled the start of a new era of Mavericks basketball. Playing under new team owner Mark Cuban, the Mavs finally broke their decade-long playoff drought. Dallas, the worst team in basketball just a handful of seasons before, suddenly became an NBA powerhouse, winning more than 50 games a season every year from

DALLAS

MAVERICKS

At 6-foot-7 and 225 pounds, Michael Finley had the quickness of a guard and the strength of a forward

Josh Howard's quickness, long reach, and high energy level made him a standout at both ends of the court

2000–01 to 2004–05. Finley, slick-passing point guard Steve Nash, and sharp-shooting forward Dirk Nowitzki worked fans in Dallas's new American Airlines Center into a frenzy season after season, but the Mavs always fell short of the NBA Finals in the playoffs.

That changed in 2005–06. Finley and Nash were gone, but new coach Avery Johnson found quality replacements in speedy guards Jason Terry and Josh Howard. It was Nowitzki, though, who was the real story that season. The German forward blossomed into one of the game's brightest stars, leading the team to a 60–22 record and three playoff series victories (including one over the defending NBA champion San Antonio Spurs).

Dallas fans began dreaming of victory parades when their team crushed the Miami Heat in the first two games of the 2006 NBA Finals. But the Heat, led by electrifying young guard Dwyane Wade, then broke hearts in Texas by storming back to win the next four games. Painful though the defeat was, Coach Johnson quickly turned Dallas's focus to the next season. "We aimed high this year, and I told my players that a lot of teams have to go through this [loss]," he said. "This will really hurt this summer, but I'm ready to try it again."

After rising up to become one of the NBA's top teams in the 1980s, the Mavericks endured much heartache in the 1990s. But thanks to new heroes such as Dirk Nowitzki and Josh Howard, "Big D" is once again a rocking basketball city ... and a big problem for opponents. Today's Mavericks hope to soon break away from the NBA herd and run all the way to their first world championship.

GERMANY'S FINEST

Before the year 2000, the greatest NBA player to hail from Germany was probably Detlef Schrempf, a forward who was drafted by the Mavericks in 1985 and went on to star for several other teams. But Schrempf has been surpassed as the greatest German hoopster of all time by Dallas forward Dirk Nowitzki, who entered the league in 1998. A 7-footer with the skills of a guard, Nowitzki posed serious matchup problems for opposing teams. He would often sky for an easy rebound, dribble up the court like a point guard, and sink a three-pointer. "Teams aren't putting their power forwards on Dirk any more," Mavericks coach Avery Johnson said of the German sensation, whose grasp of English developed along with his talent. "Dirk wears power forwards and centers out."

DALLAS

MAVERICKS

A soft touch and fiery attitude made German-born Dirk Nowitzki one of the NBA's elite scorers

INDEX

COORDINATION CHEMISTRY—21

Some Other IUPAC Titles of Interest from Pergamon Press

Books

ANANCHENKO: Frontiers of Bioorganic Chemistry and Molecular Biology

BANERJEA: Coordination Chemistry—20

BOND & HEFTER: Critical Survey of Stability Constants and Related Thermodynamic Data of Fluoride Complexes in Aqueous Solution

CIARDELLI & GIUSTI: Macromolecules—Structural Orders in Polymers and Biopolymers

FRANZOSINI & MANESI: Thermodynamic and Transport Properties of Organic Acids

FREIDLINA & SKOROVA: Organic Sulfur Chemistry

GOETHALS: Polymeric Amines and Ammonium Salts

HÖGFELDT: Stability Constants of Metal-Ion Complexes, Part A: Inorganic Ligands

LAIDLER: 28th International Congress of Pure and Applied Chemistry

PARRY: Boron Chemistry—4

PERRIN: Stability Constants of Metal-Ion Complexes, Part B: Organic Ligands

POPOVYCH: Tetraphenylborates

RIGAUDY & KLESNEY: Nomenclature of Organic Chemistry

STEC: Phosphorus Chemistry Directed Towards Biology

TROST & HUTCHINSON: Organic Synthesis—Today and Tomorrow

VARMAVUORI: 27th International Congress of Pure and Applied Chemistry

Journals

CHEMISTRY INTERNATIONAL, the news magazine for chemists in all fields of specialization in all countries of the world

PURE AND APPLIED CHEMISTRY, the international research journal publishing proceedings of IUPAC conferences, nomenclature rules and technical reports

INTERNATIONAL UNION OF PURE AND APPLIED CHEMISTRY
(Inorganic and Organic Chemistry Divisions)

in conjunction with

Centre National de la Recherche Scientifique
Laboratoire de Chimie de Coordination, Toulouse
Université Paul Sabatier, Toulouse

COORDINATION CHEMISTRY—21

Proceedings of the
21st International Conference on Coordination Chemistry
Toulouse, France, 7-11 July 1980

Editor

J. P. LAURENT

Laboratoire de Chimie de Coordination du CNRS, Toulouse, France

PERGAMON PRESS

OXFORD · NEW YORK · TORONTO · SYDNEY · PARIS · FRANKFURT

U.K. — Pergamon Press Ltd., Headington Hill Hall, Oxford OX3 0BW, England

U.S.A. — Pergamon Press Inc., Maxwell House, Fairview Park, Elmsford, New York 10523, U.S.A.

CANADA — Pergamon Press Canada Ltd., Suite 104, 150 Consumers Rd., Willowdale, Ontario M2J 1P9, Canada

AUSTRALIA — Pergamon Press (Aust.) Pty. Ltd., P.O. Box 544, Potts Point, N.S.W. 2011, Australia

FRANCE — Pergamon Press SARL, 24 rue des Ecoles, 75240 Paris, Cedex 05, France

FEDERAL REPUBLIC OF GERMANY — Pergamon Press GmbH, 6242 Kronberg-Taunus, Hammerweg 6, Federal Republic of Germany

First edition 1981

British Library Cataloguing in Publication Data

International Conference on Coordination Chemistry (*21st: 1980: Toulouse*)
Coordination chemistry-21. - (IUPAC symposium series)
1. Coordination compounds - Congresses
I. Title II. Laurent, J. P.
III. International Union of Pure and Applied Chemistry. *Inorganic Chemistry Division.*
IV. International Union of Pure and Applied Chemistry. *Organic Chemistry Division.*
V. Series
541.2'242 QD474

ISBN 0-08-025300-8

In order to make this volume available as economically and as rapidly as possible the author's typescript has been reproduced in its original form. This method has its typographical limitations but it is hoped that they in no way distract the reader.

Printed in Great Britain by A. Wheaton & Co. Ltd., Exeter

CONTENTS

*Previously published in *Pure and Applied Chemistry*, Vol. 52, No. 10, October 1980

Contents

Organizing Committee

Chairman

F. Gallais

Members

J. Dehand, R. Hugel, Y. Jeannin
O. Kahn, R. Poilblanc, J.-G. Riess
J. Tirouflet, I. Tkatchenko, R. Weiss

INTERNATIONAL UNION OF PURE AND APPLIED CHEMISTRY

IUPAC Secretariat: Bank Court Chambers, 2-3 Pound Way,
Cowley Centre, Oxford OX4 3YF, UK

PREFACE

This volume contains the lectures given during the course of the XXIst I.C.C.C. which was held in Toulouse from 7 to 11 July 1980.

The Conference was somewhat more classical in its form than some of the previous ones in the sense that sufficient time was reserved for oral communications - notwithstanding the posters - so that the number of lectures was necessarily limited.
There should have been five plenary lectures and eleven section lectures but the untimely loss of Professor Paolo CHINI from Milano deprived the Conference of the up to date panorama of clusters chemistry he had been expected to draw. The four other plenary lectures were devoted quite naturally to general subjects which for various reasons have now a great interest.

Professor R. MASON, FRS, first described the state of the art in the field of electronic structure of metal complexes. It was certainly appropriate to do so at a time when access to "ab initio" calculations is such that controversies about older calculation methods tend to be obsolete while X-ray and neutron diffraction experiments provide us with accurate maps of electronic densities.

Professor F.A. COTTON,in a sense, had a similar concern when he compared experimental work and the results of calculations (SCF - Xα - SW method) on a variety of cluster compounds and binuclear species with multiple metal to metal bonds, insisting on the mutual interaction between experiments and calculations.

Professor H.B. GRAY when he spoke about solar energy storage reactions involving metal complexes was also exploring a field which has recently received much attention. The properties of the complex systems of ruthenium he described are promising inasmuch as their irradiation by visible or ultraviolet light in aqueous solutions leads to the production of hydrogen through redox reactions.

Finally Professor H.C. FREEMAN found in the mechanism of electron transfer in blue copper proteins (namely in platocyanin and azurin) the pretext he needed to draw attention at the same time to the importance which is now recognised to inorganic biochemistry and to the progress of crystal chemistry. He showed how crystal structural results provide useful bench-marks for the discussion of kinetic, thermodynamic, spectroscopic and theoretical studies.

The eleven other lectures were given in the frame of one of the five sections and are more or less directly related to the corresponding topics.

Section 1 dealt with "Electronic stucture of coordination compounds : theoretical and experimental approaches". In his lecture, Professor P. COPPENS reported the results obtained in the way of electron density distribution by X-ray and neutron diffraction for a number of organometallic and coordination compounds. While he found evidence for covalent metal-ligand interaction in some complexes such as $Cr(CO)_6$ for example, it is striking that he could not, as a rule, observe a significant density accumulation in the regions where metal-metal bonds should be found.
For his part Professor K. SAITO, an expert in Inorganic Molecular Dissymmetry, has discussed circular dichroism of some oxo complexes of early transition elements which play a part in some biological systems. He has shown the importance in this case of an asymmetrical distortion of the ligands which overcomes the classical effects of configuration and environment.

Section 2 was devoted to "Unusual properties of coordination compounds in the solid state". An example of such properties in terms of magnetism was given by Professor D.N. HENDRIKSON who has studied the unusual way in which some spin-crossover transition metal complexes magnetic moment decreases with temperature.
On the other hand electrical properties were the basis of Doctor L.V. INTERRANTE lecture on π-donor-acceptor compounds derived from the interaction of coordination compounds with various organic molecules. A number of such new compounds have novel solid state properties, mainly a high one-dimensional electric conductivity.

Section 3 was concerned with "Coordination Chemistry in solutions" which has perhaps not received in the last years the consideration it still deserves. Professor A.A. VLCEK analysing the set of data characteristic of a redox series discussed the difference in potential drops connected with the removal of an electron from a doubly or singly occupied orbital and explained how some chemically reversible systems can be electrochemically irreversible.

This last property, as well as the influence of substituents on the redox active centers offer new means of modifying the stability and reactivity of individual members of redox series. Professor R.C. MEHROTRA reviewed the researches he has conducted with his team on alkoxides of later 3d transition elements ; he showed that, while the simple derivatives of these metals are all polymeric, insoluble and not volatile compounds, they may lead to monomeric bimetallic alkoxides, $M[Al(OR)_4]_n$ which are volatile, soluble in organic solvents and may behave as new polydentate ligands.

In section 4 : "Ligand reactivity in transition metal complexes, applications to synthesis and catalysis", synthesis and reactivity received effectively a great deal of attention and were introduced by three lectures. Professor M.L.H. GREEN spoke of the reactivity of some simple hydrocarbon ligands attached to transition metal, mainly cyclopentadiene and bis-arene derivatives ; Professor J.A. IBERS of the interaction of small molecules with transition metals (but diazofluorene, diazocyclopentadiene and norbornadiene, are they really small molecules ?) and Professor L.M. VENANZI reviewed the identified pathways for the insertion reaction of alkenes and alkynes into transition metal hydrides.

The 5th and last section was reserved for the "Application of Coordination Chemistry to Biology".

Professor M.E. VOL'PIN put forward the idea that synthetic metal complexes can be used for regulation of certain biochemical processes in a living cell and so compete with enzymes. And he gave successful examples of that nature concerning some redox processes at the level of D.N.A. and cytochrome C.

The topic treated by Professor B. SARKAR was well defined as it was the biological coordination chemistry of nickel(II). This is in fact a medical problem as workers engaged in nickel mining have a high level of metal in their serum and seem at the same time specially exposed to carcinogenesis. Professor SARKAR has succeded in identifying the Ni(II) transport site of human albumine and has shown that triethylenetetramine and D-penicillamine are most efficient for the removal of Ni from rats after toxic accumulation. No doubt that human intoxication will find it's remedy very soon.

As may be understood from this brief review the fifteen lectures given in the course of the XXIst I.C.C.C. offer a large variety and cover most of what is now the field of true Coordination Chemistry. It is hoped that they will convey a genuine appreciation of the way in which this discipline is now so rapidly developing.

Toulouse, France

F. GALLAIS

VALENCE ELECTRON DISTRIBUTIONS IN TRANSITION METAL COMPLEXES: STATE OF THE ART STUDIES

R. Mason and J. N. Varghese

School of Molecular Sciences, University of Sussex, Brighton BN1 9QJ, UK

ABSTRACT

A study of valence electron density distributions in transition metal complexes is described using the novel method of polarised neutron diffraction.

INTRODUCTION

Some thirty years of researches have taken discussions of bonding in transition metal complexes from the simple crystal field theories - with their early useful rationalisation of some magnetic,spectral and associated properties of complexes - through semi-empirical models and, finally, to ab-initio molecular orbital theories; the early success of the valence bond theory has not been followed up, largely on account of computational convenience. Running through all of this is the recognition that the redistribution of the valence electrons on bond formation, on which chemistry is based, can be assessed only by indirect evidence. Experimental studies of bonding have nearly always related to molecular energy levels, it being relatively rare that direct conclusions can be drawn on the spatial relationships of electrons in bonds. Spectroscopic experiments provide, albeit with certain assumptions, molecular eigenvalues; only diffraction experiments provide a direct link between observations (reflexion intensities) and molecular eigenfunctions.

The history of the application of X-ray diffraction to studies of electron densities in crystals goes back many years - sodium chloride and diamond featured early. Dawson's work on diamond (Ref.1) was particularly noteworthy for it showed, for the first time, how 'forbidden' X-ray intensities could be explained on the basis of aspherical electron densities at each carbon atom. Even in 1960, two dimensional X-ray photography with visually estimated intensities could demonstrate, in addition to hydrogen atoms, nitrogen lone pair features in a largish organic molecule (Ref.2) (Fig.1). In the 1970's we have seen improvements in data

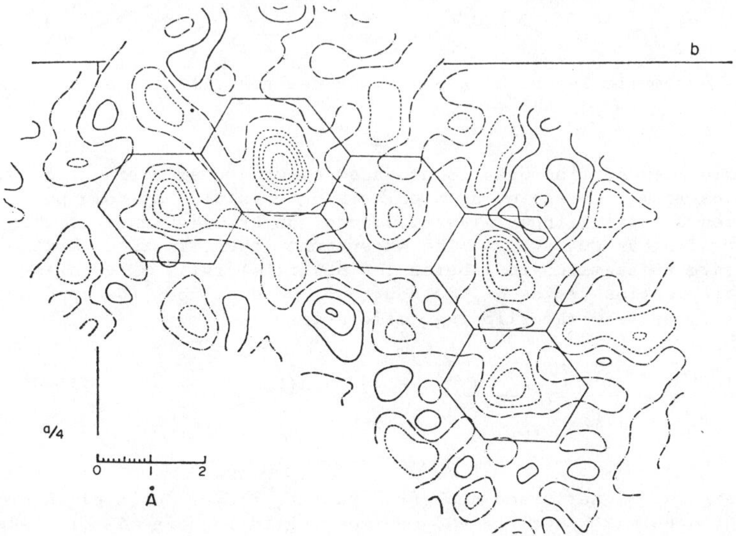

Fig.1. The electron density of 1.2:8.9-dibenzacridine from which all atoms have been subtracted (Ref.2).

accuracy and, coupled with conventional neutron scattering experiments, a number of reports (Ref.3) have described the distribution of electrons in small molecules containing elements from the first row of the Periodic Table. When we move on to complexes of transition metal ions, the X-ray experiments begin to have the rather obvious limitations associated with the significant determination of small electronic redistribution in the presence of the high local densities associated with the metal ions. Even so a significant corpus of observations is to hand (Ref.4) which, inter alia, have demonstrated aspherical electron densities around the metal atoms in simple complexes and the lack of significant density between the metal atoms in molecules where for a variety of reasons (18-electron accountancy; metal to metal separation and so on) one infers direct metal to metal bonding. The status of the X-ray method is being reviewed by P.Coppens at this Conference (Ref.5) and so little more needs saying here. Rather we shall focus on the exploration of what has been one of the most significant physical properties of transition metal complexes: paramagnetism; and the determination of some eigenfunctions of open shell molecules using the very novel method of polarised neutron scattering.

The experiment

The polarised neutron technique provides an extremely sensitive method for studying magnetisation distributions in crystalline materials. A neutron interact with atomic nuclei through the strong nuclear interaction and with electrons by virtue of its magnetic moment. The magnetisation density in a crystal is due both to the intrinsic magnetic moment of electrons (spin) and to the magnetic moment generated by moving electrons (orbital magnetisation). The magnetisation density due to spin reflects the spatial distribution of the unpaired electrons, but that due to their orbiting motion is less simply interpreted.

An instrument for doing polarised neutron diffraction experiments is illustrated in Fig.2.

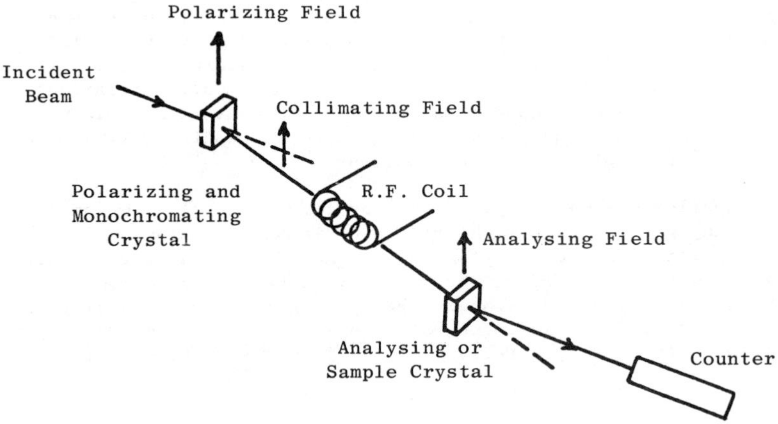

Fig.2. A schematic layout of a polarised neutron diffraction experiment.

A monochromatic polarised neutron beam is produced by Bragg reflection of polychromatic unpolarised neutrons from the reactor by a polarising crystal. At some point in the flight path to the specimen a 'spin flipper' is introduced: an RF coil (tuned to the Larmor frequency) or one of a number of other devices. The experiment, then, is to determine a 'flipping ratio' for each Bragg reflection, that being the numerical ratio of counting rates for the 'up' and 'down' polarisation states of the neutrons incident upon the specimen. In the case of a centrosymmetric crystal, the flipping ratio R is

$$R = \frac{N^2 + M^2 + 2NM}{N^2 + M^2 - 2NM} = \left(\frac{1+\gamma}{1-\gamma}\right)^2 \quad \text{where } \gamma = \frac{M}{N}$$

here M and N are the magnetic and nuclear structure factors of a given Bragg reflection; N is determined by a normal (unpolarised) neutron scattering experiment. When magnetic neutron scattering is much weaker than nuclear scattering we have

$$R = 1 + 4\gamma$$

Derivation of spin densities

Early use of magnetic structure factors was confined to detailed studies of the form (scattering) factors of simple systems such as the metals iron, cobalt and nickel (Ref.6). With increasing sophistication of equipment, increasing neutron fluxes and a developing formalism for calculating magnetic structure factors, the study of more complex magnetic systems having chemical interest has become possible.

We need then to set down some relevant approaches and the theoretical models that allow them to be developed. We noted earlier that the magnetisation density in a crystal reflects spin and orbital contributions. Where, as in some of the examples we discuss below, we have complex ions with orbitally non-degenerate ground states, we can associate the magnetisation density largely with the appropriate 1-electron spin density functions. The spin distribution may be expressed in terms of the partial occupation of molecular orbitals, accompanied by some polarisation of fully occupied orbitals.

Quite the simplest utilisation of the Bragg magnetic structure factors is to produce their Fourier transform. Two illustrations of this procedure are shown in Figs. 3 and 4. Figure 3 is the Fourier series which gives the magnetisation density in the CrF_6^{3-} ion in crystals of K_2NaCrF_6 (Ref.7); Fig.4 is the corresponding (two dimensional) density in a copper(II) dimer (Ref.8). But the limitations attached to quantitative interpretations of Fourier

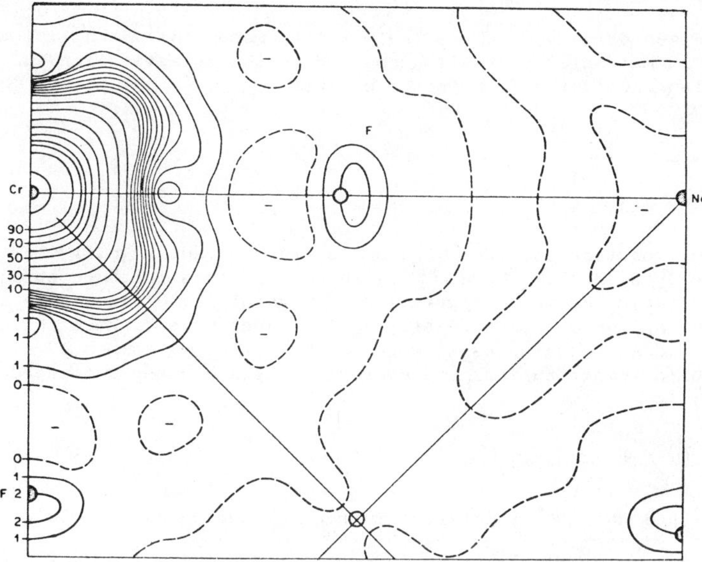

Fig.3. Fourier section through the Cr and F sites obtained from magnetic data on K_2NaCrF_6 (Ref.7).

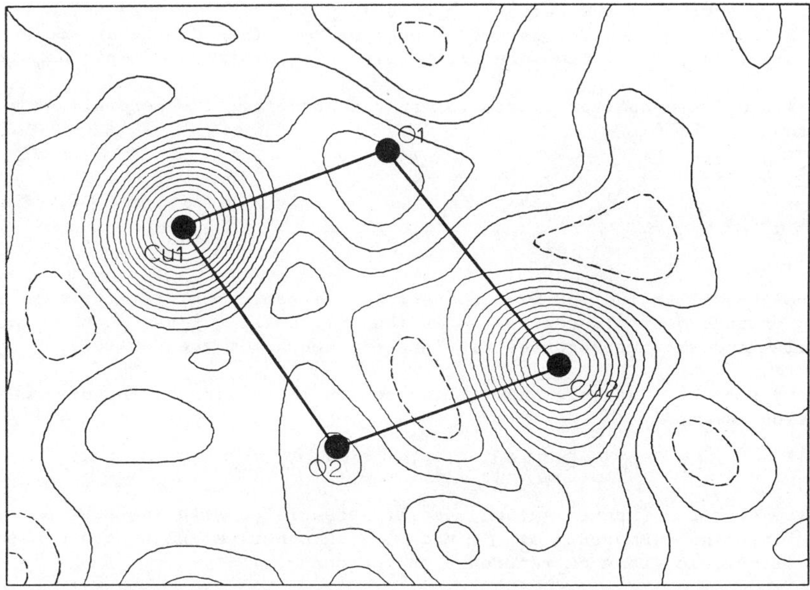

Fig.4. Fourier projection on the a b plane obtained from magnetic scattering data of aquabis(bipyridyl)di-μ-hydroxo-sulphato dicopper(II) (Ref.8).

series are well-known - they are, for the most part, concerned with series termination effects. In conventional crystallography, quantitative data can be obtained by Difference Fourier methods or least squares methods; we emphasise the second approach.

The magnetic structure factor is readily expressed as

$$\underset{\sim}{M}(\underset{\sim}{k}) = \sum_n f_n(\underset{\sim}{k}) \underset{\sim}{M}_n \exp\{i\underset{\sim}{k}\cdot\underset{\sim}{r}_n\}$$

with $f(\underset{\sim}{k})$ a magnetic form factor for a given atom, n, being

$$f(\underset{\sim}{k}) = \frac{\int m(\underset{\sim}{r}) \exp(i\underset{\sim}{k}\cdot\underset{\sim}{r})\, dr^3}{\int m(\underset{\sim}{r})\, dr^3}$$

$m(\underset{\sim}{r})$ is the atom's magnetisation density. $\underset{\sim}{M}_n$ is the magnetic moment of the nth atom positioned at $\underset{\sim}{r}_n$ from the origin. The summation is over all atoms. When the magnetisation is due to electrons in a single unfilled shell, the form factor becomes

$$f(\underset{\sim}{k}) = \sum_{\ell} A_{\ell}(\hat{\underset{\sim}{k}}) \langle j_{\ell}(|\underset{\sim}{k}|)\rangle$$

where

$$\langle j_{\ell}(\underset{\sim}{k})\rangle = \int_0^{\infty} U^2(r)\, j_{\ell}(kr)\, r^2\, dr$$

$j_{\ell}(kr)$ is the spherical Bessel function of order ℓ and $U^2(r)$ the radial distribution function of electrons in the open shell. The $A_{\ell}(\hat{\underset{\sim}{k}})$ are coefficients which depend on the scattering vector $\underset{\sim}{k}$ and on the magnetic configuration. In general, 'd' electrons have three coefficients A_0, A_2 and A_4 which are non-zero; A_0 is a coefficient which reflects spherical symmetry while A_2 and A_4 contain, as it were, quantisation of spin and 'directionality' of bonding. When orbital contributions are present, they are often estimated via a dipole approximation (Ref.9)

$$f(\underset{\sim}{k}) = 2S\langle j_0(\underset{\sim}{k})\rangle + L(\langle j_0(k)\rangle + \langle j_2(k)\rangle)$$

We showed, in an early note (Ref.10), how polarised neutron scattering data could define non-spherical d- and p-electron distributions: for the $(CrF_6)^{3-}$ ion a configuration of $t_{2g}^{2.61(2)}$ was defined with delocalisation of 0.11(3)e on to each fluorine atom; for $COCl_4^{2-}$, Figgis, Reynolds and Williams (Ref.11) have similarly modelled the spin density with a determination of the cobalt 3d orbital population as t_2 2.71(15) e 0.0 ± 0.1 spins and the spin population in each chlorine being mainly in the p σ orbital (0.06 ± 0.01 spins). This early approach had definitional value - it indicated the intrinsic sensitivity of the magnetic scattering data to non-spherical features of the metal's spin density and to covalence parameters. We now describe (Ref.12,13) a more general way of presenting results and, in particular, of making comparisons with, say, <u>ab initio</u> molecular orbital calculations of spin densities.

Whether we have X-ray, neutron-nuclear or neutron-spin scattering, the generalised structure factor can be written

$$F(\underset{\sim}{k}) = \sum_{Cell} f_j(\underset{\sim}{k}) \exp\{-i2\pi\underset{\sim}{h}\cdot\underset{\sim}{x}_j - \underset{\sim}{h}^T\cdot\underset{\approx}{\beta}_j\underset{\sim}{h}\}$$

where $\underset{\sim}{k} = 2\pi(h\underset{\sim}{a}^* + k\underset{\sim}{b}^* + \ell\underset{\sim}{c}^*)$

$\underset{\sim}{h} = (h, k, \ell)$ are the Miller indices with respect to the reciprocal lattice cell edges $\underset{\sim}{a}^*$, b^*, c^*; the run extends over all centres j in the unit cell; $\underset{\sim}{x}_j$ and $\underset{\approx}{\beta}_j$ are the positional coordinates and the mean squares displacement tensor of the centre j.

The scattering (form) factor f_j associated with the centre j is given by the one centre density representation as

$$f_j(\underset{\sim}{k}) = \int \rho(r,\theta,\phi) \exp(i\underset{\sim}{k}\cdot\underset{\sim}{r})\, d\tau = f_j(S,\alpha,\beta)$$

ρ_j is the one centre electron (magnetisation) density associated with the centre j; (r,θ,ϕ) and (S,α,β) are the components of $\underset{\sim}{r}$ and $\underset{\sim}{k}$ in spherical polar coordinates with respect to a local orthogonic frame of reference on the centre j.

In a multipole expansion (Ref. 12) the density is expanded as a linear sum of density fragments

$$\rho_{\ell m}(r,\theta,\phi) = M_\ell^m N_\ell^m Z_\ell^m(\theta,\phi) R(r)$$

$$\ell = 0,1,2,3,4,\ldots$$

$$-\ell \leq m \leq \ell$$

R(r) is the radial density distribution describing the density around the centre j , Z_ℓ^m are multipole functions (Surface or Tesseral Harmonics) given by

$$Z_\ell^m(\theta,\phi) = Y_\ell^{|m|}(\cos\theta)\cos(|m|\phi) \qquad m \geq 0$$

$$= Y_\ell^{|m|}(\cos\theta)\sin(|m|\phi) \qquad m < 0$$

Y_ℓ^m are associated Legendre functions and N_ℓ^m a normalisation factor which requires

$$\int |\rho_{\ell m}|\, d\tau = 2$$

M_ℓ^m is the population of the multipole fragment $\rho_{\ell m}$ and is normalised so that it becomes a measure of the number of electrons transferred from the negative to positive lobes of the surface harmonic (Ref.14).

Fourier transforms of multipole density fragments are

$$f_{\ell m}(S,\alpha,\beta) = \int \rho_{\ell m}(r,\theta,\phi)\exp(-i\,\underset{\sim}{k}\cdot\underset{\sim}{r})\,d\tau$$

$$= i^\ell M_\ell^m N_\ell^m 4\pi \langle j(Sr)\rangle Z_\ell^m(\alpha,\beta)$$

where

$$\langle j_\ell(Sr)\rangle = \int_0^\infty R(r) j_\ell(Sr) r^2 dr$$

and

$$S = |\underset{\sim}{k}| = 4\pi \sin\theta\, \lambda^{-1}$$

and j_ℓ are spherical Bessel functions.

Thus the structure factor can be recast in multipole terms as

$$F(\underset{\sim}{k}) = \sum_{\substack{\text{Cell} \\ \text{Centres } n}} \left\{ \sum_{\ell=0}^{\infty} \sum_{m=-\ell}^{\ell} i^\ell M_{n,\ell}^m N_\ell^m 4\pi \langle j_{n,\ell}\rangle Z_\ell^m(\alpha,\beta)\cdot \exp(-i\, 2\pi \underset{\sim}{h}\cdot\underset{\sim}{x}_n - \underset{\sim}{h}^T\cdot\underset{\approx}{\beta}_n\cdot\underset{\sim}{h}) \right\}$$

For the most part, this expression is adequate if terms up to hexadecupoles are included. There are often times when the number of non-zero multipoles is determined by local (crystallographic) symmetry arguments. A least squares convergence of the set of F(S) to the observed structure factors is via the optimisation of $M_{n,\ell}^m$, the $\underset{\sim}{x}_n$ and $\underset{\approx}{\beta}_n$ having been established by a conventional neutron scattering experiment. The radial function R(r) is constructed from Hartree-Fock or, perhaps, simple Slater functions; flexibility can be achieved via Kappa refinement methods (Ref.15) or by a Taylor expansion technique (Ref.16).

We have shown (Ref.17) how it is possible to interpret multipole populations in terms of chemical 'orbital' populations: by a simple linear transformation 'orbital' populations determined from one-centred orbital scattering factors are constrained multipole refinements - for 'd' orbitals up to hexadecupole level and for 'p' orbitals up to the quadrupole level. In determining 'orbital' populations one must remember that two centre orbital product terms are projected into one-centre terms, so any one-centre density representation will have built into it the projected two-centre density functions. 'Orbital' populations obtained by single centre density functions are related to the diagonal elements of the Dirac density matrix and should reflect the spin state of the metal ion.

But we believe a more valuable interpretation of multipole parametrisations of the spin density comes from a reconstruction of the total spin density from the multipole density fragments via the equation (Ref.12,13)

$$\rho(\underset{\sim}{r}) = \sum_{\substack{\text{Sphere}\\\text{centres } j}} \sum_{l,m} \rho^{j}_{lm}(r,\theta,\phi)$$

where the sum is over a sphere which contributes to the density of the cluster.

The results

Our first example of the quality of information that can be obtained from experiment and the correlation with theories of open shell molecules is summarised, in effect, by Fig.5. The experimental spin density (Fig.5a) shows typical 'd' orbital spin density around the chromium ion, a transfer of spin density to a fluorine 2pπ orbital and a negative spin density in the Cr - F σ- antibonding orbital. The transformation (Ref.17) of the multipole populations into 'local orbital' populations demonstrated a $t_{2g}^{2.76(1)}$configuration on the metal, no significant population in the 'e' orbitals, and a spin density of 0.31(0) in a metal 4s orbital; there is a spin transfer to the fluorine ligands which effectively includes a redistribution of 0.02e from the σ- to the π- bond framework with a negative $p_z(P(\sigma))$ orbital population of 0.05e (and a consequent +0.03e in the 2pπ(x,y) orbitals). Spin polarised Hartree-Fock calculations give the spin transfer coefficients for Cr(III) in CrF_6^{3-} as -0.022e and +0.026e for $f\sigma^*$ and $f\pi$ (semi-empirical molecular orbital) (Ref.19) and -0.048e and +0.010e from an X-α calculation (Ref.20). More conveniently Figs. 5b and 5c summarise our calculations, at a double zeta level, based on restricted and

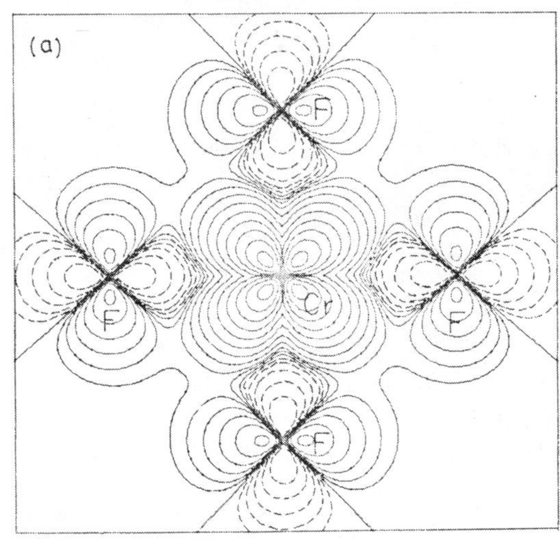

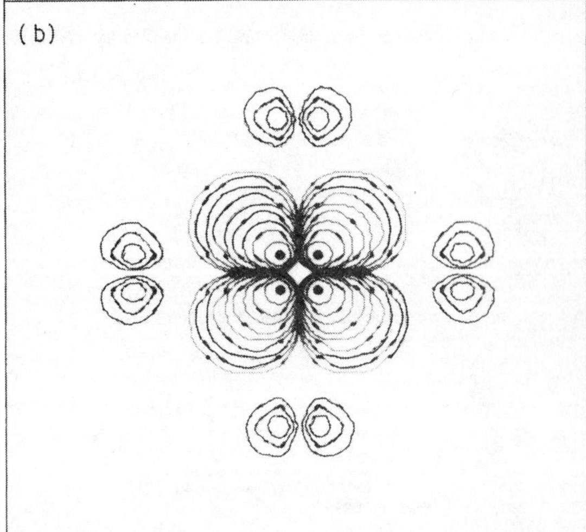

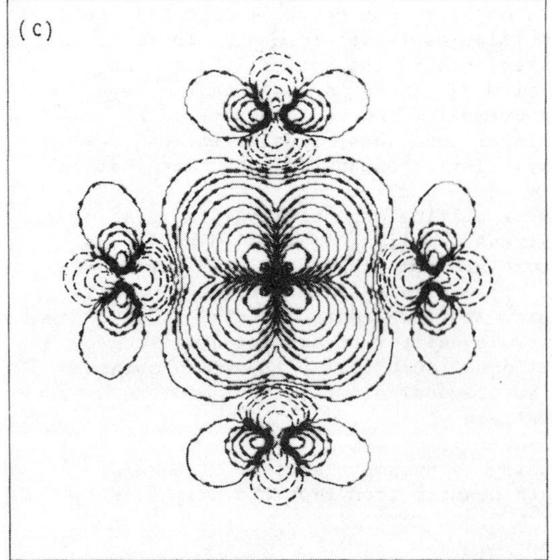

Fig.5. The spin density in the $[CrF_6]^{3-}$ ion obtained from (a) a multipole analysis (Ref.17) of the magnetic data (Ref.7), (b) restricted and (c) unrestricted Hartree-Fock ab initio calculation at a double zeta level (Ref.18), through a plane containing the Cr centre and four F centres.

unrestricted Hartree-Fock theories; the comparison shows the importance of unrestricted Hartree-Fock in representing adequately the exchange correlation effects ($p\sigma$ versus $p\pi$) which are so evident from experiment. (It is worth noting here that the calculated wave-functions are a much more sensitive test of theory than the corresponding eigenvalues.)

Next we look at the spin density in the $CoCl_4^{2-}$ determined from the multipole analysis (Ref.21) of magnetic and structure factors (Ref.22) provided by diffraction from magnetically polarised crystals of Cs_3CoCl_5. Figure 6 shows 'mouse ears' of spin density centred

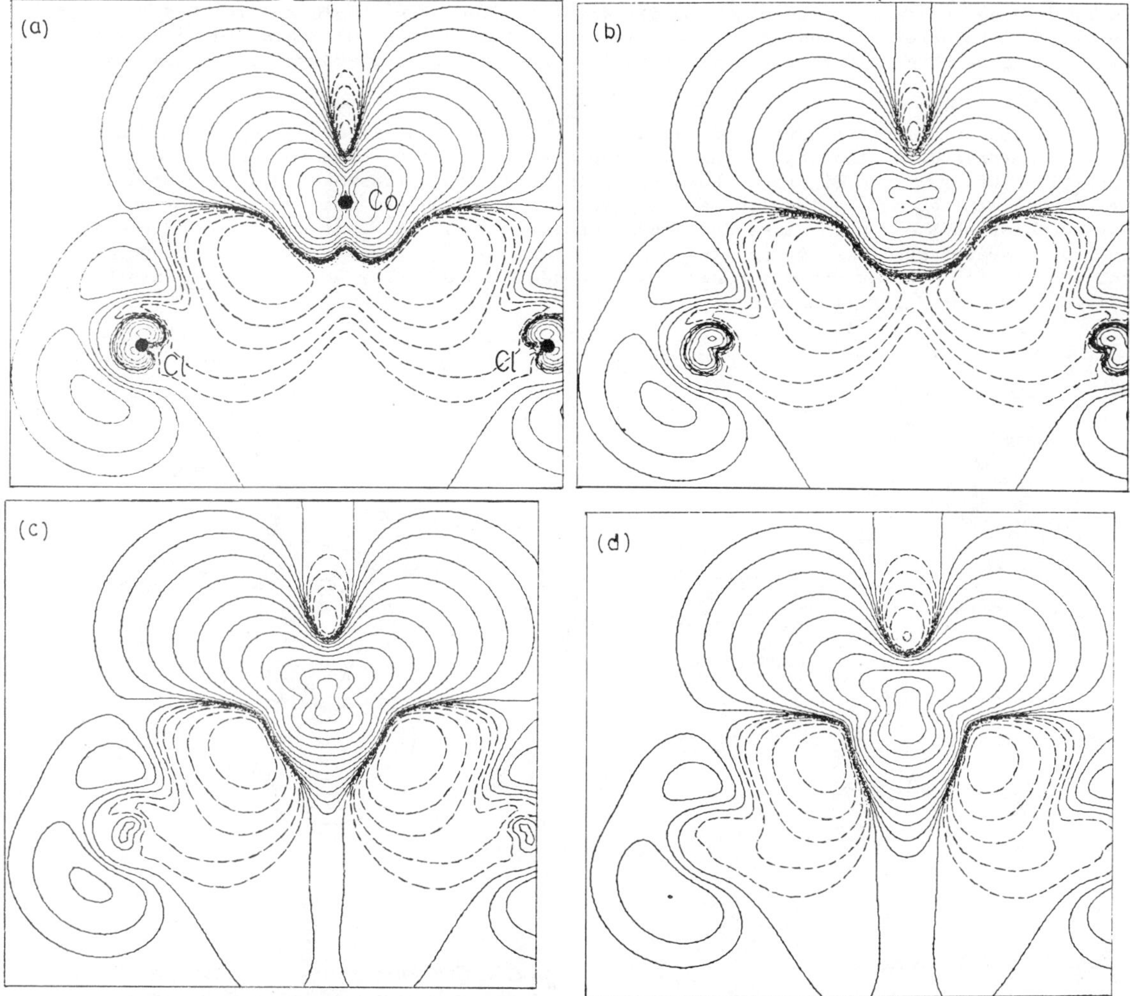

Fig.6. The spin density in the $(CoCl_4)^{2-}$ ion in Cs_3CoCl_5 obtained from a multipole analysis (Ref.21) of magnetic data (Ref.22) for (a) in the plane parallel to the c-axis of Co and two chlorine, (b) at 0.2Å, (c) 0.4Å, (d) 0.6Å above the plane.

at the cobalt, a sharp concentration of density at the chlorine centres and, once more, a significant negative spin density in the metal-ligand σ - framework. The succeeding maps show the spin densities in sections of 0.2Å, 0.4Å etc. above the plane containing the Cl - Co - Cl nuclei and show the emergence of the σ- antibonding state with its positive spin density directed away from the ligand and the negative spin density directed towards the chlorines. The orbital populations determined by appropriate transformation of the multipole population parameters are

$$d_{xy}^{\,0.88(8)} \quad d_{xz,yz}^{\,0.87(7)} \quad d_{x^2-y^2}^{\,0.16(8)} \quad d_{z^2}^{\,-0.02(6)}$$

in other words, essentially $t_2^{\,2.62(7)}\ e^{0.14(7)}$

with the chlorine calculating at

$$p_x^{\,-0.01(2)},\ p_y^{\,0.03(2)},\ p_z^{\,0.06(1)}$$

There is no significant population of the metal 'e' orbitals although a population of $d_{x^2-y^2}$ would be consistent with the deviation from Td symmetry; σ-bonding is significant; π-bonding is at least three times less so. We shall compare the experimental (Ref. 21) and theoretical spin densities in detail elsewhere (Ref. 18).

So much then for the quantitative information that we can now obtain experimentally on the eigenfunctions of open-shell molecules and the quality of theories that are needed to match these data. But we can add that while we have chosen, for obvious reasons, to look at 'natural' paramagnetic molecules (and hence at only, at best, non-bonding spin density distributions) we can anticipate the move towards studies of cationic species and hence of the orbital character of bonding states. An examination of multiple bond orders between metals would be of high interest and feasibility studies of bond orders of 3.5 has begun. (Ref. 25).

The most complex system we have studied, and it illustrates a different emphasis of application of polarised neutron scattering, is aquabis(bipyridyl)di-μ-hydroxo-sulphato di-copper(II) (Ref. 8, 23). Figure 6 shows the spin densities corresponding to the experimentally determined multipoles: in (a) only the scalar, dipoles, quadrupoles, octupoles and hexadecupoles on the copper atoms and scalar moments on the oxygenations were refined in the least squares analysis; in (b) two dipole moments on the oxygen atoms were added to the analysis; in (c) two quadrupole moments were added to the scalar and dipole moments being refined on the bridging ligands.

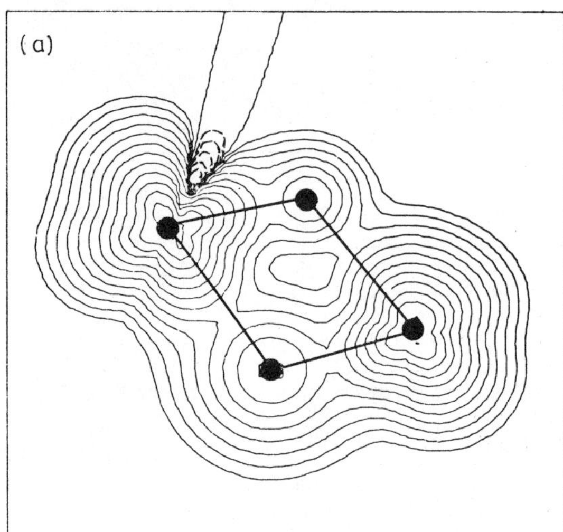

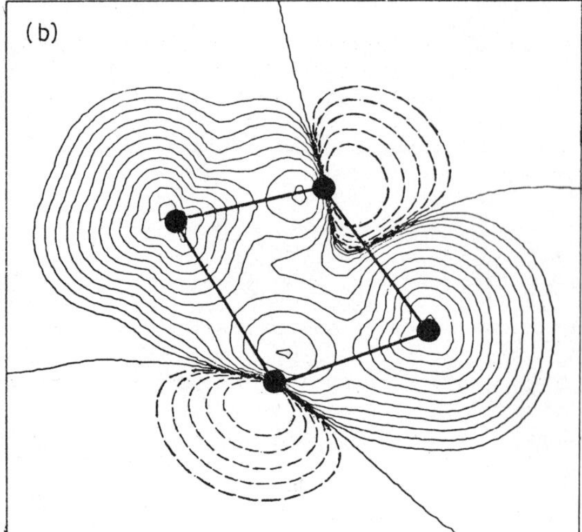

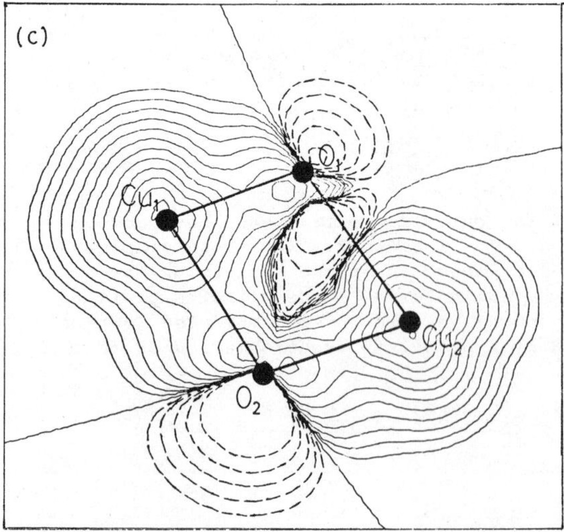

Fig.7. The spin density projected on to the a-b plane of aquabis(bipyridyl)-di-μ-hydroxo-sulphato di copper(II) obtained from a multipole analysis, (Ref.23) with (a) scalars (b) scalars and dipoles (c) scalars, dipoles and quadrupoles on the bridging oxygens, of magnetic data (Ref.8).

Figures 7a - 7c show essential invariance and equivalences of the spin densities in the $d_{x^2-y^2}$ obitals of the copper ions while the similar features of the oxygen spin densities in Figs. 7b and 7c indicate that inclusions of higher multipoles on the oxygen atoms is unnecessary. Quantitatively, the experimental spin densities and, in particular, the large negative spin densities directed away from the oxygen atoms can be understood in terms of usual exchange correlation effects.

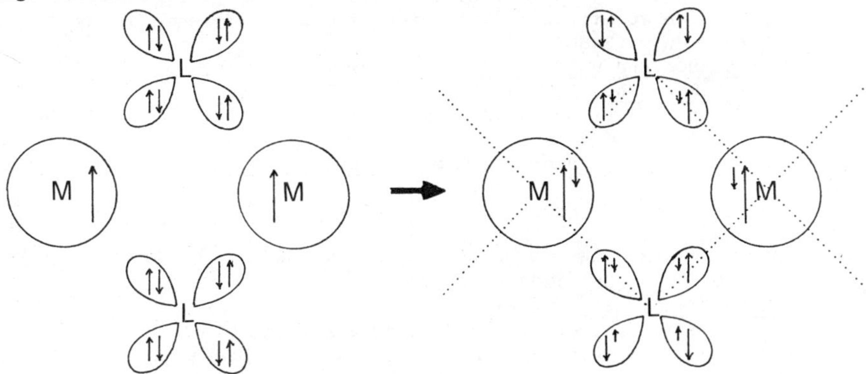

Analysis of the multipole moments show that the orbital populations are 0.90(1)e and 0.10(1)e respectively on the copper and oxygen atom. Obviously the system is too complex to analyse by the sophisticated theories we have invoked earlier; but we can clearly see that neutron scattering experiments can clarify exchange processes in discrete binuclear systems and, indeed, in extended ferromagnetic molecular crystals such as phthalocyaninato manganese(II) (Ref. 24).

The way ahead

We have demonstrated that the relatively new technique of polarised neutron scattering is capable of giving experimental information on the chemical bond in simple complexes such as CrF_6^{3-} and $CoCl_4^{2-}$. The data represent a critical test for theory, only unrestricted Hartree-Fock calculations providing eigenfunctions of sufficient accuracy to match experiment. It is of obvious interest to now begin thinking what form of semi-empirical, if not 'back of envelope', theory can meet the stringent test of experiment. So far as more complex molecules are concerned: under study at present are phthalocyaninato cobalt(II) ($s = \frac{1}{2}$) and phthalocyaninatomanganese(II) ($s = \frac{3}{2}$); at present our view is that, even with fairly extensive experimental data, it will be fairly difficult to provide comprehensive spin densities in as weak a paramagnet as the cobalt(II) complex but this situation could change quite quickly as new higher-flux neutron sources become available.

We can obviously anticipate a growing contribution of these studies to exchange phenomena in finite and infinite arrays and, no doubt, a better understanding between magnetic properties and exchange mechanisms. In a similar way, mixed valence compounds and electron transfer processes and reactions are amenable to much more direct examination. The high selectivity of magnetic scattering also points to studies of very large molecular systems (such as metalloenzymes) in that specific information on the transition metal site may be obtained without recourse to a total structural analysis.

It is salutary, therefore, to recognise the paradox that one of the most powerful probes of the chemical bond in transition metal complexes resides in essentially non-bonding, unpaired electrons. The magnetochemical criterion of stereochemistry has evolved into a comprehensive description of the very subtle features underlying the formation of metal-ligand bonds.

Acknowledgement - This work was supported by a grant from the Science Research Council, U.K.

REFERENCES

1. B. Dawson, Proc. Roy. Soc. A298, 264, 379, 395 (1967).
2. R. Mason, Proc. Roy. Soc. A258, 302 (1960).
3. P. Coppens, Measurement of Electron Densities in Solids by X-ray Diffraction, MTP. Inter. Rev. of Science, Phys. Chem. Series, Butterworth, London (1975).
4. R. Mason and J.N. Varghese, J. Organometal. Chem. 181, 159 (1979).
5. P. Coppens. Paper to be submitted at XXI International Conference on Coordination Chemistry, Toulouse, July (1980).
6. B.C. Tofield, Structure and Bonding, Springer-Verlag, Berlin, Vol.21 (1975).
7. F.A. Wedgwood, Proc.Roy. Soc. London, A349, 447 (1976).
8. B.N. Figgis, R. Mason, A.R.P. Smith, J.N.Varghese and G.A. Williams , to be published (1980).
9. W. Marshall and S.W. Lovesy, Theory of Thermal Neutron Scattering, Oxford, Clarendon Press (1971).
10. B.N. Figgis, R. Mason, A.R.P. Smith and G.A. Williams, J. Amer. Chem. Soc. 101, 3673 (1979).
11. B.N. Figgis, P.A. Reynolds and G.A. Williams, J.C.S. Dalton, in press (1980).
12. RF. Stewart, J. Chem. Phys. 58, 1668 (1973).
13. R.F. Stewart, Acta Cryst. A32, 565 (1976).
14. P.F. Price, Ph.D. Thesis, University of Western Australia (1976).
15. P. Coppens, T.N. Guru Row, P. Leung, E.D. Stevens, P.J. Becker and Y.W. Yang, Acta. Cryst. A35, 63 (1978).
16. J.N. Varghese and E.N. Maslen, unpublished results (1975).
17. J.N. Varghese and R. Mason, Proc. Roy. Soc. in press (1980).
18. R. Mason and J.N. Varghese, to be published (1980).
19. R.D. Brown and P.G. Burton, Theoret. Chim. Acta. (Berl.) 18, 309 (1970).
20. A. Tang Kai and S. Larsson, Int. J. Quantum Chem. 13, 375 (1978).
21. R. Mason, A.R.P. Smith, J.N. Varghese, to be published (1980).
22. B.N. Figgis, R. Mason, P.A. Reynolds, A.R.P. Smith, J.N. Varghese and G.A. Williams, J.C.S. Dalton, in press (1980).
23. R. Mason, A.R.P. Smith and J.N. Varghese, to be published (1980).
24. G.A. Williams, B.N. Figgis and R. Mason, to be published (1980).
25. F.A. Cotton and R. Mason, private communication.

COORDINATION COMPOUNDS WITH METAL TO METAL BONDS: THE CONSTRUCTIVE INTERACTION OF THEORY AND EXPERIMENT

F. A. Cotton

Department of Chemistry, Texas A & M University, College Station, Texas 77843, USA

Abstract - The weakness of the δ component of a quadruple bond, resulting from the rather small overlap of the d orbitals concerned, leads to some interesting problems in reconciling theory and experiment. However, when all sides of the theoretical picture as well as sufficient experimental data are properly considered, a very satisfactory constructive interaction between theory and experiment is achieved.

INTRODUCTION

The desideratum for all scientific investigation is to achieve that maximally productive marriage of the noumenal and phenomenal aspects of the enterprise. When the optimal blend of theory and experiment exists, the two move forward in tandem, each sector stimulating progress in the other. In this lecture I shall show that in the investigation of metal atom cluster compounds and multiple bonds between metal atoms, there has been a high degree of mutually beneficial interaction between theory and experiment. By theory I do not necessarily always mean high-powered calculations on a big computer, though this will most often be the case.

From the outset, in the early 1960's, the field of transition metal compounds with metal-to-metal (M-M) bonds, of whatever order, has posed special and interesting challenges for bonding theory. Most simplified bonding models that have been successfully applied to transition metal complexes are so structured that they can apply only to Werner complexes - which in the broadest sense means one-center or mononuclear complexes. Thus we have the valence-bond hybridization model of Pauling, the crystal field theory, the ligand field theory and the angular overlap model, all of which emphasize - and, indeed, limit themselves to - the question of how the interaction of ligands with a metal atom (ion) may be represented.

When we turn to the new, non-Wernerian transition metal chemistry in which covalent bonds between metal atoms are the key feature, all models based on the symmetry properties of orbitals in a unicentric system, i.e., on the mathematics of spherical harmonics, become useless. We must turn back to fundamentals and develop new approaches suited to the new material.

There are also three additional difficulties.

(1) Many of the M-M bonded compounds are formed by the heavier transition elements and are rather large systems. Even today the computational capacity needed to treat them by the conventional Hartree-Foch (HF) method is often beyond practical reach.

(2) For the compounds formed by the third transition series it is necessary to introduce relativistic corrections if quantitative results are needed. Many interesting species, e.g., $[Ta_6Cl_{12}]^{n+}$, $W_2Cl_4(PR_3)_4$, $[Re_2Cl_8]^{2-}$, Os_2(2-oxopyridine)$_4Cl_2$, are in this category.

(3) In all cases, even for compounds of 1st transition series metals (e.g., chromium, which will not be discussed in detail here) at least some of the components of the bonding are weak enough so that the HF result is inadequate and may even be qualitatively wrong. Electron correlation must be introduced, usually by the configuration interaction (CI) procedure.

In this lecture I shall focus on a few related problems, namely, difficulties associated with correctly assigning and calculating the energy and intensity of $\delta \rightarrow \delta^*$ transitions.

THE NATURE OF $\delta \rightarrow \delta^*$ TRANSITIONS

Multiple M-M bonds of orders 3 to 4 may be of the following five types:

Type	Bond Order	Configuration	Lowest Excited Configuration
a	3	$\sigma^2\pi^4$	$\sigma^2\pi^3\delta$
b	3.5	$\sigma^2\pi^4\delta$	$\sigma^2\pi^4\delta^*$
c	4	$\sigma^2\pi^4\delta^2$	$\sigma^2\pi^4\delta\delta^*$
d	3.5	$\sigma^2\pi^4\delta^2\delta^*$	$\sigma^2\pi^4\delta\delta^{*2}$
e	3	$\sigma^2\pi^4\delta^2\delta^{*2}$	$\sigma^2\pi^4\delta^2\delta^*\pi^*$

For the quadruple bonds (c) and the two types of bond with a formal bond order of 3.5 (b,d) the lowest excited state derives from a configuration that is reached from the ground state by a $\delta \rightarrow \delta^*$ promotion of one electron. As an optical transition, this is electric-dipole allowed in polarization parallel to the M-M bond axis. This transition has indeed been observed in all compounds containing bonds of types b, c and d, but in attempting to reconcile the observations with theory, two general problems have arisen.

First, in all cases the intensities are surprisingly low, considering that the transitions are orbitally allowed. Second, in the bonds of type c the transition is always observed at a far higher energy than that calculated despite the fact that the same calculation may give a rather accurate energy for all (or most) other electronic transitions in the same molecule. For cases b and d, however, the calculations predict the energy of the $\delta \rightarrow \delta^*$ transition just as well as they do for the other transitions.

The intensity problem is actually not difficult to resolve. As Trogler and Gray[1] have observed, the overlap of the two d orbitals that form the δ bond is quite small. Moreover, as Mulliken showed[2] many years ago, oscillator strength in a transition of this nature is approximately proportional to the square of the overlap integral. Thus, low intensity is a straightforward consequence of the weakness of the δ bond, and using Mulliken's relation the correct order of magnitude of the intensity can be calculated. In this instance, available theory easily resolves an apparent experimental anomaly.

The accurate theoretical estimation of the energy of the $\delta \rightarrow \delta^*$ transition has led to interesting theoretical developments. The first attempts to calculate this energy employed the SCF-Xα-SW method and were quite unsatisfactory. For $[Mo_2Cl_8]^{4-}$ the observed and calculated energies are[3] 18.8×10^3 cm^{-1} and 9.2×10^3 cm^{-1}, respectively, and for $[Re_2Cl_8]^{2-}$ the band is observed at 14×10^3 cm^{-1} and calculated[4] at 4.5×10^3 cm^{-1}. On the other hand, for $[Tc_2Cl_8]^{3-}$ the observed[5] and calculated[6] values, 5.9×10^3 cm^{-1} and 6.0×10^3 cm^{-1}, respectively, agree very well. In the closed shell species (type c) there are both singlet-singlet and singlet-triplet transitions possible, whereas for $[Tc_2Cl_8]^{3-}$ only a doublet-doublet transition is possible. However, it has been shown that even when the type c species are treated entirely correctly as regards the spin multiplicity,[3,7] there is still a large discrepancy between observed and calculated energies, with the latter being far too low.

The difficulty with the $\delta \rightarrow \delta^*$ energy calculation is now recognized to have its origin in the electron correlation phenomenon. It is not immediately obvious how to formulate this simply in the SCF-Xα-SW formalism, but it is easily explained in terms of conventional LCAO MO theory. Considering only the δ and δ^* orbitals and two electrons, it is clear[8] that the four possible states can be expressed in the standard Slater determinental form as follows, where normalizing factors are omitted.

Ground State:

$$\psi_1(^1A_{1g}) = |\delta\bar{\delta}| = |\delta\delta|\alpha\beta$$

Singly Excited States:

$$\psi_2(^1A_{2u}) = |\delta\bar{\delta}^*| + |\bar{\delta}\delta^*| = [\delta\delta^* + \delta^*\delta](\alpha\beta-\beta\alpha)$$

$$\psi_3(^3A_{2u}) = |\delta\delta^*| \begin{matrix}(\alpha\alpha) \\ (\alpha\beta + \beta\alpha) \\ (\beta\beta)\end{matrix}$$

Doubly Excited State:

$$\psi_4(^1A_{1g}) = |\delta^*\delta^*|\alpha\beta$$

The wave functions δ and δ^* are defined in terms of the two d_{xy} orbitals, χ_A and χ_B, as follows, where we neglect the overlap, S, which is $<<1$.

$$\delta = 2^{-1/2}(\chi_A + \chi_B)$$

$$\delta^* = 2^{-1/2}(\chi_A - \chi_B)$$

From here the argument is essentially that given years ago by Coulson[9] with respect to the approach to the dissociation limit of H_2. Now, however, the δ bond, even at the equilibrium internuclear distance of the ground-state, is subject to the same problems. Let us expand ψ_1, ignoring here, and later, normalizing factors.

$$\psi_1 = \{[\chi_A(1)\chi_A(2) + \chi_B(1)\chi_B(2)] + [\chi_A(1)\chi_B(2) + \chi_B(1)\chi_A(2)] \ (\alpha\beta-\beta\alpha)$$

$$\psi_{ionic} + \psi_{covalent}$$

In pictorial terms we may write:

$$\psi_1 = \underbrace{\overset{\uparrow\downarrow}{A}\text{—}B + A\text{—}\overset{\uparrow\downarrow}{B}}_{\text{ionic}} + \underbrace{\overset{\uparrow}{A}\text{—}\overset{\downarrow}{B} + \overset{\downarrow}{A}\text{—}\overset{\uparrow}{B}}_{\text{covalent}}$$

From this it is clear that ψ_1 vastly overestimates the ionic contribution to the ground state; it is quite out of the question that the true electron density distribution could put both electrons at the same nucleus as much as half of the time.

We note, however, that ψ_4 also defines a $^1A_{1g}$ state and, analogously, this too will consist of equal contributions from ionic and covalent parts:

$$\psi_4 = \overset{\uparrow\downarrow}{A}\text{—}B + A\text{—}\overset{\uparrow\downarrow}{B} - \overset{\uparrow}{A}\text{—}\overset{\downarrow}{B} - \overset{\downarrow}{A}\text{—}\overset{\uparrow}{B}$$

We note, though, that the algebraic signs are different so that $\psi_1 + \psi_4$ is a pure ionic function while $\psi_1 - \psi_4$ is purely covalent. This means that if instead of using simply ψ_1 to represent the $^1A_{1g}$ ground state we use $\psi_1' = \psi_1 - \lambda\psi_4$ we can lessen the ionic character of the ground state to whatever degree we wish by choosing the magnitude of λ.

For the singlet excited state, ψ_2, we obtain, upon similar expansion, the results:

$$\psi_3 = [\chi_A(1)\chi_A(2) - \chi_B(1)\chi_B(2)](\alpha\beta-\beta\alpha)$$

$$\overset{\uparrow\downarrow}{A}\text{—}B - A\text{—}\overset{\uparrow\downarrow}{B}$$

Thus, this state is totally ionic.

The following diagram shows the relationship that all of this has to the calculation of the energy of the $\delta^2\rightarrow\delta\delta^*$ ($^1A_{2u} \leftarrow {}^1A_{1g}$) transition.

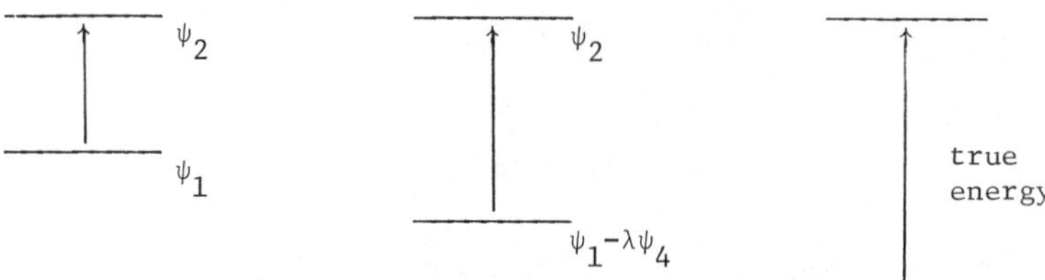

When we use the simple, heavily ionic wave function, ψ_1, we obtain too high an energy for the ground state and hence too low an energy difference between ψ_1 and ψ_2. Mixing in some of ψ_4 to make the ground state less ionic increases its stability and gives a better approximation of the true energy difference. This mixing is an example of using configuration interaction (CI) to correct a simple LCAO wave function for electron correlation. However, there are other CI contributions to the ground state wave function and also CI contributions to the wave function for the excited state, and the argument just given is greatly oversimplified from a quantitative point of view. Nevertheless, it probably deals with the principal effect, and shows the way to making improved calculations.

It is to be noted that the above argument is consistent with the fact that for $\delta\rightarrow\delta^*$ ($^2B_{1u} \leftarrow {}^2B_{2g}$) and $\delta^2\delta^* \rightarrow \delta\delta^{*2}$ ($^2B_{1u} \leftarrow {}^2B_{2g}$) good results can be obtained without CI. These are either actually or effectively one-electron systems and no correlation problems exist.

While the foregoing analysis does not apply directly to the SCF-Xα-SW approach, it is in the nature of any one-electron MO theory that it will, for reasons of electron correlation, describe a pair of electrons improperly in the limit of weak coupling between them.[10-12] It was with the problem of treating the weak δ interactions as one specific objective that several interesting new approaches to handling the correlation problem have been devised. The classical method of allowing for electron correlation is to mix appropriate excited state wave functions into the ground state (just as we did above in the almost trivial case of mixing the $|\delta^*\delta^*|\alpha\beta$ wave function, ψ_4, with $|\alpha\alpha|\alpha\beta$, ψ_1. While in principle this is always possible and in the limit this configuration interaction (CI) treatment will converge to give an accurate result, its full implementation is extremely cumbersome and expensive.

SOME RECENT RESULTS

Let us now look at some recent experimental results concerning $\delta\rightarrow\delta^*$ transitions and see how they compare with theoretical expectation at either a qualitative or a quantitative level. We turn first to a situation that allows us to examine, rather simply, the effect of decreasing the d-orbital overlap in a δ bond while keeping other factors essentially the same. This is done using data for a type of quadruply-bonded ditungsten compound[13,14] that has only recently been made and characterized. The availability of the dimolybdenum homolog makes possible an informative comparison. The molecules in question, which have been studied structurally and spectroscopically in detail[15] are:

```
          PR3
        ,'
  Cl—M—Cl
    /||||
R3P ||||  Cl
     |||| ,'
R3P—M—PR3
    /
  Cl
```

Mo-Mo(Å) = 2.130(1)Å

W-W(Å) = 2.262(1)Å

The basis of the argument in comparing the two compounds is that the outer $\underline{d}$ orbitals of the molybdenum and tungsten atoms are very similar in size, but because of the presence of an additional 32 electrons in the tungsten core, two tungsten atoms cannot approach as closely as two molybdenum atoms. As indicated above, the actual difference in bond lengths is ~0.13Å. This difference causes the δ-δ overlap to be appreciably smaller for the tungsten compound and we should expect this to be reflected clearly in both the energies and intensities of the $\delta\rightarrow\delta^*$ transitions. As shown in Fig. 1, the observations are in excellent accord with these expectations. The $\delta\rightarrow\delta^*$ transition lies at much lower energy and is considerably weaker for the tungsten compound.

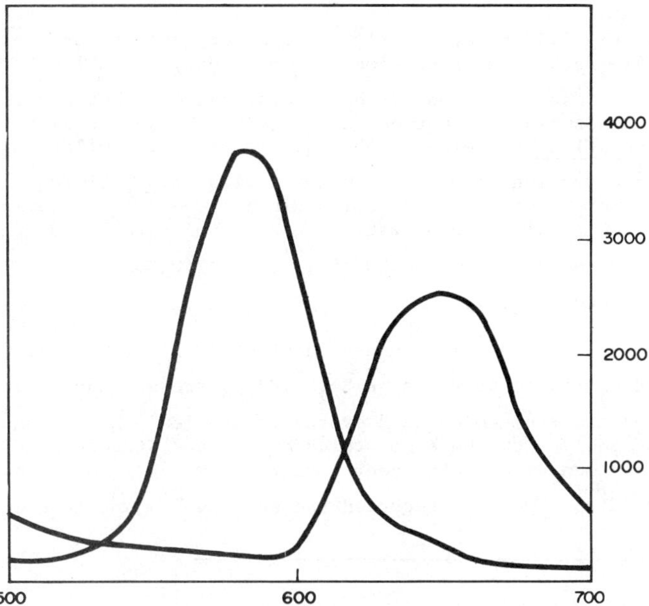

Fig. 1. The δ→δ* absorption bands for the homologous $M_2Cl_4(PMe_3)_4$ molecules. The abscissa scale is in nanometers and the ordinate gives molar extinction.

In the preceding example, we have not attempted to justify the assignment of the bands as δ→δ* transitions. In view of the fact that a direct calculation of the energy may, for the reasons discussed earlier, be expected to give a prediction far below the experimental value, how do we know, in general as well as in this particular case, that the assumption is correct? A complete answer to that question is beyond the scope of this article, but one type of evidence will be discussed since it adds further to our theme of the interaction of theory and experiment.

When a δ→δ* transition is measured at low temperature and in an oriented single crystal theory predicts that it should consist of a resolved vibrational progression in the M-M stretching frequency and that it should have a well-defined polarization parallel to the metal-metal bond; both of these features are observed in certain simple cases and such observations provide powerful evidence for the correctness of the assignment.[1] However, in other cases far more complex behavior has been observed and this has called for a more sophisticated extension of theory. It is pertinent to the theme of this paper that this extension is based, qualitatively, on the fact that the δ→δ* transition, though formally an orbitally allowed transition, has an intrinsically small dipolar contribution to its transition moment because the δ-δ overlap is small.

To understand how this affects the appearance of the absorption band (other than making it very weak) we must consider in detail the following expression for the transition moment:

$$\mathbf{M}_{fg}(Q) = \mathbf{M}_0 + \mathbf{m}_i Q_i \text{ where } \mathbf{m}_i = \left(\frac{\delta M}{\delta Q_i}\right)_{Qi} = 0$$

This expression takes account of vibronic coupling to first order and must be squared to give the intensity values for each vibrational component. When this is done using the adiabatic Born-Oppenheimer approximation we obtain:

$$\begin{aligned}\mathbf{M}_{g0,fv_i'} = [&\mathbf{M}_0^2\langle g0|\,|fv_i'\rangle^2 \\ &+ 2\mathbf{M}_0 m_i\langle g0|\,|fv_i'\rangle\langle g0|Q_i|fv_i'\rangle \\ &+ \mathbf{m}_i^2\langle g0|Q_i|fv_i'\rangle^2]\prod_{j\neq i}\langle g0|\,|fv_j'\rangle^2\end{aligned}$$

The functions $\langle g0|$ and $|fv_i'\rangle$ denote the 0th vibrational level of the electronic ground state and the v_ith vibrational level of the upper electronic state, respectively.

As a normal rule, when a transition is orbitally dipole-allowed, M_o is so large that $M_o^2 >> M_o m_i >>> m_i^2$ and we see only the vibrational progression in a totally symmetric frequency represented by the first term on the RHS of the equation. Moreover, this occurs only in parallel polarization. For dipole-forbidden transitions ($M_o = 0$) only the third term survives; we then see vibronic progressions in one or both polarizations, but not in the totally symmetric frequencies. The curious situation we have with the weaker $\delta \rightarrow \delta^*$ transitions is that $M_o \approx m_i$ so that all three terms in the equation are of similar importance. We therefore see more than one progression in parallel polarization with different Franck-Condon factors and one or more vibronic progressions in perpendicular polarization of intensity comparable to those in parallel polarization. Beautiful examples of this phenomenon have recently been reported for $[Mo_2(O_2CCHNH_3)_4]^{4+}$,[16] $Mo_2(O_2CCH_3)_4$,[17] $Mo_2[(CH_2)_2P(CH_3)_2]_4$[18] and $[Mo_2(L\text{-leucine})_4]^{4+}$.[19]

Our final example concerns a $\delta^2\delta^* \rightarrow \delta\delta^{*2}$ transition in a bond of order 3.5 (type d). R. A. Walton[20] has observed that compounds of the type $Re_2X_4(PR_3)_4$ are spontaneously oxidized by oxygen and in further electrochemical and synthetic studies[21] he has shown that the product is a +1 cation, presumably with the same stoichiometry and structure. The oxidized species has a weak absorption band in the near infrared. Using a powder sample of $[Re_2Cl_4(PPr_3)_4]PtF_6$ provided by Walton, we have recorded the spectrum[22] shown in Fig 2 at 5K.

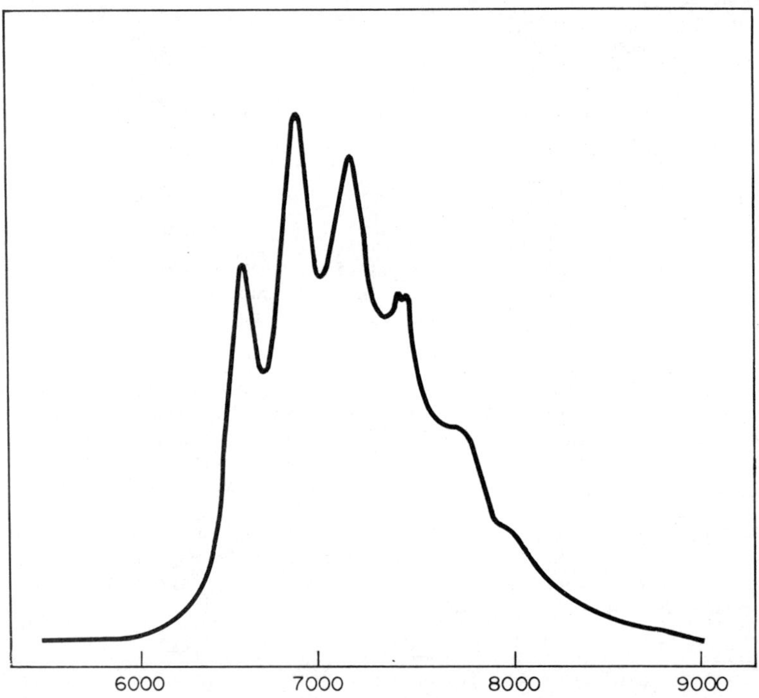

Fig. 2. The $\delta \rightarrow \delta^*$ band at 5 K for $[Re_2Cl_4(PPr_3)_4]^+$ recorded on a powder sample.

The vibrational spacing averages 275±5 cm^{-1}, consistent with expectation for an Re-Re stretching mode.

A complete calculation for $Re_2Cl_4(PH_3)_4$ by the SCF-Xα-SW method of the ground state electron configuration and the energies of the first 18 expected electronic transitions gives an excellent fit of the entire spectrum of $[Re_2Cl_4(PPr_3)_4]^+$ from 4000 to 30,000 cm^{-1}. In particular, for the $\delta \rightarrow \delta^*$ ($^2B_{1u} \leftarrow {}^2B_{2g}$) transition we obtained an energy of 5,650 cm^{-1}, which compares very well with the 0-0 transition in Fig. 2 at 6,653 cm^{-1}.

Acknowledgement - Research at the Texas A&M University on the problems discussed here was supported by the National Science Foundation and by The Robert A. Welch Foundation. I am grateful to Drs. Bruce Bursten, Brian Kolthammer and Phillip Fanwick for their help in preparing this manuscript.

REFERENCES

1. W. C. Trogler and H. B. Gray, Accounts Chem. Research, 11, 232 (1978).
2. R. S. Mulliken, J. Chem. Phys., 7, 20 (1939).
3. J. G. Norman, Jr., H. J. Kolari, H. B. Gray and W. C. Trogler, Inorg. Chem., 16, 987 (1977).
4. A. P. Mortola, J. W. Moskowitz, N. Rosch, C. D. Cowman and H. B. Gray, Chem. Phys. Lett., 32, 283 (1975).
5. F. A. Cotton, P. E. Fanwick, L. D. Gage, B. Kalbacher and D. S. Martin, J. Am. Chem. Soc., 99, 5642 (1977).
6. F. A. Cotton and B. J. Kalbacher, Inorg. Chem., 16, 2386 (1977).
7. J. G. Norman, Jr. and H. J. Kolari, J. Am. Chem. Soc., 97, 33 (1975).
8. Essentially the analysis used here is available in many elementary texts, e.g., C. J. Ballhausen and H. B. Gray, Molecular Orbital Theory, W. A. Benjamin, Inc., New York, 1964, pp. 14-15.
9. C. A. Coulson and I. Fischer, Phil. Mag., 40, 139 (1949).
10. R. K. Nesbet, Phys. Rev., A135, 460 (1964); A122, 1497 (1961).
11. P. O. Lowdin, Rev. Mod. Phys., 34, 80 (1962); 36, 968 (1964).
12. W. A. Goddard, III, et al., Accounts Chem. Research, 6, 368 (1973); J. Chem. Phys., 62, 3912 (1975).
13. P. R. Sharp and R. R. Schrock, J. Am. Chem. Soc., 101, 1430 (1980).
14. F. A. Cotton, T. R. Felthouse and D. G. Lay, J. Am. Chem. Soc., 101, 1431 (1980).
15. F. A. Cotton, M. W. Extine, T. R. Felthouse, B. R. Kolthammer, and D. G. Lay, to be published.
16. F. A. Cotton, D. S. Martin, T. R. Webb and T. J. Peters, Inorg. Chem., 15, 1199 (1976).
17. D. S. Martin, R. A. Newman, and P. E. Fanwick, Inorg. Chem., 18, 2511 (1979).
18. F. A. Cotton and P. E. Fanwick, J. Am. Chem. Soc., 101, 5252 (1979).
19. A. Bino, F. A. Cotton and P. E. Fanwick, Inorg. Chem., 19, 1215 (1980).
20. J. R. Ebner and R. A. Walton, Inorg. Chem., 14, 1987 (1975).
21. P. Brant, D. J. Salmon and R. A. Walton, J. Am. Chem. Soc., 100, 4424 (1978).
22. F. A. Cotton and P. E. Fanwick, unpublished.
23. G. G. Stanley, Ph. D. Dissertation, Texas A&M University, 1979.

SOLAR ENERGY STORAGE REACTIONS INVOLVING METAL COMPLEXES

A. W. Maverick and H. B. Gray*

Arthur Amos Noyes Laboratory, California Institute of Technology, Pasadena, California 91125, USA

Abstract - Photochemical properties of transition metal complexes are discussed as they relate to possible schemes for energy storage. Complexes of copper(I) with π-acceptor ligands have been used to sensitize isomerizations of organic molecules, and there is room for considerable further investigation in this area. Electron transfer reactions have been more intensively studied. These reactions fall into three broad categories: ionization, oxidative addition/reductive elimination, and excited state electron transfer. Experiments in the first two categories have generally led to rather poor storage efficiency and have required ultraviolet light. But long-lived excited states of coordination compounds can participate in chemical reactions with high efficiency, and such systems are promising for solar energy storage. Specific systems of this type that are discussed in detail involve electron transfer quenching of the lowest emissive excited states of $Ru(2,2'\text{-bipyridine})_3^{2+}$, $M_2(\text{diisocyanoalkane})_4^{2+}$ (M=Rh,Ir), and $Mo_6Cl_{14}^{2-}$.

INTRODUCTION

The realization that the world faces shortages of fossil fuels has spurred research into all types of alternative energy sources. Because it is plentiful and environmentally clean, solar energy has been the object of a particularly intense research campaign. However, there are two major drawbacks to its widespread use: sunlight is a dilute form of energy, meaning that a commercial installation would require large areas of collectors; and energy could only be produced intermittently by such a plant. The storage of solar energy in chemical form would help to circumvent the second of these objections. Also, if sunlight could be used to produce a fuel by a photochemical reaction, dwindling fossil fuel supplies could be replaced directly. This paper examines recent developments in the field of photochemical energy storage, concentrating on the role of transition metal complexes in causing or promoting these reactions.

THE SOLAR SPECTRUM AND ENERGY STORAGE REQUIREMENTS

Several authors have discussed [1-3] the factors limiting the performance of a photochemical energy storage system: First, the chromophore must absorb light of relatively low energy in order to make use of a significant portion of the solar spectrum. Second, the excited state formed on absorption of light must undergo subsequent reactions with high probability. And third, the exothermic reaction of the photochemical products (to give the starting materials again) must be controllable.

The second and third of these constraints are largely a function of the particular chemical system chosen for energy storage. But the nature of the solar spectrum imposes fundamental limits on the efficiency of any photochemical sequence. Most of the energy in sunlight appears as photons of relatively long wavelength [4]; only a small portion lies in the ultraviolet region of the spectrum. The maximum possible efficiency η_P of a storage system based on the reaction

$$X \xrightarrow{h\nu} X^* \qquad (1)$$

depends on the threshold wavelength λ_1, the maximum wavelength thermodynamically sufficient to cause reaction (1); here $\lambda_1 = N^0hc/\Delta G_1^0$. It is assumed in the derivation of η_P that all light of $\lambda \leq \lambda_1$ is absorbed, that the quantum yield for formation of X* is 1, and that the energy of X* is extracted and stored at the optimum rate. The values of η_P obtained for various threshold wavelengths, using a typical solar spectrum for a sunny day near noon, are given in the Table [1]. Additional considerations, such as intersystem crossing to produce

TABLE Maximum Efficiencies η_P for Various Threshold Wavelengths λ_1

λ_1/nm	η_P
400	0.04
500	0.14
600	0.22
700	0.28
800	0.31
900	0.32
1000	0.30
1100	0.31
1200	0.29
1300	0.28
1400	0.26

photoactive states, the decay of such states, and energy losses in subsequent thermal reactions of X*, reduce this figure further; Bolton suggests 0.13 as the maximum fraction of total solar energy that could be stored in a chemical system under ideal conditions [1].

We will deal here with two general types of energy storage schemes: photoisomerization, in which the endergonic reaction

$$X \rightarrow Y \qquad (2)$$

is carried out photochemically and the high-energy product Y is stored; and photoredox, where X*, or a species formed from it, undergoes an electron transfer reaction. The photoredox experiments have been designed almost exclusively with the goal of promoting reactions such as

$$H_2O \rightarrow H_2 + 1/2\ O_2\ . \qquad (3)$$

Few photochemical reactions are known for excitation wavelengths above 600 nm; most require ultraviolet light. So the aspiring solar chemist faces two challenges: to maximize the efficiency of the storage reactions, and to extend the useful region of the spectrum as far to the red as possible. Our discussion will center on the recent use of transition metal complexes to attack these two problems.

PHOTOISOMERIZATION

The photoinduced conversion of a molecule to a higher-energy, metastable isomer, as illustrated by reaction (2) above, suggests an attractive system for solar energy storage. Ideally, X should be highly photosensitive and Y inert; and a catalyst should be available for rapid conversion of Y to X when the stored energy is to be extracted again.

In practice the choice of substrates has been largely restricted to organic molecules [5], where energy differences and activation energies for isomerization are generally large. Perhaps the most-studied example is the system norbornadiene(NBD) - quadricyclane(Q), where ΔG_4^0 is 110 kJ mol^{-1} [6]:

NBD → Q (4)

Although λ_4 here is 1080 nm, suggesting that good solar energy storage efficiencies might be achievable, norbornadiene is transparent well into the ultraviolet. Based on an estimate of 300 kJ mol^{-1} for the lowest triplet state of NBD [7], conventional triplet sensitization might allow use of longer wavelengths. Both organic chromophores [8] and, more recently, Cu(I) complexes [9-12] have been employed as sensitizers. Even in these systems, however, ultraviolet light is necessary to achieve reaction (4).

The evolution of heat from high-energy materials such as quadricyclane is less difficult. Some transition metal complexes are excellent catalysts for the conversion of Q to NBD [13, 14].

Two problems seem particularly acute in this type of solar energy scheme: the short wavelengths required for the photochemical steps, and side products produced in the thermal reaction. Research with other copper(I) complexes [15] as sensitizers is addressing the first question, and a paper by Samuel [16] analyzes the problem of side products and the tolerances for a viable photoisomerization system.

PHOTOREDOX PROCESSES

Photoisomerization reactions offer a simple scheme for energy storage, but the stored energy can only be released again in the form of heat. Isomers are generally relatively close in energy and therefore have low energy storage capacity. Metastable molecules produced by redox reactions, however, are often called fuels because their combustion is so highly exothermic. Energy storage in photosynthetic organisms operates exclusively by photoredox mechanisms, and by-products of these reactions, the fossil fuels, are our most convenient and useful energy sources today. Energy storage in the form of a compact fuel [such as hydrogen, eq. (3)] would reduce transportation problems and make the stored energy available in many forms [17]. An artificial chemical system could in principle improve on natural photosynthesizers: although the energy storage process in plants has an efficiency of 6 to 8% [2], much of the stored energy is then used in metabolism. We discuss here three general ways in which transition-metal complexes have been used in photoredox reactions.

Photoionization

This type of scheme may be discussed with reference to the water-splitting reaction. We may use a metal complex, represented by M, to sensitize reaction (3) in two steps:

$$M + H^+ \rightarrow M^+ + 1/2\ H_2 \tag{5}$$

$$M^+ + 1/2\ H_2O \rightarrow M + 1/4\ O_2 + H^+ \tag{6}$$

Several metal ions, for example Mn(IV) [18] and Co(III) [19], are known to carry out reaction (6). Thus a catalytic cycle would be complete if corresponding reduced metal complexes could be made to photoreduce H^+ to H_2.

Low-valent metal complexes often exhibit intense metal to ligand charge transfer (MLCT) or charge transfer to solvent (CTTS) absorption bands. The use of far-ultraviolet light to cause reaction (5) is illustrated by work with Fe^{2+} in aqueous solution [20,21]. Similar experiments with europium(II) also gave hydrogen under 366 nm irradiation [22]; but in this case reaction (5) is exergonic. Certain copper(I) complexes also have been irradiated in the ultraviolet to induce photoionization, simultaneously producing H_2 [23,24].

The photoionization of strongly metal-metal bonded species has been studied in our laboratory [25]. Under 254 nm irradiation, quadruply-bonded $d^4 - d^4$ systems are oxidized by H^+ to mixed-valence $d^3 - d^4$ species or to dinuclear $d^3 - d^3$ complexes. One-electron oxidized products were identified for $Mo_2(SO_4)_4^{4-}$ [26,27] and $Re_2Cl_8^{2-}$ [28]; $Mo_2(aq)^{4+}$ ultimately underwent two-electron oxidation [27].

Recent results indicate that hexachloroiridate(III) could be used in a photochemical energy storage cycle. Waltz and Adamson were the first to observe photoionization of $IrCl_6^{3-}$, trapping the ejected electron with N_2O [29]. The irradiation (254 nm) of $IrCl_6^{3-}$ in dilute acid solution produces, among other products, hexachloroiridate(IV) and hydrogen [28]:

$$H^+ + IrCl_6^{3-} \rightarrow IrCl_6^{2-} + 1/2\ H_2 \tag{7}$$

Here the standard electrode potential for the $IrCl_6^{2-/3-}$ couple, 0.867 V [30], suggests that a substantial amount of energy has been stored in reaction (7). Details of this photoreaction and of possible side reactions (including aquation) are now being studied.

Another type of photoionization process, this time involving the transfer of electrons to a metal atom by LMCT excitation, has been examined by Yamase and co-workers [31,32]. Near-ultraviolet light reduces alkylammonium isopolymolybdates(VI) to persistent mixed-valence Mo(V)-Mo(VI) complexes and unidentified oxidation products both in the solid state and in solution [31]. The mixed-valence complexes (blue in solution) were also found to be photosensitive, and a galvanic cell containing the blue ion in the anode compartment and a platinum wire in the cathode compartment produced hydrogen when irradiated [32]. Questions of stoichiometry and quantum yield remain unresolved, but the system is potentially quite interesting.

Photoassisted oxidative addition and reductive elimination

These are common processes for organometallic compounds and offer possibilities for photochemical energy storage. They may be illustrated respectively by the forward and reverse directions of the following reaction:

$$M + X{-}Y \rightleftarrows X{-}M{-}Y \tag{8}$$

The oxidation state of the metal atom is formally increased by two on the addition of XY. These reactions are best known for square planar complexes M. Where XY is a halogen the concept is intuitively appealing; but where the process involves an alkyl halide or a protic acid (*e. g.*, HCl, CH_3NO_2, or PhC≡CH) the term oxidation seems less appropriate. To the extent that the oxidative-addition product H-M-Y has hydridic character, reaction with a second molecule of acid may be proposed:

$$H{-}M{-}Y + HY \rightarrow Y{-}M{-}Y + H_2 \tag{9}$$

Reaction (9) could then be followed by reductive elimination of Y—Y, regenerating the square planar starting material and catalyzing the overall reaction

$$2HY \rightarrow H_2 + Y_2 \tag{10}$$

For the hydrogen halides HCl and HBr reaction (10) is highly endergonic, and this scheme would be a useful one for energy storage.

There are few photochemical studies of simple oxidative addition and reductive elimination. Dihydro complexes of cobalt(III) [33] and iridium(III) [34] have been shown to eliminate hydrogen on ultraviolet irradiation, but no efforts have been made to incorporate these reactions into a catalytic cycle.

More encouraging results have been obtained with polynuclear complexes. Solutions of $Mo_2X_8^{4-}$ (X=Cl,Br) underwent oxidative addition of HX from aqueous solution when exposed to 254 nm light [27]. The $Mo_2X_8H^{3-}$ [not an oxidative-addition product in the sense of reaction (8), but at least one in which H^+ has formally been reduced and Mo(II) oxidized] then decomposed, giving H_2 and a dinuclear Mo(III) species.

Geoffroy has reviewed [35] the photochemistry of metal hydride complexes, and finds the dissociation of H from monohydro complexes to be rare. A more common photoprocess is the dissociation of other ligands [*e. g.*, carbon monoxide from $HCo(CO)_4$]. One compound that produces H_2 photochemically is $HIr(PF_3)_4$, giving the dinuclear species $Ir_2(PF_3)_8$ (an overall bimolecular reductive elimination) [36]. It was claimed that the dinuclear Ir product could be converted back to $HIr(PF_3)_4$ on reaction with water, but the details of the chemistry of this system have not been reported.

Recently, infrared and nmr evidence has been obtained for HY adducts of iridium(I) bridging-isocyanide complexes [Y = Cl, $CH(CN)_2$] [37]. Adducts such as these were originally thought to be present in the blue solutions made by adding $Rh_2b_4^{2+}$ (b = 1,3-diisocyanopropane) to aqueous acid [38]; this would have provided a close analogy to the halogen oxidation products described earlier [39]. Studies of the blue Rh species have been conducted using flash kinetic spectroscopy [40,41], redox titrimetry [42], and X-ray crystallography [43]. These have established that $Rh_2b_4^{2+}$ is oxidized in acidic solution to give a tetranuclear $Rh_4b_8^{6+}$ ion. Thus the evolution of hydrogen from solutions of $Rh_4b_8^{6+}$ is not a photochemical reaction of a metal hydride. In aqueous sulfuric acid, where hydrogen is not produced, the primary photoprocess is homolytic cleavage to two $Rh_2b_4^{3+}$ radicals [40,41]:

$$Rh_4b_8^{6+*} \rightarrow 2Rh_2b_4^{3+} \tag{11}$$

The radicals may in turn be trapped by oxidation, for example, with Fe^{3+}:

$$Rh_2b_4^{3+} + Fe^{3+} \rightarrow Rh_2b_4^{4+} + Fe^{2+} \tag{12}$$

Experiments conducted in hydrochloric acid solution demonstrate that redox reactions occur even in the absence of added oxidants [41,44,45]. Whereas a complete analysis of the kinetics has not been possible, it is reasonable to propose that heterolytic cleavage, or photodisproportionation, also occurs [42]:

$$Rh_4b_8^{6+*} \rightarrow Rh_2b_4^{2+} + Rh_2b_4^{4+} \qquad (13)$$

$Rh_2b_4^{2+}$ has not been observed directly under these conditions, but the product of its reaction with $Rh_4b_8^{6+}$, the hexanuclear $Rh_6b_{12}^{8+}$, does appear. Upon reduction of $Rh_4b_8^{6+}$ with Cr^{2+} in aqueous sulfuric acid solutions, Sigal observed [42] a number of $Rh_4b_8^{6+}/Rh_2b_4^{2+}$ adducts as follows:

$$Rh_2b_4^{2+} + Rh_4b_8^{6+} \rightleftharpoons Rh_6b_{12}^{8+} \qquad (14)$$

λ_{max} = 540nm 550nm 780nm

$$2Rh_6b_{12}^{8+} \rightleftharpoons Rh_{12}b_{24}^{16+} \qquad (15)$$

1300nm

$$Rh_2b_4^{2+} + Rh_6b_{12}^{8+} \rightleftharpoons Rh_8b_{16}^{10+} \qquad (16)$$

960nm

Direct reaction of $Rh_2(TMB)_4^{2+}$ (TMB = 2,5-diisocyano-2,5-dimethylhexane) with $Rh_4b_8^{6+}$ in aqueous sulfuric acid solution gave analogous polynuclear rhodium cations [46].

We had hoped [47] that oxidative addition and related electron transfer reactions could be promoted photochemically, as a means of energy storage, in complexes with low-lying MLCT excited states. Photooxidation of six-coordinate isocyanide complexes of Cr, Mo, and W has indeed been observed in chlorocarbon solvents [48], but experiments more directly related to energy storage have not been successful.

Reactions of long-lived excited states

Transition metal complexes have been known for many years whose excited states are sufficiently long-lived to participate in bimolecular reactions. Reactions of molecular excited states, including primarily energy and electron transfer, are well known for organic molecules but have only recently been examined in metal complexes. Balzani and co-workers have published two excellent reviews on the subject, emphasizing energy [49] and electron transfer [50].

An excited state M* of a metal complex M may undergo oxidation or reduction on reaction with an electron acceptor A or donor D, respectively:

$$M^* + A \rightarrow M^+ + A^- \qquad (17)$$

$$M^* + D \rightarrow M^- + D^+ \qquad (18)$$

A reaction of the former type (17) was first observed by Gafney and Adamson in 1972 [51]. Many other examples of both (17) and (18) have confirmed that M* is thermodynamically both a better oxidant and a better reductant than M, which is readily understood in terms of simple molecular orbital descriptions of electronic structure. Endergonic redox reactions of metal complexes may therefore be made exergonic by using M* instead of M.

Basic processes. Reactions (17) and (18) may be applied readily to an energy storage scheme. For example, if the system is to produce hydrogen, the reactions

$$A^- + H^+ \rightarrow A + 1/2\ H_2 \quad \text{or} \qquad (19)$$

$$M^- + H^+ \rightarrow M + 1/2\ H_2 \qquad (20)$$

may be used. Products D^+ or M^+ might then produce an oxidant (such as O_2) in other steps. A major obstacle to achievement of energy storage is that the products of reactions (17) and (18) tend to react with each other again, converting the stored energy to heat:

$$M^+ + A^- \rightarrow M + A \qquad (21)$$

$$M^- + D^+ \rightarrow M + D \quad (22)$$

In Gafney and Adamson's work [51], M was $Ru(bpy)_3^{2+}$ (bpy = 2,2'-bipyridine) and A was $Co(NH_3)_5Br^{2+}$. Here the A^- complex [presumably $Co(NH_3)_5Br^+$] decomposed rapidly in aqueous solution, giving $Co(OH_2)_6^{2+}$. Thus substantial concentrations of $Ru(bpy)_3^{3+}$ could accumulate without interference from (21).

Since these early experiments efforts to use excited state redox reactions in energy storage have most often used $Ru(bpy)_3^{2+}$ as photoreceptor [$\tau(Ru(bpy)_3^{2+*})$ = 0.62 μs in aqueous solution] [49]. Whitten has reviewed recent progress in this area [52].

Lehn and Sauvage used [53,54] a rhodium(III) complex as electron acceptor and triethanolamine to reduce the $Ru(bpy)_3^{3+}$ produced in reaction (17). By far the most popular reagent for oxidative quenching of $Ru(bpy)_3^{2+*}$ has been methylviologen (1,1'-dimethyl-4,4'-bipyridinium, or "paraquat"; abbreviated here as MV^{2+}):

$$Ru(bpy)_3^{2+*} + MV^{2+} \rightarrow Ru(bpy)_3^{3+} + MV^+ \quad (23)$$

$$Ru(bpy)_3^{3+} + MV^+ \rightarrow Ru(bpy)_3^{2+} + MV^{2+} \quad (24)$$

The rate constants k_{23} and k_{24} are respectively 2.4 x 10^9 [55] and 8.1 x 10^9 $M^{-1}s^{-1}$ [56], so that either $Ru(bpy)_3^{3+}$ or MV^+ must be efficiently scavenged to prevent reaction (24). Amines such as EDTA have been shown to reduce $Ru(bpy)_3^{3+}$, leading ultimately to degradation of EDTA into inert products. Matsuo and co-workers showed that this MV^{2+}-based system could be used as a homogeneous photoreductant [57,58].

Whitten and co-workers have investigated [59] the reductive quenching of $Ru(bpy)_3^{2+}$ and its derivatives by amines. The rate of back electron transfer (22) could be drastically reduced by using substituted bipyridines as ligands, so much so that M^- persisted in solution for days at room temperature.

The products of the excited state reaction may also be separated physically. Matsuo *et al.* showed [60] that the yield of electron transfer products in the reductive quenching of a $Ru(bpy)_3^{2+}$ derivative by *N*,*N*-dimethylaniline (DMA) was increased by incorporating the Ru complex into a cationic micelle. Presumably the high positive charge of the Ru(I)-containing micelle inhibits back electron transfer to DMA^+. The opposite strategy was followed by Brugger and Grätzel, who used 1-methyl-1'-tetradecyl-4,4'-bipyridinium ($C_{14}MV^{2+}$)

as electron acceptor in the presence of cationic micelles [61]. $C_{14}MV^{2+}$ itself was unaffected by the micelles; but its one-electron reduction product was sufficiently hydrophobic to be taken up, and was thereby isolated from $Ru(bpy)_3^{3+}$. The back electron transfer rate constant was decreased by some two orders of magnitude in this way.

Utilization in Energy Storage. The use of the strongly reducing and oxidizing properties of molecular excited states to split water into H_2 and O_2 is attractive, not only because H_2 is a convenient fuel but also because gaseous oxidation and reduction products can be removed easily from the irradiated solution. Research into photochemical water decomposition has concentrated most heavily on the sensitized reduction of protons to hydrogen; but success has been reported recently in photooxidizing water to O_2 as well.

The principal problem in generation of hydrogen is that two electrons are needed for each molecule. Direct two-electron transfer processes are rare; the only alternative appears to be the generation of radical intermediates. Such radicals are often unstable to disproportionation or other reactions, and so their generation invites energy-wasting processes.

1. $Ru(bpy)_3^{2+}$ as sensitizer

Sutin and co-workers first sensitized the homogeneous evolution of hydrogen from weakly acidic solutions [62]. Their experimental strategy was to initiate a two-electron reaction by the transfer of a single electron. Having established that $Ru(bpy)_3^{2+}$ could be reduced efficiently by Eu^{2+}, they added a macrocyclic Co(II) complex and observed the following reactions:

$$Ru(bpy)_3^+ + Co(II) \rightarrow Ru(bpy)_3^{2+} + Co(I) \quad (25)$$

$$Co(I) + 2H^+ \rightarrow Co(III) + H_2 \quad (26)$$

The Co(III) complex was then reduced to Co(II) again by a second Eu^{2+} ion. Similar experiments with ascorbic acid, which also quenches $Ru(bpy)_3^{2+*}$ reductively, also led to hydrogen production, but with substantially lower efficiency. Whereas the reduction of protons by Eu^{2+} is exergonic (E^0 = 0.43 V) under their conditions, that by ascorbic acid is not ($E \sim$ -0.4 V).

The $Ru(bpy)_3^{2+}$-sensitized oxidation of water to O_2 by $Co(NH_3)_5Cl^{2+}$ has also been claimed [63], but this has yet to be incorporated into a full cycle for the decomposition of water.

The remainder of the experiments in the sensitized reduction of water have used heterogeneous catalysts, particularly colloidal noble metals and noble metal oxides. These materials catalyze the reduction of H^+ to H_2 (perhaps *via* adsorbed H atoms) by one-electron reductants. Catalysis by platinum black of the redox equilibrium

$$2MV^+ + 2H^+ \rightleftharpoons 2MV^{2+} + H_2 \quad (27)$$

has been known since 1934 [64]. A platinum catalyst has been used [65] by Kagan and coworkers to generate H_2 from the MV^+ produced by oxidative quenching of $Ru(bpy)_3^{2+*}$. A similar mechanism, but using a Rh bipyridine complex as electron relay, is presumably involved in the system studied by Lehn and Sauvage [53,54]. And in DeLaive and Whitten's work [66], Adams' catalyst (PtO_2) allowed $Ru(bpy)_3^+$ to reduce protons to hydrogen. All of the experiments in which amines (including EDTA) are the electron donors have in common the following overall reaction:

$$RCH_2NR'R'' + H_2O \rightarrow RCHO + HNR'R'' + H_2 \quad (28)$$

In the case of triethylamine, for example, reaction (28) is endothermic by *ca.* 58 kJ mol^{-1} [66]. Under optimum conditions DeLaive and Whitten were able to obtain 37% hydrogen yield, *i.e.*, every 100 photons absorbed led to the formation of 37 molecules of H_2. A system based on this reaction could, if all photons with $\lambda \leq 500$ nm were absorbed and converted to H_2 with the same efficiency, achieve storage of *ca.* 2% of available solar energy.

The experiments described above have involved the reduction of water by a mild reductant. The report by Kalyanasundaram and Grätzel of simultaneous production of hydrogen and oxygen from water, using a two-catalyst system, therefore represents a major advance [67]. Methylviologen was the oxidative quencher for $Ru(bpy)_3^{2+}$ in their experiments, and H_2 was produced from MV^+ at a Pt catalyst in the usual manner. But $Ru(bpy)_3^{3+}$ is also capable of oxidizing water to O_2 [E^0 for $Ru(bpy)_3^{3+/2+}$ is 1.26 V] [68]. They achieved this by adding RuO_2 as a second heterogeneous catalyst.

2. Other complexes as sensitizers

The tris(bipyridine) complexes of ruthenium offer a number of advantages in photoredox experiments. The excited states are long-lived and of high energy, and readily undergo electron transfer reactions; the complexes are substitution-inert in all three readily accessible oxidation states; and the corresponding Ru(I) and Ru(III) species are powerful reducing and oxidizing agents, respectively. Not all photoredox energy storage schemes involve $Ru(bpy)_3^{2+}$, however; many other complexes have been examined with solar energy storage applications in mind.

Other polypyridine complexes

The properties of other conventional low-spin d^6 polypyridine complexes are closely analogous to those of $Ru(bpy)_3^{2+}$ (see, for example, refs. 68 and 69) and will not be discussed here. Recently, Watts and co-workers have examined the novel iridium(III) complex $(bpy)_2Ir(bpy)(OH_2)^{3+}$, in which one of the bpy ligands is monodentate and a water molecule occupies the sixth coordination site [70,71]. They find its excited state some ten times longer-lived than that of $Ru(bpy)_3^{2+}$, and are now exploring its redox photochemistry.

Chromium(III) complexes have long been popular subjects for photochemical studies. Lifetimes exceeding 50 μs are known for the ^2E excited states of a number of Cr(III) complexes. Electron transfer to $Cr(bpy)_3^{3+*}$ from $Fe(OH_2)_6^{2+}$ and $Ru(bpy)_3^{2+}$ was demonstrated by flash kinetic spectroscopy in 1976 [72]. In the latter case $Cr(bpy)_3^{2+}$ and $Ru(bpy)_3^{3+}$ were produced by reaction both of $Ru(bpy)_3^{2+*}$ with $Cr(bpy)_3^{3+}$ and of $Cr(bpy)_3^{3+*}$ with $Ru(bpy)_3^{2+}$. Systems in which $Cr(bpy)_3^{2+}$, produced by reductive quenching of $Cr(bpy)_3^{3+*}$, is used to reduce H^+ to H_2 are now being examined [73]. The chemical reductant $Cr(bpy)_3^{2+}$ is unfortunately somewhat substitution-labile in aqueous solution; this interferes with efficient catalysis, as the aquated species are photoinert. However, chromium could be favored in an industrial process over ruthenium for economic reasons even if it were less durable. The photooxidation of bis(2,9-dimethyl-1,10-phenanthroline)copper(I) by cobalt(III) complexes, while it proceeds with rather low efficiency [74], is of interest because the Cu(I) complex may be irradiated in the 450-500 nm range.

Metalloporphyrins

Two research groups have reported that zinc porphyrin complexes sensitize the reduction of H^+ to H_2 by EDTA in the presence of a Pt catalyst. The Zn-based sensitizer is relatively efficient for excitation wavelengths above 500 nm and is more durable and more active than $Ru(bpy)_3^{2+}$ under similar conditions [75]. Kalyanasundaram and Grätzel found several additional features of interest in their experiments [76]: The reaction apparently proceeds by both reductive(EDTA) and oxidative(MV^{2+}) quenching of the metalloporphyrin excited state. Large variations in the quenching rates were observed on changing from anionic to cationic substituents in the porphyrin ring. And the system can be made to produce hydrogen without MV^{2+}.

Other complexes

We have also turned our attention to the redox chemistry of excited states. The intensely phosphorescent triplet excited states of two dinuclear rhodium(I) isocyanide complexes have long lifetimes in acetonitrile solution [77]. The $^3A_{2u}$ lifetimes of $Rh_2b_4^{2+}$ and $Rh_2(TMB)_4^{2+}$ are respectively 8.5 μs and 25 ns at room temperature. The $Rh_2b_4^{2+}$ excited state energy was estimated at 1.7 eV by energy transfer experiments, and electron transfer quenching studies were conducted for both it and $Rh_2(TMB)_4^{2+}$ using reductive and oxidative quenchers. Characteristic absorption maxima for reduced (Rh_2^+) and oxidized (Rh_2^{3+}) species were identified from transient difference spectra.

We hope to make use of the excited state properties in two ways. First, since the Rh_2^+ species are also known to be powerful reductants [78], we envision a cycle in which Rh_2^+ could be produced by reductive quenching and then function as a two-electron donor:

$$Rh_2^+ + 2H^+ \rightarrow Rh_2^{3+} + H_2 \tag{29}$$

Such a system would be similar to that of Sutin *et al.* [62] except that the chromophore would also participate directly in proton reduction. So far we have observed only back electron transfer to regenerate Rh_2^{2+} (22). Second, the oxidative quenching system also offers advantages, especially for $Rh_2b_4^{2+}$. In the reaction system

$$Rh_2b_4^{2+*} + MV^{2+} \rightarrow Rh_2b_4^{3+} + MV^+ \tag{30}$$

$$Rh_2b_4^{3+} + MV^+ \rightarrow Rh_2b_4^{2+} + MV^{2+} \tag{31}$$

k_{30} is probably larger than k_{31}; in addition, reaction (11) might allow competitive removal of $Rh_2b_4^{3+}$. Both of these factors should improve the chances of efficient production of MV^+. The adaptation of this system to hydrogen-producing reactions is now under investigation.

Photoredox behavior has also been observed for two other types of complexes. The phosphorescence of $Ir_2(TMB)_4^{2+}$ is quenched by *N,N,N',N'*-tetramethyl-*p*-phenylenediamine(TMPD) with reduction of the iridium complex [37]. The Ir system, with a strong absorption at 625 nm, extends the photoredox response for these isocyanide complexes into the red region of the visible spectrum. Solutions of the molybdenum(II) cluster species $Mo_6Cl_{14}^{2-}$ are also luminescent [79]. Here oxidative quenching occurs in acetonitrile solution with electron acceptors such as MV^{2+}, and the $Mo_6Cl_{14}^-$ ion produced is an extremely strong oxidant ($E_{\frac{1}{2}} \sim$ 1.6 V *vs.* SCE in CH_3CN).

PROSPECTS

Much of the theoretical groundwork concerning electron transfer in molecular ground and excited states has now been laid. Many of the results described here suggest that a relatively efficient system for photochemical energy storage should be achievable. It seems that several areas in particular would benefit from more intense study. Systems capable of multielectron transfer are not common, and an effort should be made to design them and incorporate them into photochemical studies. Such experiments might also lead to new catalysts for gas evolution. In this regard we would do well to examine species such as $Co(CN)_5^{3-}$, which is already known [80,81] to catalyze gas-solution redox equilibria. Experiments with photoinduced oxygen evolution [82] might also be useful in this respect. But an almost totally unexplored area is the redox photochemistry of small molecules other than water. Whereas such reactions (*e.g.*, N_2H_4/NH_3; $C_2O_4^{2-}/CO_2$) might ultimately have applications in energy storage, they could also be adapted to the photochemical promotion of other simple reactions.

The future of photoredox chemistry is, so to speak, bright!

Acknowledgment - For several years our research in inorganic and organometallic photochemistry has been supported by grants from the National Science Foundation (Chemical Dynamics Program). The solar energy storage work involving inorganic molybdenum and iridium photoreceptors has been supported by the Department of Energy (Advanced Technology Projects, Office of Energy Research). Collaboration with Drs. R. Ryason and A. Gupta at the Jet Propulsion Laboratory has been aided by grants from the JPL Director's Discretionary Fund and from the DOE. Instrumentation was obtained with grants from NSF (CHE78-10530) and from the Union Oil Company of California Foundation. The rhodium and iridium salts required in our research have been loaned to us by Johnson Matthey, Inc. (formerly Matthey Bishop, Inc.). One of us (A.W.M.) acknowledges an NSF Graduate Fellowship (1977-80).

REFERENCES

1. J. Bolton, Science 202, 705-711 (1978).
2. H.-D. Scharf, J. Fleischhauer, H. Leismann, I. Ressler, W. Schleker, and R. Weitz, Angew. Chem. Int. Ed. Engl. 18, 652-662 (1979).
3. V. Balzani, L. Moggi, M. F. Manfrin, F. Bolletta, and M. Gleria, Science 189, 852-856 (1975).
4. K. W. Böer, Solar Energy 19, 525-538 (1977).
5. W. H. F. Sasse in J. Bolton, ed., "Solar Power and Fuels," Academic, New York (1976).
6. K. B. Wiberg and H. A. Connon, J. Am. Chem. Soc. 98, 5411-5412 (1976).
7. N. J. Turro, W. R. Cherry, M. F. Mirbach, and M. J. Mirbach, J. Am. Chem. Soc. 99, 7388-7389 (1977).
8. G. S. Hammond, N. J. Turro, and A. Fischer, J. Am. Chem. Soc. 83, 4674-4675 (1961).
9. D. P. Schwendiman and C. Kutal, J. Am. Chem. Soc. 99, 5677-5682 (1977).
10. C. Kutal, Advan. Chem. Ser. 168, 158-173 (1978).
11. P. A. Grutsch and C. Kutal, J. Am. Chem. Soc. 101, 4223-4233 (1979).
12. C. Kutal, D. P. Schwendiman, and P. A. Grutsch, Solar Energy 19, 651-655 (1977).
13. H. Hogeveen and H. C. Volger, J. Am. Chem. Soc. 89, 2486-2487 (1967).
14. E. M. Sweet, R. B. King, R. M. Hanes, and S. Ikai, Advan. Chem. Ser. 173, 344-357 (1979).
15. C. A. Kutal and P. A. Grutsch, Advan. Chem. Ser. 173, 325-343 (1979).
16. O. Samuel, A. Moradpour, and H. B. Kagan, Solar Energy 23, 543-545 (1979).
17. D. P. Gregory, Sci. Am. (Jan.) 13-21 (1973).
18. M. Anbar and I. Pecht, J. Am. Chem. Soc. 89, 2553-2556 (1967).
19. T. S. Dzhabiev, V. Ya. Shafirovich, and A. E. Shilov, React. Kinet. Catal. Lett. 4, 11-20 (1976).
20. L. G. Heidt, M. G. Mullin, W. B. Martin, Jr., and A. M. J. Beatty, J. Am. Chem. Soc. 66, 336-341 (1958).
21. J. Jortner and G. Stein, J. Am. Chem. Soc. 66, 1258-1271 (1958).
22. P. R. Ryason, Solar Energy 19, 445-448 (1977).
23. K. L. Stevenson and D. D. Davis, Inorg. Nucl. Chem. Lett. 12, 905-909 (1976).
24. D. D. Davis, K. L. Stevenson, and C. R. Davis, J. Am. Chem. Soc. 100, 5344-5349 (1978).
25. W. C. Trogler and H. B. Gray, Acc. Chem. Res. 11, 232-239 (1978).
26. D. K. Erwin, G. L. Geoffroy, H. B. Gray, G. S. Hammond, E. I. Solomon, W. C. Trogler, and A. A. Zagars, J. Am. Chem. Soc. 99, 3620-3621 (1977).
27. W. C. Trogler, G. L. Geoffroy, D. K. Erwin, and H. B. Gray, J. Am. Chem. Soc. 100, 1160-1163 (1978).
28. P. Slusser, unpublished results.
29. W. L. Waltz and A. W. Adamson, J. Phys. Chem. 73, 4250-4255 (1969).
30. R. N. Goldberg and L. G. Hepler, Chem. Rev. 68, 229-252 (1968).
31. T. Yamase and T. Ikawa, Bull. Chem. Soc. Japan 50, 746-749 (1977).
32. T. Yamase and T. Ikawa, Inorg. Chim. Acta 37, L529-L531 (1979).
33. A. Camus, C. Cocevar, and G. Mestroni, J. Organomet. Chem. 39, 355-364 (1972).
34. G. L. Geoffroy and R. Pierantozzi, J. Am. Chem. Soc. 98, 8054-8059 (1976).
35. G. L. Geoffroy, Prog. Inorg. Chem. 27, 123-151 (1980).
36. T. Kruck, G. Sylvester, and I. P. Kunan, Angew. Chem. Int. Ed. Engl. 10, 725 (1971).
37. T. P. Smith and H. B. Gray, INOR, 180th ACS National Meeting, San Francisco, CA, Aug. 24-29, 1980.
38. K. R. Mann, N. S. Lewis, V. M. Miskowski, D. K. Erwin, G. S. Hammond, and H. B. Gray, J. Am. Chem. Soc. 99, 5525-5526 (1977).
39. N. S. Lewis, K. R. Mann, J. G. Gordon, II, and H. B. Gray, J. Am. Chem. Soc. 98, 7461-7463 (1976).
40. V. M. Miskowski, I. S. Sigal, K. R. Mann, H. B. Gray, S. J. Milder, G. S. Hammond, and P. R. Ryason, J. Am. Chem. Soc. 101, 4383-4385 (1979).
41. S. J. Milder, Ph.D. thesis, University of California, Santa Cruz, 1978.
42. I. S. Sigal, K. R. Mann, and H. B. Gray, J. Am. Chem. Soc., in press.

43. K. R. Mann, M. J. DiPierro, and T. P. Gill, J. Am. Chem. Soc., in press.
44. J. P. Chesick, unpublished results.
45. K. R. Mann and H. B. Gray, Advan. Chem. Ser. 173, 225-235 (1979).
46. I. S. Sigal and H. B. Gray, to be submitted for publication.
47. H. B. Gray, K. R. Mann, N. S. Lewis, J. A. Thich, and R. M. Richman, Advan. Chem. Ser. 168, 44-56 (1978).
48. K. R. Mann, H. B. Gray, and G. S. Hammond, J. Am. Chem. Soc. 99, 306-307 (1977).
49. V. Balzani, L. Moggi, M. F. Manfrin, F. Bolletta, and G. S. Laurence, Coord. Chem. Rev. 15, 321-433 (1975).
50. V. Balzani, F. Bolletta, M. T. Gandolfi, and M. Maestri, Topics Curr. Chem. 75, 1-64 (1978).
51. H. D. Gafney and A. W. Adamson, J. Am. Chem. Soc. 94, 8238-8239 (1972).
52. D. G. Whitten, Acc. Chem. Res. 13, 83-90 (1980).
53. J.-M. Lehn and J.-P. Sauvage, Nouv. J. Chim. 1, 449-451 (1977).
54. M. Kirch, J.-M. Lehn, and J.-P. Sauvage, Helv. Chim. Acta 62, 1345-1384 (1979).
55. C. R. Bock, J. A. Connor, A. R. Gutierrez, T. J. Meyer, D. G. Whitten, B. P. Sullivan, and J. K. Nagle, J. Am. Chem. Soc. 101, 4815-4824 (1979).
56. P. J. DeLaive, C. Giannotti, and D. G. Whitten, J. Am. Chem. Soc. 100, 7413-7415 (1978).
57. K. Takama, M. Kajiwara, and T. Matsuo, Chem. Lett. 1199-1202 (1977).
58. K. Takuma, Y. Shuto, and T. Matsuo, Chem. Lett. 983-986 (1978).
59. P. J. DeLaive, J. T. Lee, H. W. Sprintschnik, H. Abruña, T. J. Meyer, and D. G. Whitten, J. Am. Chem. Soc. 99, 7094-7097 (1977).
60. Y. Tsutsui, K. Takuma, T. Nishijima, and T. Matsuo, Chem. Lett. 617-620 (1979).
61. P.-A. Brugger and M. Grätzel, J. Am. Chem. Soc. 102, 2461-2463 (1980).
62. G. M. Brown, B. S. Brunschwig, C. Creutz, J. F. Endicott, and N. Sutin, J. Am. Chem. Soc. 101, 1298-1300 (1979).
63. V. Ya. Shafirovich, N. K. Khannanov, and V. V. Strelets, Nouv. J. Chim. 4, 81-84 (1980).
64. D. E. Green and L. H. Strickland, Biochem. J. 28, 898-900 (1934).
65. A. Moradpour, E. Amouyal, P. Keller, and H. Kagan, Nouv. J. Chim. 2, 547-549 (1978).
66. P. J. DeLaive, B. P. Sullivan, T. J. Meyer, and D. G. Whitten, J. Am. Chem. Soc. 101, 4007-4008 (1979).
67. K. Kalyanasundaram and M. Grätzel, Angew. Chem. Int. Ed. Engl. 18, 701-702 (1979).
68. C.-T. Lin, W. Böttcher, M. Chou, C. Creutz, and N. Sutin, J. Am. Chem. Soc. 98, 6536-6544 (1976).
69. C. Creutz, M. Chou, T. Netzel, M. Okumura, and N. Sutin, J. Am. Chem. Soc. 102, 1309-1319 (1980).
70. S. F. Bergeron and R. J. Watts, J. Am. Chem. Soc. 101, 3151-3156 (1979).
71. R. J. Watts, M. Finlayson, and P. C. Ford, INOR, 178th ACS National Meeting, Washington, DC, Sept. 9-14, 1979.
72. R. Ballardini, G. Varani, F. Scandola, and V. Balzani, J. Am. Chem. Soc. 98, 7432-7433 (1976).
73. D. Miller and G. McLendon, J. Am. Chem. Soc., in press.
74. B.-T. Ahn and D. R. McMillin, Inorg. Chem. 17, 2253-2258 (1978).
75. G. McLendon, D. Miller, and T. Guarr, INOR, 179th ACS National Meeting, Houston, TX, Mar. 23-28, 1980.
76. K. Kalyanasundaram and M. Grätzel, Helv. Chim. Acta 63, 478-485 (1980).
77. S. J. Milder, H. B. Gray, R. A. Goldbeck, and D. S. Kliger, J. Am. Chem. Soc., submitted for publication.
78. J. S. Najdzionek, unpublished results.
79. A. W. Maverick and H. B. Gray, INOR, 180th ACS National Meeting, San Francisco, CA, Aug. 24-29, 1980.
80. G. G. Strathdee and M. J. Quinn, Can. J. Chem. 50, 3144-3153 (1972).
81. D. L. Reger and M. M. Habib, Advan. Chem. Ser. 173, 43-49 (1979).
82. G. L. Geoffroy, G. S. Hammond, and H. B. Gray, J. Am. Chem. Soc. 97, 3933-3936 (1975).

ELECTRON TRANSFER IN 'BLUE' COPPER PROTEINS

H. C. Freeman

Department of Inorganic Chemistry, University of Sydney, Sydney 2006, Australia

Abstract - Recent crystal structural results for plastocyanin and azurin, two proteins with 'blue' copper centres, are reviewed in relation to biological electron-transfer between metalloproteins. The molecules of both plastocyanin and azurin have a single Cu atom with a distorted tetrahedral coordination geometry. The ligands in each case are the imidazole N_δ atoms of two histidine residues, the thiolate S atom of a cysteine residue, and the thioether S atom of a methionine residue. In plastocyanin the Cu-ligand bond-lengths have been determined to relatively high precision (estimated standard deviations = 0.05Å) for both the oxidised [Cu(II)] and reduced [Cu(I)] states of the protein. By repeating the diffraction measurements and refinement calculations for crystals prepared at different pH's it has been found that the structure of Cu(II)-plastocyanin is pH-independent whereas the reduced protein is an equilibrium mixture of a redox-active form, Cu(I)-plastocyanin, and a protonated redox-inactive form, HCu(I)-plastocyanin. The crystal structural results from plastocyanin and azurin provide useful bench-marks for the discussion of kinetic, thermodynamic, spectroscopic and theoretical studies of electron-transfer reactions involving metalloproteins which have 'blue' copper centres.

INTRODUCTION

Electron-transfer is a central (and conceptually simple) process in chemistry and biology. It is, however, easier to write

$$A + B \rightarrow A^+ + B^-$$

than to describe this process quantitatively for the case where A and B are real chemical entities. When A and B are metalloprotein molecules, each with a thousand or more carbon, nitrogen and oxygen atoms in addition to a redox-active metal centre, the number of parameters which may affect the electron-transfer reaction is obviously very large. In this lecture we shall examine the current status of our understanding of electron-transfer reactions involving a particular class of metalloproteins, namely those which have 'blue' copper centres (Table 1). Some recent relevant review articles are cited as Refs. 1-4

'Blue' or 'Type 1' Cu centres

'Blue' or 'Type 1' Cu centres occur (Table 2) both in copper-proteins where the molecule contains only one Cu atom and in multi-Cu enzymes where 'Type 1' centres are associated with other Cu centres described as 'Type 2' and 'Type 3'. The 'blue Cu centres are characterised by

(i) an intense absorption band near 600 nm (ε_{max} ~5000 $M^{-1}cm^{-1}$, compared with ~50 $M^{-1}cm^{-1}$ for the *d-d* transitions of 'normal' Cu(II) complexes with low-MW ligands),

(ii) a very small hyperfine splitting in the $g_\parallel$ region of the EPR spectrum ($A_\parallel$ = 0.003-0.006 cm^{-1} instead of 0.013-0.020 cm^{-1}), and

TABLE 1. Classification of proteins with 'blue' copper centres

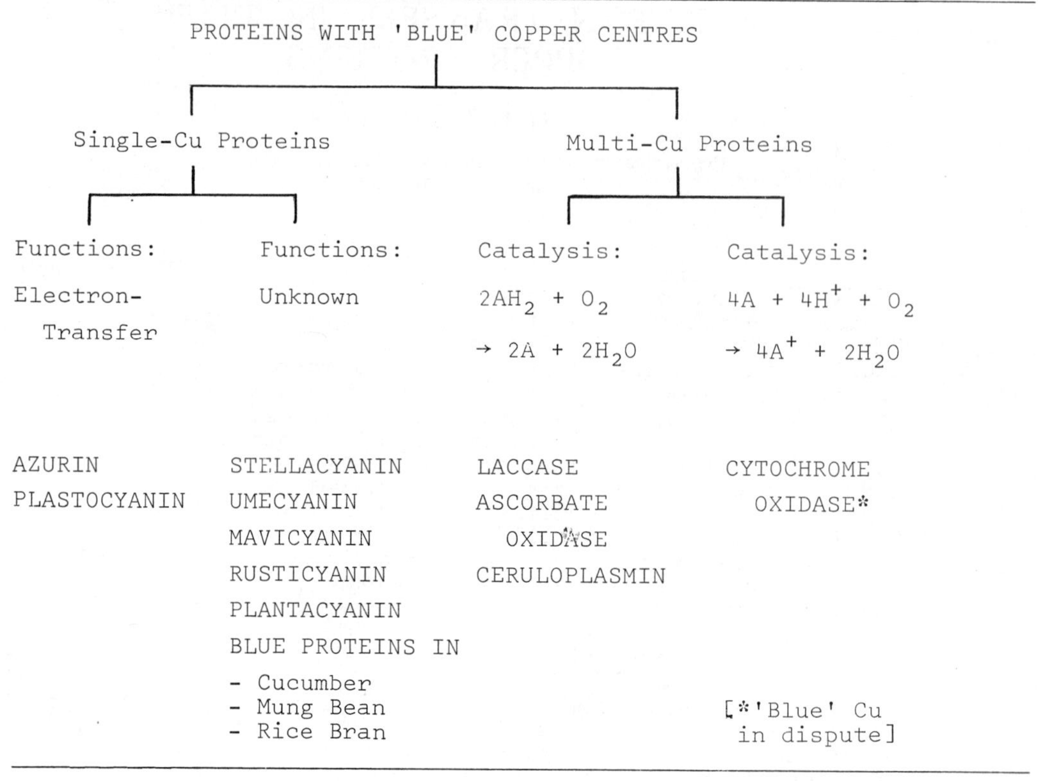

(iii) an unusually high redox potential (Table 2). E_0' lies - with one exception - in the range 300-800 mV, compared with 170 mV for the Cu(II)/Cu(I) couple in aqueous solution.

Among these three properties, the redox potential is the one which is directly related to the biological function of the 'blue' Cu centres. In all cases where such a function has been identified it is electron-transfer. It seems that Nature has used the protein molecules to tune the redox potentials of the Cu centres to values which are appropriate for the biological processes in which they participate.

Some general comments on metalloprotein structures

At the risk of saying the obvious, I remind you of several properties of proteins and metalloproteins which are relevant to the discussion of electron-transfer.

The ligands by which the metal atoms in metalloproteins are coordinated are of course very much larger than those in conventional coordination compounds. The MW's of the ligands in the examples given in Table 2 span the range 10,000-14,000 d. A trivial result of the large sizes of the protein molecules is that - depending on the distance of a metal centre beneath the molecular surface - the electron-transfer pathways to and from the metal may be much longer than in low-MW complexes. A less trivial result is that it may not be valid for many purposes to treat metalloprotein molecules as uniformly charged particles. The surfaces are structured just as the interiors are. Positive, negative and non-polar groups may occur in patches on the molecular surface. Such patches may help to orient a protein molecule in relation to its environment (e.g., a membrane) or to achieve specificity in its reactions with biological redox partners.

All proteins are polymers built up from amino-acid sub-units, $-[NH-CHR-CO]_n-$. The amino-acid sequence of a protein is called the *primary* structure. From a structural view-point there are advantages in treating the protein as a sequence of tetrahedral, chiral C_α atoms alternating with planar, rigid amide ('peptide') groups, $^+NH_3....C_\alpha HR-CONH-C_\alpha HR'-CONH-...COO^-$. To a good

TABLE 2. Some properties of proteins with 'blue' copper centres.

Protein	Source	M.W.	E_0' of 'Blue' Cu mV(pH)	'Blue' Cu: Total Cu
Single-Cu Electron-Transfer Proteins				
AZURIN	Bacteria	14,000	330(6.4)	
PLASTOCYANIN	Plants, green algae, some blue-green algae	10,500	370(7.0)	
Single-Cu Proteins without known functions				
STELLACYANIN	Lacquer tree	20,000	184(7.1)	
UMECYANIN	Horseradish roots	14,600	283(7.0)	
MAVICYANIN	Squash	18,000	285(7.0)	
RUSTICYANIN	*Th. ferro-oxidans*	16,500	680(2.0)	
BASIC BLUE PROTEIN (= PLANTACYANIN?)	Cucumber	10,100	317(6.8)	
BLUE PROTEIN	Rice bran	18,300	275(7.4)	
BLUE PROTEIN	Mung bean	24,000	-	
Multi-Cu Enzymes				
LACCASE	Fungi *(Polyporus)*	64,000	767	1:4
LACCASE	Lacquer tree *(Rhus)*	100,000	415	1:4
ASCORBATE OXIDASE	Squash, cucumber	140,000	-	2:9±1
CERULOPLASMIN	Blood serum	130,000	490,580	2:7±1
CYTOCHROME *c* OXIDASE	Mitochondria			1?:2

approximation, the local conformation (*secondary* structure) of the polypeptide backbone can then be described in terms of only two parameters per C_α atom, namely the torsion angles about the N-C_α and C_α-C bonds.

Steric factors and hydrogen-bonding make certain types of secondary structure energetically favourable. For example, an extended and slightly puckered conformation ('β-structure') causes successive side-chains to lie alternately on opposite sides of the polypeptide backbone (Fig. 1). Parallel or anti-parallel alignment of polypeptide chains which are in the β-conformation provides ideal geometrical conditions for hydrogen-bonding, and leads to the formation of β-sheets (Fig. 1) in many protein structures. A β-sheet may be bent to enclose a space, in which case a 'β-barrel' or 'β-sandwich' may result. Since alternate side-chains lie on opposite sides of the polypeptide chain in the β-conformation, the side-chains of a β-barrel point alternatively towards the interior and the exterior.

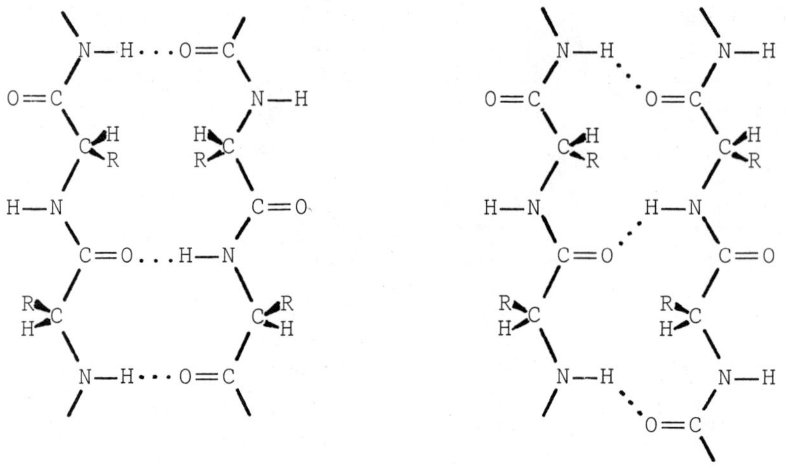

Fig.1 Schematic representation of *(a)* anti-parallel and *(b)* parallel β-sheets.

The structure of a protein as determined by X-ray diffraction is a time-averaged structure. The positions in which the atoms or groups are found are, if all goes well, the most probable positions. The crystallographic vibrational parameters of highly refined structures tell us qualitatively that the atoms and groups are in thermal motion (which is difficult to distinguish from disorder). Quantitative information about the extent and time-scale of this motion is beginning to become available from spectroscopic measurements. For example, we know from ^{1}H NMR spectra that the phenolic side-chains of the Tyr residues in plastocyanin flip at a rate which is rapid on the NMR time scale (5). (See Note a). A study by time-resolved fluorescence polarisation spectroscopy, using synchrotron radiation as a pulsed light source, has shown that the bulky aromatic side-chain of a Trp residue in azurin rotates within a cone of semi-angle 34° and with a periodicity of 0.51 *nanosecond* (6) . The significance of these results is that a protein can (but does not necessarily) have an interior that is fluid-like in the sub-nanosecond time-range, and that sub-nanosecond fluctuations about the crystallographically observed time-average may be involved in chemical/biological activity (6).

Regardless of the structural details, there are a number of reasons why metalloproteins cannot be treated merely as overgrown low-MW complexes. A protein molecule has many more hydrogen-bonded, ionic and non-polar ('hydrophobic') interactions than a ligand in a low-MW complex. The ligand in a metalloprotein is thus able to stabilize a metal centre in a coordination geometry which may not be accessible in smaller molecules with fewer intra-molecular interactions. Further, the metal centre in a metalloprotein is characteristically found in a hydrophobic environment so that information and concepts derived from model complexes in aqueous solution have to be used with caution. The kinetics and thermodynamics of electron-transfer reactions may also be influenced by functional groups remote from the metal centre (e.g., surface patches of charged or non-polar side-chains, functioning as recognition or binding sites for redox partners). There is no guarantee that inorganic redox reagents will use the same electron-transfer sites, pathways or mechanisms as the biological redox partners of a metalloprotein.

Note a. Some amino-acids (3-letter code, amino-acid, -R in -NHCHRCO-): Ala, alanine, $-CH_3$; Asn, asparagine, $-CH_2CONH_2$; Asp, aspartate, $-CH_2COO^-$; Cys, cysteine, $-CH_2SH$; Glu, glutamate, $-CH_2CH_2COO^-$; Gly, glycine, -H; His, histidine, $-CH_2$-(imidazolyl); Leu, leucine, $-CH_2CH(CH_3)_2$; Met, methionine, $-CH_2CH_2SCH_3$; Phe, phenylalanine, $-CH_2$-(phenyl); Pro, proline, cyclic $-(CH_2)_3$- from C_α to N; Trp, tryptophan, $-CH_2$-(indolyl); Tyr, tyrosine, $-CH_2$-(phenyl)-OH.

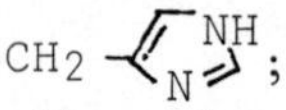

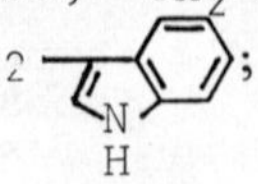

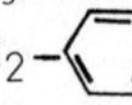

ELECTRON TRANSFER BETWEEN METALLOPROTEINS: THEORY

Tunneling

It is only a modest exaggeration to say that the development of meaningful theories for electron-transfer between metal centres in metalloproteins has been achieved by throwing the proteins away. A theoretician's view (7) of two metalloproteins just prior to electron-transfer is shown in Fig. 2.

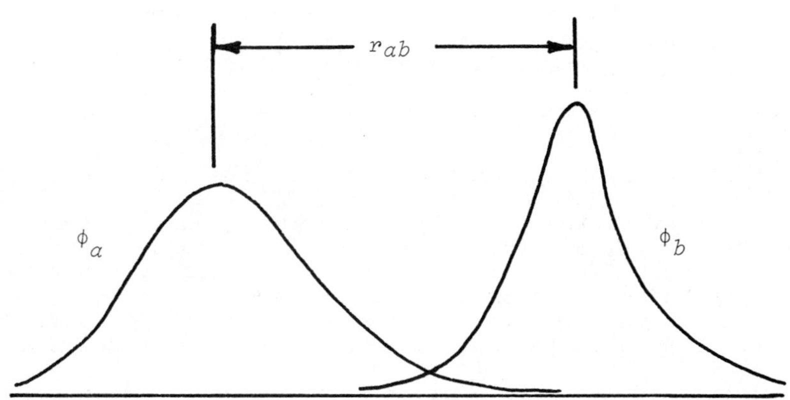

Fig. 2. Two metalloprotein molecules just prior to electron-transfer from site *a* to site *b*. The wave functions ϕ_a and ϕ_b are well separated by a distance r_{ab}, and overlap weakly. (From Ref. 7).

The problem is reduced to getting an electron from a metal centre *a*, where its behaviour is described by a wave function ϕ_a, to a metal centre *b*, where its behaviour is described by a wave function ϕ_b. For electron-transfer to occur, ϕ_a and ϕ_b must overlap, even if only weakly. In this event there is a matrix element T_{ab} of the Hamiltonian between the two one-electron states. T_{ab} is small due to the exponential decrease of the wave functions in the region between the sites *a* and *b* - the region which constitutes the barrier against electron-transfer. The transfer process thus involves 'tunneling', and T_{ab} as been clled the tunneling matrix element. An excellent overview of the present state of tunneling theory is presented in Ref. 8, which includes important contributions by Hopfield (9) and Marcus (10). In calculating the rate of tunneling w_{ab} (7), it is necessary to include the effects of vibronic coupling (because this gives an energy width to electronic states which would otherwise be infinitely sharp). Development of the theory for Gaussian atoms embedded 'in a more or less rigid matrix' leads (7) to -

$$w_{ab} = (2\pi/h)|T_{ab}|^2(\tfrac{1}{2}\pi\sigma^2)^{\frac{1}{2}}\exp[-(E_a - E_b - \Delta)^2/2\sigma^2]$$

where $\sigma^2 = (\tfrac{1}{2}k_a x_a^2)\kappa T_a \coth(T_a/2T) + (\tfrac{1}{2}k_b x_b^2)\kappa T_b \coth(T_b/2T)$

and $\Delta = \tfrac{1}{2}k_a^2 x_a^2 + \tfrac{1}{2}k_b x_b^2$

In these expressions -

x_a, x_b = vibration coordinates with electron in states ϕ_a, ϕ_b

k_a, k_b = curvatures of states ϕ_a, ϕ_b

T = temperature of observation

T_a, T_b = 'characteristic' temperatures

$E_a - E_b$ = potential difference between the two sites

Δ = vibronic coupling parameter reflecting the shape of the PE surface for a reaction centre

κ = collision frequency factor

Because the vibronic coupling parameter Δ is positive and on a scale of 1 eV, electron-transfer is *slow* unless it is "downhill", i.e., unless $E_a - E_b$ is appreciable. In the event that $E_a - E_b \approx \Delta$ short-circuiting transfers downhill can be very fast, but this effect can be avoided if the proteins use stereo-chemistry to keep T_{ab} small. Transfers downhill by about 2Δ are slow in any case. Hopfield (7) has concluded that "these simple qualitative features must dominate the structural and stereochemical disposition of electron-transfer components in photosynthetic and mitochondrial assemblies".

Application of the theory to real protein systems leads to credible results, For the rate of electron-transfer from a cytochrome *c* to bacteriochlorophyll in the photosynthetic bacterium *Chromatium* the available data are fitted by $E_a - E_b = 0.45$ V, $\Delta = 1.7$ eV, $T_{ab} = 4 \times 10^{-4}$ eV, $T_a = T_b = 350^oK$. Further, given a number of additional reasonable assumptions and approximations, T_{ab} can be used to derive an approximate donor-acceptor distance. If the donor and acceptor molecules are separated by an edge-to-edge distance R, if the barrier height represented by the surrounding material is 2 eV, and if the edge atoms of both molecules are carbon atoms in aromatic (e.g., haem) groups, then

$$T_{ab} \approx 2.7 \exp(-0.72R)$$

In the cited example it is necessary to include a normalisation factor to take into account the numbers of atoms in the aromatic ring systems of the donor and acceptor molecules. When this is done, the value $T_{ab} = 4 \times 10^{-4}$ eV corresponds to a separation R = 8Å between the edges of the donor and acceptor molecules.

The restriction of the theoretical treatment to Gaussian atoms is not essential (11). Various authors differ in their current estimates of R, but most of the estimates fall in a range of $0 < R < 30$Å. Although an elegant experimental verification of the preceding theory (the discovery of a predicted near-IR charge transfer band) has recently been found to have a different explanation (12), there is substantial agreement that electrons can tunnel over quite large distances. It is interesting that computerised model-building experiments for the reaction between cytochromes *c* and b_5, two haem proteins whose structures are known from X-ray diffraction, indicate a contact geometry in which the edges of the electron-donating and accepting groups are separated by 9Å (13).

Tunneling theory makes it respectable for electron-transfer to occur even when the metal centres in two metalloprotein molecules are separated by quite large distances. In its present form the theory treats the material between the metal sites as a continuum. This leaves the proteins with functions which are concerned entirely with *control*: Protein molecules may (*i*) use ligand groups or coordination geometry to tune the E_0' of a metal to a required value, (*ii*) use surface structural features to ensure specificity of interaction, and/or (*iii*) determine rates of electron-transfer by setting a lower limit to the distances over which electrons must be transferred. It remains to be proven that these *are* the functions for which Nature has designed such complicated molecules, and that the structural details of the material between the metal centres are largely irrelevant to the electron-transfer process itself.

Thermodynamic aspects
A considerable number of kinetic and thermodynamic parameters for oxidations and reductions of 'blue' Cu-proteins have been reported. Structural interpretations have been given for some of them. A recent review by Sutin (14) provides an excellent perspective for the discussion of metalloprotein redox reactions in the context of our present understanding of simpler systems.

Electron-exchange reactions. One of the examples treated by Sutin is an inorganic electron-exchange reaction without overall chemical change,

$$Fe(H_2O)_6^{2+} + Fe(H_2O)_6^{3+} \rightleftharpoons Fe(H_2O)_6^{3+} + Fe(H_2O)_6^{2+}$$

The free energy of activation $\Delta G^{\ddagger}$ for such a reaction, and hence the rate constant k, may be calculated *a priori* if adequate theremodynamic quantum-mechanical and stereochemical data are available:

$$k = (kT/h)\exp(-\Delta G^{\ddagger}/RT)$$

$$\Delta G^{\ddagger} = w_r + \Delta G^{\ddagger}_{trans} + \Delta G^{\ddagger}_{in} + \Delta G^{\ddagger}_{out}$$

Here w_r is the work required to bring the reactants together, G_{trans} is the free energy of formation of the transition state from the two non-interacting reactants, and $\Delta G^{\ddagger}_{in}$ and $\Delta G^{\ddagger}_{out}$ are the free energies required to reorganise the inner and outer coordination shells, respectively. The physical data which are used in the calculation of the free energy terms (14) are given in Table 3. In the case of the $Fe(H_2O)_6^{2+/3+}$ reaction, the calculations indeed predict the kinetics correctly. The kinetics are shown to be consistent with an adiabatic, outer-sphere model in which nuclear tunneling and other quantum effects are small. On the other hand, the calculations fail to reproduce the ionic strength dependences of the enthalpy and entropy of activation (14). It is of course obvious that even for such a simple reaction as electron-exchange the *a priori* calculations cannot easily be extended to metalloproteins. Some of the reasons have been included as comments in Table 3 - not to criticise thermodynamic theory, but to emphasise significant differences between metalloproteins and low-MW complexes.

Marcus cross-relations. In electron-transfer reactions where the reactants and products are not identical, e.g.,

$$Fe(H_2O)_6^{2+} + Ru(bpy)_3^{3+} \rightarrow Fe(H_2O)_6^{3+} + Ru(bpy)_3^{2+}$$

the Marcus cross-relations enable the kinetic and thermodynamic parameters of the cross-reaction (subscripted '12) to be expressed in terms of the parameters of the self-exchange reactions of the components (subscripted '11' and '22'). The equation relating the rate constants is

$$k_{12} = (k_{11}k_{22}K_{12}f_{12})$$

$$\text{where } \log f_{12} = (\log K_{12})^2/4 \log(k_{11}k_{22}/Z^2)$$

$$\text{and } K_{12} = \text{equilibrium constant}$$

The Marcus cross-relations have been widely used in the discussion of the kinetic and thermodynamic parameters measured for the reactions of metalloproteins with other metalloproteins and with inorganic redox reagents. In cases where *different* self-exchange rates are obtained from the cross-reactions of a metalloprotein with a number of redox partners, *differences* between the electron-transfer pathways are inferred (see, e.g., Refs. 15-17). For example, the self-exchange rates k_{11} calculated for plastocyanin from the cross-reactions with cytochrome *f*, cytochrome *c* and $Fe(edta)^{2-}$ are ~4×10^{10}, 2×10^6 and 10 $M^{-1}s^{-1}$, respectively; the values calculated for azurin from the rates of reduction by cytochrome c_{551} cytochrome *c* and $Fe(edta)^{2-}$ are 8×10^7, 2×10^4 and 7×10^{-3} $M^{-1}s^{-1}$, respectively (15). From these results it has been suggested that the Cu site in azurin is

TABLE 3. Free energy terms and basic data required for the prediction of free energies of activation and rate constants in inorganic electron-exchange reactions, with some comments illustrating major differences between low-MW complexes and metalloproteins.

SYMBOL	EXPLANATION	COMMENTS
Free energy terms		
w_r	Work required to bring the reactants together (calc. by Debye-Hückel expression)	In biological reactions, the reactants may already be membrane-bound; or one may be membrane-bound while the other diffuses in 2 or 3 dimensions from site to site.
$\Delta G^{\ddagger}_{trans}$	Free energy of formation of transition state from the two non-interacting reactants	
$\Delta G^{\ddagger}_{in}$ $\Delta G^{\ddagger}_{out}$	Free energy required to reorganise the inner and outer coordination shells of the reactants	What is the 'outer coordination shell' when (*i*) a reactant is bound in or on a membrane? (*ii*) a metal centre is buried some distance below the surface of a protein molecule?
Physical data for calculation of free energy terms*		
Z	Collision frequency of two uncharged particles in solution.	See comment on w_r
q_i	Charges on reactants	When two proteins react specifically, the overall charges may be less important than local concentrations of charge on the molecular surfaces.
a_i	Radii of reactants	The metal centre in a metalloprotein is usually located unsymetrically, i.e., the distance to the molecular surface depends on the direction.
d	Distance between the centres of the reactants in the activated complex	Minimum values (i.e., values based on favourable inter-molecular contacts) can be predicted for metalloproteins when molecular structures for both reactants are known from crystal structure analyses.
f_i	Breathing force constants of the reactants	A single force constant per reactant may be inadequate for calc. of $\Delta G^{\ddagger}_{in}$ since metal atoms in metalloproteins usually have unsymmetrical coordinations by 4-6 ligands; and the force-fields at the metal atoms may fluctuate due to the dynamics of the non-ligand side-chains in the interior of the molecules.
μ n D_s	Ionic strength, refractive index, and static dielectric constant of the 'medium'	The 'medium' between electron-transfer centres in metalloproteins may include structured protein as well as liquid/membrane material; a description in terms of a continuum with isotropic properties may be inadequate.

* The data required for the free-energy terms are: w_r - q_i, D_s, d, μ; $\Delta G^{\ddagger}_{trans}$ - Z; $\Delta G^{\ddagger}_{out}$ - q_i, a_i, d, n, D_s; $\Delta G^{\ddagger}_{in}$ - f_i, a_i

significantly less accessible to redox partners than is the Cu site in plastocyanin, and that the cytochromes (presumably using their haem edges) are able to penetrate the hydrophobic regions around the Cu centres more easily than $Fe(edta)^{2-}$ (15). The k_{11} values found for both plastocyanin and azurin with $Co(phen)_3^{3+}$ are also larger than with $Fe(edta)^{2-}$, again suggesting that $Co(phen)_3^{3+}$ makes the more favourable contacts with the Cu sites (16).

The *converse* argument has also been used. The k_{12} values derived via the Marcus relations for the oxidations of cytochrome c_{551} and azurin by $Co(phen)_3^{3+}$ agree with the observed rates. This has been taken to imply "that the interactions of $Co(phen)_3^{3+}$ with cytochrome *c* or with azurin resemble very closely those of cytochromes *c* with themselves or with azurin". This resemblance has been attributed to the presence in both $Co(phen)_3^{3+}$ and cytochromes of the exposed edges of hydrophobic, π-bonded ligands (18). In a comprehensive study of 13 protein-protein redox reactions involving cytochromes *c*, c_{551}, c_{553} and *f*, three azurins and three plastocyanins (19), a good fit between observed and calculated k_{11} values was obtained by the use of six k_{11} values (one for each cytochrome except *f*, two for two types of azurin, one for the plastocyanins). It was concluded that there is no evidence for kinetic selectivity between any of the 13 reaction partners analysed. (The numerical values of the k_{11} values used in this work differed from those in Ref. 15. In particular, the order of the k_{11} values for azurin and plastocyanin was reversed.)

Structural inferences from thermodynamics. The preceding discussion has concentrated on only two aspects of the kinetics and thermodynamics of metalloprotein redox reactions. Nothing has been said about the large amount of information which is now available for the enthalpies and entropies of reaction and activation. Neither has justice been done to a number of authors who have expressed reservations about the applicability of the Marcus cross-relations to protein electron-transfer reactions (20, 41) and about the validity (or rather uniqueness) of mechanistic interpretations based only on thermodynamic parameters (e.g., the use of activation entropies to discriminate between adiabatic and non-adiabatic reactions)(3(*b*)). On the whole it seems desirable to proceed cautiously in this area. For example, the disagreement between the rate equations and rate constants found by two groups of authors for the azurin—$Co(phen)_3^{3+}$ system (16, 21) suggests that the use of the Marcus cross-relations could lead to the creation of a body of hypotheses which are only coincidentally self-consistent.

THE STRUCTURE AND FUNCTION OF PLASTOCYANIN - PART I

Biological function

Plastocyanin, a single-Cu protein with MW = 10,500 d (Tables 1 and 2), has a relatively well-defined function in photosynthetic electron-transport (Fig. 3). The protein occurs in all higher plants, in many green

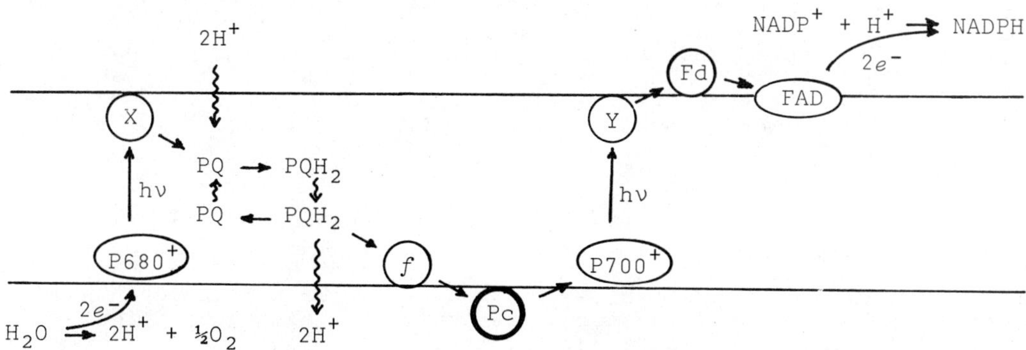

Fig. 3. Photosynthetic electron-transfer chain (simplified), showing the positions which the components are thought to occupy in relation to the thylakoid membrane. $P680^+$, $P700^+$ = chlorophyll pigments of photosystems II, I; X, Y = primary electron-acceptors of photosystems II, I; PQ, PQH_2 = plastoquinone, plastoquinol; *f* = cytochrome *f*; Pc = plastocyanin; Fd = ferredoxin; FAD = flavine adenine dinucleotide. Movement of protons and plastoquinol/one is indicated by ⟿.

algae, and in some blue-green algae (cyanobacteria). It acts as an oxidant for a membrane-bound cytochrome (cytochrome *f*, MW ~33,000) and as a reductant for P700, the double chlorophyll pigment of photosystem I. The extensive literature on photosynthesis is reviewed in Ref. 22.

The sites where photosynthesis takes place are highly convoluted 'thylakoid' membranes inside particles called chloroplasts. A thylakoid membrane encloses a space, so that it has an interior and an exterior. Cytochrome *f* and pigment P700 are membrane-bound, probably close to the interior thylakoid surface. The location of plastocyanin is still a matter for debate. The weight of current opinion favours a location *on* the interior thylakoid surface. There are arguments supporting an attachment which permits the plastocyanin molecules to diffuse 2-dimensionally along the surface. It is possible that plastocyanin attached to the membrane is in equilibrium with plastocyanin dissolved in the liquid inside the thylakoid. Some investigators prefer plastocyanin to exist purely as a solute. It is therefore not yet clear whether plastocyanin molecules are associated on the thylakoid surface with specific cytochrome *f* and P700 partners, or whether they act as electron-shuttles by moving along the thylakoid surface or through the intra-thylakoid liquid.

The photosynthetic electron-transport process in which plastocyanin takes part is *vectorial* in the sense that it results in the transfer of electrons from the interior to the exterior of the thylakoid membrane. This electron-transport is linked with the generation of protons inside the thylakoid (by the oxidation of H_2O) and with proton-transport from the exterior to the interior by plastoquinol. According to the chemiosmotic hypothesis of Mitchell, the proton-translocating electron transport system and ATP-synthetase are linked to form a phosphorylating proton circuit. The evidence for, and consequences of, this hypothesis have recently been reviewed (22, 23).

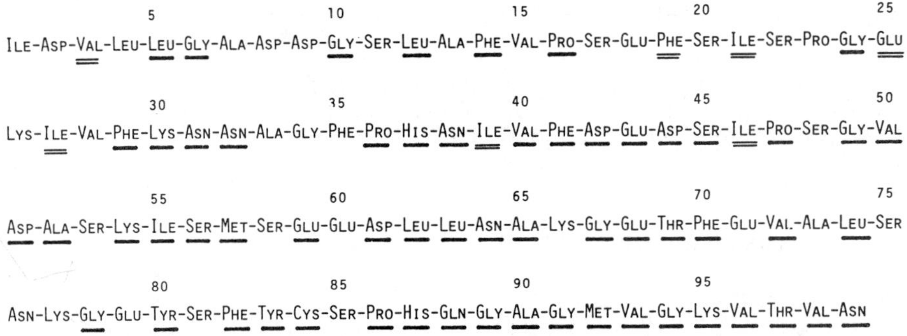

Fig. 4 Amino-acid sequence of poplar (*Populus nigra* var. *italica*) plastocyanin, showing 67 residues which are invariant (——) or conservatively substituted (══) in 67 plant plastocyanins. If three algal plastocyanins are included, the number of invariant or conservatively substituted residues is 39. Residue 45 is Ser in poplar, Glu in other plant plastocyanins; residue 70 is Phe in poplar, Tyr in other plastocyanins.

Complete or partial aminoacid sequences have been determined for 67 higher plant plastocyanins and 3 algal plastocyanins. These show a surprising degree of conservation (Fig. 3). Among 13 complete sequences (99 residues) and 54 partial sequences (*ca.* 40 residues) for plant plastocyanins, 60 residues are invariant and 7 residues are conservatively substituted, in each case with at most one exception. If three complete algal plastocyanin sequences are included, the numbers of invariant and conservatively substituted residues are 33 and 6, respectively. The high degree of conservation is important for two reasons. Firstly, it suggests that structural information derived from one plastocyanin should be valid for the family as a whole. This hypothesis is confirmed by the close similarity of the ^1H NMR spectra of the Cu(I)-plastocyanins from a variety of plant sources, as well as by the corresponding (Cu(I)- minus Cu(II)-plastocyanin) NMR difference spectra (5). Secondly, there is the likelihood that highly conserved residues have been conserved either because they are essential for the function of the protein, or because they are essential for a structural feature which is essential for the function of the protein. Highly conserved residues may therefore, in the light of the molecular structure, provide clues concerning the electron-transfer pathways and mechanisms of the protein.

The crystal structure of Cu(II)-plastocyanin

General description. The crystal structure of plastocyanin in the oxidised state [i.e. Cu(II)-plastocyanin = Cu(II)Pc] was originally solved at a resolution of 2.7Å (24). The crystals were obtained from the plastocyanin of poplar trees (*Populus nigra*, var. *italica*). They were large, deep blue, mechanically robust, and stable under the conditions of X-irradiation used for diffraction measurements. These features are relevant since they contributed to the precision of the diffraction data and therefore to the precision with which the structure could be refined. The present description is based on the refinement at 1.6Å resolution (25). The conventional crystallographic residual *R* is 0.168, which is regarded as highly respectable in protein crystal structure analysis. The estimated standard deviations of the Cu-ligand bond-lengths are 0.05Å, and those of the ligand-Cu-ligand bond-angles are 3°. The sites of 42 H_2O molecules on the exterior of the protein have been found.

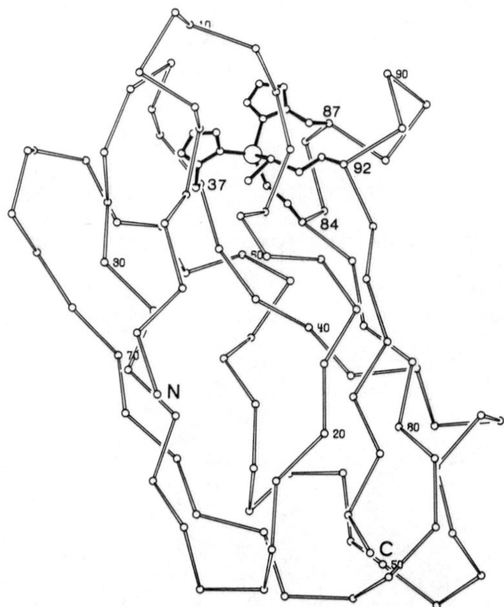

Fig. 5 Molecular structure of poplar plastocyanin. The polypeptide backbone is represented by the C_{α} atoms. Every tenth residue is numbered. The four Cu-binding side-chains are shown.

The molecular structure (Fig.5) comprises eight strands of polypeptide backbone and seven connecting loops. Seven of the strands have segments in the β-conformation. One strand (the fifth, starting from the NH_2-terminus of the chain) is irregular and has no β-character. There are several prominent kinks in three of the strands (at residues 14-17, 42-45, 52-56 and 57-61]). The Cu site is near the "northern" end of the molecule in the orientation of Fig.5.

The refinement at 1.6Å resolution is sufficiently precise to make possible a detailed description of the hydrogen bonding interactions, both between backbone amide groups and between side-chain functional groups. An analysis of the contacts between the side-chains inside the molecule has also been made. Details will be published elsewhere.

The Cu site. The Cu atom is coordinated by the side-chains of His37, Cys84, His87 and Met92 (Fig.5). The coordination is considerably distorted from a tetrahedral geometry (Fig.6). The metal-ligand bond-lengths are: Cu—N(His37) = 2.04Å, Cu—S(Cys84) = 2.13Å, Cu—N(His87) = 2.10Å,

Cu—(Met92) = 2.90Å. The smallest bond-angle is N(His37)—Cu—S(Met92) = 85°, and the largest is N(His37)—Cu—S(Cys84) = 132°. The Cu atom lies 0.72° from the plane of N(His37), S(Cys84) and S(Met 92); this plane has no special significance but the deviation of the Cu atom from it is a useful measure of tetrahedrality. In comparison with Cu(II)—ligand bond-lengths in model complexes with similar ligands but with more conventional coordination geometries the two Cu—N bonds in Cu(II)-Pc are normal, the Cu—S(thiolate) is somewhat short, and the Cu—S(thioether) bond is unusually long (25). A recent EXAFS study has yielded Cu—N(His) and Cu—S(Cys) distances which are in excellent agreement with the crystallographic results (26). The long Cu—S(Met) distance is not unequivocally determined by EXAFS.

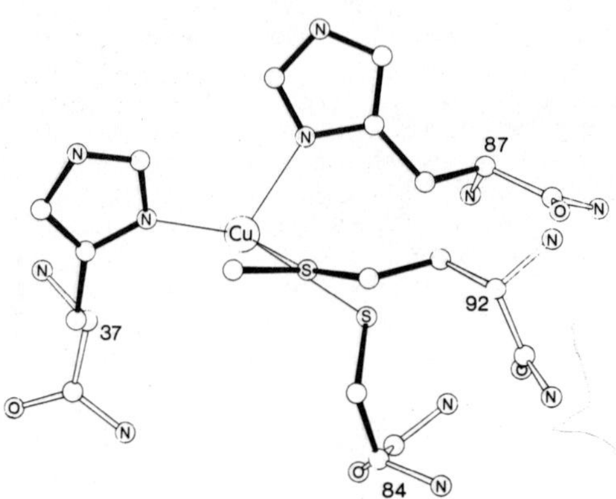

Fig. 6. The Cu site in poplar plastocyanin showing the protein backbone segments and side-chains at His37, Cys84, His87 and Met92.

The Cu site lies in a depression or pocket between three loops in the polypeptide backbone. The walls and rim of the pocket in which the Cu site lies are lined by conserved hydrophobic residues (Fig. 7). The phenyl ring of Phe14 lies beneath (just "south" of) the side-chain of the ligand Met92. The side-chains of Pro36, Pro86 and Leu63 form parts of the wall of the hydrophobic pocket. In the northerly direction, only the imidizole ring of His87 lies between the Cu atom and the molecular boundary.

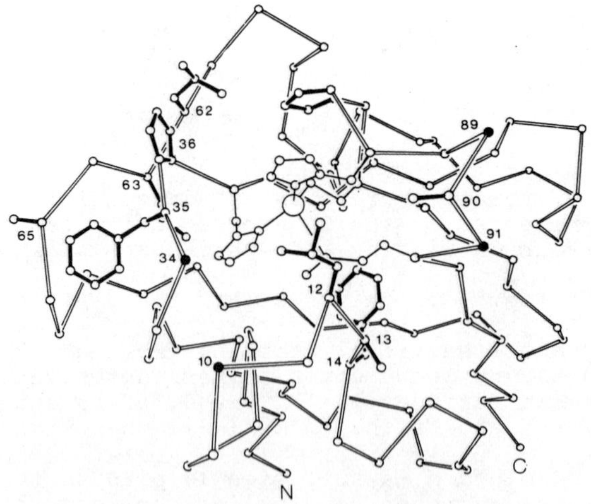

Fig. 7. View of the plastocyanin molecule, looking down on the 'northern' end. The imidazole ring of His87 is seen above the Cu atom, that of His37 to the left. The side chains of conserved hydrophobic residues near the Cu site are shown in black (Leu12, Ala13, Phe14, Phe35, Pro36, Leu62, Leu63, Ala65, Pro86, Ala90). The black C_{α} atoms belong to conserved glycine residues (Gly10, Gly34, Gly89, Gly91).

The pseudo-aromatic imidazole ring, coordinated to the Cu atom on one side and exposed to the solvent on the other, has obvious attractions as a putative electron-transfer pathway. The structure provides (necessarily circumstantial) evidence in favour of such a pathway. Not only is the northern end a highly conserved region of the molecule, but the side-chains of several conserved residues - Leu12, Ala13, Phe35, Leu62 and Ala90 - together with the exposed edges of Pro36 and Pro86 form a distinctive hydrophobic surface around the Cu site. (The residues Ala13 and Phe35 are somewhat less rigorously conserved than the rest). The hydrophobic patch probably acts as a recognition site for redox partners or for orienting groups on a membrane (24).

A number of glycine residues at the northern end of the molecule are also invariant - Gly10, Gly34, Gly89 and Gly91. All four occur at bends in the backbone, and may be conserved for that reason. However, the first three lie at the extreme end of the molecule; their side-chains, if they were larger than R = H, would protrude from the existing molecular boundary and make the molecule bigger in the northerly direction. It is possible that these glycine residues are conserved so as to keep the molecular boundary where it is in relation to the Cu site. (In this context, the 'molecular boundary' is envisaged to be a surface over which an atomic ball would roll without penetrating the Van der Waals radii of the external atoms).

For the case of negatively charged inorganic redox reagents there is experimental evidence that the northern end of the molecule is indeed a binding site. Observations of the perturbation of the ^{1}H NMR spectrum of Cu(I)-plastocyanin by $Cr(CN)_6^{3-}$ show that this complex is bound at or near His87 (27, 28). $Cr(CN)_6^{3-}$ is a paramagnetic, redox-inactive analogue of $Fe(CN)_6^{3-}$. It may be inferred that the oxidation of Cu(I)-plastocyanin by $Fe(CN)_6^{3-}$, and therefore the reduction of Cu(II)-plastocyanin by $Fe(CN)_6^{4-}$, proceed via His87.

Two other features of the Cu site require comment. Firstly, the exposed edge of the His87 imidazole ring is almost precisely level with the molecular boundary. A proposal (based on an imaginative use of Marcus theory) that the 'active site' in plastocyanin lies at least 2.6Å below the surface of the protein (29) is therefore not supported by the structural results, at least for electron-transfer reactions where the imidazole ring of His87 is involved. Secondly, electron-density maps and electron-density difference maps provide no evidence for any H_2O molecules at the Cu site or anywhere else inside the plastocyanin structure. Careful examination of a space-filling model, simulated on a computer graphics system, suggests that the packing of side-chains around the Cu site is in fact so compact that no H_2O molecules can be accommodated in that vicinity. The explanation recently given (30) for the large negative ΔS^{o} values for the electron-transfer reactions of plastocyanin,

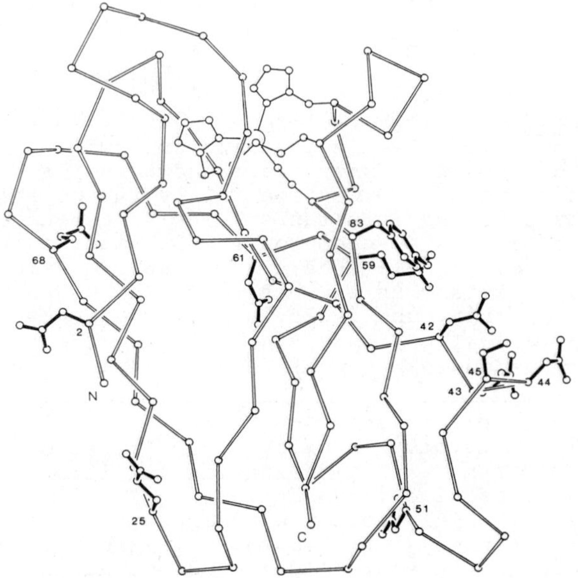

Fig. 8. Poplar plastocyanin, showing side-chains which are acidic in all plant plastocyanins. Tyr83 is seen projecting into the solvent near the acidic region on the right of the figure. (Residue 45 is Ser in poplar but Glu in other plant plastocyanins.)

azurin and stellacyanin (that "any partially disordered water molecules near the +1 site will be converted to a highly ordered state (an internally hydrogen-bonded network of very low entropy) in the reduced protein") therefore requires modification.

The acidic patch. As in most globular proteins, the side-chains inside the plastocyanin molecule are hydrophobic or neutral. The charged side-chains are on the surface and in contact with the solvent. There is a striking imbalance in the distribution of the charges. There are only three conserved lysines, so that basic residues play a minor role. None of the ten conserved acidic residues lies in the top one-third of the molecule. Six of them (Fig. 8) are concentrated on two kinks in the protein backbone at residues 42-45 and 59-61. These two groups of residues have their negatively charged side-chains directed into the solvent, and form an elongated acidic patch. Near the middle of the acidic patch, a conserved tyrosine (Tyr83) also has its side-chains directed into the solvent.

The existence of this surface concentration of conserved acidic residues is such a striking feature of the structure that a functional significance has been sought for it. Like the hydrophobic patch at the northern end of the molecule, the acidic patch and Tyr83 may be a recognition or binding site for redox partners (24). Experimental verification has come from ^{1}H NMR line-broadening experiments similar to those which have already been mentioned (27, 28). When $Cr(phen)_3^{3+}$ - a paramagnetic, redox-inactive analogue of the oxidant $Co(phen)_3^{3+}$ - is added to Cu(I)-plastocyanin, the ^{1}H NMR resonances which are broadened include those of the ring protons of Tyr83. The binding-site for $Cr(phen)_3^{3+}$ and $Co(phen)_3^{3+}$ must therefore be close to Tyr83 and the acidic patch. It is important to note that this result demonstrates that electron-transfer can take place from a site which is 10-15Å from the Cu atom (see Note b).

The demonstration that plastocyanin has two binding sites for inorganic redox reagents, possibly correlated with the charges on the reagents, is consistent with the results of reaction rate measurements (20). Two different binding sites for biological redox partners would also not be unexpected, since biological electron-transfer has to be specific and controlled (32). Nevertheless, there is as yet no proof that the binding site near the acidic patch is used for electron-transfers between plastocyanin and either cytochrome *f* or P700. The arguments from amino-acid sequence invariance are not as strong in the case of the acidic patch as they are in the case of the hydrophobic patch near His87. While residues 42-45, 51, 59 and 61 are acidic (with only one recorded exception) in the known sequences of higher plant plastocyanins, only residues 42 and 51 remain invariant and acidic if three algal plastocyanin sequences are included in the comparison. Algal plastocyanin molecules do not have an acidic patch. The structure of the closely related protein azurin also contains no acidic patch. In the azurin molecule, access to the corresponding site is in fact blocked (see below).

Conserved aromatic residues. It has already been stated that the interior of the barrel-like plastocyanin molecule contains predominantly hydrophobic side-chains. The conserved aromatic residues are shown in Fig. 9. With one exception (Phe35) they lie south of the Cu site. Only two of them (Phe35, Tyr83) have their side-chains pointing into the solvent. A sequence of aromatics extends from below the Met92 side-chain of the Cu site to the southern end of the molecule: Phe14, Phe82, Phe19, Phe41 and Tyr80. Residues Phe14, Phe41 and Tyr80 are totally invariant in all plastocyanins; Phe82 is replaced by Tyr in one algal plastocyanin; and Phe19 is conservatively substituted by other hydrophobics in several plastocyanins. In azurins, the residues at the sequence positions corresponding to Phe14 and Phe82 are always aromatic;

Note b. The worrying possibility of a 'dead-end' mechanism, i.e., the formation of an unproductive plastocyanin-oxidant complex at one site on the protein while electron-transfer takes place during collisions elsewhere, cannot be excluded on the basis of kinetic evidence (20, 29). Dr. P.E. Wright has pointed out to me that his high-field ^{1}H NMR experiments do not favour the 'dead-end' mechanism. $Cr(phen)_3^{3+}$ blocks the oxidation of Cu(I)-plastocyanin by $Co(phen)_3^{3+}$ (20). In the case of a 'dead-end' mechanism, the bound $Cr(phen)_3^{3+}$ would have to affect the $Co(phen)_3^{3+}$ reaction at a distance. Conformational changes would presumably be required to transmit the effect. Such changes should result in shifts of the ^{1}H resonances of the relevant side-chains. No such shifts have been detected in the high-field NMR spectrum of any plastocyanin-Cr(III) complex studied so far (31).

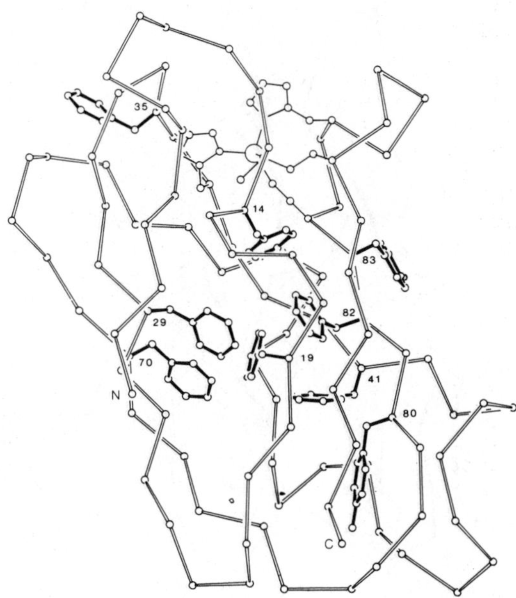

Fig. 9. Poplar plastocyanin, showing conserved aromatic residues. (Residue 70 is Phe in poplar but Tyr in other plant plastocyanins.)

those corresponding to Phe19 and Phe41 are conservatively hydrophobic; and a Tyr corresponding to Tyr80 is totally invariant. The orientation of the phenol ring of Tyr80 in plastocyanin is fixed by means of a O—H...O hydrogen bond to the peptide carbonyl oxygen of residue 76. The immediate environment of the Tyr80 phenol ring also seems to be conserved: two invariant residues, Gly78 and Pro47, make a close contact between backbone strands 7 and 4 just level with the phenol ring. Any side-chain more bulky than R = H at residue 78 would create a bigger spacing between strands 7 and 4 in this region. The invariance of Tyr80, its location at an extremity of the molecule, and the evidence for conservation of the structure in its vicinity and between it and the Cu centre, all suggest that this residue has a function. There is no evidence what that function is, but participation in electron-transfer is clearly a possibility.

THE STRUCTURE AND FUNCTION OF AZURIN

Biological function

Apart from the plastocyanins, the best characterised group of 'blue' single-Cu proteins are the azurins. These proteins occur in some pseudomonad bacteria where they have an electron-transport function. It is not yet entirely clear what that function is. The plausible sequence

$$\text{cytochrome } c_{551} \rightarrow \text{azurin} \rightarrow \text{cytochrome } cd \rightarrow O_2$$

has been queried on the grounds that the reaction between cytochrome c_{551} and azurin shows no kinetic selectivity (19). It is possible that cytochrome c_{551} and azurin provide alternate electron-transfer routes to the oxidase (cf. c_{552} and plastocyanin). Numerous studies of the kinetics and thermodynamics of electron-transfer to and from azurin have been made (see, e.g., Refs. 15, 17, 19, 21, 29, 30, 33).

Sequence homologies indicate an evolutionary relationship between the azurin and plastocyanin families, as well as between those families and stellacyanin, ceruloplasmin and sub-unit II of cytochrome *c* oxidase (34). The azurin molecule (128 amino-acid residues, MW ~14,000 d) is larger than plastocyanin (99 amino-acid residues). A plot of the additional residues in azurin on a diagram of the plastocyanin structure shows that most of the insertions have taken place at positions remote from the Cu site in plastocyanin, mainly in the irregular fifth strand and at bends between the strands of the backbone (24).

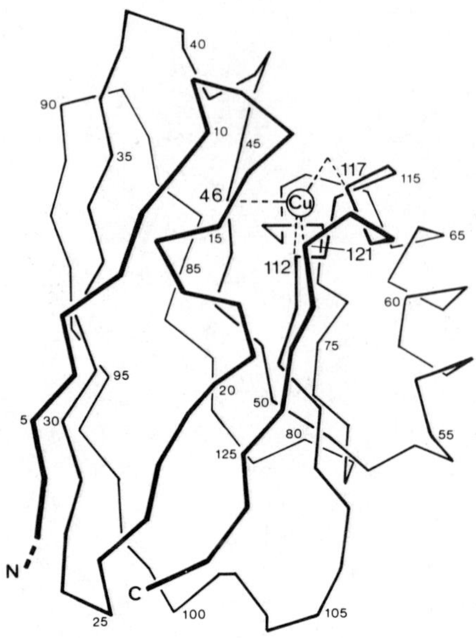

Fig. 10. Molecular structure of *Pseudomonas aeruginosa* azurin. Small numerals identify the C_α atom of every fifth residue. Large numerals identify the C_α atoms of the four Cu ligands (His46, Cys112, His117 and Met121).

The crystal structure analysis of Cu(II)-azurin

The crystal structure analysis of azurin from *Pseudomonas aeruginosa* at 3Å resolution (35) required the location of five times as many atoms as the structure analysis of plastocyanin: the azurin molecule is 25% larger than plastocyanin and there are four molecules in the asymmetric unit of the crystals. For this reason and other technical reasons connected with the quality of the crystals, our knowledge of the azurin structure is not yet as detailed as in the case of plastocyanin. The structure of azurin from *Alcaligenes denitrificans* is under investigation (37). The present description of *Pseudomonas* azurin is based on an improved model of the structure at 2.7Å resolution (36). In the construction of this model, the dimensions of the Cu site have been assumed to be the same as in plastocyanin (36). An earlier, puzzling difference between the topologies (i.e., folds of the polypeptide backbones) of azurin and plastocyanin has been resolved. The two proteins are seen to be closely related in structure as well as amino-acid sequence (Fig. 10).

The eight strands of the azurin polypeptide chain are again arranged to form a somewhat distorted barrel. Parts of the backbone have pronounced β-character (the three strands of backbone on the left of Fig. 10 form a classical β-sheet with the appropriate left-handed twist). The most striking departure from the plastocyanin structure is the addition of a flap between residues 53 and 78. This flap, which includes some helical turns, hangs outside the body of the rest of the molecule. It seems to be an expansion of the irregular fifth strand in plastocyanin.

The Cu site

The Cu atom is coordinated by four residues which are the exact analogues of the ligand residues in plastocyanin - His46, Cys112, His117 and Met121. The Cu site lies in a hydrophobic pocket. Its environment is highly conserved. Among 26 residues with centres of gravity within 10Å of the Cu atom, the 4 ligands and 7 nearest neighbours are invariant, and 8 of the 15 next-nearest neighbours are invariant or conservatively substituted. None of these 26 residues is charged in *Ps. aeruginosa* azurin. (Two of the residues, 18 and 19, can be charged in other species).

A large hydrophobic surface is formed at the northern end of the molecule by a group of invariant or conservatively substituted side-chains. Met44, Phe114 and Pro115 are near the ligand His117. The surface is extended in one

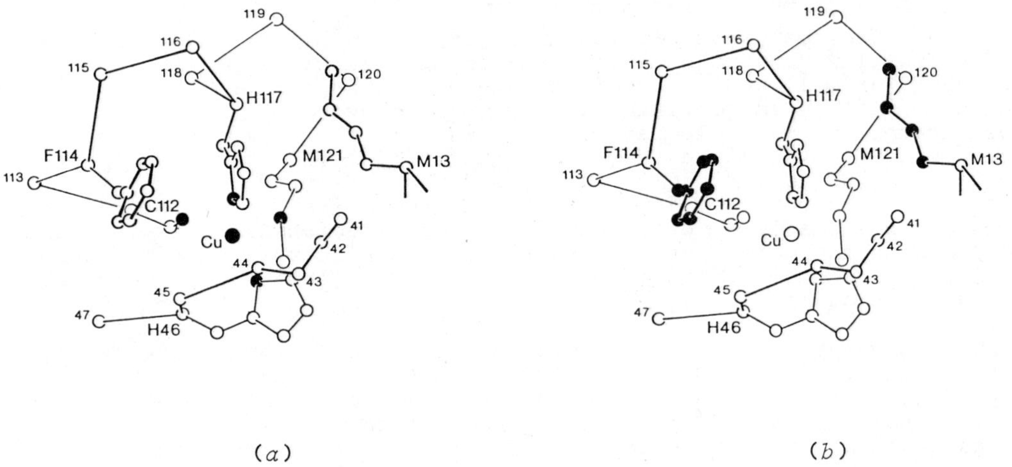

(*a*) (*b*)

Fig. 11. The Cu site in azurin, seen from above the molecule in Fig. 9. (*a*) The Cu atom and the four atoms to which it is bonded are shown in black. (*b*) The side-chains of Met13 and Phe114, which may sterically hinder access to the Cu site, are shown in black.

direction by Leu120, and in the opposite direction by Met13, Val43, Leu39, Pro40, Met64 and Leu68. This feature clearly resembles the hydrophobic surface in plastocyanin. There is, however, an important difference between the Cu sites in the two proteins. In azurin, the side-chains of Met13, Met44 and Phe114 shield the Cu site from the solvent (Fig. 11). A structural reason accordingly exists for the order of "kinetic accessibility", azurin < plastocyanin, derived from kinetic data (17, 29).

Other structural features.

The polypeptide chain has a pronounced bend between residues 15 and 18 (in strand 2). An analogous bend occurs at residues 14-17 in plastocyanin. In both proteins, the first residue in the bend is an invariant Phe which has its phenyl ring close to the side-chain of the ligand Met. The close resemblance between the backbone conformations of azurin and plastocyanin is all the more remarkable since, apart from the two Phe's, the sequences are not homologous in the region of the bend. The aromatic rings of Phe15 (azurin) and Phe14 (plastocyanin) are clearly essential in some way for the function of the Cu sites.

Two further observations reported by the azurin investigators (36) have implications in relation to electron-transfer mechanisms. Firstly, there is no concentration of surface changes. With few exceptions, the invariant basic groups (Lys) and acidic groups (Asp, Glu) occur in pairs. The formation of thermodynamically stable precursor complexes during reactions with $Fe(CN)_6^{3-/4-}$ must therefore have a cause other than the suggested "existence of a cluster of positively charged groups" (33). Secondly, the acidic patch in plastocyanin is replaced in azurin by a hydrophobic surface which faces the helical flap and is matched by invariant or conservatively substituted hydrophobic residues on the flap. If we hypothesise that azurin and plastocyanin interact in similar ways with their respective biological electron-transfer partners, then the absence of an acidic patch in azurin casts doubt on the mechanistic significance of the acidic patch in plastocyanin.

THE STRUCTURE AND FUNCTION OF PLASTOCYANIN - PART II

The crystal structure of Cu(I)-plastocyanin

Background: The fact that plastocyanin performs a biological electron-transfer function generates an interest in the structure of the protein in its reduced, as well as its oxidised, state. It is fortunate that the crystals of Cu(II)-plastocyanin can easily be reduced by ascorbate. In the reduced state, the crystals can be kept exposed to the air for long periods without oxidation (provided that they are kept in contact with mother-liquor - see Note c). They are rapidly re-oxidised under X-irradiation, but this problem can be overcome by carrying out the reduction with a large excess of ascorbate. Presumably a sufficient excess of reductant remains in the mother-liquor between the molecules in the crystals to keep the protein reduced. The failure of the crystals to split or crack when they are reduced tells us that reduction causes no major conformational changes in the protein.

The physical robustness of the plastocyanin crystals, their excellent diffracting properties, and the accessibility of two oxidation states extend over a wide pH-range. This combination of properties has recently enabled us (38) to test the hypothesis that the pH-dependences of the redox potential and redox kinetics of plastocyanin are correlated with structural changes.

The first step in the work was a re-investigation of Cu(II)Pc at pH 4. The original data had been recorded at pH 6. Crystals were gradually equilibrated against mother-liquor at the lower pH. A complete set of diffraction data to 1.9Å resolution was recorded. Refinement of the structure using these data converged with a residual R= 0.157. There were no significant changes in the structure at all: the structure of Cu(II)Pc is, within the precision of the structure analysis, the same at pH 4 as it is at pH 6. Small conformational changes due to proton equilibria of peripheral groups cannot be ruled out, but there is no doubt that the Cu(II) site remains intact and unchanged. Any pH-dependent structural changes must therefore be associated with the reduced state of the protein.

The Cu site in Cu(I)-plastocyanin

In the study of Cu(I)-plastocyanin (38), diffraction data were recorded from crystals at pH 3.8, 4.4, 5.1, 5.9 and 7.0. Depending on the quality of the various specimens, resolutions between 1.7 and 2.1Å were achieved. Each structure was refined, care being taken to avoid biassing the final results in the direction of a particular model. The five refinements accordingly give independent determinations of the structure. The final crystallographic residuals R are all in the range 0.163-0.178. A sixth data set, using crystals at pH 7.8, is still in the process of being recorded.

There are scarcely any significant differences between the five refined structures of the reduced protein, or between them and the structure of the oxidised protein, except *at the Cu site*. A comparison between the structures of the reduced and oxidised proteins at, say, pH 6 shows that reduction causes the Cu atom to move away from His87 and towards Met92; the His87 imidazole ring moves 0.2Å away from the Cu atom and towards the molecular surface; the Cys84 side-chain follows the Cu atom; His37 and Met92 remain unchanged.

Quantitatively, the changes in coordination are much larger than expected for a metal which is involved in *rapid* electron-transfer. For example, at pH ~6 the bond-lengths are:

Bond:	Cu(II)Pc:	Cu(I)Pc:
Cu—N(His37)	2.04Å	2.07Å
Cu—N(His87)	2.10	2.82
Cu—S(Cys84)	2.13	2.11
Cu—S(Met92)	2.90	2.68

Note c: The plastocyanin crystals are grown from a solution containing 70% saturated ammonium sulphate solution plus buffer. This solution occupies 36% of the internal volume of the crystals - the spaces between the protein molecules. For X-ray diffraction measurements a moist crystal is sealed in a capillary together (but not in contact) with a drop of mother-liquor which keeps the relative humidity of the air in the capillary constant.

The apparent changes in Cu—N(His87) and Cu—S(Met92) are highly significant in relation to the estimated standard deviations (0.05Å). Such large changes imply far too high Franck-Condon reorganisation barriers.

To add to the improbability of the situation, comparisons between the atomic positions at the five pH values show that the movement of the Cu atom away from His87 and towards Met92 is a smooth function of the pH. A gradual movement of the Cu atom would be believable only if it were the cumulative result of several pH-dependent changes with different pK's elsewhere in the molecule. There is no evidence for such changes.

The explanation of the pH effects is that the structure observed at each pH (e.g., pH 6, above) is the *weighted mean of two structures*. In Fig. 12 the bond-length changes which are observed between pH 3.8 and pH 7.0 are extrapolated to low-pH and high-pH limits. The *high-pH* limit clearly represents a geometry which is not very different from that of the Cu site in Cu(II)Pc. We have labelled this high-pH form "Cu(I)Pc". The Cu-ligand bond-lengths are 0-0.2Å larger in this form than in Cu(II)Pc. These differences are compatible with rapid outer-sphere electron-transfer (14). The extrapolated distance of the Cu atom from the $N_{37}S_{84}S_{92}$ plane is 0.7Å, as in Cu(II)Pc.

Extrapolation of the Cu(I) geometry to *low pH* produces a structure in which the Cu atom has become dissociated from the His87 imidazole ring. The Cu···N(His87) distance, ~3.4Å, is sufficient to accommodate a Van der Waals contact between the Cu atom and a proton on the imidazole N_{δ} atom. We have accordingly labelled the low-pH form "HCu(I)Pc". The Cu atom is now coplanar with N_{37}, S_{84}, and S_{92}. The Cu—S(Met) bond has an extrapolated length of 2.5Å, which is only slightly greater than the average in model complexes. The coordination geometry is trigonal-planar with almost classical Cu(I)-ligand bond-lengths. The stabilisation of Cu(I) under these conditions should be sufficient to make HCu(I)Pc redox-inactive with respect to biological redox partners and most inorganic redox reagents.

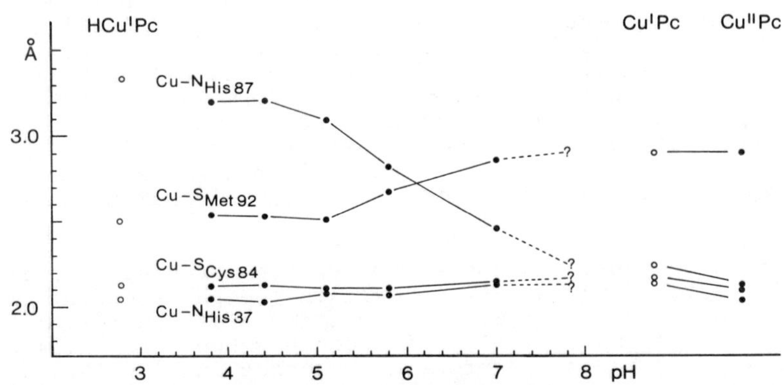

Fig. 12. Changes of the Cu coordination geometry in plastocyanin as a function of pH and oxidation state. The bond-lengths in oxidised plastocyanin ["Cu(II)Pc"] are taken from the refined structure at 1.6Å resolution. The values shown under "HCu(I)Pc" and "Cu(I)Pc" are obtained by extrapolation from the apparent Cu—ligand bond-lengths in reduced plastocyanin at five pH values in the range 3.8-7.0. (The Figure comprises unpublished results which are subject to minor modifications).

Our present dimensions for the three forms of plastocyanin are shown in Fig. 13.

In the preceding description and discussion, all the pH values were obtained by conventional measurements. They were uncorrected for the extremely high ionic strength of the mother-liquor with which the crystals are necessarily saturated (see Note c). It is assumed that no gross errors are introduced by equating "pH_{meas}" with pH.

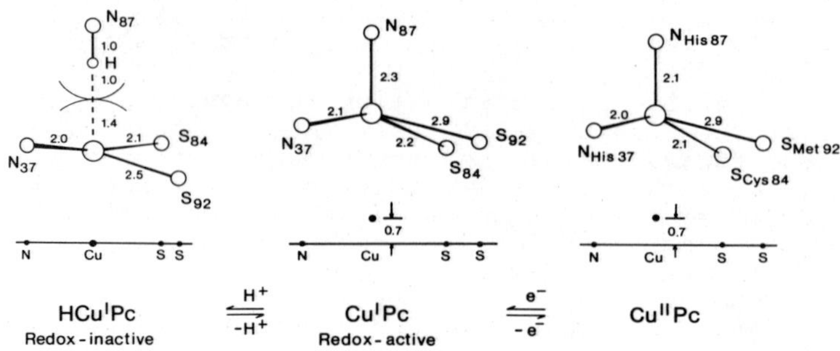

Fig. 13. Dimensions of the Cu site in HCu(I)Pc (protonated, redox-inactive), Cu(I)Pc (redox-active) and Cu(II)Pc (redox-active). The bond-lengths for the reduced protein are derived from the extrapolations in Fig. 10. The lower portion of each diagram shows the deviation of the Cu atom from a plane fitted to N_{37}, S_{84} and S_{92}.

Comments on pH dependence of structure

The lack of significant pH effects at the Cu site of Cu(II)Pc is as it should be. The Cu(II)—N(His87) bond is strong enough - the crystal-field stabilisation of Cu(II) with the nitrogen ligand is large enough - to prevent the protonation of the imidazole nitrogen. Any changes of the Cu(II)Pc structure as a function of pH are accordingly limited to changes which are not detected by the crystal structure analysis, e.g., changes in the protonation, hydrogen-bonding or preferred conformations of surface side-chains. Effects of this kind must be invoked to account for the modest increases in the rates of reduction of Cu(II)Pc by $Fe(edta)^{2-}$ (15) and by $Fe(CN)_6^{4-}$ (20) at low pH.

In the reduced protein, on the other hand, the comparative weakness of the Cu(I)—N(His87) bond and the absence of crystal-field stabilisation enable protons to compete successfully against Cu(I) for the N(His87) lone pair. The protein exists as an equilibrium mixture of the redox-inactive form HCu(I)Pc and the redox-active form Cu(I)Pc. The "bond-length titration" curves of Fig. 12 show that the redox-inactive form is dominant at pH 4, thus accounting for the observed cut-off in electron-transfer to inorganic and biological oxidants at low pH (20, 41). At the pH which is of biological interest (pH 5.5, the pH inside the thylakoid), the redox-inactive form of plastocyanin is an important component in the equilibrium mixture. It makes a significant contribution even at pH 7.

The existence of a protonated, redox-inactive form of plastocyanin was proposed already by Katoh (39) in 1962 to explain the pH-dependent increase of the redox potential below pH ~5.5. A suggestion that the E_o'-pH behaviour is consistent with the protonation of an imidazole group which dissociates from the Cu(I) atom when it becomes protonated was made in 1964 (40). Sykes and co-workers have subsequently shown that the kinetics of electron-transfer from Cu(I)-plastocyanin to some inorganic oxidants are consistent with an equilibrium between a protonated and an unprotonated form of the reduced protein, and that the rates of electron-transfer from the protonated form are low or zero (41). It is somewhat disconcerting that the redox-inactive behaviour has been attributed to a failure to form productive protein-oxidant complexes at low pH, rather than to a change at the redox centre of the protein (20). This interpretation of the kinetics seems to clash with the new crystallographic results which not only show that the protonated form HCu(I)Pc really exists, but also provide an excellent reason - the stabilisation of the Cu(I) site - why the rates of electron-transfer from it should be very low.

Biological implications

Our final task is to review the structural results in the light of what was said earlier about the biological function of plastocyanin. The distorted tetrahedral co-ordination geometry and the N,N,S,S ligands have presumably evolved for two reasons. Firstly, they give the Cu centre in plastocyanin a redox potential (370 mV) between those of its redox partners, cytochrome *f* (360 mV) and P700 (520 mV). Secondly, they facilitate rapid electron-transfer by producing a Cu centre which has almost the same geometry and Cu-ligand dimensions in the Cu(II) and Cu(I) states. A potential pathway for electron-transfer exists at the northern end of the molecule, where the exposed edge of the His87 imidazole ring seems to satisfy all the requirements of current electron-transfer theory for contacts with redox partners. The presence of a highly conserved hydrophobic region on the surface of the molecule near His87 reinforces the impression that this part of the molecule is functionally important.

These conclusions, if they are correct, must certainly apply with only minor numerical changes to azurin as well as plastocyanin.

The hydrophobic surface in plastocyanin may be a recognition patch used to ensure specificity of reaction with one redox partner (or with both partners, alternately), or it may have the function of orienting plastocyanin appropriately with respect to the thylakoid membrane. At this point our speculations are hampered by two uncertainties. We do not know whether plastocyanin is stationary in relation to its redox partners, or whether it shuttles back and forth between them; and we do not know whether reduction and oxidation proceed *via* the same or different electron-transfer pathways.

If plastocyanin, cytochrome *f* and P700 are all relatively fixed on or near the thylakoid surface, then the use of separate electron-transfer pathways in and out of plastocyanin is conceptually more satisfying than, say, a 'wobble' mechanism in which a membrane-bound plastocyanin points a single electron-transfer site alternately towards its two redox partners. On the other hand, if plastocyanin accepts an electron from cytochrome *f* and diffuses (2-dimensionally along the membrane surface or 3-dimensionally through the intra-thylakoid liquid) until it collides with a P700 centre, then there may be no need for more than one electron-transfer site or pathway. It is conceivable that one site, such as the northern end of the molecule, is capable of making specific and productive collisions with both cytochrome *f* and P700. It is even possible that the current oxidation state of the plastocyanin molecule, i.e., whether it is waiting to accept or deliver an electron, is signalled by the position of the His87 imidazole ring edge in relation to the molecular surface: as described earlier, reduction causes a small but significant movement (0.2Å) of the imidazole ring in the direction of the outside of the molecule.

The structural results cannot provide answers to the preceding questions. On the contrary, the question whether plastocyanin has two electron-transfer pathways or only one arises partly from the observation that more than one portion of the molecule has distinctive and conserved structural features. In addition to the hydrophobic patch around His87 at the 'northern' end, we have the aromatic/hydrophobic channel from the Cu atom to the rigorously conserved Tyr80 at the 'southern' end, and (in higher plant plastocyanins) the acidic patch around Tyr83.

We must ask, finally, whether the equilibrium between HCu(I)Pc and Cu(I)Pc in the reduced state of plastocyanin has any biological significance. The pH inside the thylakoid is believed to be about 5.5. At this pH, the redox-inactive form HCu(I)Pc represents a significant proportion of the reduced plastocyanin molecules (Fig. 12). The proportion of redox-inactive HCu(I)Pc increases as the pH is lowered, until the reduced protein is present substantially in the redox-inactive form at pH 4-4.5.

It follows that electron-transfer between photosystems II and I should depend on the pH inside the thylakoid. This is known to be the case (23, 42). The observed pH-dependence of electron-transport in chloroplasts has a pK near 5.5 (42). Plastocyanin is therefore seen to participate in photosynthetic electron-transfer in two ways. It acts as an electron carrier between cytochrome *f* and P700; and it controls electron-transport as a function of the pH inside the thylakoid. Such a control mechanism is necessary because, as we saw earlier, electron-transport across the thylakoid membrane in an outward direction is linked with proton transport in the opposite direction.

It is true that the control of electron-transport between photosystems II and I as a function of pH has hitherto been attributed to plastoquinol (the reductant of cytochrome *f*. The evidence for this control mechanism is, however, derived from the agreement between the observed electron-transfer kinetics and kinetics calculated from appropriate rate-equations. At the time of the experiments and calculations there was no reason to suspect that plastocyanin might be involved, and this hypothesis was not tested. In the light of the structural results it is clear that when plastocyanin is present it *must* exert control over electron-transfer as a function of pH, whether control also occurs at plastoquinol or not.

Finally, the fact that plastocyanin occurs naturally under conditions where the reduced form Cu(I)Pc is in equilibrium with HCu(I)Pc suggests a reason for the long bond between the Cu atom and S(Met92) in Cu(I)Pc and Cu(II)Pc. A functional significance for the S(Met92) ligand, possibly as part of the E_0'-tuning mechanism, is of course not eliminated. Structurally it is unlikely that the long Cu—S(Met92) bond, 2.9Å, contributes much to the stability of the Cu site. In the low-pH form HCu(I)-plastocyanin this situation is changed. The formation of a strong Cu—S(Met92) bond, 2.5Å compensates for the dissociation of the His87 ligand. The real significance of Met92 may be that it stabilises the Cu site whenever the reduced protein is in its low-pH form.

Acknowledgements - I am indebted to my colleagues Dr Mitchell Guss, Dr Mitsuo Murata, Miss Valerie Norris and Mr Peter Harrowell, who have been responsible for the crystallographic work on plastocyanin since our 1978 *Nature* paper. In particular, the refinement calculations are the work of Dr Mitchell Guss. Professor Lyle Jensen and Dr Elinor Adman kindly made their manuscript describing the structure of azurin at 2.7Å resolution available prior to publication; Dr Adman especially prepared line-drawings on which Figs. 10 and 11 are based. Dr Allen Hill and Professors Harry Gray, John Hopfield, Joshua Jortner and Rudolph Marcus sent copies of recent, and in some cases unpublished, papers: due to limitations of space, only some of this material has been explicitly cited here. Helpful discussions with Professors Geoffrey Sykes and Harry Gray on reaction mechanisms, with Dr Derek Bendall on photosynthesis, and with Drs James Beattie, Peter Wright and Tony Larkum on electron-transfer in biological systems, are gratefully acknowledged. The research on protein structure analysis at the University of Sydney is supported by Grant 74/15398 from the Australian Research Grants Committee.

REFERENCES

1. R.A. Holwerda, S. Wherland and H.B. Gray, Ann. Rev. Biophys. Bioeng. 5, 363-396 (1976).
2. I. Pecht, O. Farver and M. Goldberg in K.N. Raymond (Ed.), Bioinorganic Chemistry II, pp. 179-206, Amer. Chem. Soc. Adv. in Chem. Series, No. 162 (1977).
3. (*a*) C. Greenwood and D. Barber in H.A.O. Hill (Ed.), Inorganic Biochemistry, Vol. 1, pp. 236-246, Chemical Society, London (1979).
   (*b*) R.D. Cannon in A. McAuley (Ed.), Inorganic Reaction Mechanisms, Vol. 6, pp. 5-17, Chemical Society, London (1979).
4. A.E.G. Cass and H.A.O. Hill in The Biological Roles of Copper (CIBA Foundation Symposium 79), to be published in Excerpta Medica.
5. H.C. Freeman, V.A. Norris, J.A.M. Ramshaw and P.E. Wright, FEBS Lett., 86, 131-135 (1978).
6. I. Munro, I. Pecht and L. Stryer, Proc. Natl. Acad. Sci. USA 76, 56-60 (1979).
7. J.J. Hopfield in E. Roux (Ed.), Electrical Phenomena at the Biological Membrane Level, pp. 471-492, Elsevier, Amsterdam (1977).
8. B. Chance *et al.* (Eds.), Tunneling in Biological Systems, Academic Press, New York (1979).
9. J.J. Hopfield in Ref. 8, pp. 417-432.
10. R.A. Marcus in Ref. 8, pp. 109-127.
11. J. Jortner, J. Chem. Phys., 64, 4860-4867 (1976).
12. R.H. Austin and J.J. Hopfield, unpublished work cited in Abstract IV-11, Symposium on Interaction between Iron and Proteins in Oxygen and Electron-Transport, Airlie House, Virginia, April 1980.

13. (*a*) F.R. Salemme, Ann. Rev. Biochem. 46, 299-329 (1977).
(*b*) F.R. Salemme in Ref. 8, pp 523-540.

14. N. Sutin in Ref. 8, pp 201-224.

15. R.C. Rosenberg, S. Wherland, R.A. Holwerda and H.B. Gray, J. Amer. Chem. Soc. 98, 6364-6369 (1976).

16. R.A. Holwerda, D.B. Knaff, H.B. Gray, J.D. Clemmer, R. Crowley, J.M. Smith and A.G. Mauk, J. Amer. Chem. Soc. 102, 1142-1146 (1980).

17. J.V. McArdle, C. Coyle, H.B. Gray, G.S. Yoneda and R.A. Holwerda, J. Amer. Chem. Soc. 99, 2483-2489 (1977).

18. J.V. McArdle, K. Yocom and H.B. Gray, J. Amer. Chem. Soc. 99, 4141-4145 (1977).

19. S. Wherland and I. Pecht, Biochemistry, 17, 2585-2591 (1978).

20. A.G. Lappin, M.G. Segal, D.C. Weatherburn and A.G. Sykes, J. Amer. Chem. Soc. 101, 2297-2301 (1979).

21. A.G. Lappin, M.G. Segal, D.C. Weatherburn, R.A. Henderson and A.G. Sykes, J. Amer. Chem. Soc. 101, 2302-2306 (1979).

22. A.R. Crofts and P.M. Wood in D.R. Sanadi and L.P. Vernon (Eds.), Current Topics in Bioenergetics, Vol 7: Photosynthesis, Part A, pp. 175-244. Academic Press, New York (1978).

23. D.S. Bendall in D.H. Northcote (Ed.), Int. Rev. Biochem, Vol. 13, Plant Biochemistry II, pp. 41-78, University Park Press, Baltimore (1977).

24. P.M. Colman, H.C. Freeman, J.M. Guss, M. Murata, V.A. Norris, J.A.M. Ramshaw and M.P. Venkatappa, Nature 272, 319-324 (1978).

25. J.M. Guss and H.C. Freeman, unpublished work.

26. T.D. Tullius and K.O. Hodgson, personal communication.

27. D.J. Cookson, M.T. Hayes and P.E. Wright, Nature 283, 682-683 (1980).

28. P.M. Handford, H.A.O. Hill, R.W.-K. Lee, R.A. Henderson and A.G. Sykes, J. Inorg. Biochem., in press (1980).

29. A.G. Mauk, R.A. Scott and H.B. Gray, J. Amer. Chem. Soc. 102, 4360-4363 (1980).

30. N. Sailasuta, F.C. Anson and H.B. Gray, J. Amer. Chem. Soc. 101, 455-458 (1979).

31. P.E. Wright, personal communication.

32. G.R. Moore and R.J.P. Williams, Coord. Chem. Rev. 18, 125-197 (1976).

33. M. Goldberg and I. Pecht, Biochemistry 15, 4197-4208 (1976).

34. (*a*) L. Ryden and J.O. Lundgren, Nature 261, 344-346 (1976).
(*b*) L. Ryden and J.O. Lundgren, Biochimie 61, 781-790 (1979).

35. E.T. Adman, R.E. Stenkamp, L.C. Sieker and L.H. Jensen, J. Mol. Biol. 123, 35-47 (1978).

36. E.T. Adman and L.H. Jensen, Isr. J. Chem. in press (1980).

37. G.E.Norris, B.F. Anderson, E.N. Baker and S.V. Rumball, J. Mol. Biol. 125, 309-312 (1979).

38. H.C. Freeman, J.M. Guss, P. Harrowell, M. Murata and V.A. Norris, unpublished results.

39. S. Katoh, I. Shiratori and A. Takamiya, J. Biochem. (Tokyo) 51, 32-40 (1962).

40. A.S. Brill, R. B. Martin and R.J.P. Williams in B. Pullman (Ed.), Electronic Aspects of Biochemistry, pp. 519-557, Academic Press, New York (1964).

41. M.G. Segal and A.G. Sykes, J. Amer. Chem. Soc. 100, 4585-4592.

42. U. Siggel in M. Avron (Ed.), Proceedings of the Third International Congress on Photosynthesis, pp. 645-654, Elsevier, Amsterdam (1974).

EXPERIMENTAL CHARGE DENSITY DISTRIBUTION IN METAL-METAL AND METAL-LIGAND BONDS

P. Coppens

Chemistry Department, State University of New York at Buffalo, Buffalo, New York 14214, USA

Abstract - Experimental charge densities on distorted octahedral and tetrahedral transition metal complexes show charge density accumulation in directions away from ligand atoms. The maps are analyzed quantitatively in terms of orbital occupancies and show evidence for partially covalent bonding in FeS_2. Metal-metal bonding studies show broad areas of excess density in strong metal-metal bonds, but absence of deformation density in weak bonds. Agreement with ab-initio theoretical calculations is good at a qualitative level.

INTRODUCTION

X-ray crystallography is known for its ability to provide three-dimensional atomic structure. But in addition more basic information can be extracted from elastic x-ray scattering, which is the distribution of the electronic charge in solids. As x-ray scattering is due to the interaction of electromagnetic radiation with the electrons in the crystal, the charge distribution is the primary information, while the assignment of atomic positions to maxima in the charge distribution is conjectural, but not always correct in detail.

We will refer to the literature for a description of techniques such as the use of neutron and high order data to obtain structural parameters unbiased by the electron distribution (Refs. 1-3), the derivation of properties like molecular dipole moments and electrostatic potentials (Refs. 4-6), and the fitting of atom-centered spherical harmonic density functions to obtain an analytical descrition of the charge density (Refs. 7-9). Summarizing the activity of the past 10-15 years we note that experimental charge density studies have now reached a stage at which for light atom molecules almost quantitative agreement is reached with large basis set theoretical calculations (see for example refs. 10 and 11), while semi-empirical or approximate ab-initio calculations have been shown to be inadequate (refs. 12-13).

For molecules containing heavier atoms, such as transition metal elements, additional experimental difficulties are encountered, which result from the larger ratio of core versus valence electrons. This means that the effect of chemical bonding on the electron distribution is a smaller part of the total signal that is being measured. But a detailed analysis shows that heavier atom structures can be studied provided absorption effects are carefully accounted for (see the last section for a further discussion of errors). On the theoretical side the large number of atomic orbitals involved dictates the use of restricted basis sets or other approximations. Furthermore many transition metal complexes have low-lying virtual orbitals so that a single determinant SCF wave function may be inadequate for describing the system. Such uncertainties increase the need for comparison with experiment.

The x-ray experiment leads to the total charge density, which is the sum of the 'spin up' and 'spin down' electron distributions

$$\rho_{total} = \rho_{\uparrow} + \rho_{\downarrow} \qquad (1)$$

On the other hand with polarized neutrons it is possible to measure the magnetization density which in the absence of an orbital moment may be written as the spin density:

$$\rho_{spin} = \rho_{\uparrow} + \rho_{\downarrow} \qquad (2)$$

The combination of (1) and (2) should be an unusually powerful tool in studying non-diamagnetic materials. Due to the slowness of the polarized neutron experiment no complete studies of his kind have been reported so far.

The density maps which we will discuss here are charge deformation densities defined by

$$\Delta\rho = \rho_{total} - \rho_{promolecule} = \rho_{observed}/k - \sum_{\substack{all \\ atoms}} \rho_{spherical\ atom} \quad (3)$$

where k is the scale of the experimental data, and $\rho_{observed}$ is obtained by a Fourier summation over the experimental structure factors. In the centrosymmetric case the signs of the observed and promolecule density structure factors may be assumed equal, but phase differences must be taken into account when deformation densities of non-centrosymmetric crystals are calculated (Refs. 14,15).

A limited number of studies on crystals containing transition metal atoms have been completed; a selection is listed in Tables 1 and 2. A number of these are discussed in the following sections.

ASPHERICITY OF THE ELECTRON DISTRIBUTION AROUND METAL ATOMS

A list of some single-metal atom complexes of which the charge density has been studied experimentally is given in Table 1. Peaks of electron density corresponding to electrons in ligand-field stabilized 3-d orbitals are commonly found around the metal atoms. In the octahedral field these are the t_{2g} orbitals d_{xy}, d_{xz}, d_{yz}. When equally occupied these orbitals give an electron distribution which peaks in the body diagonal direction of the octahedral field. Such peaks are observed for $Cr(CO)_6$, $Co(NH_3)_6Co(CN)_6$, $Co(NH_3)_6Cr(CN)_6$ and FeS_2, all of which have octahedral or distorted octahedral coordination.

TABLE 1. Studies of complexes with a single transition metal atom

$Cr(CO)_3C_6H_6$	Rees & Coppens (1973)	(17)
$Co(NH_3)_6Co(CN)_6$	Iwata & Saito (1973)	(18)
Ni_2SiO_4	Marumo, Isobe, Saito, Yagi & Akimoto (1974)	(19)
$Cr(NH_3)_6Co(CN)_6$	Iwata (1977)	(20)
$Cr(CO)_6$	Rees & Mitschler (1976)	(21)
$CoAl_2O_4$	Toriumi, Ozima, Akoagi & Saito (1978)	(22)
αK_2CrO_4	Toriumi & Saito (1978)	(23)
$NaK_2Co(NO_2)_6$	Ohba, Toriumi, Sato & Saito (1978)	(24)
FeS_2	Stevens, DeLucia & Coppens (1980)	(25)
$KFeS_2$	Stevens (1979)	(26)
$Fe(C_5H_4COOH)_2$	Takusagawa & Koetzle (1979)	(27)
$Ru(C_6H_6)_2$	Takusagawa & Koetzle (1980)	(28)
Co porphyrin	Stevens (1980)	(29)

In a tetrahedral surrounding the e_g orbitals are lowest in energy; accordingly in the maps of $KFeS_2$ density is accumulated along directions bisecting the Fe-S bonds (with the exception of the bisectors pointing towards the iron atoms). For metal atoms coordinated with aromatic C_6 or C_5 rings the density accumulation corresponds to preferential occupancy of the d_{z^2} orbitals pointing towards the center of the ring, as in benzene chromiumtricarbonyl, ruthenocene and bis (dicarbonyl-π cyclopentadienyl iron). A detailed analysis of the bonding in the last compound is given in Ref. 34. The observed asymmetry is in good agreement with an approximate theoretical calculation and indicates the largest occupancies for d_{z^2} and $d_{x^2-y^2}$, and a larger occupancy for d_{yz} than for d_{xz}, where the x axis lies in the mirror plane of the complex (Fig. 1) parallel to the cyclopentadienyl ring, and the z axis is perpendicular to the ring.

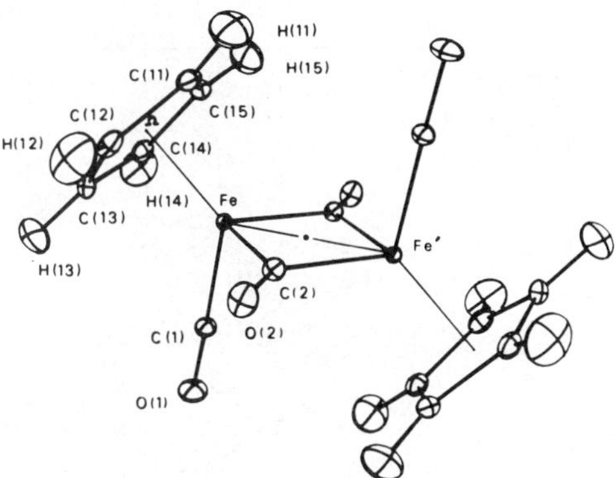

Fig. 1 Geometry of bis (dicarbonyl-π-cyclopentadienyliron) at 74K (Ref. 34)

A more quantitative analysis of the orbital occupancies has been made for iron pyrite, (Ref. 25) in which the iron atom is surrounded by a trigonally distorted octahedron of sulfur atoms at 2.2633(2)Å (Fig. 2). Magnetic susceptibility and Mossbauer data indicate a

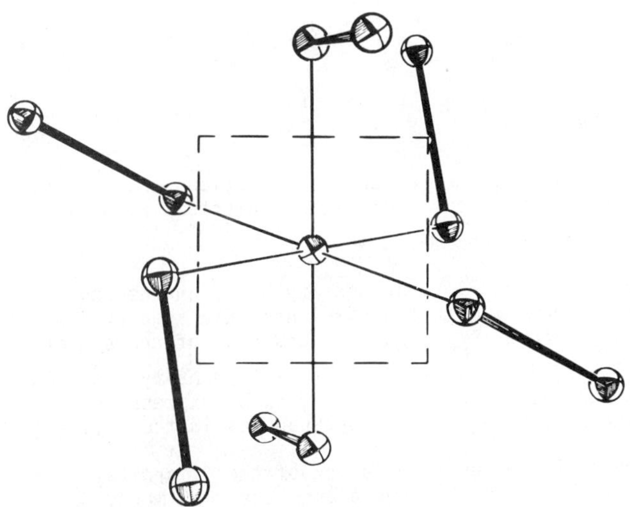

Fig. 2. Coordination geometry of disulfide ions around iron in pyrite. The dashed lines define the section of the electron density distribution plotted in Fig. 3 (Ref. 25)

low-spin state for iron, suggesting a population of the t_{2g} orbitals by all d electrons. The large asymmetry of the electron distribution is indeed confirmed by the experimental electron deformation density (Fig. 3), which shows accumulation in directions not pointing to the sulfur ligands. The S-Fe-S angles of the distorted octahedron are 94.355(4) and 85.645(2)°. A larger accumulation is observed along the direction bounded by the larger S-Fe-S angles. In the distorted octahedral field the octahedral t_{2g} orbital is split into a doubly degenerate e_g and a non-degenerate a_g orbital, while the octahedral e_g orbital, here labelled e_g', retains its multiplicity. If a common radical function R(r) is assumed, the d orbital density may be expressed in terms of the populations P_1, P_2 and P_3 of the a_g, e_g and e_g' orbitals:

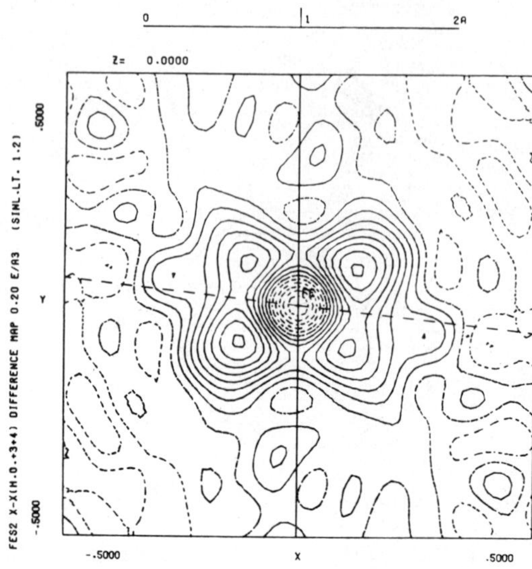

Fig. 3. Experimental deformation density around the iron atom in FeS_2 calculated with X-ray structure factors to a resolution of $(\sin\theta)/\lambda = 1.2Å^{-1}$. Contours at $0.2eÅ^{-3}$ intervals. Zero and negative contours broken. (Ref. 25).

$$\rho_d(r) = [R(r)]^2[P_1 y_{a_b}{}^2 + \frac{1}{2} P_2(y_{e_{g+}}{}^2 + y_{e_{g-}}{}^2) + \frac{1}{2} P_3(y_{e_{g+'}}{}^2 + y_{e_{g-'}}{}^2) + P_4(y_{e_{g+}} + y_{e_{g-}})(y_{e_{g+'}} + y_{e_{g-'}})] \quad (4)$$

in which the y's are the symmetry adepted angular functions and the cross product represents the mixing of the e_g species. As this expression neglects mixing with ligand orbitals it is valid in the crystal field approximation.

An alternative description of the electron density based on the experimental data is given by the aspherical atom refinement with spherical harmonic angular functions (Ref. 9). The population parameters P_{lm} such as P_{00}, P_{20}, P_{40} and P_{43+} of the symmetry allowed monopolar, (l = 0), quadrupolar (l = 2) and hexadecapolar (l = 4) density functions are directly related to the orbital populations P_1, P_2, P_3 and P_4 of expression (4) (Ref. 31). They can therefore be used to derive the orbital occupancies in the crystal field approximation.

Results of the refinement with a zero population of the 4s orbital, but variable 3d orbital exponent are listed in Table 2, which shows a considerable improvement in the agreement with the introduction of the aspherical atom functions (refinement II). Additional variation of the total d shell occupancy (refinement III) does not lead to a further reduction of the

TABLE 2. Orbital occupancies of Fe in pyrite from refinement of x-ray data

	Refinement		
	(I)	(II)	(III)
$\zeta(a.u.^{-1})$	3.73(3)	3.79(3)	3.93(4)
$P_{3d}(=P_1 + P_2 + P_3)$	6.00	6.0	5.22(13)
$P(S_2)$	2.00	2.0	2.77(13)
P_1	1.2	1.98(12)	1.82(13)
P_2	2.4	3.36(15)	3.06(17)
P_3	2.4	0.66(15)	0.34(17)
P_4	0.0	-0.04(16)	0.02(16)
R(F)(%)	2.35	1.81	1.79
R_w(F)(%)	1.92	1.31	1.29

agreement indices. The results in column II indicate full occupancy of the lowest lying a_g orbital, but less than complete population of the e_g orbital. The latter result which is in apparent contradication to the observed diamagnetism, is probably due to partial covalent bonding between the transition metal and the ligand molecules. Thus, 0.76 out of 6 electrons, i.e. 13%, are in an orbital which would not be populated according to the purely electrostatic theory.

For comparison the numbers in $KFeS_2$ are listed in Table 3 (from Ref. 26). The iron atom in this mineral is in a distorted tetrahedral environment and has a high spin configuration. The population analysis show a very small (though statistically significant according to the R factor ratio test (Ref. 32)) depopulation of the d_{z^2} orbital pointing towards a second Fe atom at 2.701(1) Å. As expected on the basis of the high spin state, deformation density maps show much less pronounced asphericities than in the case of the low spin iron atom in pyrite.

TABLE 3. Orbital occupancies in $KFeS_2$ from refinement of X-ray data⁺ (Ref. 26)

	Refinement (I)	Refinement (II)		Refinement (I)	Refinement (II)
ζ(a.u.$^{-1}$)		3.64(4)	$P_3(d_{xy})$	1.0	0.99(5)
$P_{3d}(=P_1+P_2+P_3+P_4)$	5.00	5.00	$P_4(d_{xz},d_{yz})$	2.0	2.09(11)
$P_1(d_{x^2-y^2})$	1.0	1.11(5)	R(F)(%)	3.87	3.67
$P_2(d_{z^2})$	1.0	0.81(8)	R_w(F)(%)	3.36	3.16

⁺ z axis along the Fe-Fe direction, x and y perpendicular z, bisecting SFeS angles

ELECTRON DISTRIBUTION IN METAL-METAL BONDS

At present few electron density studies of metal cluster compounds have been completed. The listing in Table 4 shows two chromium, four nickel and a manganese binuclear cluster and one trinuclear cobalt compound. Conspicuously lacking at present are complexes with metal-hydrogen interactions, but such a study is now being undertaken in our laboratory. Three compounds for which parallel theoretical calculations have been done by Benard (Refs. 37, 46) are discussed below.

TABLE 4. Experimental charge density studies of metal-metal bonding

compound	reference	
μ(HC≡CH)$(CpNi)_2$	Wang & Coppens (1976)	(33)
$[(CO_2)_2CpFe]_2$	Mitschler, Rees & Lehmann (1978)	(34)
μ(cyclooctaene)$(CpCr)_2$	Kruger (1978)	(35)
$[Cr(CH_2COO)_2 \cdot 2H_2O$	DeLucia, Stevens & Coppens (1978)	(36,37)
$[C_4H_7NiOCH_3]_2$	Kruger (1980)	(38)
$[C_3H_5NiSCH_3]_2$	Kruger (1980)	(38)
$[C_5H_9NiCH_3]$	Kruger (1980)	
$[Mn(CO)_5]_2$	Mitschler & Rees (1980)	(39)

Dichromium tetraacetate $[Cr(CH_3COO)_2]_2$ is of interest because its chromium atoms are linked by a quadruple bond, consisting of one sigma ($d_z{}^2$-$d_z{}^2$), two pi (d_{xz}-d_{xz} and d_{yz}-d_{yz}) and a delta (d_{xy}-d_{xy}) component (z parallel to Cr-Cr). A reinvestigation of its structure (Ref. 43) showed the bond in dichromium tetraacetate dihydrate to be 2.36Å, considerably shorter than had been reported previously, while even shorter Cr-Cr bonds have been discovered more recently (Ref. 42).

The electron density in dichromiumtetraacetate was determined at liquid nitrogen temperature

(Ref. 36,37). The deformation density map shows peaks near the chromium atoms in one of the acetate planes which are not present in the second, chemically equivalent plane, and may be due to anharmonic motion effects. The deformation densities in the plane of the acetate group and in the plane bisecting the acetate planes, are shown in Figs. 4a and 5a respectively. They are obtained after averaging over chemically equivalent planes and left-right averaging permitted by the D_{4h} symmetry. Peak heights of 0.2-0.4 $e\AA^{-3}$ are found in all four Cr-O acetate bonds, while density also accumulates between oxygen and carbon, between adjacent carbon atoms and in the lone pair regions at the back of the acetate oxygen atoms. The Cr-Cr region, however, does not show pronounced peaks of electron density, but contains a broad area of excess density with a maximum height of 0.10-0.15$e\AA^{-3}$ off the bond axis (Figs. 4 and 5). As the standard deviation of the averaged density away from the nuclear positions is estimated to be 0.02$e\AA^{-3}$ the accumulations are statistically significant and may be interpreted as evidence for the presence of π and σ bonding between the chromium atoms. The electron deficiency of the region around the internuclear axis suggests the absence of sigma bonding and is probably related to the presence of axial ligands in dichromium tetraacetate dihydrate.

Theoretical calculations on dichromiumtetraformate have been performed by Benard (Ref. 37, 40) using a double zeta basis set for the transition metal valence shells and a minimal basis set for the other orbitals. The calculation shows the non-correlated SCF wavefunction to have very small weight (18%) in the multideterminant expansion of the CI (configuration interaction) wavefunction, with the large contributions of antibonding Cr-Cr orbitals tending to reduce the strength of the Cr-Cr bond. But even the strongly bonding SCF wavefunction does not lead to any sharp peak in the Cr-Cr bond region, a feature attributed to the diffuse character of the metal d orbitals. The maps obtained from the CI wavefunction (Figs. 4b and 5b) have a density maximum of about 0.1$e\AA^{-3}$ in the Cr-Cr bond compared with 0.2$e\AA^{-3}$ for the SCF calculation. They are in good qualitative agreement with the experimental results except near the bond axis where differences may be expected due to the absence of an axial ligand in the complex on which the calculation was performed.

The electron density in bis(dicarbonyl-π-cyclopentadienyl iron) $(C_5H_5Fe(CO)_2)_2$ has been determined by the combined use of x-ray and neutron diffraction (Ref. 30). Its molecular geometry is shown in Fig. 1, while the electron density distribution in a plane containing the Fe-Fe bond and the terminal carbonyl is given in Fig. 6.

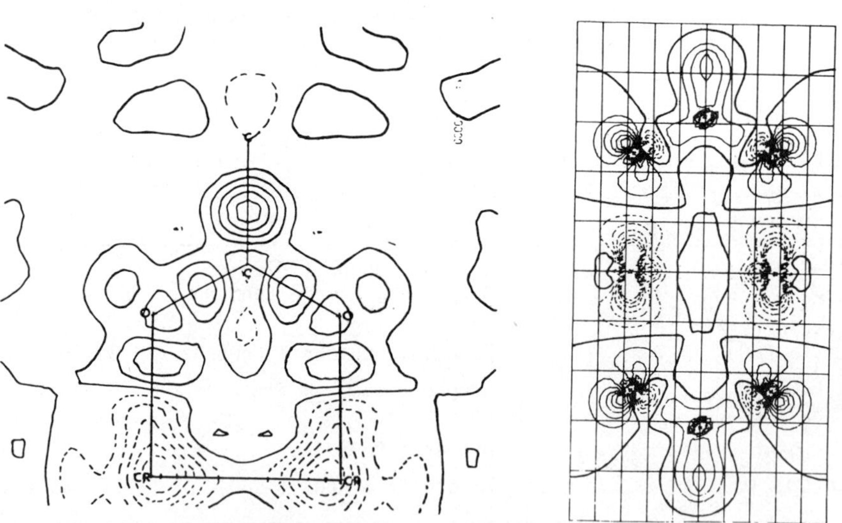

Fig. 4. Deformation density in the plane of the acetate group. a) Experimental. Contours at 0.10$e\AA^{-3}$ intervals. Negative contours broken. b) Theoretical from limited CI wavefunction. Contours interval 0.03e(au)$^{-3}$ ($\sim$ 0.2$e\AA^{-3}$), the bold line is the zero contour and negative contours are broken. (Ref. 37)

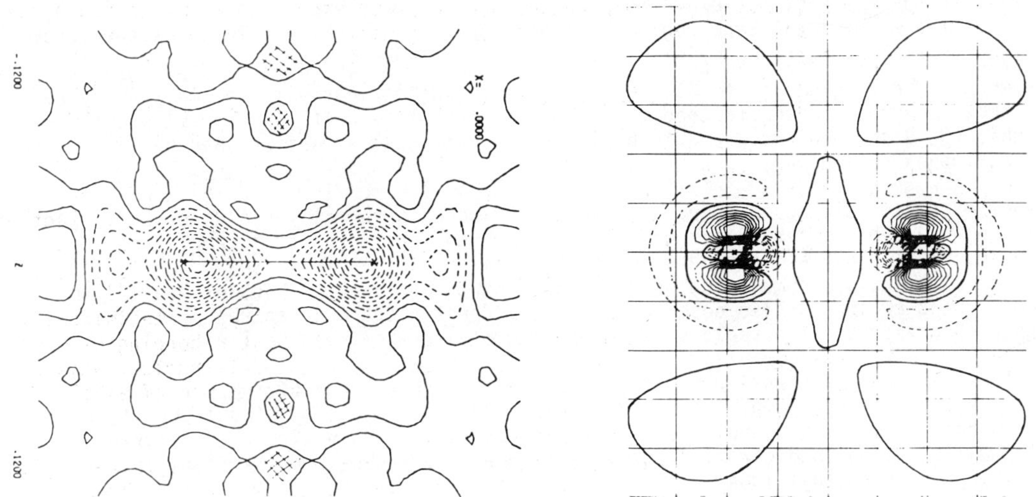

Fig. 5. As Fig. 4 in the plane bisecting the planes of two adjacent acetate groups a) Experimental. Contours at 0.05eÅ^{-3} intervals. b) Theoretical, contours as in Fig. 4. (Ref. 37)

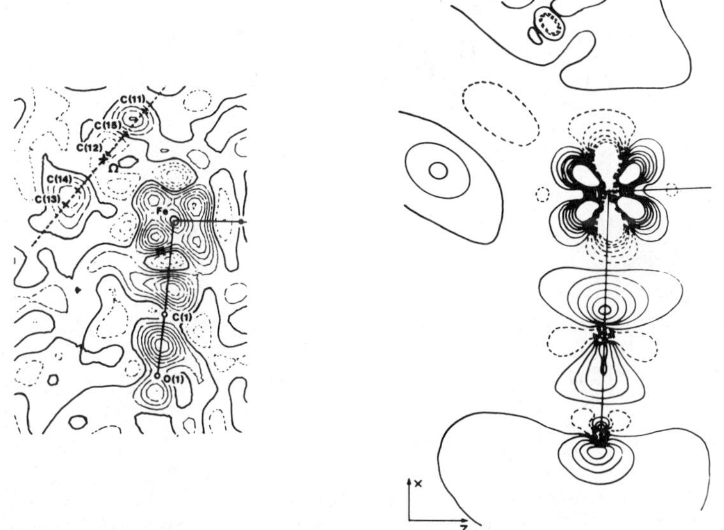

Fig. 6. Deformation density in bis(dicarbonylcyclopentadienyl)iron in plane containing the Fe-Fe bond and the terminal CO group

a) Experimental, Contour interval 0.1eÅ^{-3}. Bold line is zero contour. Negative contours broken.

b) Theoretical. Contour interval 0.03 e(au)$^{-3}$. Deformation densities beyond $\pm$ 0.18 e(au)$^{-3}$ are not represented. Broken contours negative (Ref. 34)

The metal-metal bond in this complex is different from the bond in dichromium tetraacetate. Here the 18 electron rule requires only a single bond to explain the observed diamagnetism. The experimental results indicate a complete absence of density accumulation in the metal-metal bonding region and give an agreement with an SCF theoretical density by Benard, which is remarkable in view of the limitations of the basis set and the absence of thermal smearing in the theoretical density (Fig. 6b). The Mulliken population analysis of the SCF wavefunction gives a small negative value for the overlap population between the iron atoms and thus suggests that the metal-metal bonding is of a multicenter type involving the carbonyl linkages (Ref. 46).

In contrast to the two previous examples a discrepancy between experimental and theoretical densities of the metal-metal bond region is found for $(C_5H_5Ni)_2CH{\equiv}CH$. This was the first binuclear complex to be analyzed and the only one studied so far which does not have a centrosymmetric space group (Ref. 33). Though uncertainties in the phases may reduce peak heights they are not expected to lead to serious quantitative differences. It seems more likely that the discrepancies are due to either observational errors or inadequacies in the theoretical wavefunction.

As in the Fe complex discussed previously the Ni-Ni bond is formally a single bond. The calculation with a basis set as discussed above does not show density accumulation in the bond region, while two peaks are observed between the nickel atoms in the experimental map with relatively little accumulation near the bond center (Fig. 7). Lack of density in the metal-metal bond region is also observed in methylidenetricobalt nonacarbonyl $Co_3CH(CO)_9$, which does show accumulation regions representing metal-carbon binding (Ref. 41).

The available evidence, which further includes a very recent study of the non-bridged diamanganese decacarbonyl complex (Ref. 37) points to the absence of strong density accumulations in bonds involving d-orbitals. There is nevertheless a noticeable difference between the multiple bond in dichromiumtetraacetate and a very weak bond as found in bis-(dicarbonylcyclopentadienyl iron).

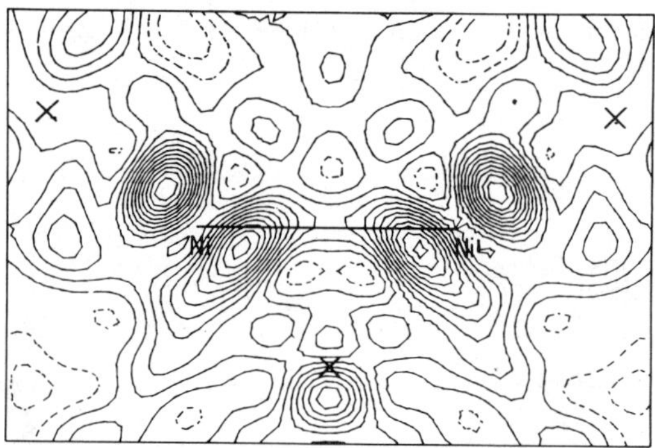

Fig. 7. Experimental deformation density in μ acetylene-bis(cyclopentadienylnickel) in the plane containing two nickel atoms and the midpoint of the acetylene CC bond. Contours as in Fig. 4a. Crosses indicate the centers of the cyclopentadienyl rings, and the C≡C bond. (Ref. 33).

PERTURBATION OF LIGAND DENSITIES

The acetylene molecule in μ acetylene bis(cyclopentadienyl nickel) is strongly perturbed, the molecule deviating from linearity by more than 30° at each of the carbon atoms. Both the theoretical and the experimental electron density maps show a displacement of the bond peak from the bond axes in a direction away from the nickel atoms, an indication that the C-C bond may be bent such as to increase overlap between metal orbitals and bonding hybrids on the carbon atoms involved in carbon-metal bonding.

A smaller but equally significant perturbation of the ligand density has been observed in chromium-hexacarbonyl (Ref. 21). When a prepared chromium atom, with a configuration corresponding to the observed density, and a thermally smeared theoretical density for CO are subtracted from the experimental distribution a difference map is obtained which shows depletion of the highest occupied σ (5σ) and gain in the lowest occupied π (2π) orbitals, in agreement with the accepted σ-bonding π backbonding mechanism (Fig. 8).

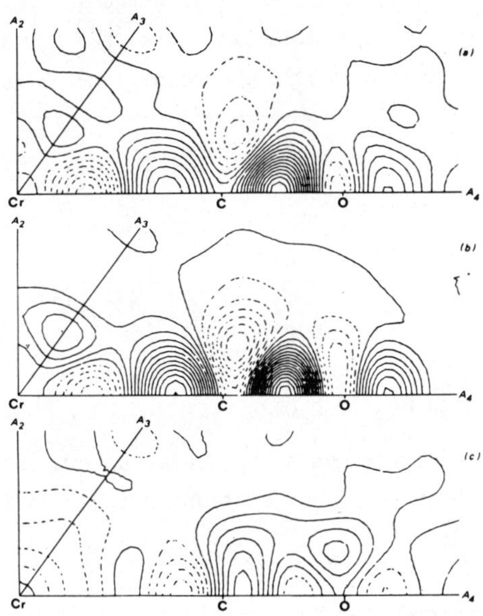

Fig. 8. Deformation density in $Cr(CO)_6$. Plane containing one CO group and the bisector of the two other CO groups. Contours 0.05 $e\text{Å}^{-3}$, negative contours broken.
a) Observed density b) Calculated density molecular model (chromium in configuration $3d(t_{2g})^{3.8}$ $3d(e_g)^{1.2}$ 4s + carbon monoxide molecules) minus free atoms.
c) Observed minus calculated for molecular model (Ref. 21).

SOURCES OF ERROR IN EXPERIMENTAL DENSITIES

Assuming that systematic errors have been minimized through careful control of experimental conditions and adequate corrections for effects such as absorption and extinction we can estimate the experimental errors using statistical theory. Contributions to random errors in the deformation density arise from errors in the structure factors included in the calculation of ρ_{obs}, from errors in the positional and thermal parameters used in the derivation of $\rho_{promolecule}$ and from errors in the scale factor k, used to bring ρ_{obs} and $\rho_{molecule}$ on a common scale (eq. 3) (Refs. 44,45). The error in ρ_{obs} is fairly constant over the unit cell, except at special positions where it increases by a factor which is the square root of the multiplicity of the position. The effect of the parameter errors on the other hand is strongly position dependent and much larger near nuclear positions. The numbers in Table 5 illustrate the dominant effect of temperature factor and scale factor errors in limiting precision near the nuclear positions. Collection of extensive data sets including very high order reflections is recommended to reduce errors in the region near the nuclei.

TABLE 5. Sources of error in the density in the vicinity of a Cr atom (σ_x = 0.00016Å, σ_U = 0.00007Å^2, $\sigma(k)/k$ = 0.0017, temperature factors of 100K structure determination)

distance from Cr nucleus Å	total error	$\sigma(\rho_{obs})$	$\sigma(\rho_{calc,k})^+$	$\sigma_x(\rho_{calc})$	$\sigma_U(\rho_{calc})$	$\sigma_k(\rho_{calc})$
0	0.47eÅ^{-3}	0.04eÅ^{-3}	0.47eÅ^{-3}	0.00eÅ^{-3}	0.53eÅ^{-3}	0.37eÅ^{-3}
0.2	0.26	0.04	0.25	0.10	0.22	0.25
0.4	0.10	0.04	0.09	0.05	0.01	0.07
0.6	0.05	0.04	0.03	0.01	0.01	0.02
0.8	0.04	0.04	0.01	0.00	0.00	0.00

+$\sigma(\rho_{calc},k)$, the total error due to parameter uncertainties, may be smaller than its components because of correlations between parameters; $\sigma_x(\rho_{calc})$ is error due to $\sigma(x)$ etc.

When a similar analysis is performed for heavier atoms such as Mo or W only a slight increase in errors near the atomic positions is found, as an increase in derivatives such as $d\rho/dx$ is compensated by a reduction in the standard deviations of parameters derived from high order data. A more serious limitation is caused by the increase in the absorption correction, which requires an increasingly accurate description of the boundary planes of the specimen crystal. This limitation may be counterbalanced by the use of more penetrating X-rays, though for large unit cells short wavelengths may give diffraction patterns with overlapping reflections.

CONCLUSIONS

The experiment does not yield information on the individual molecular orbitals, which often must be considered to understand details of bonding in a complex. But the electron density is a uniquely defined observable unlike the M.O.'s and it may be linked to the individual molecular orbitals through a theoretical calculation calibrated by its agreement with experiment.

As larger complexes are to be studied experimental demands in terms of diffractometer time and computing capability become exceedingly severe. Use of more intense sources such as synchrotron beams and on-line computer analysis should allow further development of this field.

ACKNOWLEDGEMENTS

I would like to thank my coworkers who participated in the part of the work performed at SUNY/Buffalo. Support by the National Science Foundation is gratefully acknowledged.

REFERENCES

1. P. Coppens, MTP Int. Rev. Sci. Ser 2, 11, 21.
2. P. Coppens, Ang. Chemie 16, 32 (1977).
3. P. Coppens, in Neutron Diffraction H. Dachs Ed. Springer, Berlin (1979).
4. R. F. Stewart, J. Chem. Phys. 58, 1668 (1973).
5. R. F. Stewart, Chem. Phys. Letters 65, 335 (1979).
6. P. Coppens, G. Moss & N. K. Hansen in Crystallographic Computing, N. Venkatesan and S. Ramaseshan Ed.. Ind. Inst. Science (1980).
7. F. L. Hirshfeld, Isr. J. of Chem. 16, 226 (1977).
8. R. F. Stewart, Acta Cryst A32, 565 (1976).
9. N. K. Hansen and P. Coppens, Acta Cryst. A34, 909 (1978).
10. E. D. Stevens, J. Rys and P. Coppens, J. Am. Chem. Soc. 100, 2324 (1978).
11. E. D. Stevens and P. Coppens, Acta Cryst B36 In Press.
12. J. W. McIver Jr., P. Coppens and D. Nowack, Chem. Phys. Letters 11, 82 (1971).
13. J. Bicerano, D. S. Marynick and W. N. Lipscomb, J. Am. Chem. Soc. 100, 732 (1978).
14. P. Coppens, Acta Cryst B30, 225 (1974).
15. J. M. Savariault and M. S. Lehmann, J. Am. Chem. Soc. 102, 1298 (1980).
16. J. O. Thomas, Acta Cryst A34, 819 (1978).
17. B. Rees and P. Coppens, Acta Cryst B29, 2516 (1973).
18. M. Iwata and Y. Saito, Acta Cryst B29, 822 (1973).
19. F. Marumo, M. Isobe, Y. Saito, T. Yagi and S. Akimoto, Acta Cryst B30, 1904 (1974).
20. M. Iwata, Acta Cryst B33, 59 (1977).
21. B. Rees and A. Mitschler, J. Am. Chem. Soc. 98, 7918 (1976).
22. K. Toriumi, M. Ozima, M. Akaogi and Y. Saito, Acta Cryst B34, 1093 (1978).
23. K. Toriumi and Y. Saito, Acta Cryst B34, 3149 (1978).
24. S. Ohba, K. Toriumi, S. Sato and Y. Saito, Acta Cryst B34, 3535 (1978).
25. E. D. Stevens, M. L. DeLucia and P. Coppens, Inorg. Chem. 19, 813 (1980).
26. E. D. Stevens, unpublished results.
27. F. Takusagawa and T. F. Koetzle, unpublished results.
28. F. Takusagawa and T. F. Koetzle, ACA Program and Abstracts Series 2, 7, 16 (1980).
29. E. D. Stevens, ACA Program and Abstracts Series 2, 7, 17 (1980).
30. A. Mitschler, B. Rees and M. S. Lehmann, J. Am. Chem. Soc. 100, 3390 (1978).
31. E. D. Stevens and P. Coppens, Acta Cryst A35, 536 (1979).
32. W. C. Hamilton, Acta Cryst 18, 502 (1965).
33. Y. W. Wang and P. Coppens, Inorg. Chem. 15, 1122 (1976).
34. A. Mitschler, B. Rees and M. S. Lehmann,, J. Am. Chem.Soc. 100, 3390 (1978).
35. W. Geibel, G. Wilke, R. Goddard, C. Kruger and R. Mynott, J. Organomet. Chem., 160 139 (1978).
36. M. L. DeLucia, Thesis, State University of New York at Buffalo (1977).
37. M. Benard, P. Coppens, M. L. DeLucia and E. D. Stevens, Inorg. Chem. In press.
38. C. Kruger, Abstracts Darmstaedter Symposium on Structure Analysis and Theoretical Chemistry p 54 (1980).
39. A. Mitschler and B. Rees, to be published.
40. M. Benard, J. Am. Chem. Soc. 100, 2354 (1978).
41. P. Leung and P. Coppens, unpublished results.
42. F. A. Cotton, Accounts of Chem. Research 11, 225 (1978).
43. F. A. Cotton, B. DeBoer, M. LaPrade, J. Pipal and D. Ueko Acta Cryst. B27, 1664 (1971).
44. E. D. Stevens and P. Coppens, Acta Cryst. A32, 915 (1976).
45. B. Rees, Acta Cryst. A32, 483 (1976).
46. M. Benard, J. Am. Chem. Soc., 100, 7740 (1978).

CIRCULAR DICHROISM OF ASYMMETRICALLY DISTORTED COMPLEXES OF TRANSITION ELEMENTS

K. Saito

Chemistry Department, Faculty of Science, Tohoku University, Sendai 980, Japan

Abstract — Oxo complexes of molybdenum(V) and vanadium(IV) give considerable asymmetric distortion whenever optically active multidentate ligands are coordinated. X-Ray crystallography disclosed that the distortion is due to the respulsion between oxo and other ligating atoms, and to the stress caused by the chelate formation. The distorsion of the binuclear Mo^V complexes with $Mo_2O_2L_{b(1)}L_{b(2)}{}^{2+}$ core (L's are O^{2-} or S^{2-}) may be designated by the torsion angle between the two octahedrons projected across the Mo-Mo axis. For uninuclear $V^{IV}O^{2+}$ complexes and mixed valence binuclear $V^{IV}V^{V}O_3{}^{3+}$ complexes with centre of symmetry, the deviation of the ligating atoms from the plane parpendicular to the V=O bond can be a criterion of distortion. Circular dichroism (CD) peaks of the binuclear Mo^V complexes in the visible and UV region correspond to the four absorption peaks which are reckoned to be of charge transfer nature within the binuclear core. The second and the third peaks are best correlated to the torsion angle and the fourth (highest wave number) seems to be related with the configuration of asymmetric carbon of the ligand. The CD peaks of V^{IV} complexes corrsponding to the four d-d transition peaks. The mixed valence complex gives, besides these, a large CD peak around 10000 cm^{-1} corresponding the intervalence absorption. Their pattern is rather common regardless of the ligand, but seems to be governed by the configuration of chelates.

INTRODUCTION

Circular dichroism (CD) spectra of coordination compounds are governed by various factors including (i) the configuration of ligands particularly of chelates around the central metal ion, (ii) the absolute configuration of asymmetrically ligating atoms, (iii) that of remote asymmetric atoms such as asymmetric carbon of organic ligands, (iv) conformation of puckered chelate rings, and (v) deviation of coordinated atoms from regular polyhedron. Importance of the last contribution was demonstrated by the crystallographic data of some cobalt(III) complexes including tris(1,2-cyclopentanediamine)cobalt(III) (*1*) and tris(2,4-pentanediamine)cobalt(III) (*2-4*). The examples are, however, limited to Co^{III} complexes and to other complexes with Schiff bases, although there are theoretical discussions. (*5 - 7*)

Examination of the reported X-ray structure of the complexes of *S*-cysteinate (*S*-cys), its methyl- (*S*-mecys) and ethylester (*S*-etcys) and *S*-histidinate (*S*-hist), $[Mo_2O_4(S\text{-cys})_2]$ (*8*) $[Mo_2O_2S_2(S\text{-cys})_2]$ (*9*), $[Mo_2O_4(S\text{-etcys})_2]$ (*10*), $[Mo_2O_2S_2(S\text{-mecys})_2]$ (*11*), $[Mo_2O_4(S\text{-hist})_2]$ (*12*), and $[Mo_2O_2S_2(S\text{-hist})_2]$ (*13*), disclosed that the distortion of the ligands around the Mo_2 core is considerably different from one another despite of the common *S*-configuration of the aminocarboxylates. We have measured their CD spectra in various organic solvents and in KBr disks, and found that the CD pattern also differs remarkably from one another and correlated with the distortion. We have prepared new optically active complexes of *R*-propylenediaminetetraacetate (*R*-pdta), $[Mo_2O_4(R\text{-pdta})]^{2-}$, $[Mo_2O_3S(R\text{-pdta})]^{2-}$ and $[Mo_2O_2S_2(R\text{-pdta})]^{2-}$, measured CD spectra, determined the X-ray structure and found the same correlation between the CD pattern and distortion, despite of the different location of asymmetric carbon and bridging structure.

Optical activity of square pyramidal and octahedral oxovanadium(IV) complexes has been studied only with Schiff bases (*14-18*), lactate and tartrate (*14*). There is no information concerning the absolute configuration around V^{IV} and conformation of the chelates. We have synthesised new oxovanadium(IV) complexes with *S*-1-(2-pyridyl)ethylamino-*N*,*N*-diacetate (*S*-peida^{2-}), *S*-1-{*N*,*N*-bis(carboxylatomethyl)amino}propionate (*S*-alaninediacetate, *S*-alada^{2-}), *S*-1-{*N*,*N*-bis(phosphonatomethyl)amino}propionate (*S*-alaninedimethylenediphosphonate, *S*-admdp^{5-}), 1,2-{*N*,*N*-bis(*S*-propionato)diamino}ethane (ethylenediamine-*N*,*N*-dipropionate, *S*,*S*-eddp^{2-}) and 1,2-bis(*S*-2-carboxylato-1-pyrrolidinyl)ethane (ethylenebis(*N*-*S*-prolinate), *S*,*S*-ebp^{2-}). Their visible and UV absorption and CD spectra were recorded in water and in KBr disks. We demonstrated the formation of oxo-bridged binuclear deep blue complex of vanadium with nitrilotriacetate (nta^{3-}) between the blue $[V^{IV}O(nta)(H_2O)]^-$ and yellow $[V^{V}O_2(nta)]^{2-}$ in water and the existence of a mixed valence state in the $V_2O_3{}^{3+}$ core with only one d

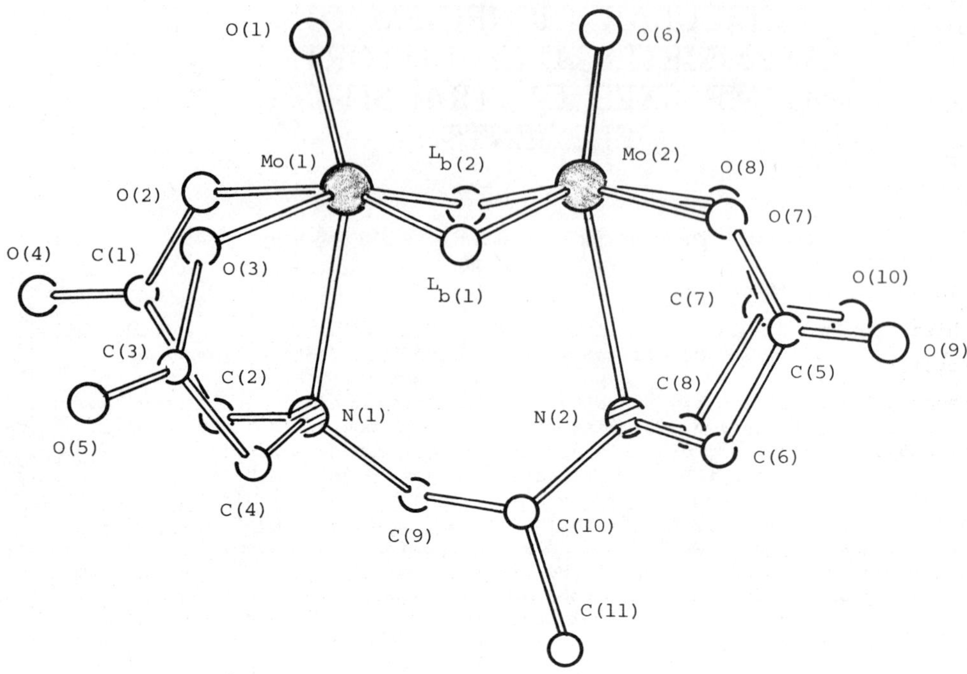

Fig. 1 A perspective drawing of $[Mo_2O_4(R\text{-pdta})]^{2-}$ anion with atom numbering (The same numbering is used for $[Mo_2O_3S(R\text{-pdta})]^{2-}$ and $[Mo_2O_2S_2(R\text{-pdta})]^{2-}$ $L_{b(1)}$ and $L_{b(2)}$ standing for the bridging O and S.)

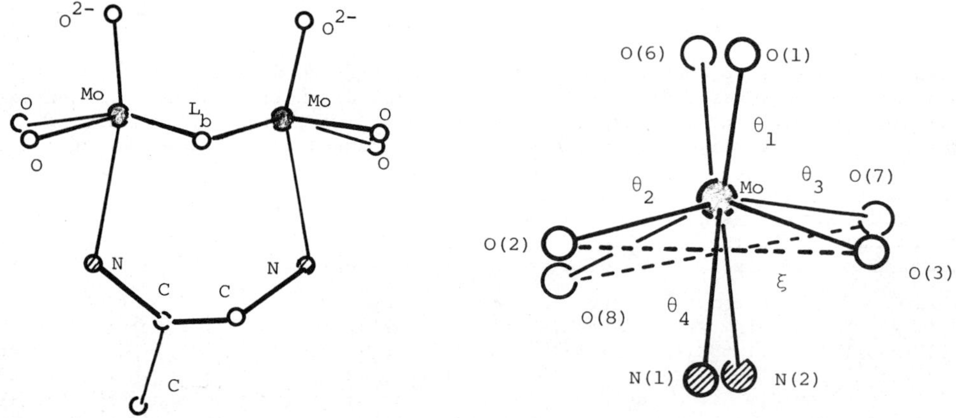

Fig. 2 Projection of $[Mo_2O_4(R\text{-pdta})]^{2-}$ from the axis conneting two bridgingj oxides, $L_{b(2)}$ (over the paper) and $L_{b(1)}$

Fig. 3 Definition of the torsion angles (projected on the plane across the Mo-Mo)

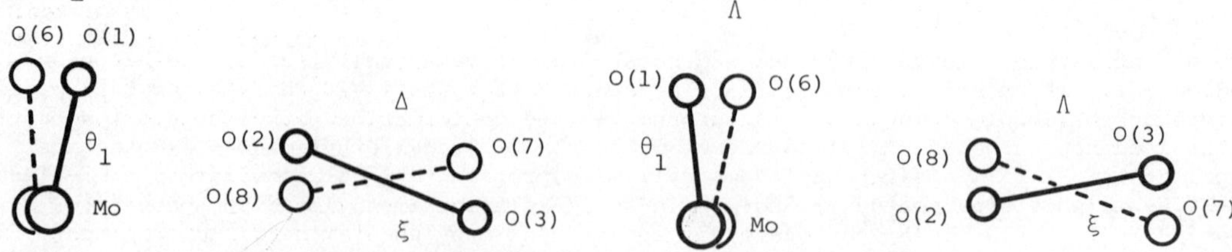

Fig. 4 Definition of the chirality (tentative names; *cf. Ref. 20*)

Table 1 Torsion angles, chirality of the corresponding twist and the conformation of gauche-like chelate rings of $Mo_2O_2L_{b(1)}L_{b(2)}{}^{2+}$ complexes

Complex	Torsion angle a,b) $\vert\theta_1\vert$	$\vert\theta_2\vert$	$\vert\theta_3\vert$	$\vert\theta_4\vert$	$\vert\xi\vert$	Chelate ring
$Na_2[Mo_2O_4$(*R*-pdta)]·$3H_2O$	5.4 (8) Δ	8.6(10) Δ	6.8(11) Δ	5.4 (6) Δ	8.6(7) Δ	λ
$Na_2[Mo_2O_3S$(*R*-pdta)]·$4H_2O$	0.2 (3)*Δ	10.0 (3) Δ	11.6 (4) Δ	9.1 (2) Δ	11.5(2) Δ	λ
$Na_2[Mo_2O_2S_2$(*R*-pdta)]·$4H_2O$	0.2 (6)* Λ	9.3 (6) Δ	9.2 (7) Δ	10.8 (4) Δ	10.4(5) Δ	λ
$Na_2[Mo_2O_4$(*S*-cys)$_2$]·$5H_2O$	4.0 (8) Δ	1.5 (7) Δ	1.7 (7) Δ	11.7 (5) Λ	0.1(4)*Δ	δ
$Na_2[Mo_2O_2S_2$(*S*-cys)$_2$]·$2H_2O$	4.7(14) Δ	1.4(11) Δ	0.6(11)*Δ	10.9 (8) Λ	0.2(8)* Λ	δ
$[Mo_2O_2S_2$(*S*-hist)$_2$]·$1.5H_2O$	2.5 (4) Δ	0.8 (5) Δ	7.5 (4) Δ	4.6 (3) Λ	4.5(3) Δ	—
$[Mo_2O_4$(*S*-etcys)$_2$]	6.7(11) Λ	22.1 (8) Λ	24.3 (7) Λ	—	28.4(6) Λ	δ
$[Mo_2O_2S_2$(*S*-mecys)$_2$]	9.2(15) Λ	30.1(13) Λ	26.8(14) Λ	—	35.9(11) Λ	λ

a) for the signs see Figs. 3 and 4 *b)* estimated standard deviations in parentheses
*) too small to be discussed

electron (*19*). Similar mixed valence complexes have been prepared with *S*-peida^{2-} and *S*-alada^{2-} and their absorption and CD spectra recorded. X-Ray crystallography of some of these complexes indicated that considerable distortion exists around the VO^{2+} and $V_2O_3{}^{3+}$ core.

This paper gives the X-ray crystallographic data of these asymmetrically distorted complexes, and the source of distortion is discussed. The relationship between the CD pattern and the X-ray structure is discussed with special reference to the nature of the absorption bands to which the CD peaks are assigned.

CRYSTAL STRUCTURE OF THE DISTORTED COMPLEXES

Structure of binuclear molybdenum(V) complexes

The structure of $[Mo_2O_2L_{b(1)}L_{b(2)}(R\text{-pdta})]^{2-}$ is schematically illustrated in Fig. 1. (L_b's are O^{2-} and S^{2-}) Change in th bridging species from O to S does not cause big change in the overall structure. When one looks at the complex through the axis connecting the bridging L_b's, the edges connecting the carboxylate oxygens are distorted to give δ distortion. Fig. 3 illustrates such a distortion; the two terminal oxides are not parallel to each other. Such a distortion is tentatively designated by Δ and Λ as shown in Fig. 4. (*20*) The complex anion $[Mo_2O_3S(R\text{-pdta})]^{2-}$ gives two geometrical isomers, but only one was prepared selectively, in which the S is at $L_{b(1)}$. Examination of the crystal data of other aminocarboxylato complexes with $Mo_2O_2L_{b(1)}L_{b(2)}{}^{2+}$ core disclosed the existence of such distortions which are expressed by a similar manner (*9-13*). Table 1 gives the torsion angles designated in Fig. 3, and the conformation of the chelate rings two coordiantion sites of the binuclear core.

Source of distortion

The R-pdta complexes The distortion should arise from the strain caused by chelate formation. If there were no chelate, the two Mo, two terminal O and the two apical ligating atoms should lie on one plane. The coordinated *R*-pdta^{2-} takes λ conformation at the 1,2-propanediamine moiety to make the methyl equatorial with respect to the idealised Mo-Mo-Z-Z' plane. Hence the three N-C bonds cannot be symmetrical with respect to this plane, and the NC_3 portion rotates unticlockwise about the Mo-N vector until the torsion angle N-C-C-N becomes 94 to 98°. Such a rotation brings about upper shift of Y and Y' (Fig. 5) [O(2) and O(7) in Fig 1] and down shift of X and X' (Fig. 5) [O(3) and O(8) in Fig. 1], to make the edge X-Y slant to X'-Y'. Thus a Δ configuration is caused at the $Mo_2O_2L_{b(1)}L_{b(2)}{}^{2+}$ core, and the strain of the *R*-1,2-propanediamine and glycinate rings may be alleviated. The distance between the terminal oxides and Y and Y' (2.67 to 2.72 Å) are significantly shorter than those between the terminal oxides and X and X' (2.70 to 2.88 Å) for the three complexes. The displacement of X and Y from the idealised basal plane is *ca.* 0.10 Å on an average. The terminal oxide ions should move to keep the distance with X (and X') and Y (and Y') to bring about Δ twist at the O=Mo-Mo=O moiety. Such a displacement is much smaller for the S-bridged complexes, presumably because of the longer Mo-Mo and N-N distance. (*21*)

The S-cysteinato and S-histidinato complexes The torsion angles and the conformation were calculated on the basis of the crystal data in the literatures and listed in Table 1. These complexes have a common framework shown in Fig.5, and the chelate ring spans as schematically shown in Fig. 6. Since the asymmetric carbon of the aminocarboxylates has *S*-configuration the three ligating atoms S,N and O of *S*-cys^{2-} and N(ring), N and O of *S*-hist^{2-} should be located clockwise in this order (Y,X and Z and Y',X' and Z'), when the Mo^V ion is looked at from the asymmetric carbon of the ligands. Formation of a chelate ring between X and Z shifts X towards Z to make the terminal O distant from X. The terminal O will be thus inclined towards X, and Y may approach terminal O to make the interatomic distances O-X and O-Y optimal. Such a distortion results in rotation of the triangle OXY (O'X'Y') to bring

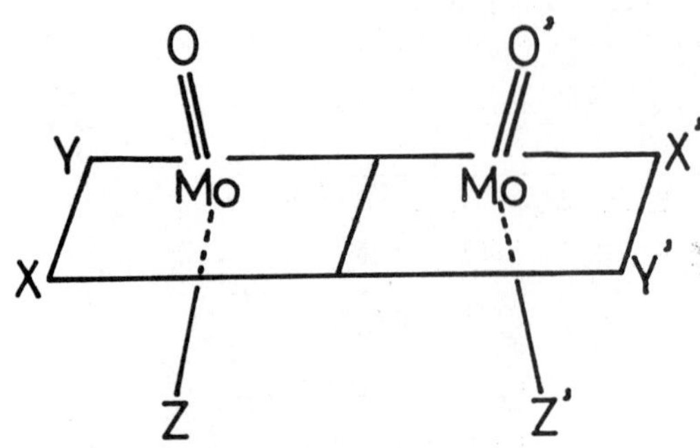

Fig. 5 Distortion around the binuclear molydenum(V) core

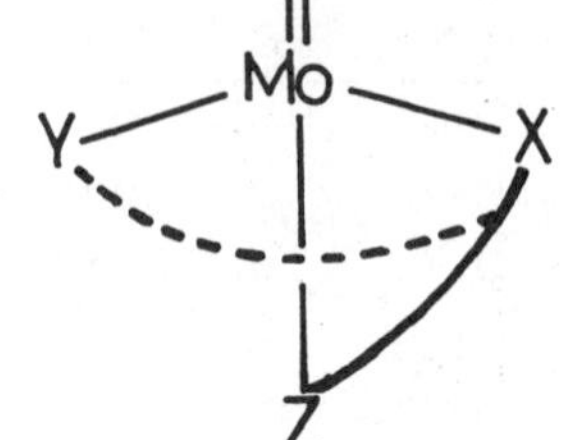

Fig. 6 Chelate formation around molybdenum(V)

about a twist in the O=Mo-Mo=O' core as well as that of the edges X-Y and X'-Y'.

In the absence of chelate between X and Z (X' and Z') in the *S*-mecys$^-$ and *S*-etcys$^-$ complexes, such a shift cannot be expected. Since the distance between terminal O and S (Y and Y', *ca.* 3.4 Å) is significantly longer than that between terminal O and N (X and X', *ca.* 2.9 Å), the greater repulsion between O and S results in the distortion of the triangle OXY (O'X'Y') in the reversed direction to bring about Λ distortion. Such a repulsion should be effected in the *S*-cys^{2-} complex, but overwhelmed by the more marked influence due to chelate formation.

All these results indicate that the $Mo^{V}_{2}O_{2}L_{b(1)}L_{b(2)}{}^{2+}$ core is readily subject to distortion to either Δ or Λ direction depending on the strain on chelate formation, or on different repulsions between the terminal oxide and the ligating atoms. There seems to be an overall trend towards greater distortion in the following sequence.

$$S\text{-hist}^- < R\text{-pdta}^{4-} \simeq S\text{-cys}^{2-} < S\text{-etcys}^- \simeq S\text{-mecys}^-$$

Structure of vanadium(IV) and vanadium(IV,V) complexes

No X-ray crystallographic study has been reported concerning the absolute configuration of optically active complexes of oxovanadium(2+). We have so far determined the crystal structure of the optically active complexes, $[V^{IV}O(S\text{-peida})(H_2O)]$, $[V_2O_3(S\text{-peida})_2]^-$, $[V^{IV}O(S,S\text{-ebp})(H_2O)]$ and $[V_2O_3(S\text{-alada})_2]^{3-}$ (for the abbreviated formulae of the ligands see "Introduction"). Figures 7 and 8 show the structure of of the uni- and binuclear complexes of *S*-peida^{2-}. The V^{IV} complex has three geometrical isomers, but our preparation gave only one of them with the tertiary nitrogen at the apical (trans to oxo) site. The *S*,*S*-ebp^{2-} complex has Δ-cisα configuration around V^{IV}.

As exemplified by Figs. 7 and 8, considerable distortion is seen for all the complexes. (*22*) There can be several baselines upon which the distortion is expressed. We have tentatively chosen the V=O bond as the base for both the uni- and binuclear complexes. Figures 9 and 10 show the deviation from the base plane. which passes the the V ion and is parpendicular to the V=O bond. The example is too few to generalise the discussion, but we tend to consider that the source of distortion might be similar to that for the binuclear Mo(V) complexes; *i.e.* the repulsion between the terminal O and the ligating atoms at the basal sites, and the stress caused by the chelate formation.

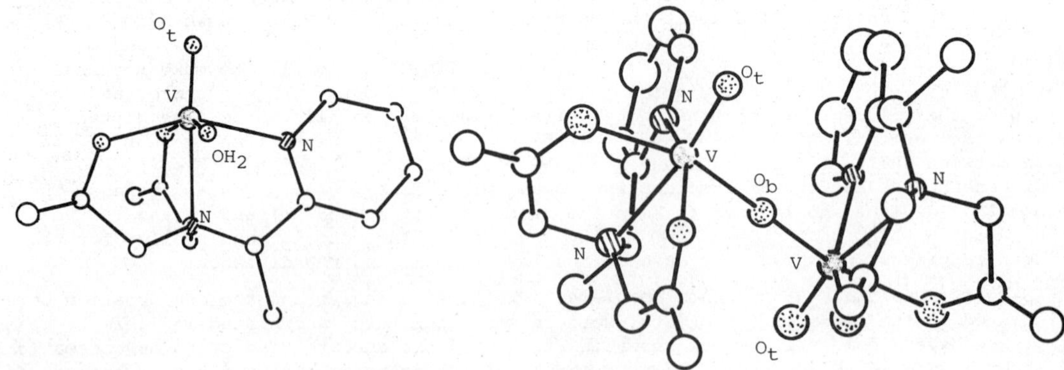

Fig. 7 Structure of $[V^{IV}O(S\text{-peida})(H_2O)]$

peida^{2-} = $^-$OOC-CH$_2$ / $^-$OOC-CH$_2$ >N-CH(CH$_3$)-C (HC=CH, CH, N—CH ring)

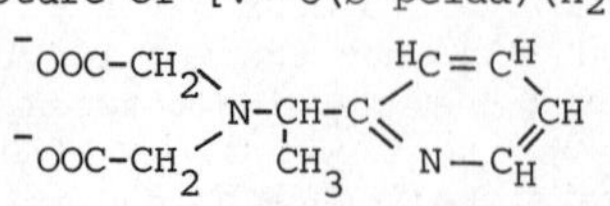

Fig.8 Structure of $[V_2O_3(S\text{-peida})_2]^-$

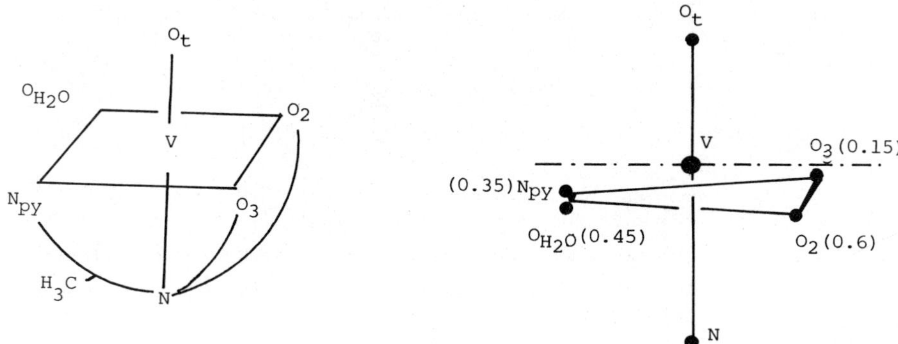

Fig. 9 Distortion of $[V^{IV}O(S\text{-peida})(H_2O)]$ expressed with the V=O bond as the base

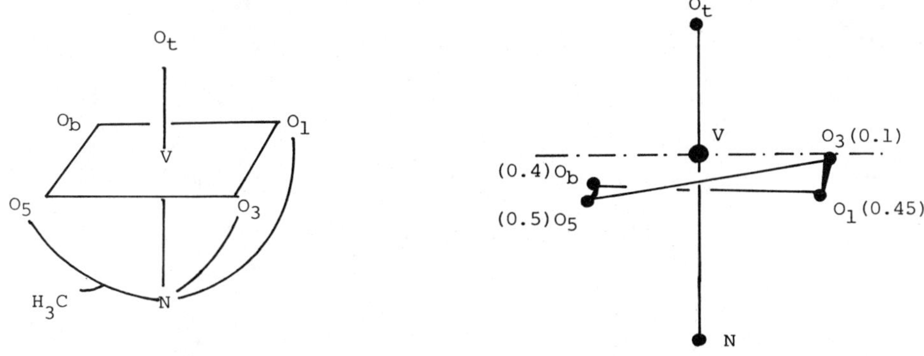

Fig. 10 Distortion of $[V_2O_3(S\text{-alada})_2]^{3-}$ expressed with the V=O bond as the base
(The bridging O $[O_b]$ is the pseudo centre of symmetry)

The binuclear complexes provide interesting examples of mixed valence state in the form of discrete species. There is a pseudo centre of symmetry at the bridging oxide. However, closer examination indicates that the two V-O_b distances are slightly different from each other. (1.762Å and 1.876 Å) There can be an influence of packing in the crystal, but other structural parameters around each nuclear core are very similar to each other. (23)

CIRCULAR DICHROISM OF THE COMPLEXES

CD Pattern of the molybdenum(V) complexes

The *R*-pdta complexes give rather complicated absorption pattern in the visible and UV region. (Fig. 11) The oxo bridged species have two peaks at 25800 and 33600 cm^{-1} and several shoulders. Those bridged by O and S and two S ions have more complicated pattern. All the other complexes containing other aminocarboxylates show more or less similar pattern. (*24*) Brown, Perkins and Stewart calculated the electronic transition energies of $[Mo_2^VO_4(S\text{-cys})_2]^{2-}$ by the SCF-MO method and gave five transition energies, 13250, 20320, 27390, 30870 and 35700 cm^{-1}. These were assigned to the transitions involving the orbitals located mainly on the two Mo^V ions, and claimed to be common to other $Mo_2O_4^{2+}$ complexes. (*25*) The observed CD peaks are listed in Table 2. All of them are naturally related to the absorption peaks, and correspond to those predicted by Brown *et al.* except that at 13250 cm^{-1}, which was observed in none of the present complexes in less than 0.1 mol dm^{-1} solution. The observed four bands are tentatively named Bands I, II, III and IV from the lower wave number. A large absorption band with log 3.5 to 4 appears around 45000 cm^{-1} and is accompanied by CD peaks (Band V).

Relationship between the structure and the CD pattern Figure 12 exemplifies the influence of the medium upon the CD pattern. Since the curves are similar to one another in KBr disks and in the soulutions, the complex should maintain the same structure as in the crystalline state. This is also true for all the other complexes. The CD pattern in the solutions can be discussed on the basis of the crystal structure.

The CD peaks at Band I are small and very sensitive to the environment. The CD patterns in Band II and Band III region seem to differ considerably from one another; *e.g.* the *S*-cys and *S*-etcys complexes give reversed signs despite of the common *S*-configuration of asymmetric carbon. However, when one looks at the distortion around the Mo_2 core (*vide supra*), a very good correlation is obvious, which is tabulated in Table 3.

Table 2 Circular dichroism peaks of binuclear molybdenum(V) complexes with a core $Mo_2L_{b(1)}L_{b(2)}{}^{2+}$ (wave number in cm^{-1}, $\Delta\varepsilon$ in parentheses) *a)*

Complex	Band I	Band II	Band III	Band IV	Band V
$[Mo_2O_4(R\text{-pdta})]^{2-}$	20.8s(-0.48)	26.0 (-5.5)	33.3 (+5.1)	37.1 (-1.6)	40.6 (+3.9) 45.2 (-5.1)
$[Mo_2O_3S(R\text{-pdta})]^{2-}$	20.1 (-0.45) 22.5 (+0.51)	26.1 (-11.1)	30.8 (+2.8) 34.0 (+2.2)	36.5 (-5.4)	40.7 (+16.4) 45.5 (-3.5)
$[Mo_2O_2S_2(R\text{-pdta})]^{2-}$	20.2 (+0.78)	25.6 (-12.3) 28.0s (-6.4)	31.7 (+7.4) 34.4s (+0.9)	36.0 (-1.8) 39.1 (+22.5)	45.2 (+10.5)
$[Mo_2O_4(S\text{-cys})_2]^{2-}$	19.2 (+0.07)	26.1 (-12.2)	31.7 (+2.6)	36.0 (+3.1)	43.8 (+9.3)
$[Mo_2O_2S_2(S\text{-cys})_2]^{2-}$	19.3 (-0.04)	25.0 (+4.0) 27.8 (-7.9)	31.5 (+15.7)	37.8 (-16.8)	42.9 (+48.2) 47.6 (-36.9)
$[Mo_2O_4(R\text{-pen})_2]^{2-}$ *b)*	18.6 (-0.07)	26.6 (+11.4)	31.9 (-4.4)	35.8 (-4.9)	43.6 (-11.7)
$[Mo_2O_4(S\text{-hist})_2]$ *c)*	20.4 (+0.14)	26.9 (-3.0)	33.6 (+3.9)	38.0 (+7.3)	—
$[Mo_2O_4(S\text{-etcys})_2]$ *d)*	22.2 (+1.03)	28.8 (+30.5)	34.4 (-21.5)	37.4 (+10.2)	40.4 (-4.6) 44.0 (+10.0) 46.7 (-6.5)
$[Mo_2O_2S_2(S\text{-mecys})_2]$ *d)*	20.2 (+1.08) 23.6 (+2.18)	28.2s (+17.2) 30.1 (+20.4)	34.2 (-22.1)	38.0 (+17.0)	44.0 (+40.0) 49.1 (+13.2)

a) s, shoulder; in water unless otherwise stated
b) pen, penicillaminate
c) in dimethylsulphoxide
d) in acetonitrile

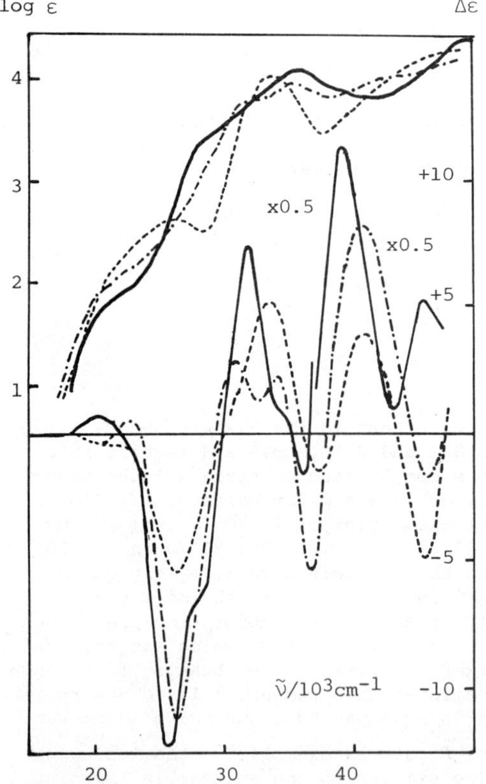

Fig. 11 Absorption and CD spectra of $[Mo_2O_2L_{b(1)}L_{b(2)}(R\text{-pdta})]^{2-}$ in water
---- L = O, O —·—·— L = O, S
—— L = S, S

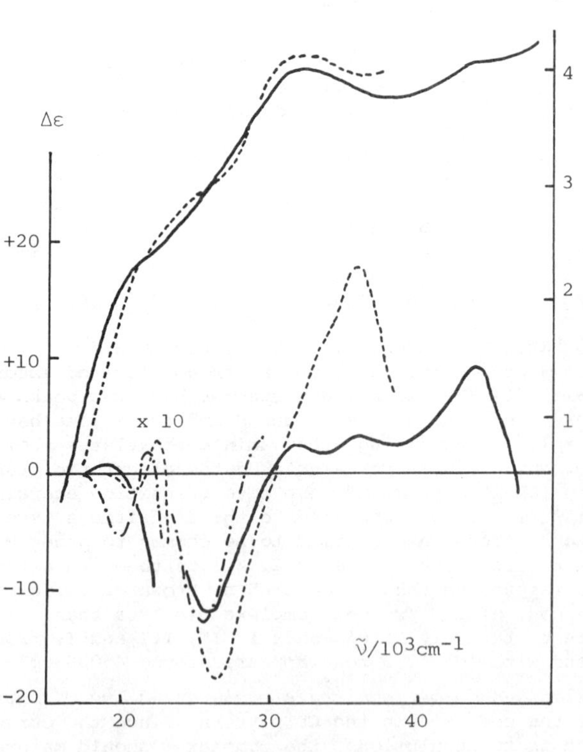

Fig. 12 Absorption and CD pattern of $[Mo_2O_4(S\text{-cys})_2]^{2-}$
—— in water —·—·— in KBr disk
----- in dimethylformamide

Table 3 Relationship between the CD signs in Band II and Band III region and the distortion of the $Mo_2O_2L_{b(1)}L_{b(2)}{}^{2+}$ core

Complex	in *a)*	CD sign at *b)* Band II	CD sign at *b)* Band III	Distorsion of Mo_2 core	Configuration of asym. C	conformation of chemate
$[Mo_2O_4(R\text{-pdta})]^{2-}$	water	- (26.0)	+ (33.3)	Δ	*R*	λ
$[Mo_2O_3S(R\text{-pdta})]^{2-}$	water	- (26.1)	+ (30.8)	Δ	*R*	λ
$[Mo_2O_2S_2(R\text{-pdta})]^{2-}$	water	- (25.6)	+ (31.7)	Δ	*R*	λ
$[Mo_2O_4(S\text{-cys})_2]^{2-}$	water	- (26.1)	+ (31.7)	Δ	*S*	δ
$[Mo_2O_2S_2(S\text{-cys})_2]^{2-}$	water	- (27.8)	+ (31.5)	Δ	*S*	δ
$[Mo_2O_4(R\text{-pen})_2]^{2-}$	water	+ (26.6)	- (31.9)	(Λ) *c)*	*R*	λ
$[Mo_2O_4(S\text{-hist})_2]$	DMSO	- (26.9)	+ (33.6)	Δ	*S*	—
$[Mo_2O_4(S\text{-etcys})_2]$	AN	+ (28.8)	- (34.4)	Λ	*S*	δ
$[Mo_2O_2S_2(S\text{-mecys})_2]$	AN	+ (28.2)	- (34.2)	Λ	*S*	λ

a) the solvent; DMSO, dimethylsulphoxise, AN, acetonitrile
b) The wave number at which the CD sign was examined in parenthesis in $10^3 cm^{-1}$.
c) not crystallographically determined

Δ-Configuration of the Mo_2 core gives negative and positive CD peaks at Band II and Band III, respectively, regardless of the absolute configuration of asymmetric carbon and conformation of the chelate ring involving asymmetric carbon. Change in the bridging species form oxide to sulphide brings about slight change of CD pattern. However, it is understood by considering that new CD peaks with rather small Δε/ε values appear near the Band II. Table 1 shows that ξ values for the S-cys^{2-} complexes are almost zero. For most other complexes, however, they are bigger than $|\theta_1|$. On the other hand $|\theta_1|$ is almost zero for R-pdta^{4-} complexes with O,S- and S_2- bridges. It is seen that neither the twist of Mo=O bonds nor the tetrahedral distortion of the basal plane can be individually responsible for the CD sign of Band II and Band III region. The CD sign must reflect the overall distortion around the Mo_2 core (*24*).

The CD sign in the Band IV region seems to be more or less related to the absolute configuration of asymmetric carbon. Nothing decisive can be stated at the present stage concerning the CD sign in the region > 40000 cm^{-1}.

Absorption and CD spectra of vanadium(IV) and vanadium(IV,V) complexes

Vanadium(IV) complexes The V^{IV} complexes give four absorption peaks or shoulders in the region from 10000 to 45000 cm^{-1}. The d-d transition is schematically shown in Fig. 13. The three absorption bands at 11000 to 15000 (doubly degenerated), 17000 to 18000 and 28000 to 30000 cm^{-1} are assigned to the three d-d transitions. The band at 40000 to 45000 cm^{-1} are reckoned to be of charge transfer nature. (*26*)

The absorption and CD spectra are shown in Fig. 14. As exmplified by the CD pattern of [VO (S-peida)(H_2O)], the medium affects the pattern to a modest extent. The CD peaks are listed in Table IV, in which the CD strength is expressed by Δε/ε . They correspond well to the absorption bands, and a distinct splitting is seen in the degenerated Band I. The sign of CD peaks at Band Ib (the higher wave number of the split peak), II and III is common for all the complexes regardless of the chelate structure. On the other hand, the CD peaks at Band Ia (the lowest wave number) differ from one another. It seems that the two complexes with S,S-eddp^{2-} and S,S-ebp^{2-} which have configurational asymmetry Δ-cisα structure exhibit large positive peaks at *ca.* 12000 cm^{-1}. Falmer and Urbach measured the CD spectra of $V^{IV}O^{2+}$ complexes with a variety of Schiff bases formed between S,S-cyclohexanediamine or S-propylenediamine and acetylacetone and salicylaldehyde, and demonstrated that the CD signs are governed mainly by the conformation of the diamine moiety of the ligands. (*27*) Our complexes have different location of asymmetric carbon from theirs and from one another. The X-ray structure is known only for a few of them and the source of asymmetry cannot be discussed in more detail.

Mixed valence binuclear complexes The binuclear complexes give, besides the d-d bands, very large absorption peaks at *ca.*10000 cm^{-1}, which are assigned to intervalence transfer band. The pattern is illustrated in Fig. 15 together with the CD pattern. Since the binuclear complex is in equilibrium with the VO^{2+} and $VO_2{}^{+}$ species (*19*), the CD pattern is known only in the visible region, where the absorption and CD intensity of the V^{IV} and V^{V} species are not overwhelming. The S-alada^{3-} complex gives different patterns in KBr disk and in aqueous solution. The skeletal structure may change in these two media. The S-peida^{2-} complex provides an interesting example of CD corresponding to intervalence transfer band.

Table 4 Absorption and CD peaks of oxovanadium(IV) complexes with aminocarboxylates in water *a)*

Complexes	*b,c)*	Band I	Band II	Band III	Band IV
$[VO(S\text{-peida})(H_2O)]$	AB	13.2 (27.3)	17.7 (16.5)	28.2 (357)	38.8 (4970)
	CD	11.9 (-14) 14.3 (-19)	18.1 (+34)	28.5 (+9.6)	
$[VO(S\text{-alada})(H_2O)]$	AB	12.4 (16.5)	16.5 (8.68)	30.0s (19.2)	40.0s (918) 48.8s (6020)
	CD	12.3 (-0.12) *d)*	16.7 (+1.0)	29.0 (+2.7)	
$[VO(S\text{-admdpH})(H_2O)]^{2-}$	AB	11.7 (24.7)	15.4 (12.4)	28.6 (19.1)	40.2 (1940)
	CD	11.0 (-4.0) *d)*	15.6 (-0.13)	28.8 (+0.57)	
$[VO(S,S\text{-ebp})(H_2O)]$	AB	13.1 (25.4)	17.6 (12.0)	30.4s (25.7)	40.6s (978)
	CD	11.8 (+45.2) 14.2 (-24.5)	16.7 (-20.5)	29.3 (+4.4)	
$[VO(S,S\text{-eddp})(H_2O)]$	AB	13.1 (24.9)	17.6 (15.4)	30.3s (30.0)	41.1s (927)
	CD	11.8 (+16) 14.2 (-12)	17.5 (-23)	30.0 (+1.8)	

a) wave numbers in $10^3 cm^{-1}$; s, shoulder *b)* AB, absorption, ε values in parentheses
c) CD strength, $10^3\Delta\varepsilon/\varepsilon$ in parentheses *d)* split of Band I is not obvious

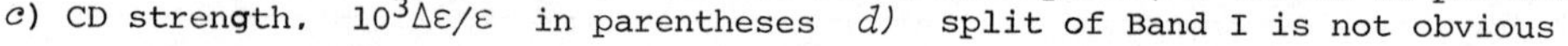

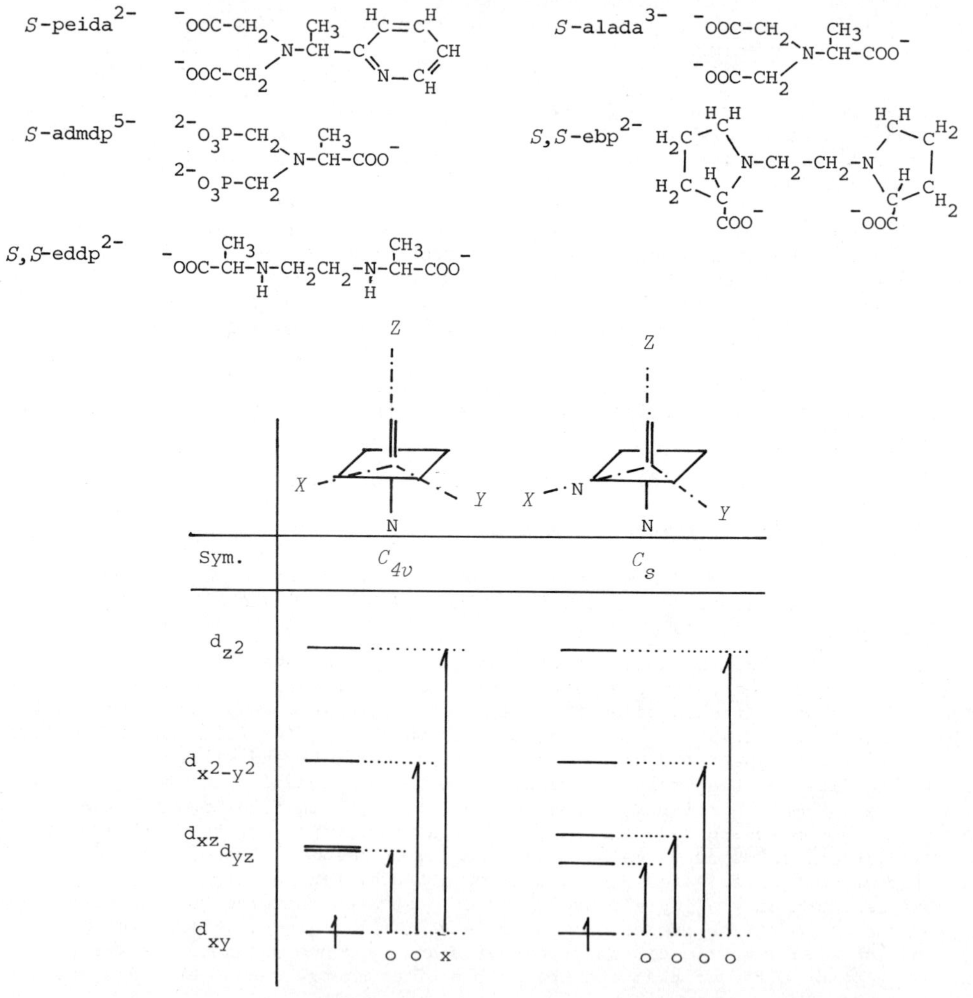

Fig. 13 Splitting of the d orbitals in $[V^{IV}O(O_4N)]$ and $[V^{IV}O(O_3N_2)]$ type complexes.

(o magnetic dipole allowed, x magnetic dipole forbidden)

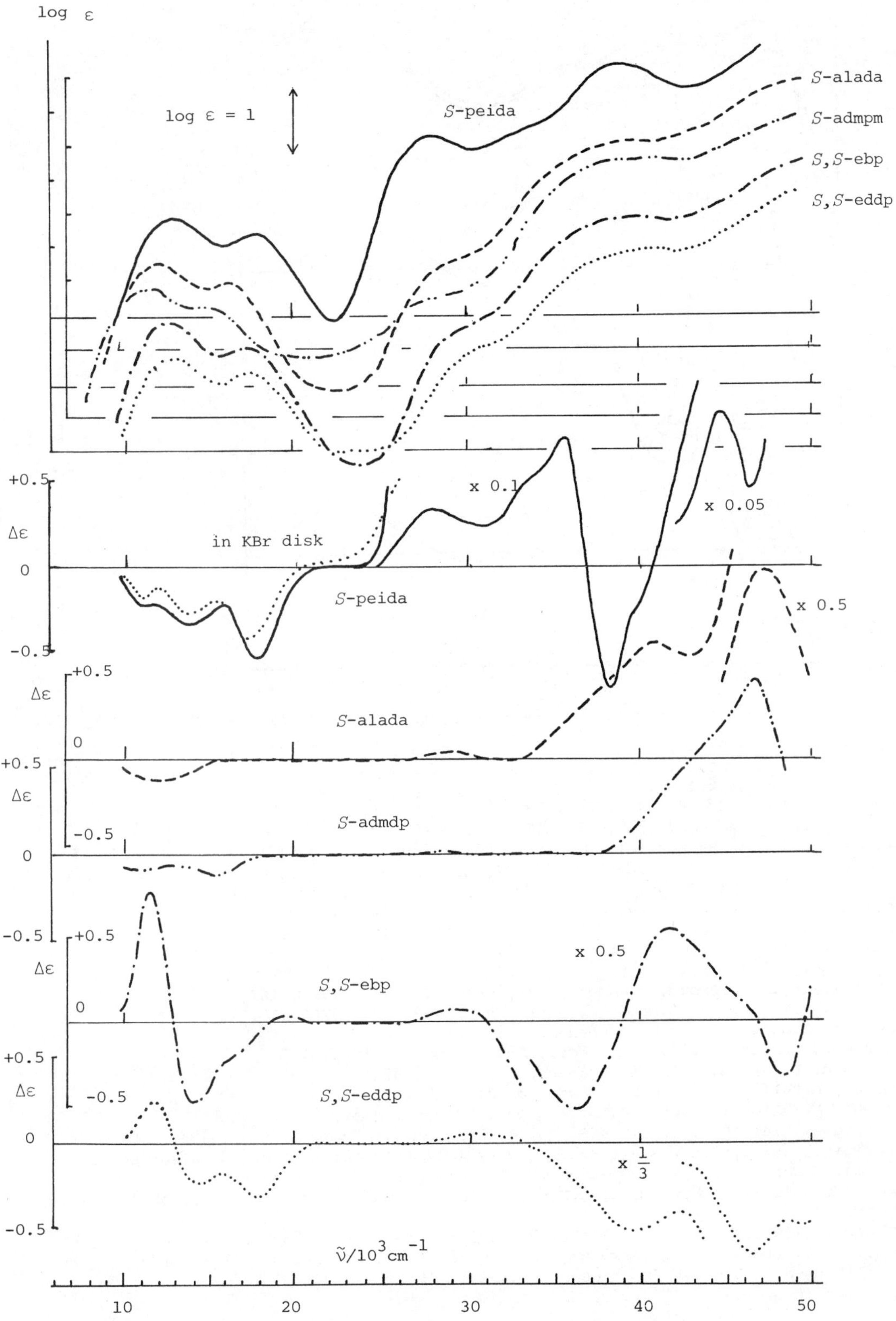

Fig. 14 Absorption and CD spectra of vanadium(IV) complexes of the type $[VO(L)(H_2O)]$ (L, optically active quadridentate ligands) in water (the abbreviated formulae of the ligands, see Table 4)

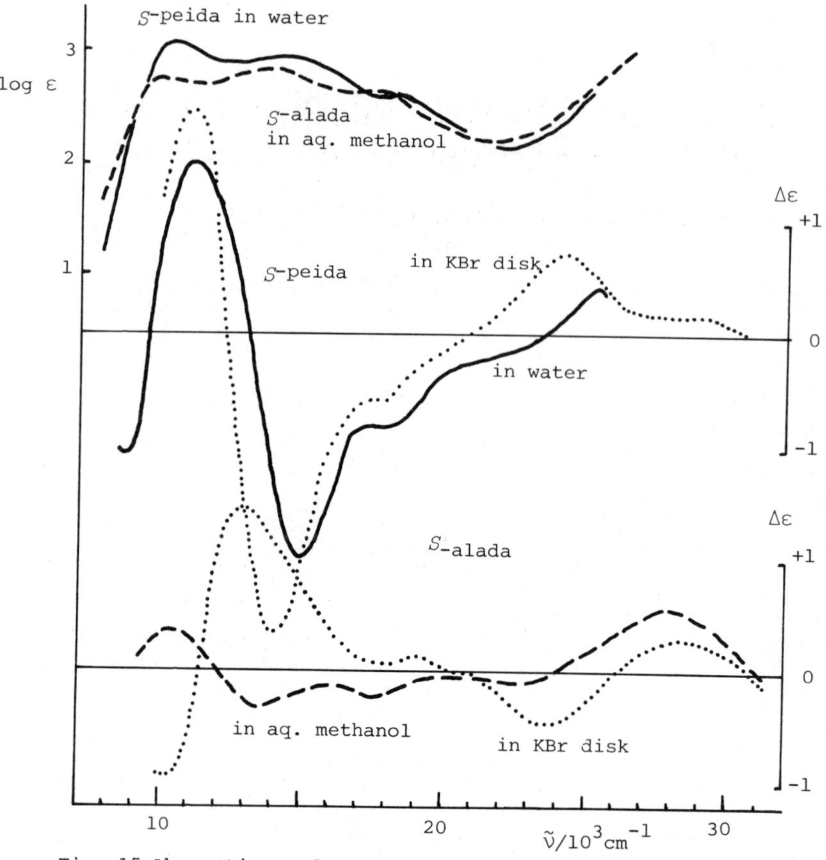

Fig. 15 Absorption and CD spectra of the mixed valence complex $[V_2O_3(L)_2]$

1) M.Ito, F.Marumo, Y,Saito, *Acta Crystallog., Ser. B.*, 27, 2187 (1971)
2) A.Kobayashi, F.Marumo, Y.Saito, *Ibid. B* 28,3591 (1972)
3) *Idem., Ibid., B* 29, 2443 (1973)
4) S.Sato, Y.Saito, *Ibid. B* 34, 420 (1978)
5) F.S.Richardson, *Chem. Rev.*, 79, 17 (1979)
6) B.Bosnich, J. MacB. Harrowfield, *J. Amer. Chem. Soc.*, 94, 3425 (1972)
7) R.M.Wing, R. Weiss, *Ibid.*, 92, 1929 (1970); N.C.Payne, *Inorg. Chem* ., 12, 1151 (1973); A.Pasini, M.Gullotti, R.Ugo, *J. Chem. Soc., Dalton Trans.*, 1977, 346.
8) J.R.Knox, C.K.Prout, *Acta Crystallogr., Ser. B.* 25, 1857 (1969).
9) D.H.Brown, J.A.D.Jeffereys, *J. Chem. Soc., Dalton Trans.*, 1973, 732.
10) M.G.B.Drew, A.Kay, *J. Chem. Soc., A*, 1971, 1846
11) *Idem., Ibid.*, 1971, 1851
12) L.T.J.Delbaere, C.K.Prout, *J. Chem. Soc., Chem. Commun.*, 1971, 162
13) B.Spivack, A.P.Gaughan, Z.Dori, *J. Amer. Chem. Soc.*, 93, 5266 (1971)
14) K.M.Jones, E.Larsen, *Acta Chem. Scand.*, 19, 1210 (1965)
15) R.F.Falmer, F.L.Urbach, *J. Chem. Soc., Chem. Commun.*, 1970, 1515.
16) H.P.Jensen, E.Larsen, *Acta Chem. Scand.*, 25, 1439 (1971)
17) A.Pasini, M.Gullotti, *J. Coord. Chem.*, 3, 319 (1974)
18) A.Pasini, M.Gullotti, R.Ugo, *J. Chem. Soc., Dalton Trans.*, 1977., 346.
19) M.Nishizawa, K.Hirotsu, S.Ooi, K.Saito, *J. Chem. Soc., Chem. Commun.*, 1979, 707
20) The original definition was extended. New symbols τ(+) and τ(-) may be also useful.
21) A.Kojima, S.Ooi, H.Kuroya, K.Z.Suzuki, Y.Sasaki, K.Saito, in preparation
22) S.Ooi, M.Nishizawa, K.Matsumoto, H.Kuroya, K.Saito, *Bull. Chem. Soc. Jpn.*, 52,452 (1979)
23) A.Kojima, S.Ooi, in preparation
24) K.Z.Suzuki, Y.Sasaki, S.Ooi, K.Saito, *Bull. Chem. Soc. Jpn.*, 53, 1288 (1980)
25) D.H.Brown, P.G.Perkins, J.J.Stewart, *J. Chem. Soc., Dalton Trans.*, 1972, 1105
26) C.J.Ballhausen, H.B.Gray, *Inorg. Chem.*, 1, 111 (1962)
27) R.L.Falmer, F.L.Urbach, *Ibid.*, 9, 2562 (1970)

The content of this paper comes from our joint studies with Dr. Yoichi Sasaki, Mr. Ken-ichi Okazaki and Miss Kimiko Z. Suzuki in our Department, and Dr. Shun'ichiro Ooi and Mr. Akinobu Kojima of Osaka City University, to whom sincere thanks are due.

CURIOSITIES OF SPIN-CROSSOVER FERRIC SCHIFF-BASE COMPLEXES

D. N. Hendrickson, M. S. Haddad, W. D. Federer and M. W. Lynch

School of Chemical Sciences, University of Illinois, Urbana, Illinois 61801, USA

Abstract - Ferric spin-crossover transition metal complexes exhibit unusual properties in the solid state. In many cases a Boltzmann distribution over electronic states is not seen. In several cases incomplete transitions are seen. Variable-temperature magnetic susceptibility, ^{57}Fe Mössbauer and EPR data are presented for a particular series of ferric spin-crossover complexes in an effort to understand the origin of these non-equilibrium effects. It has been found that mechanically grinding the ferric compounds which normally show complete transitions yields compounds exhibiting incomplete transitions. A certain percentage of the molecules in each ground sample persists in the high-spin state even at very low temperatures. Grinding the sample also makes the transition more gradual. Doping the ferric complexes into the isostructural cobalt(III) and chromium(III) complexes has a similar effect. It appears that all of the effects of grinding or doping a spin-crossover complex and the factors that determine whether a given complex exhibits a gradual or sudden transition can be explained by the nucleation and growth mechanism of phase transitions in solids. One of our complexes is unique in having a spin-flipping rate commensurate with the reciprocal of the ^{57}Fe Mössbauer timsecale.

INTRODUCTION

Several iron(III) complexes exhibit properties characteristic of "spin-equilibrium" complexes, where a high-spin excited state is within thermal energy of the low-spin ground state (Ref. 1). Magnetic susceptibility data for spin-crossover ferric complexes in solution yield approximately linear log K vs. 1/T plots, consistent with a dynamic equilibrium between the two spin states where K is the equilibrium constant (Ref. 2). "Spin-equilibrium" compounds in the solid state seldom give linear plots of log K vs. 1/T. Several curiosities are observed for the spin-crossover ferric complexes in the solid state:

1. The variation of the effective magnetic moment (μ_{eff}) per iron ion vs. temperature for a given complex does not correspond simply to a Boltzmann distribution over the thermally populated high-spin and low-spin states.
2. Incomplete spin-crossover transitions are seen where, instead of decreasing to a value appropriate for a low-spin complex, μ_{eff} per iron(III) ion decreases to an intermediate value at some temperature and further reduction of the sample temperature does not lead to a decrease in μ_{eff}/Fe. A "plateau" in the μ_{eff}/Fe vs. temperature curve develops.
3. The history of the spin-crossover sample can be important.
4. The presence of solvate molecules can be important.

Probably the first significant step to understand the nature of spin-crossover transitions observed in the solid state was made by Sorai and Seki (Ref. 3). As a consequence of heat capacity and other measurements on two iron(II) compounds, they suggested that the spin transition in these solid state complexes is a cooperative phenomenon and occurs via significant coupling between the electronic structure of the metal ion and the phonon system consisting of intramolecular and intermolecular vibrations. It was further suggested that the transition involves the formation of a domain (small region) of low-spin molecules in a crystallite of the high-spin phase. The size of the low-spin domains affects the degree of cooperativity and therefore the shape of the μ_{eff}/Fe vs. temperature curve. Recent work by the groups of Gütlich (Ref. 4) and König (Ref. 5) have contributed to an understanding.

It is our hypothesis that all of the curiosities observed for solid-state spin-crossover complexes can be explained by the general nucleation and growth mechanism of phase transitions in solids (Refs. 6 and 7). According to this mechanism, the transformation from high spin to low spin would involve the formation of domains of the low-spin phase in the high-spin crystallite and the subsequent growth of the low-spin domains. The rate of growth of critical-size domains of low-spin molecules determines the nature of the spin-crossover phase transition. Thus, in general there is not a "spin-equilibrium" in the solid state, but there is kinetic control of the spin-crossover phase transition. Kinetic control could result by virtue of the fact that the growth of a low-spin domain involves the incorporation into the low-spin domain of high-spin molecules on the boundaries of the domain. If the boundary of the low-spin domain encounters a defect in the crystal, then the activation energy for further growth of the low-spin domain will be increased.

Data are presented in this paper for a series of ferric complexes with the composition $[Fe(X\text{-}SalEen)_2]Y$, where X-SalEen is the monoanion of the condensation product of salicylaldehyde (or a substituted salicylaldehyde) and a substituted ethylenediamine (propylenediamine), and Y is NO_3^-, PF_6^-, ClO_4^- or BPh_4^-. As communicated recently (Ref. 8), the various types of μ_{eff} vs. temperature curves are found for this series and the compounds can be examined for evidence of the nucleation and growth mechanism. We find it most convenient to discuss the mechanism(s) of spin-crossover transitions within the general framework of the two somewhat artificial categories of equilibrium considerations and non-equilibrium considerations. For an isolated complex it is important to determine what factors control the rate at which the complex converts from one state to another. It is also important to understand the cooperativity seen for spin-crossover complexes in the solid state.

EQUILIBRIUM CONSIDERATIONS FOR ISOLATED COMPLEX

In octahedral symmetry a ferric complex can have two low-lying electronic states, the low-spin $^2T_{2g}$ state and the high-spin $^6A_{1g}$ state. The combined effects of molecular distortion and spin-orbit interaction split the $^2T_{2g}$ state into three Kramers doublets which could be energetically well separated. The $^6A_{1g}$ state is also split into three Kramers doublets, but the splittings between these three doublets generally are very small, i.e., less than 1 cm^{-1}. In a ferric spin-crossover complex, the ground state is found to be the lowest energy Kramers doublet which is derived from the $^2T_{2g}$ state. In Fig. 1 are shown the potential energy curves for this ground state and for the array of three $^6A_{1g}$ Kramers doublets (represented by one curve). The energy gap,

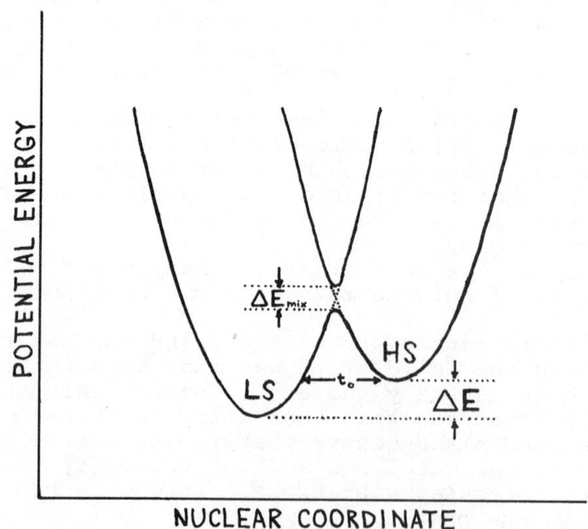

Fig. 1. One-dimensional potential energy diagram for a spin-crossover system.

ΔE_{mix}, is a measure of the extent of mixing of the electronic wavefunctions of the two states via spin-orbit coupling, vibronic interactions, and covalency in the metal-ligand bonding. Metal-ligand bond lengths are smaller in the low-spin state than in the high-spin state and, consequently the potential well for the high-spin state is displaced along the nuclear coordinate relative to that for the low-spin state.

A spin-crossover transformation for an isolated ferric complex is, in effect, an intramolecular electron transfer reaction. Relaxation techniques have been used to measure "spin-flipping" rates for complexes in solution (Refs. 9-11). Variable-temperature kinetic studies in which the "spin-flipping" rate constants, k(LS→HS) and k(HS→LS), were determined would serve as the most valuable probe into the mechanism(s) of spin-state interconversion. When ΔE_{mix} is not small (i.e., greater than ca. 200 cm^{-1}), a complex could convert from low spin to high spin by going over the barrier. Absolute rate theory would predict linear plots of log k versus 1/T for this unimolecular reaction, with an intercept corresponding to k=0 at absolute zero. However, ΔE_{mix} is expected to be small for spin-crossover complexes. The $^2T_{2g}$ and $^6A_{1g}$ states cannot interact directly via a spin-orbit interaction, but interact only via a mutual spin-orbit interaction with a $^4T_{1g}$ excited state. An intriguing possibility not covered by the classical theory is that of quantum-mechanical nuclear and/or electron tunneling. In a recent article, Jortner et al. (Ref. 12) predict non-classical temperature dependence of the rate constants (i.e., non-vanishing k at low temperatures) for a number of spin-crossover complexes using the quantum theory of radiationless multiphonon processes.

Previous to this time, no spin-crossover complex has been reported to show pronounced temperature dependence (i.e., line broadening and coalescence) of either EPR, ^{57}Fe Mössbauer, or NMR signals. All ferric spin-crossover complexes with N_4O_2 and $N_2O_2S_2$ ligand sets interconvert between the two spin states at a rate which is less than the inverse of the ^{57}Fe Mössbauer timescale. In the case of each compound separate distinct quadrupole-split doublets are seen for molecules in either the low-spin or high-spin states. The ferric dithiocarbamates have S_6 ligand sets. The increased metal-ligand covalency and spin-orbit interaction in these complexes leads to a greater rate of interconversion. Apparently the tris-dithiocarbamates (Ref. 13) and their monothio analogues (Ref. 14) are the only ferric spin-crossover complexes which give Mössbauer spectra wherein distinct high-spin and low-spin signals are not seen but rather one average signal is seen that is the result of spin flipping faster than the inverse of the ^{57}Fe Mössbauer timescale. The EPR technique can potentially sense rates of interconversion that are greater than those gauged with ^{57}Fe Mössbauer spectroscopy. Unfortunately, the EPR signals for the ferric tris-dithiocarbamate complexes are very difficult to see and are not well understood (Ref. 15).

We have been fortunate enough to prepare the first known example of an iron spin-crossover complex suitable for line-broadening studies with ^{57}Fe Mössbauer spectroscopy. The compound $[Fe(SalAPA)_2]ClO_4$ contains a pair of tridentate SalAPA ligands bound to ferric ion, as shown in Fig. 2. Various pieces of

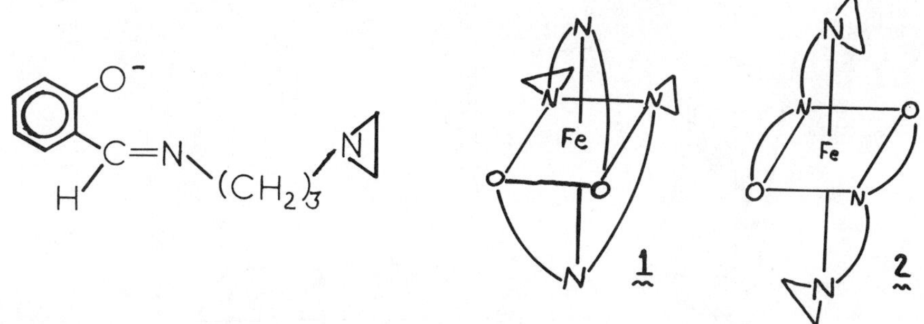

Fig. 2. Structures of the ligand SalAPA and two possible geometric isomers of the complex $[Fe(SalAPA)_2]ClO_4$.

evidence indicate that the complex exists as the centrosymmetric isomer 2. A solid sample of this compound exhibits a gradual spin-crossover transformation, where the μ_{eff}/Fe vs. temperature curve decreases gradually from 4.5μ_B at 286°K to 2.2μ_B at 4.2°K.

An EPR signal is seen at g=4.2 for those molecules in the high-spin state and a pattern of g=2.31, 2.13, and 2.00 is seen for the molecules in the low-spin ground-state Kramers doublet. Least-squares fitting of the observed g-values for the ground-state Kramers doublet to the theoretical equations indicates that the unpaired electron resides in an orbital basically d_{xy} in character and that the three Kramers doublets from the $^2T_{2g}$ state are spaced at roughly equal intervals of ca. 900 cm^{-1}. All of the other $[Fe(X\text{-}SalEen)_2]Y$ spin-crossover complexes that we have investigated are based only on a two-carbon ethylenediamine Schiff-base ligand and could be structured as isomer 1. The

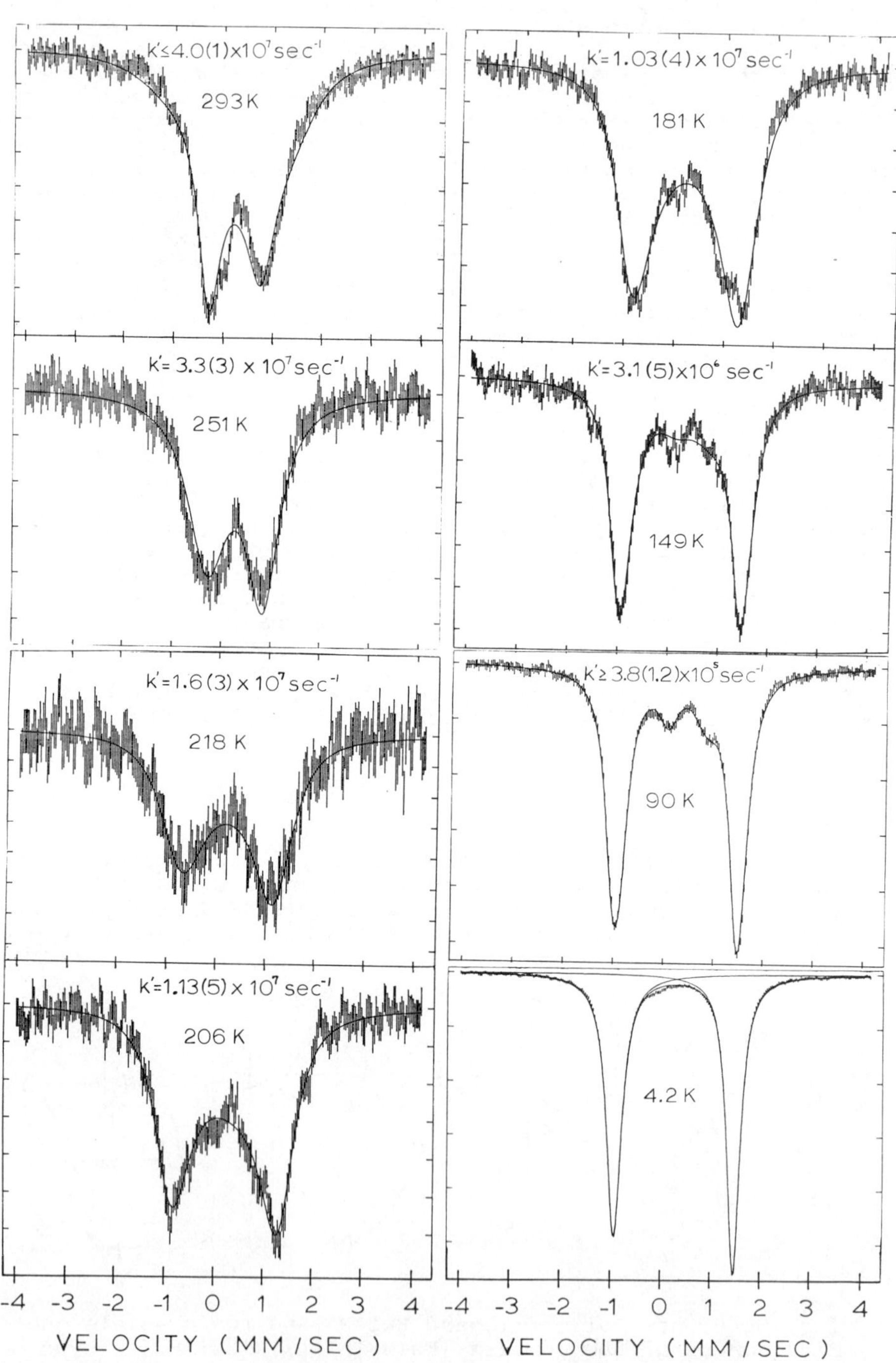

Fig. 3. The ^{57}Fe Mössbauer spectra of $[Fe(SalAPA)_2]ClO_4$ at various temperatures. All but the spectrum at 4.2°K are fit to a two-state relaxation model. Relaxation rates deduced from least-squares fitting of the spectra are given above each spectrum.

three-carbon propylenediamine construction in $[Fe(SalAPA)_2]ClO_4$ leads to increased rhombicity and this moves the second $^2T_{2g}$ Kramers doublet closer to the array of three $^6A_{1g}$ doublets. It could be this feature that leads to an increased rate of spin flipping in $[Fe(SalAPA)_2]ClO_4$ relative to the other complexes with N_4O_2 ligand sets. An examination of the variable-temperature ^{57}Fe Mössbauer data illustrated in Fig. 3 for $[Fe(SalAPA)_2]ClO_4$ shows that this complex is indeed interconverting between the two different spin states at a rate that is commensurate with the reciprocal of the ^{57}Fe Mössbauer timescale. At 4.2°K almost all of the iron ions in $[Fe(SalAPA)_2]ClO_4$ are in the low-spin Kramers doublet and one quadrupole-split doublet is seen in the spectrum. It can be seen that this doublet tends to broaden and coalesce with the high-spin doublet as the temperature of the sample is increased. At 181°K, it is still possible to discern the two different quadrupole-split doublets in the spectrum, however, by 218°K it appears that the two doublets have coalesced into one broadened doublet.

The spectra in Fig. 3 were fit to a two-state relaxation model. The solid lines in Fig. 3 represent the simulated spectra obtained by a least-squares fitting procedure using solutions to the steady-state Bloch equations (Ref. 16). The parameters of this model include a quadrupole splitting, isomer shift (corrected for the second-order Doppler effect), and internal magnetic field for each of the two states, as well as the zero-point energy difference and relaxation rate between the two states. The relaxation rates obtained by least-squares fitting are given above each spectrum. An equilibrium constant was calculated at each of the indicated temperatures from the variable-temperature magnetic susceptibility data. The equilibrium constants, together with the relaxation rates, were used to calculate the k(LS→HS) and k(HS→LS) rate constants. The resulting Arrhenius plots are shown in Fig. 4.

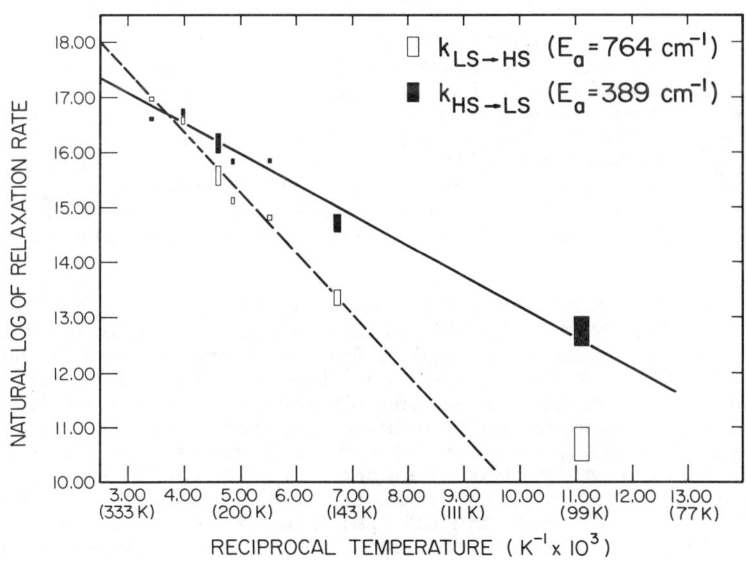

Fig. 4. Arrhenius plots of the Mössbauer kinetic data for $[Fe(SalAPA)_2]ClO_4$.

The activation energies of 764 cm^{-1} and 389 cm^{-1} were obtained from the lines in Fig. 4 and probably reflect metal-ligand stretching modes.

Spectra will have to be collected at considerably more temperatures in order to improve the precision of these activation energies and to determine if there is any deviation in the Arrhenius plots at low temperature which might signal the presence of a quantum mechanical tunneling process.

COOPERATIVITY IN SOLID STATE

Unperturbed Compounds

Complexes in the [Fe(X-SalEen)$_2$]Y series do exhibit the full range of curiosities in μ_{eff}/Fe vs. temperature curves. Fig. 5 shows the variation with temperature of the effective magnetic moment per iron ion for four of the compounds. The compound [Fe(SalEen)$_2$]NO_3 exhibits a decrease in μ_{eff}/Fe from

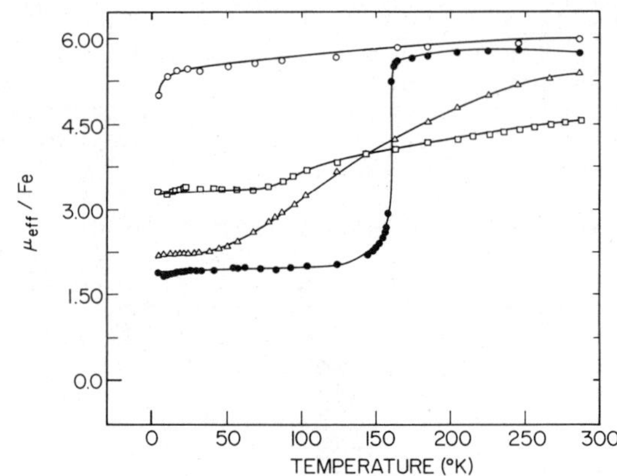

Fig. 5. Plots of effective magnetic moment per iron ion, μ_{eff}/Fe, vs. temperature for [Fe(3-OCH_3-SalEen)$_2$]PF_6, ●; [Fe(SalEen)$_2$]PF_6, △; [Fe(SalEen)$_2$]NO_3, □; [Fe(3-OCH_3-SalEen)$_2$]BPh_4, ○.

4.50μ_B at 286°K to 3.26μ_B at 4.2°K. The transition is incomplete and, as can be seen in Fig. 5, there is a "plateau" in μ_{eff}/Fe at a value of ca. 3.3μ_B when the sample temperature is less than 80°K.

A change in anion gives [Fe(SalEen)$_2$]PF_6 which exhibits a "normal" gradual spin-crossover transition. The compound [Fe(3-OCH_3-SalEen)$_2$]PF_6 plays a crucial role in this study, for it is the only complex which undergoes a relatively sudden transition from essentially high spin to essentially low spin around T_C=159°K. The transition occurs within ca. 2°K. Substitution of BPh_4^- for PF_6^- in this 3-methoxy substituted compound leads to a dramatic change as can be seen in Fig. 5. There is only a gradual decrease in μ_{eff}/Fe from 5.92μ_B at 286°K to 4.95μ_B at 4.2°K for [Fe(3-OCH_3-SalEen)$_2$]BPh_4. Other complexes were isolated in the [Fe(X-SalEen)$_2$]Y series that are either all high spin or all low spin.

Iron-57 Mössbauer data were collected for many of the [Fe(X-SalEen)$_2$]Y complexes and it is clear that only two electronic states are thermally populated for only two different quadrupole-split doublets are seen. In no case was there any evidence of a doublet which could be attributed to molecules in an intermediate-spin $^4T_{1g}$ state. A second observation is made with the Mössbauer data for these spin-crossover compounds. The ratio of the number of high-spin to low-spin molecules, as deduced from the areas found for the doublets in the spectra, is generally less than the ratio calculated from the magnetic susceptibility data. For example, from the 104°K spectrum of [Fe(3-OCH_3-SalEen)$_2$]BPh_4 it is found that the area of the high-spin molecules is calculated to be 89% from the susceptibility data. The Fe-ligand bonds are stronger in the low-spin complexes and this leads to a larger recoilless fraction for the low-spin complexes. Except for [Fe(SalAPA)$_2$]ClO_4, no occurrences of line broadening or coalescence were seen, although only limited temperature dependence of spectra were investigated. The fourth piece of information available from the Mössbauer spectra for these complexes comes from the fact that, in all cases, the negative-velocity component of the low-spin doublet is broader than the positive-velocity component. This indicates that the principal electric-field gradient V_{zz}<0, which indicates that the ground state Kramers doublet for these complexes is the doublet where the unpaired electron is in the d_{xy} orbital.

EPR data for the [Fe(X-SalEen)$_2$]Y complexes are also in agreement with the assessment that the unpaired electron in the ground-state Kramers doublets is in d_{xy} orbital. EPR signals are also seen for complexes in only two electronic states--a low-spin signal centered at g=2.0 and a high-spin signal at g=4.3. One interesting exception is found. The sudden spin-crossover complex [Fe(3-OCH_3-SalEen)$_2$]PF_6 gives a high-spin signal at g=7.5, which indicates that the high-spin complexes in this compound are experiencing a distortion which is in some way different than those experienced by the other high-spin [Fe(X-SalEen)$_2$]Y complexes.

What explanations can be given for the variations in shape of μ_{eff} vs. temperature curves from one complex to another and for the plateaus in some of these same curves? As with other such spin-crossover complexes, we have also found that the properties of these compounds can vary from one sample preparation to another. At the outset of this work it was hypothesized that all of the curiosities observed for spin-crossover complexes in the solid state could be explained by the general nucleation and growth mechanism of phase transitions in solids. Small domains (homogeneous regions) of low-spin complexes form in the crystallite of high-spin molecules. Before a low-spin domain can persist and continue to grow, it has to attain a critical size. The critical size is generally believed to be temperature dependent. The rate at which critical-size domains of low-spin complexes grow in crystallites of high-spin complexes is rate determining. Crystal defects play a major role in the nucleation and growth mechanism. On the one hand they serve as preferred sites for the initial formation of low-spin domains. On the other hand the presence of crystal defects inhibits the growth of critical-size low-spin domains.

The growth of the low-spin domains occurs, of course, by incorporating into the low-spin domain high-spin molecules on the boundaries of the domain. If the boundary of the low-spin domain encounters a defect in the crystal, then the activation energy for further growth of the low-spin domain will be increased. This sensitivity to defects could explain why different preparations of a given compound can have different characteristics. In this study, defects were introduced into the microcrystalline [Fe(X-SalEen)$_2$]Y spin-crossover complexes by mechanically grinding the compounds, by doping them into isostructural cobalt(III) and chromium(III) hosts, and by intentionally preparing powdered samples of some of the compounds.

Effects of Grinding Compounds

The effects of grinding spin-crossover complexes were investigated in various experiments. A microcrystalline sample of [Fe(3-OCH_3-SalEen)$_2$]PF_6 was divided into three fractions. One fraction was left unperturbed, a second was ground for a few minutes with mortar and pestle, and the third was more thoroughly ground in a ball mill for a period of 30 min. As can be seen in Fig. 6, variable-temperature magnetic susceptibility data show that sample grinding does affect the spin-crossover transition.

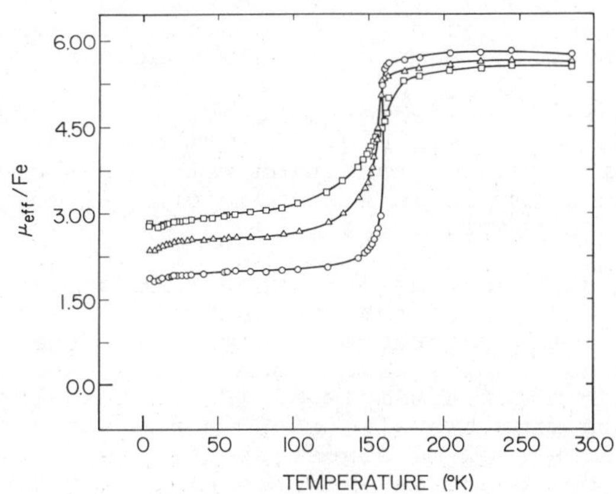

Fig. 6. Effective magnetic moment per iron ion vs. temperature curves for [Fe(3-OCH_3SalEen)$_2$]PF_6: ○, unperturbed microcrystalline solid; △, same solid ground with mortar and pestle; □, same solid ground in a ball mill.

A comparison with data for the unperturbed sample shows that grinding a sample leads to various changes that can be listed:

1. Grinding leads to an incompleteness of the transition, i.e., a plateau in the μ_{eff}/Fe vs. temperature curve.
2. The transition becomes more gradual.
3. There are more low-spin molecules in the ground samples at higher temperatures.
4. The temperature at which there are equal numbers of low-spin and high-spin molecules shifts to a lower value upon sample grinding.

The above effects of sample grinding were found to be reproducible.

In a second experiment another sample of $[Fe(3\text{-}OCH_3\text{-}SaleEen)_2]PF_6$ was prepared by rapid precipitation to give a powdered sample that to the eye appeared not to be microcrystalline. In Fig. 7 it can be seen that this powdered sample shows a low-temperature plateau at $2.70\mu_B$ in the plot of μ_{eff}/Fe vs. temperature.

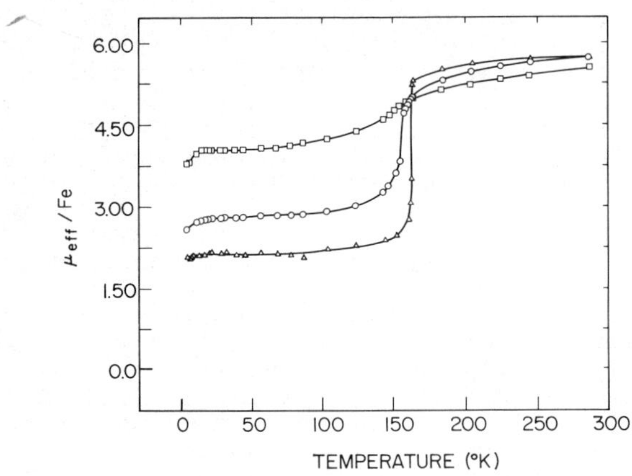

Fig. 7. Effective magnetic moment per iron ion vs. temperature curves for an apparently non-crystalline sample of $[Fe(3\text{-}OCH_3\text{-}SalEen)_2]PF_6$: ○, unperturbed powder; □, same powder ground in a ball mill; △, ground sample recrystallized by evaporating a methanol solution to dryness.

It was interesting to find that grinding this sample made the transition even more gradual and moved the plateau to $\mu_{eff}/Fe=4.0\mu_B$. This ground sample was then recrystallized by dissolving the ground sample in absolute methanol and evaporating the solution to dryness. It can be seen in Fig. 7 that this recrystallized sample shows a sudden and complete phase transition as was found for the other microcrystalline sample of this compound.

The compound $[Fe(SalEen)_2]PF_6$ undergoes a gradual, but complete, spin-crossover transition, as can be seen in Fig. 5. Grinding this compound in a ball mill also leads to an incomplete transition with a plateau at $2.9\mu_B$. The transition for the ground sample is also more gradual compared to that for the original microcrystalline sample.

Several physical techniques were used to show that compound grinding does not result in a structural change and that the same two electronic states are present that were found for the unperturbed compounds. The x-ray powder patterns of unperturbed and ground samples were found to be essentially identical. Mössbauer spectra were run for a sample of $[Fe(3\text{-}OCH\ SalEen)_2]PF_6$ ground in a ball mill. Only signals from two electronic states can be seen for this ground sample. A comparison of Mössbauer spectra for the ground and unperturbed samples of this compound is shown in Fig. 8, where it can be seen that only the relative amounts of high-spin and low-spin signals are changed at a given temperature.

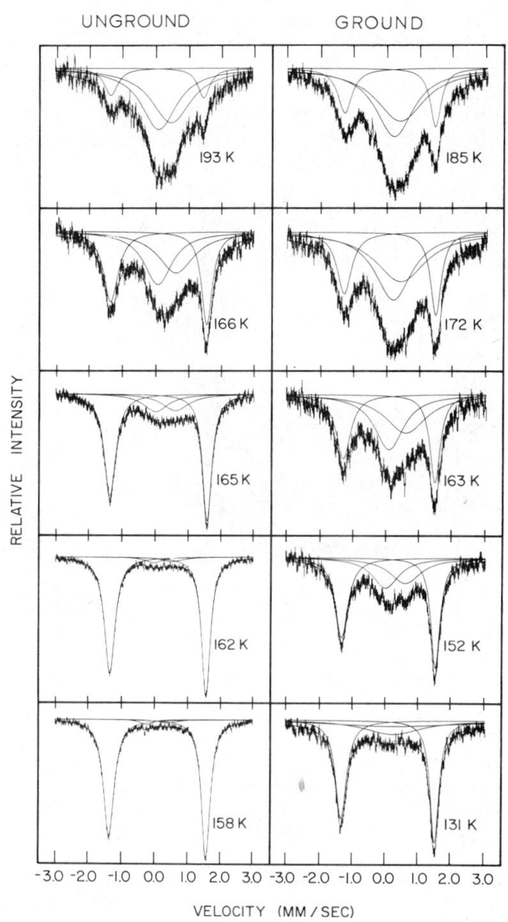

Fig. 8. Temperature variation of ^{57}Fe Mössbauer spectrum for $[Fe(3\text{-}OCH_3\text{-}SalEen)_2]PF_6$. Spectra were initially recorded for a microcrystalline sample and then it was ground in a ball mill and reexamined with Mössbauer spectroscopy.

Similar effects were seen with EPR comparisons of ground and unperturbed samples. Only in one case was a new signal seen upon grinding a sample. Grinding samples of $[Fe(3\text{-}OCH_3\text{-}SalEen)_2]PF_6$, which in the original microcrystalline form gave only a high-spin signal at g=7.5 in addition to a low-spin signal, converted some part of the high-spin g=7.5 signal into a new high-spin signal at g=4.3. It would be interesting to know where in the ground crystallites the high-spin complexes that give this g=4.3 signal are located. The above observations on ground samples of spin-crossover complexes are explicable in terms of the nucleation and growth mechanism of phase transitions in solids. Grinding a microcrystalline sample would be expected to lead to defect structure in the microcrystals such as fissures, cracks, or irregular features that develop on the crystal surfaces as well as internal dislocations. If the concentration of defects is increased upon sample grinding, there will be a greater concentration of low-spin nucleation sites in the ground sample than in the unground sample. This could explain the formation of more low-spin molecules at high temperatures for the ground samples (see Fig. 6). It is also possible to explain why grinding a ferric spin-crossover complex makes the transition more gradual and shifts the transition temperature to a lower value. There is kinetic control because the growth of the low-spin domains is rate determining in the nucleation and growth mechanism.

The increased defect concentration in the ground sample leads to more impingement of the boundaries of low-spin domains with defects and this increases the activation energy for the growth of such domains. The tendency to exhibit an incomplete spin-crossover transition is also due to the increased activation for growth of low-spin domains in the ground samples. The growth is slowed down to such a slow rate that as the sample temperature is further decreased there is very little change in relative amounts of low-spin and high-spin complexes.

Effect of Doping Complexes

The incorporation of metal ions other than iron(III) into the crystals of [Fe(X-SalEen)$_2$]Y spin-crossover complexes is another means of introducing defects. Isostructural cobalt(III) and chromium(III) complexes have been prepared. X-ray powder diffraction patterns for the iron(III) and chromium(III) complexes are almost superimposable. Fig. 9 illustrates the variation with temperature of μ_{eff}/Fe for [Fe_xCr_{1-x}(3-OCH_3-SalEen)$_2$]PF_6 with x=1.00, 0.65, 0.50 and 0.40. As the chromium(III) concentration is increased the sharpness

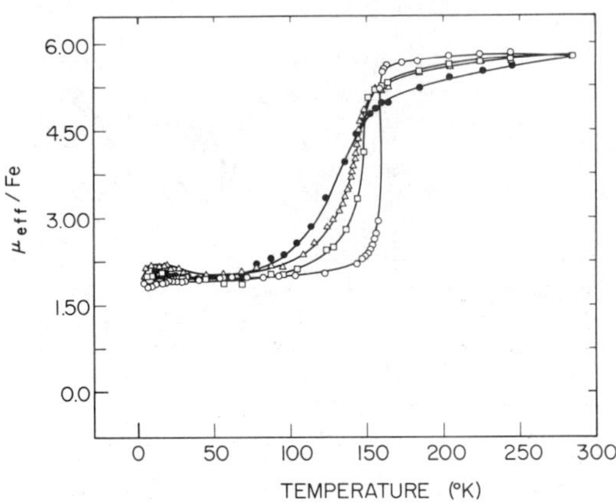

Fig. 9. Effective magnetic moment per iron ion vs. temperature curves for microcrystalline [Fe_xCr_{1-x}(3-OCH_3-SalEen)$_2$]PF_6: ○, x=1; □, x=0.65; Δ, x=.50; ●, x=0.40.

of the transition decreases and the transition temperature shifts to lower temperature. It appears that the effects of doping are similar to some of the effects of grinding the sample. In a doped sample, as a given low-spin domain grows it can encounter a chromium(III) complex at the domain boundary. The activation barrier for the movement of the domain boundary is increased by such an encounter. It is understandable, then, why the spin-crossover phase transition becomes more gradual as the concentration of chromium(III) host is increased.

As an outgrowth of the idea that sample grinding and doping might be similarly affecting the spin-crossover transition, the effect of grinding a doped sample was explored. A crystalline sample of [$Fe_{0.50}Cr_{0.50}$(3-OCH_3-SalEen)$_2$]PF_6 was ground in a ball mill for 30 minutes and variable-temperature magnetic susceptibility data were collected. As we communicated (Ref. 8), the effect of grinding the doped compound is dramatic. The ground compound shows a low-temperature plateau in the μ_{eff}/Fe vs. temperature at ca. 4.5μ_B. The effect of grinding this compound can also be reversed by recrystallizing the ground sample from an absolute methanol solution.

The effect of doping [Fe(3-OCH_3-SalEen)$_2$]PF_6 into the diamagnetic cobalt(III) host is illustrated in Fig. 10. The data show that, as for the chromium(III) case, the transition becomes more gradual as the cobalt(III) concentration is increased. However, unlike the chromium(III) case, the transition temperature is shifted to a higher temperature as the concentration of cobalt(III) is increased. As was shown by the comparison of x-ray powder patterns (vide infra), the ionic radius of the high-spin iron(III) ion r(Fe)=0.65Å, is comparable to the ionic radius of the chromium(III) ion, r(Cr)=0.63Å. On the other hand, the ionic radius of the cobalt(III) ion, r(Co)=0.53Å, is significantly smaller than the radii for the other two ions. This agrees with the fact that the peaks in the x-ray powder pattern of [Co(3-OCH_3-SalEen)$_2$]PF_6 are shifted to higher θ values compared to the corresponding peaks in the pattern for the iron(III) complex. With a cobalt(III) host, a larger percentage of the iron (III) complexes are forced into the low-spin state at 286°K than in the pure iron(III) complex. It was also found that grinding a cobalt-doped compound leads to dramatic effects as found for the chromium-doped systems.

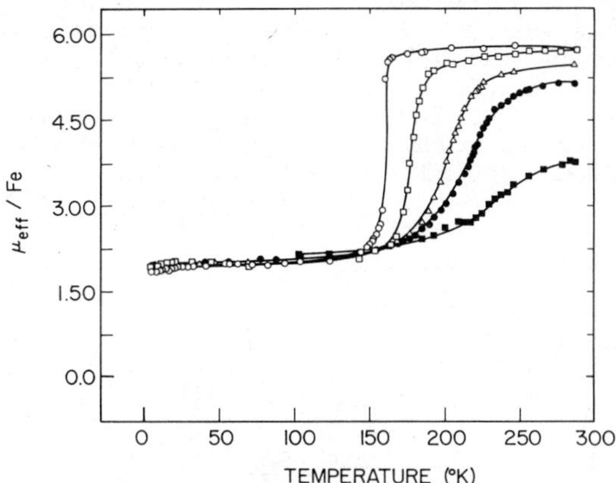

Fig. 10. Effective magnetic moment per iron ion vs. temperature for microcrystalline $[Fe_xCo_{1-x}(3\text{-}OCH_3\text{-SalEen})_2]PF_6$: O, x=1; □, x=0.77; Δ, x=0.69; ●, x=0.60; ■, x=0.50.

Two interesting observations were noted in the EPR spectra of the iron(III) complexes doped in the diamagnetic cobalt(III) host. At room temperature, $[Fe(3\text{-}OCH_3\text{-SalEen})_2]PF_6$ shows a low-spin signal at g=2.0 and a high-spin signal at g=7.5. Doping this complex into the analogous cobalt(III) complex gives a new high-spin signal at g=5.5, as can be seen in Fig. 11 which shows the spectrum for $[Fe_xCo_{1-x}(3\text{-}OCH_3\text{-SalEen})_2]PF_6$. The intensity of this new signal increases from one doped sample to another as the concentration of cobalt(III) is increased. This just underscores the suggestion made above that the effective system $[Fe(3\text{-}OCH_3\text{-SalEen})_2]PF_6$ is unusual and susceptible to changes by grinding and doping.

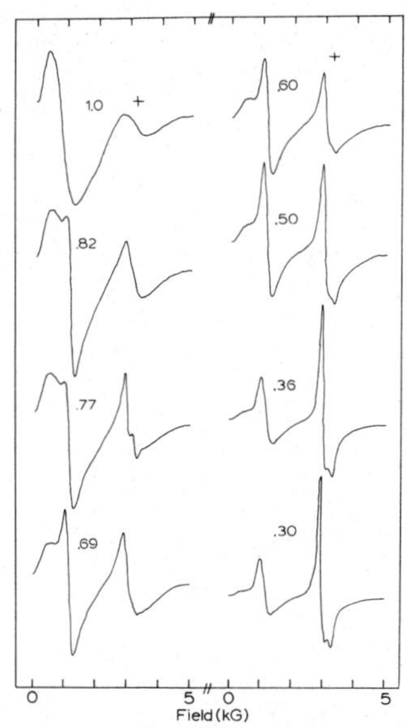

Fig. 11. Room-temperature X-band EPR spectra of microcrystalline $[Fe_xCo_{1-x}(3\text{-}OCH_3\text{-SalEen})_2]PF_6$ for various values of x.

In the case of $[Fe(SalEen)_2]PF_6$, an apparently axial low-spin signal is seen at 77°K with broad "perpendicular" and "parallel" signals at g=2.177 and g= 2.015, respectively. As the cobalt(III) content is increased it becomes apparent that there really is more than one type of low-spin signal. The spectrum of $[Fe_{0.36}Co_{0.64}(SalEen)_2]PF_6$, for example, shows a distorted "derivative" at g=2.209 and "bumps" at g=2.140, 2.009 and 1.936.

Acknowledgment - This work was supported by the National Institutes of Health (HL 13652).

REFERENCES

1. For the most recent reviews see:
   a) H. A. Goodwin, Coord. Chem. Rev., 18, 293 (1976).
   b) R. H. Martin and A. H. White, Trans. Met. Chem., 4, 113 (1968).
2. R. H. Petty, E. V. Dose, M. F. Tweedle and L. J. Wilson, Inorg. Chem., 17, 1064 (1978).
3. M. Sorai and S. Seki, J. Phys. Chem. Solids, 35, 555 (1974).
4. P. Gütlich, H. Köppen, R. Link and H. G. Steinhäuser, J. Chem. Phys., 70, 3977 (1979), and references therein.
5. E. König, G. Ritter, W. Irler and S. M. Nelson, Inorg. Chim. Acta, 37, 169 (1979), and references therein.
6. C. N. R. Rao and K. J. Rao, Phase Transitions in Solids, McGraw-Hill, New York (1978).
7. J. W. Christian, The Theory of Transformations in Metals and Alloys, Pergamon Press, Oxford, 2nd ed., part I (1975).
8. M. S. Haddad, W. D. Federer, M. W. Lynch and D. N. Hendrickson, J. Am. Chem. Soc., 102, 1468 (1980).
9. E. V. Dose, M. A. Hoselton, N. Sutin, M. F. Tweedle and L. J. Wilson, J. Am. Chem. Soc., 100, 1141 (1978).
10. J. K. Beattie, R. A. Binstead, and R. J. West, J. Am. Chem. Soc., 100, 3044 (1978).
11. R. A. Binstead, J. K. Beattie, E. V. Dose, M. F. Tweedle and L. J. Wilson, J. Am. Chem. Soc., 100, 5609 (1978).
12. E. Buhks, G. Navon, M. Bixon and J. Jortner, J. Am. Chem. Soc., 102, 2918 (1980).
13. P. B. Merrithew and P. G. Rasmussen, Inorg. Chem., 11, 325 (1972).
14. K. R. Kunze, D. L. Perry and L. J. Wilson, Inorg. Chem., 16, 594 (1977).
15. G. R. Hall and D. N. Hendrickson, Inorg. Chem., 15, 607 (1976).
16. H. H. Wickman, Mössbauer Effect Methodology, 2, 39 (1966).

COORDINATION COMPOUNDS AS A SOURCE OF ELECTRICALLY CONDUCTIVE SOLID STATE MATERIALS

L. V. Interrante

General Electric Corporate Research and Development, Schenectady, NY 12301, USA

Abstract - Coordination compound systems with appreciable electrical conductivity and other unusual solid state properties are reviewed and discussed. The various modes of solid state electronic interaction in such systems are described and a classification scheme for coordination compounds whose properties are significantly influenced by such interactions is presented. Specific examples from our work are used to illustrate the structural features and solid state properties of these compounds.

INTRODUCTION

The subject of this paper is a group of coordination compound-containing materials whose properties in the solid state do not conform to the usual description of such compounds as molecular systems comprised of discrete, electronically and magnetically, isolated units. These materials, along with certain organic compounds, are currently the object of intense scientific interest, particularly within the solid state physics community, and have been the subject of a large number of recent meetings and review articles (1). We will focus here, in particular, on coordination compound systems which are of interest for their unusual electrical properties in the solid state and will survey briefly, from the perspective of our own work in this area, the salient structural features and properties of these materials.

The concept of coordination compound solids as materials in which intermolecular electronic interactions play little or no role in determining properties such as absorption spectra and magnetic susceptibility has always had its exceptions. Among the most notable of these were compounds such as Prussian Blue (2), Magnus' Green Salt (3), and nickel dimethylglyoxime (4), which were recognized quite early to have anomalous colors and spectral properties as compared with those of the constituent ions or molecules in solution. The unusual spectral features of these and other coordination compounds in the solid state have continued to attract considerable scientific interest and there have been a number of detailed studies in recent years which have significantly advanced the general understanding of the solid state interactions in these materials and the consequences of these interactions on the spectral properties (5).

The prospect that such intermolecular electronic interactions could give rise to novel electrical properties for coordination compound solids first received attention in the mid 1960's (6) and the subsequent identification of significant conductivities and other novel electrical behavior for these systems a few years later (7) provided a further stimulus and new direction for the growing interest in such materials. The discovery of one dimensional (1-D) metal-like characteristics for certain members of this group of compounds, (8) and the suggestion that systems of this type could fulfill the criteria for a high temperature superconductor set forth by Little (9), also contributed in an important way to this growing interest. Eventually this work on coordination compound systems became effectively merged with the rapidly advancing efforts on organic molecular conductors leading to the development of what is now a major sub-branch of solid state physics and chemistry research which actively involves scientists from industrial, governmental, and academic institutions literally all over the world.

In terms of their electrical conductivity, molecular solids have traditionally been viewed as insulators with conductivities typically below $10^{-7}ohm^{-1}cm^{-1}$ (Figure 1). Indeed, the observation of conductivities greater than $\sim 10^{-3}ohm^{-1}cm^{-1}$ for a molecular solid is still considered noteworthy and there are relatively few such materials presently in this category. The observation of conductivities in the range $10^{2} \rightarrow 10^{5}ohm^{-1}cm^{-1}$ for several members of this new group of molecular solids is therefore quite remarkable and clearly deserving of interest, both from a scientific and, potentially, a technological viewpoint. Moreover, for many of these materials the conductivity actually increases with decreasing temperature in a manner characteristic of metallic substances, in contrast to the usual thermally activiated (semi-conductor-like) conductivity behavior generally found for molecular solids.

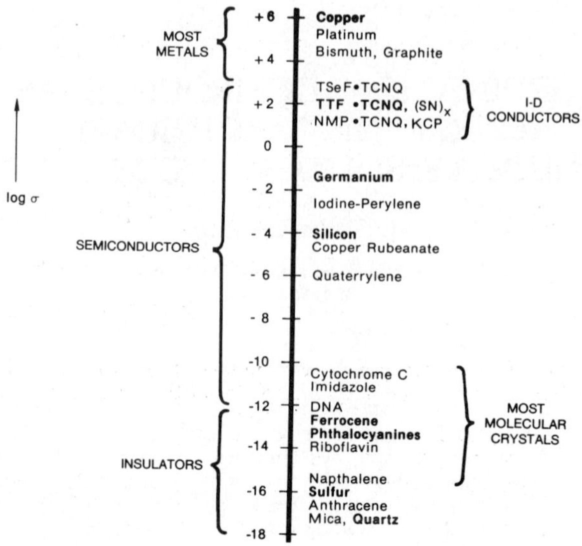

Fig. 1. Conductivity scale for some representative materials ($\log \sigma_{25^\circ C}$).

The reason for the exceptionally high conductivities of this class of molecular solids continues to occupy much attention as does the question of whether it might be possible to raise this level of conductivity even further, perhaps to values comparable to that of copper or aluminum. Other sources of continuing interest are the highly anisotropic physical properties and unique structural phase-transitions that many of them exhibit, which result directly from the quasi-1-D character of the solid state interactions. The study of such effects and their consequences on the physical properties constitutes an important aspect of the current solid state physics research on these materials.

From the viewpoint of the synthetic coordination chemist, this area offers some unique research opportunities. The enormous structural flexibility of both organic and coordination compound systems are potentially available here for preparing new materials which perhaps will display new and interesting solid state physics, and a means of varying and controlling the physical properties of solids through subtle variations in molecular structure.

METHODS FOR GENERATING ELECTRONICALLY SIGNIFICANT SOLID STATE INTERACTIONS IN COORDINATION COMPOUNDS

Among the various types of coordination compounds which are known to exhibit unusual solid state properties, there seem to be basically two ways in which electronically significant interactions between metal complex units develop. One of these involves the sharing of a bridging ligand group, either a monoatomic or polyatomic species, by two or more metal ions in such a manner so as to generate a one-, or less commonly, two-, or three-dimensional network of directly connected metal complex units. Typical bridging ligands are the halide and pseudo-halide (CN^-, SCN^-, etc.) ions and bifunctional organic ligands such as pyrazine.

The other main avenue to electronically significant interactions between metal complex units in the solid state involves the direct overlap of non-bonding or π-bonding valence orbitals on adjacent planar complexes in a parallel stacking arrangement. These orbitals can be either d-orbitals localized on the metal or π-orbitals associated with the ligand system of the metal complex. In either case one obtains an effectively one dimensional array of interacting units along one direction in the solid. (Fig. 2).

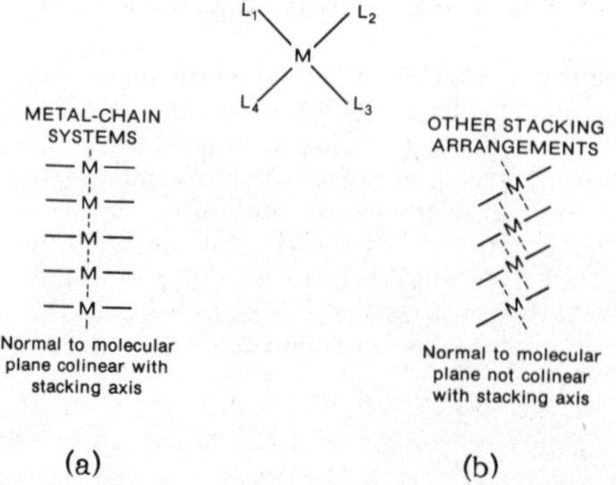

Fig. 2. Solid state stacking arrangements for planar metal complexes.

Table 1. Classification of coordination compound systems with extended solid state interactions.

I. Metal Chain Complexes

Integral valence compounds

Examples: $Pt(NH_3)_4PtCl_4$(MGS) (10)

$Ir(CO)_2$(acac) (7a)

$Ir(CO)_3Cl$ (12)

$R^{2+}[M(CN)_4^{2-}]$, M = Pd, Pt (5b,c)

$M(dimethylgloxime)_2$ (M = Ni, Pd, Pt) (11)

$M(diphenylglyoxime)_2X$ (X = Br, I, ClO_4) (13)

Typical Properties: electronic spectra strongly perturbed by intermolecular interactions and highly anisotropic; diamagnetic; conductivity behavior typical of insulators or semiconductors.

Non-integral valence compounds

Examples: $K_2Pt(CN)_4Br_{0.3}\cdot 3H_2O$(KCP) (8)

$Rb_2Pt(CN)_4(FHF)_{0.40}$ (15)

$K_{1.75}Pt(CN)_4\cdot 1.5\ H_2O$ (15)

$Mg_{0.82}Pt(C_2O_4)_2\cdot 6H_2O$ (14)

$K_{1.6}Pt(C_4O_4)_2\cdot 2H_2O$ (16)

$K_{0.58}Ir(CO)_2Cl_2$ (17)

Typical Properties: metal-like reflectivity toward light polarized along metal chains; conductivities up to ~300 $ohm^{-1}cm^{-1}$ along chain direction; 1-D metallic characteristics including "Peierls transition" at low temperatures.

II. Systems Involving Ligand-Based Solid State Interactions

Ligand-bridged metal complex chain systems

Examples: Polyferrocenylene (18)

$(-Cu(OAc)_2\text{-pyrazine-})_n$ (20)

$(CH_3NH_3)_2MnCl_4$ (19)

$Fe_4[Fe(CN)_6]_3\cdot XH_2O$ (Prussian Blue) (2)

$M(A)_nX_3$, M = Pd, Pt; A = NH_3, en; X = Cl, Br, I (21)

$AuLX_2$, L = $S(CH_2C_6H_5)_2$, X = Cl, Br (22)

Typical Properties: electronic spectra in some cases perturbed by interunit interactions; strong intervalence CT transitions in mixed valence systems; magnetic superexchange interactions occur when M carries unpaired spins; conductivity behavior typical of insulators or semiconductors--considerably enhanced in $M(A)_nX_3$ and $AuLX_2$ cases at high pressures.

Systems with dominant ligand π-orbital interactions

Examples: metal phthalocyanines (MPc) (23)

$MPcI_x$ (25)

$R^{m+}_{(n-m)}MS_4C_4X_4^{n-}$ (24)

$[(Al\ Pc\ F)\ I_x]_n$ (26)

Typical Properties: Integral valence systems exhibit semiconductor and photoconductor behavior; partially oxidized compounds show 1-D metallic characteristics with conductivities at 25°C up to 550 $ohm^{-1}cm^{-1}$.

π-donor-acceptor derivatives

Examples: $(perylene)_2\ PtS_4C_4(CN)_4$ (27)

$(TTF)_2Ni(S_2C_6H_4)_2$ (29)

$TTT_{1.2}NiS_4C_4H_4$ (31)

$[FeCp_2](TCNQ)_2$ (28)

$TTF\cdot MS_4C_4(CF_3)_4$ (30)

$[Ni(TATMA)_2]_2NiS_4C_4H_4$ (32)

Typical Properties: Anisotropic conductivity reflecting directional solid state interactions; generally semiconductors-certain 1-D metallic characteristics evidenced in a few cases with conductivities 30→300 $ohm^{-1}cm^{-1}$; others exhibit novel structural features and cooperative magnetic phenomena.

Thus, for both the ligand-bridged complexes and the stacked planar systems the electronic interactions are usually highly directional and often one dimensional in character, leading to the highly anisotropic physical properties and other unusual characteristics typically observed for these materials.

CLASSIFICATION OF COORDINATION COMPOUND-CONTAINING SOLIDS WITH EXTENDED SOLID STATE INTERACTIONS

In Table 1 some examples of coordination compounds with extended solid state interactions are given along with a brief description of their general characteristics. The division into two main categories is based on the mode of the solid state interactions, i.e., whether it involves primarily the direct overlap of metal-based orbitals (I) or whether the ligand system is integrally involved (II), either as a direct interaction of ligand-based orbitals or as a bridge between the metal ions of adjacent units. Included as a special sub-group within the latter category are a collection of π-donor-acceptor compounds derived from transition metal complexes. These compounds, in general, are comprised of two different planar species (π-donor and π-acceptor) either or both of which may be involved in the extended interactions giving rise to the observed solid state properties.

Metal chain complexes - integral valence compounds

The so-called "metal chain compounds" (category I) have been divided into two sub-groups, depending on the formal valence state of the metal ion in the complex. The "integral valence" compounds are generally planar metal complexes of the d^8 metal ions which assume a columnar stacking arrangement in the solid state (Fig. 2a) so as to produce a linear chain of metal atoms along one direction in the crystal. As is suggested by the typically van der Waals separations between the adjacent units in these compounds and the results of molecular orbital calculations on representative dimer units (33, 34), this "metal chain feature" appears to be more a consequence of structural packing considerations than a source of this particular structural arrangement. Thus the magnitude of the solid state electronic interactions in these systems is relatively small and many of the observed properties, such as the absorption spectra, can be explained starting from a basically localized electronic viewpoint (5a, 35). Despite this, in addition to dramatic changes in spectral properties, several of these compounds exhibit substantial and often highly anisotropic electrical conductivity.

A case in point is the compound $Pt(NH_3)_4PtCl_4$, known as Magnus' Green Salt (MGS), for which the prospect of significant electrical conductivity along the metal chain direction in the structure was first suggested on the basis of spectral observations (6). Later work did indeed verify this prediction, indicating conductivities as high as $5 \times 10^{-4} ohm^{-1}cm^{-1}$ for polycrystalline samples of this material (7). More recent work in our laboratory (36) and at the IBM Research Laboratory (10, 37) has established that this compound is, in fact, an excellent example of an extrinsic, one-dimensional semiconductor in which small amounts of Pt(IV) complexes in the solutions used to prepare this material lead to the incorporation of "Pt(III)-like" defects which can be identified by their characteristic epr spectrum in the solid. These defects, which appear to be delocalized over several Pt sites but effectively bound to the vicinity of the interstitial charge compensating anions, apparently form energy states close to the top of the filled "d_z2-like" orbitals on the Pt(II) ions. Electrons thermally excited into these states produce "holes" in the d_z2 band which serve as the charge carriers for electrical conduction. This model was suggested by both the results of the epr studies carried out at IBM and by the detailed measurements of electrical conductivity and thermoelectric power obtained in our laboratory on single crystals grown by a silica gel diffusion method.

In the absence of these Pt(III)-like extrinsic defects it is likely that MGS would be effectively an electrical insulator due to the large d_z2 - p_z band gap anticipated from both spectral studies (35) and molecular orbital calculations (33). It is possible that the significant conductivity that has been observed for several of the other compounds in this class ($Ir(CO)_2acac$ (7a), $Ir(CO)_3Cl$ (38), etc.) may also be impurity dominated, perhaps via the same type of "partial oxidation" mechanism, and that large effective band gaps and low conductivities are a characteristic feature of the compounds of this type.

Metal chain complexes - non-integral valence compounds

In its extrinsic form MGS is seen to be actually an example of a partially oxidized Pt(II) chain system or a non-integral valence compound. As generally obtained, the concentration of the Pt(III)-like defects in MGS is apparently quite low, probably on the order of 100 ppm. On the other hand, under certain conditions, a relatively large proportion of these defects can be doped into the MGS structure, leading to a substantial increase in the electrical conductivity accompanied by a decrease in thermal activation energy and in the intrachain Pt-Pt separation (10, 37). In this case, however, at the upper limit of partial oxidation attained (ca 0.05 Pt(III)-like sites/Pt atom) the conductivity remains thermally activated and a transition to a metal-like state does not occur.

For certain other stacked, planar platinum(II) complexes namely $Pt(CN)_4^{2-}$, $Pt(C_2O_4)_2^{2-}$ and $Pt(C_4O_4)_2^{2-}$ ($C_4O_4^{2-}$=squarate) (15,16,39), and possibly some iridium(I) compounds (17), this "partial oxidation process" can be carried to the point where compounds with quasi-1-D metal-like properties are obtained. In these cases, crystalline, typically non-stoichiometric materials have been isolated, both by partial chemical or electrochemical oxidation of the Pt(II) (or Ir(I)) precursor complexes and by co-crystallization of the precursor complexes with their higher valent analogs.

The first structural study of these compounds was carried out in 1968 by Krogmann and Hausen on a compound of the stoichiometry, $K_2Pt(CN)_4Br_{0.3}\cdot 3H_2O$(KCP)(40). This study revealed a linear Pt chain structure in which the Pt ions are located in a uniform structural environment and are separated by a distance which is very close to that found in Pt metal. This structure suggested that the Pt ions were uniformly oxidized, implying a highly delocalized electronic arrangement involving a partially filled d_z2-like conduction band system. The prospect of one dimensional metal-like properties for these compounds was recognized by Krogmann and Hausen and later verified in detail by a wide range of physical property studies carried out by scientists at the Brown Boveri Research Lab and other institutions in Europe and the United States (8). These compounds, and KCP in particular, have since become the classic examples of a one-dimensional metal system, displaying not only highly anisotropic physical properties such as electrical conductivity and optical reflectivity but also the unusual features which arise as a result of the special physics associated with an effectively one-dimensional conduction band system (41).

For example, many of these compounds exhibit a metal-like conductivity temperature dependence only over a small range of temperatures near or above room temperature and at lower temperatures undergo a gradual metal-to-insulator transition which is accompanied by the "freezing-in" of periodic structural distortions which split the partially occupied d_z2-band into a set of sub-bands with an energy gap between the highest occupied and lowest unoccupied sub-bands. This observation is a basic consequence of the quasi-one dimensional character of the conduction band system and its intrinsic instability (known as the Peierls instability) toward a structural distortion of the appropriate periodicity to generate a gap at the Fermi energy of the system. In real "1-D" systems, such as KCP, other factors such as the presence of inter-chain interactions and finite structural disorder enter in, leading to actual 3-D phase transitions and complicating the detailed interpretation of physical properties such as conductivity.

In the last few years a variety of chemical varients of the KCP and partially oxidized bis-oxalato-platinum system have been prepared which have considerably extended the range of structures and properties exhibited by this class of compounds as well as adding to the fundamental understanding of their behavior (15).

Solid state interactions directly involving the ligands - ligand-bridged, metal complex chain systems

The known compounds of this type are, in general, rather poor electrical conductors, at least at atmospheric pressure, and have been of most interest from the standpoint of properties other than electrical conductivity, namely magnetic and/or spectral properties. Indeed, the general rule among these compounds is an effectively localized electronic structure with only very weak perturbations due to interactions with adjacent units in the structure (35).

This low degree of electronic coupling seems to be largely a consequence of the rather large intermolecular separations typically found for such systems, which is presumably dictated in part by non-bonding repulsive interactions arising from filled orbitals on the units, as well as the lack of specific mechanisms for strong electronic coupling between the metal centers. There are clearly at least a few examples of ligand-bridged binuclear complexes in which the metal centers are strongly coupled electronically with a considerable degree of electron delocalization (42); however, thus far the extension of this process to yield extended chain systems with a highly delocalized electronic structure has apparently not yet been achieved (43).

In certain cases, namely a series of mixed valence, halide-bridged, complexes of Pd, Pt and Au of the type, ML_nX_3 (M = Pd, Pt; L = NH_3, en; X = Cl, Br, I) and $AuS(CH_2C_6H_5)_2X_2$ (X = Cl, Br), evidence has been obtained for a substantial increase in the degree of electronic delocalization under very high pressures (21, 22); however, even here the ultimate conversion to a one dimensional metal system, formally analogous to that found for the partially oxidized metal chain compounds, apparently does not occur.

Systems involving ligand π-orbital interactions - the metal phthalocyanines and porphrins

The most notable examples of compounds of this type are the partially oxidized derivatives of macrocyclic complexes, such as the metal phthalocyanines and porphrins (25, 44). In their non-oxidized, integral-valence forms these complexes are typically insulators or semiconductors, despite their characteristic parallel stacking arrangement in the solid state (23). On partial oxidation, usually with I_2, certain of these compounds become very good electrical conductors with metal-like conductivity temperature dependence and magnetic properties, which is usually accompanied by only slight changes in the intrachain, intermolecular separations. EPR studies on these systems show g-values close to 2, indicating largely ligand-centered unpaired spins. Moreover, it has been found that even the Zn and Mg phthalocyanines as well as the metal-free species exhibit similar behavior on partial oxidation, suggesting quite strongly that it is the ligand system in these complexes which is primarily involved in the intrachain charge transport process.

π-donor-acceptor compounds involving planar metal complexes

In the final section of this paper a new group of coordination compound containing systems will be described in which the coordination compound is used as either a π-donor (D) or a π-acceptor (A) usually in combination with a planar organic molecule, to form a crystalline compound in which either or both types of molecules may be involved in extended solid state electronic interactions. In all of the known examples of these compounds, the dominant interaction pathway, when it involves the coordination compound unit, is primarily of the π-π type in which the π-orbitals are typically delocalized over both the metal ion and ligand system.

The interest in π-donor-acceptor (π-D·A) compounds is a long-standing one in the area of conducting molecular solids and in the last few years a variety of organic compounds of this type have been prepared which exhibit high metal-like conductivities as well as other novel solid state properties. A particularly notable example is the compound formed by the interaction of the organic π-donor, tetrathiafulvalene (TTF) with the π-acceptor tetracyanoquinodimethane (TCNQ), TTF·TCNQ (45).

At room temperature, TTF·TCNQ is among the best-known molecular conductors with a conductivity of nearly $10^3 ohm^{-1} cm^{-1}$ along its principal conducting (crystallographic b) axis. This conductivity increases with decreasing temperature, reaching $\sim 10^4 ohm^{-1} cm^{-1}$ at around 60° K. Like KCP it shows many of the unusual features of a one dimensional metal, including highly anisotropic reflectivity and conductivity behavior as well as a sensitivity to 1-D structural distortions which manifests itself in a metal-to-insulator transition at low temperatures.

Unlike KCP, however, this compound contains two different types of planar molecular units, both of which are capable of participating in a 1-D stacking configuration. The structure of TTF·TCNQ, in fact, contains parallel, separate stacks of TTF and TCNQ. Charge transfer from the highest occupied π-orbital of TTF to the lowest unoccupied π-orbital of TCNQ occurs to the extent of ~0.6 of an electron per unit, leading to partially occupied 1-D conduction bands on both types of stacks.

The presence of two different 1-D conduction band systems in the same solid adds further to the complexity of this material and a number of experimental and theoretical studies in recent years have focused on questions relating to the effect of interactions within and between these chains on the properties and structure of the solid. A wide variety of organic analogs of TTF·TCNQ have been prepared and examined in the last several years, in part, to obtain answers to these questions, culminating in the identification of materials with even higher electrical conductivities as well as metallic behavior which is retained down to the lowest temperatures investigated (46). One of these compounds (actually a complex salt of the selenium analog of TTF, i.e., $(\text{tetraselenofulvalene})_2 PF_6$) has recently been observed to become superconducting at high pressures and low temperatures, effectively opening up a new area to the search for new, and hopefully higher temperature, superconductors (47).

Efforts to explore coordination compound analogs of TTF·TCNQ through the preparation and study of π-donor-acceptor compounds of transition metal complexes, have been relatively few thus far. Early studies of the bis-dithiolene metal complexes, $MS_4C_4X_4$ (X = CN, CF_3) (Fig. 3), established the ability of this group of complexes to serve as π-acceptors in the formation of π-D.A compounds with certain polycyclic organic molecules and have subsequently led to several new examples of molecular solids with appreciable electrical conductivity (27, 29).

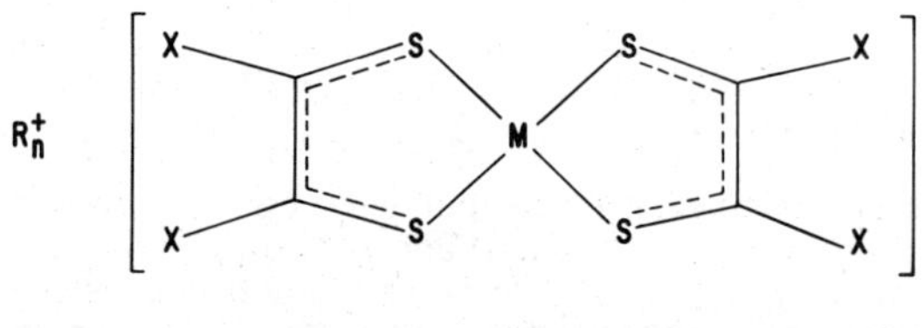

Fig. 3. Molecular structure of the bis-ethylene-1,2-dithiolene metal complexes; R^+ = various inorganic or organic cations; X = H, CH_3, CN, CF_3, C_6H_5, etc.; M = Ni, Pd, Pt, Co, Cu, Au, etc.; n = 0, 1, 2.

In our own laboratory the strongly ligand-dependent π-acceptor characteristics of this group of metal complexes has been explored in some detail over the last several years, using both TTF and tetrathiotetracene (TTT) as π-donors. This work has led to a variety of new π-D·A compounds with novel magnetic as well as electrical properties. Included here are the first experimental systems to exhibit the theoretically anticipated magnetic analog of the Peierls transition in the one dimensional metal systems, the "spin-Peierls transition". This is a progressive, magnetically driven, distortion of a quasi-1-D, antiferromagnetically coupled, spin system which leads to a dimerized phase with a singlet ground state at low temperatures. The spin system in this case consists of chains of TTF^+ ions in the compounds, TTF·$MS_4C_4(CF_3)_4$ (M = Cu, Au) (30).

In addition to these and other examples of novel magnetic systems, several new compounds with appreciable electrical conductivity and interesting structural features have been obtained, including a material ($TTT_{1.2}NiS_4C_4H_4$) with a room temperature conductivity of 30 $ohm^{-1} cm^{-1}$ and a quasi-1-D metal-like conductivity temperature dependence analogous to that observed for KCP and other one-chain, 1-D metal systems (31). In this case, as in most of the other examples of transition metal complex π-D·A compounds prepared thus far, the conducting chains are comprised of the organic component, and the bis-dithiolene metal complex units form a separate Curie-like magnetic sub-system in the structure (Fig. 4).

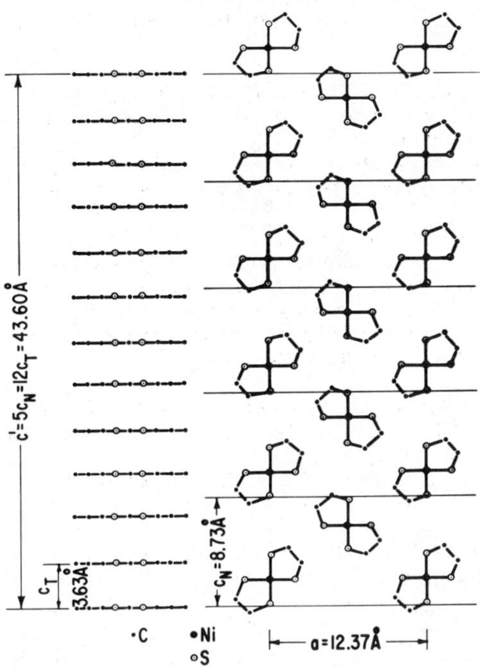

Fig. 4. View of the two subcells in the $TTT_{1.2}NiS_4C_4H_4$ structure normal to the ac plane.

With TTF, the same nickel bis-dithiolene complex, $NiS_4C_4H_4$, forms two distinct solid phases, one with the stoichiometry $(TTF)_2NiS_4C_4H_4$ and the other with a $(TTF)_2(NiS_4C_4H_4)_3$ approximate composition (48). The former phase is structurally related to the $TTT_{1.2}NiS_4C_4H_4$ compound and also consists of separate organic and metal complex sub-structures in which the organic units are stacked in a 1-D chain arrangement and the $NiS_4C_4H_4^-$ units comprise a weakly interacting 2-D magnetic network. In this compound, charge transfer from one of the two TTF units to the $NiS_4C_4H_4$ occurs leading to two potentially unpaired electron species, TTF^+ and $NiS_4C_4H_4^-$. Based on the results of magnetic susceptibility and epr measurements as well as the structural results, it appears that the TTF^+ units form an eclipsed $(TTF^+)_2$ dimer in the solid state in which the TTF^+ odd electrons are paired in a bonding molecular orbital derived from combination of the highest occupied b_{1g} orbitals on adjacent TTF^+ units (Fig. 5) (49). Subsequent to this observation, similar $(TTF^+)_2$ dimer units have been observed in other TTF^+ derivatives and evidenced in solution by spectral studies (50). As might be expected from this structural and electronic arrangement, this compound is a semiconductor with a conductivity at room temperature highest along the "TTF chain" direction in the crystal at $7 \times 10^{-3} ohm^{-1}cm^{-1}$, and a thermal activation energy of 0.2 eV.

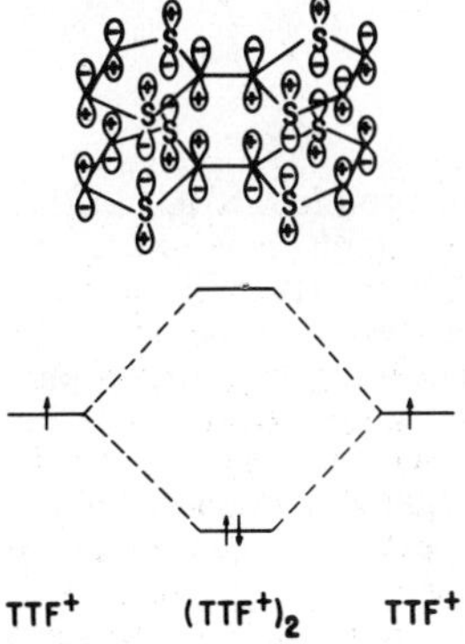

Fig. 5. Bonding in the $(TTF^+)_2$ unit.

The compound $(TTF)_2(NiS_4C_4H_4)_3$, is also a semiconductor, but, as is obvious from its structure and magnetic properties, the conductivity depends on structural and electronic features which differ substantially from that of its $(TTF)_2NiS_4C_4H_4$ relative. Unlike the 2:1 compound, this one has no net spin susceptibility or epr spectrum and infrared spectral studies show evidence for only the neutral TTF and $NiS_4C_4H_4$ species. Its structure (Fig. 6) is quite unusual for a molecular solid, consisting to the first approximation, of a disordered solid solution of the component molecules. The formation of a solid solution is presumably facilitated by the close similarity in the molecular structures of the two neutral species, which differ mainly by the replacement of a the Ni atom by a C = C unit.

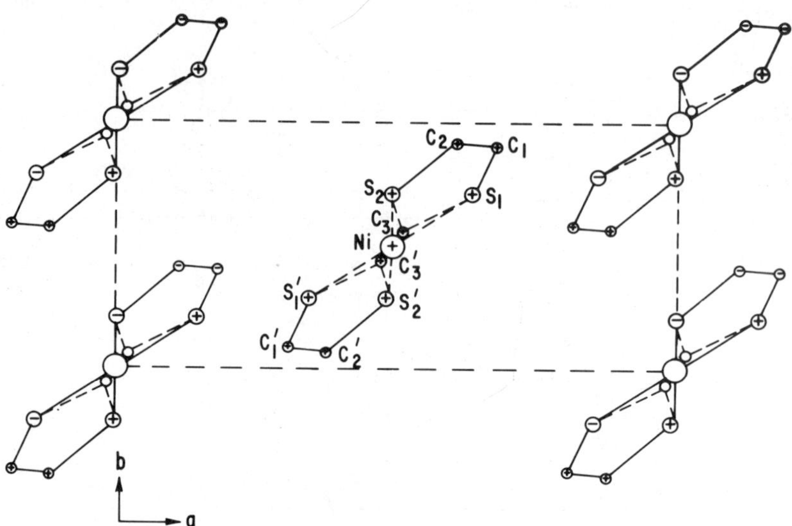

Fig. 6. Projection of the $(TTF)_2(NiS_4C_4H_4)_3$ crystal structure on the (001) plane.

As is evidenced by the occurrence of a complex pattern of weak satellite reflections, the actual structure of this material involves a sinusoidal modulation in composition along the b-axis of the monoclinic cell with a wavelength of 2.5b (subcell), modified by a modulation of wavelength 2/a* normal to b (51). While this type of solid solution structure with a modulated compositional variation is common in metal alloys it appears to be unprecedented among molecular crystals.

In addition to their novel structural and electronic features, these two phases are also noteworthy for their unusual charge transfer characteristics. The observed change from a charge-transferred π-D·A compound to a non-charge-transferred one on changing the proportion of donor to acceptor is quite remarkable and suggests an unusually close match between the effective, in situ, donor ionization potential and acceptor electron affinity in this case.

Thus far, none of the coordination compound containing π-D·A derivatives prepared in our laboratory or elsewhere have been found to exhibit the characteristic structural and electronic features of the TTF·TCNQ system. Moreover, in those cases where appreciable electrical conductivity has been observed, it is the organic component that seems to be primarily responsible for this behavior. Considering the structural flexibility and inherent advantages, in terms of the opportunity for extended solid state interactions, provided by a metal complex system as compared to a purely organic one, it is likely that this situation reflects more the relative proportion of synthesis efforts invested than any fundamental limitations and that coordination compound π-D·A systems will eventually take their place among the other examples of highly conductive molecular solids with metal-like electrical characteristics.

SUMMARY

A significant number of coordination compound systems with conductivities in excess of 1 $ohm^{-1}cm^{-1}$ and other novel solid state properties have been identified in the last few years. Most of these systems contain square planar metal complexes which have been partially oxidized, either chemically or electrochemically, and which form crystalline, typically non-stoichiometric, solids with parallel chains of stacked molecules. Overlap of metal-based (d_z2) or ligand-based (π) orbitals on the planar molecules in these stacks leads to formation of effectively one dimensional, partially filled, conduction bands and quasi 1-D metallic characteristics.

Coordination compound analogs of the organic π-donor-acceptor (π-D·A) compound, TTF·TCNQ, have not been obtained as yet; however, a variety of π-D·A compounds with novel structural features and solid state properties have been prepared.

There is still much remaining to be learned about the nature of the solid state electronic interactions in all of the systems described and further efforts directed at this question as well as the elucidation of the effects of molecular structure variations on solid state properties such as conductivity are needed.

Acknowledgment - This work was supported in part by the Air Force Office of Scientific Research (AFSC), United States Air Force, under contract F49620-79-C-0051. The United States Government is authorized to reproduce and distribute reprints for governmental purposes notwithstanding any copyright notation hereon.

REFERENCES

1. NATO Advanced Research Institute on "Molecular Metals", Les Arcs, France, 1978 [NATO Conf. Series: VI, Mats. Sci., Vol. 1; Plenum Press (1979)] ; NATO Advanced Study Institutes: Tomar, Portugal, 1979; Bolzanno, Italy, 1976; Starnberg, Germany, 1974; International Conferences on "Low Dimensional Synthetic Metals", Lo-Skolen, Helsingør, Denmark, Aug. 1980; "Quasi One-Dimensional Conductors", Dubrovnik, Yugoslavia, Sept., 1978; "Organic Conductors and Semiconductors", Siófok, Hungary, Sept. 1976 [Vols. 65 and 96 in Lecture Notes in Physics, Springer-Verlag, Berlin (1977 and 1979)]; NY Academy of Sciences Meeting on "Synthesis and Properties of Low Dimensional Materials", New York, N.Y., June 1977 [J. Miller and A. Epstein, editors, Anals NY Acad. Sci., 313 (1978)]; L.V. Interrante, editor, ACS Sympos. Ser., 5 (1974); J. Miller and A. Epstein, Progr. Inorg. Chem. 20 (1976); ibid, Scientific American, Oct. (1979) p. 52; J. Devreese, editor, Highly Conducting One Dimensional Solids, Plenum Press, New York (1979).

2. "Miscellanea Berolinensia an incrementum scientarium", Berlin, 1710, p. 377; H.J. Buser, D. Schwarzenbach, W. Petter and A. Ludi, Inorg. Chem. 16, 2704 (1977).

3. S. Yamada and R. Tsuchida, J. Chem. Soc. Japan 70, 44 (1949); S. Yamada, J. Amer. Chem. Soc., 73, 1579 (1951).

4. L.E. Godycki and R.E. Rundle, Acta Cryst., 6, 478 (1953); S. Yamada and R. Tsuchida, J. Amer. Chem. Soc., 75, 6351 (1963).

5. (a) P. Day, Inorg. Chim. Acta Reviews 3, 81 (1969); (b) D.S. Martin, ACS Sympos. Series, 5, 254 (1974); (c) P. Day, J. Amer. Chem. Soc., 97, 1588 (1975); (d) H. Yersin, G. Gliemann and V. Rossler, Solid State Commun., 21, 915 (1977).

6. J. R. Miller, J. Chem. Soc., 713 (1965).

7. (a) C.G. Pitt, L.K. Monteith, L.F. Ballard, J.P. Collman, J.C. Morrow, W.R. Roper and D. Ulkii, J. Amer. Chem. Soc., 88, 4286 (1966); (b) P.S. Gomm, T.W. Thomas, and A.E. Underhill, J. Chem. Soc.(A) 2154 (1971); (c) C.N.R. Rao and S.N. Bhat, Inorg. Nucl. Chem. Letters, 5, 531 (1969).

8. H.R. Zeller, Adv. Solid State Phys., (Festkörperprobleme) 13, 31 (1973).

9. D. Davis, H. Gutfreund and W.A. Little, Phys. Rev., 138, 4766 (1976); W.A. Little, Phys. Rev., 134, 1416 (1964).

10. G.M. Summa and B.A. Scott, Inorg. Chem., 19, 1079 (1980).

11. P.S. Gomm, T.W. Thomas, and A.E. Underhill, J. Chem. Soc.(A)., 2154 (1971).

12. A.H. Reis, Jr., V.S. Hagley and S.W. Peterson, J. Amer. Chem. Soc., 99, 4148 (1977).

13. A.E. Underhill, D.M. Watkins and R. Pethig, Inorg. Nucl. Chem. Letters, 9, 1269 (1973); J.S. Miller and C.H. Griffiths, J. Amer. Chem. Soc., 99 749 (1977); H. Endres, H.J. Keller, H. van de Sand and V. Dong, Z. Naturforsch, 33b, 843 (1978).

14. A.E. Underhill and D.J. Wood, NATO Conf. Series VI. Mats. Sci., 1, 377 (1979).

15. J.M. Williams and A.J. Shultz, NATO Conf. Series VI. Mats. Sci., 1, 337 (1979).

16. H. Toftlund, J.C.S. Chem. Commun., 837 (1979).

17. L.N. Buravov, R.N. Stepanova, M.I. Khidekel and I.F. Schchegolev, Dokl. Chem., 203, 283 (1972); K. Krogmann, et al., Abs. Amer. Chem. Soc. Mtg., 167, INOR 221 (1974); K. Krogmann, ACS Sympos. Ser., 5, 350 (1974).

18. D.O. Cowan, J. Park, C.V. Pittman, Jr., Y. Sasaki, T.K. Mukherjee, and N.A. Diamond, J. Amer. Chem. Soc., 94, 5110 (1972).

19. R.D. Willett, Anals NY Acad. Sci., 313, 111 (1978).

20. J.S. Valentine, A.J. Silverstein and Z.G. Soos, J. Amer. Chem. Soc., 96, 97 (1974); J.A.R. van Veen, H.T. Witteveen, and N.J. Verm, Solid State Commun., 13, 1235 (1973).

21. L.V. Interrante, F.P. Bundy, and K.W. Browall, Inorg. Chem., 13, 1158 (1974); L.V. Interrante and K.W. Browall, Inorg. Chem., 13, 1162 (1974).

22. L.V. Interrante and F.P. Bundy, J. Inorg. Nucl. Chem., 39, 1333 (1977).

23. S. Omiya, M. Tsutsui, E.F. Meyer, Jr., I. Bernal and D.L. Cullen, Inorg. Chem., 19, 134 (1980); G.H. Heilmeier and S.E. Harrison, Phys. Rev., 132, 2010 (1963).

24. K.W. Browall and L.V. Interrante, J. Coord. Chem., 3, 27 (1973).

25. B. Hoffman, T.E. Phillips, C.J. Schramm and S.K. Wright, NATO Conf. Series VI. Mats. Sci., 1, 393 (1979); C.J. Schramm, D.R. Stojakovic, B.M. Hoffman and T.J. Marks, Science, 200, 47 (1978).

26. P.M. Kuznesof. K.J. Wynne, R.S. Nohr and M.E. Kenney, J.C.S. Chem. Commun., 121 (1980).

27. L. Alcacer and A.H. Maki, J. Phys. Chem., 80, 1912 (1976).

28. S.R. Wilson, et al, NATO Conf. Series VI. Mats. Sci., 1, 407 (1979).

29. P. Calas, J.M. Fabre, M. Khalife-El-Saleh, A. Mas, E. Torreilles and L. Giral, Tetrahedron Letters, 4475 (1975).

30. D. Bloch, J. Voiron, J.C. Bonner, J.W. Bray, I.S. Jacobs, and L.V. Interrante, Phys. Rev. Letters, 44, 294 (1980); L.V. Interrante, J.W. Bray, H.R. Hart, Jr., J.S. Kasper and P.A. Piacente, Proc. Int'l. Conf. on Quasi One-Dimensional Conductors, Lecture Notes in Physics, 96, Vol. II, Springer-Verlag Publ., (1979) pp. 56-58; J.C. Bonner, T.S. Wei, H.R. Hart, Jr., L.V. Interrante, I.S. Jacobs, J.S. Kasper, G.D. Watkins and H.W.J. Blote, J. Appl. Phys. 49, 1321 (1978); I.S. Jacobs, H.R. Hart, Jr., L.V. Interrante, J.W. Bray, J.S. Kasper, G.D. Watkins, D.E. Prober, W.P. Wolf and J.C. Bonner, Physica 86-88B, 655 (1977); I.S. Jacobs, J.W. Bray, H.R. Hart, Jr., L.V. Interrante, J.S. Kasper, G.D. Watkins, D.E. Prober and J.C. Bonner, Phys. Rev., 14B, 3036 (1976).

31. J.W. Bray, H.R. Hart, Jr., L.V. Interrante, I.S. Jacobs, J.S. Kasper, and P.A. Piacente, Phys. Rev., 16B, 1359 (1977).

32. P. Cassoux, L.V. Interrante and J.S. Kasper, Compt. rend., to be published.

33. L.V. Interrante and R.P. Messmer, Inorg. Chem., 10, 1174 (1971).

34. L.V. Interrante and R.P. Messmer, ACS Sympos. Series, 5, 382 (1974).

35. P. Day, NATO Adv. Study Inst. Ser., Series B: Physics, Vol. 25, Plenum Press, NY, pp. 197-223 (1977).

36. L.V. Interrante, ACS Adv. in Chem. Series, 150, 1 (1976); E. Fishman and L.V. Interrante, Inorg. Chem., 11, 1722 (1972); L.V. Interrante, J.C.S. Chem. Commun., 302 (1972); L.V. Interrante and F.P. Bundy, Inorg. Chem., 10, 1168 (1971).

37. F. Mehran and, B.A. Scott, Physica 83B, 179 (1976); F. Mehran and L.V. Interrante, Solid State Commun., 18, 1031 (1976); B.D. Silverman and B.A. Scott, J. Chem. Phys., 63, 518, 523 (1975); B.A. Scott, F. Mehran, B.D. Silverman and M.A. Ratner, ACS Symp. Series 5, 331 (1974); F. Mehran and B.A. Scott, Phys. Rev. Lett., 31, 39 (1973).

38. F.N. Lecrone, M.J. Minot and J.H. Perlstein, Inorg. Nucl. Chem. Lett., 8, 173 (1972).

39. K. Krogmann, Angew. Chem. Internatl. Edit., 8, 35 (1969).

40. K. Krogmann and H.D. Hausen, Z. Anorg. Allgem. Chem., 358, 67 (1968).

41. J. Miller and A. Epstein, Progr. Inorg. Chem., 20 (1976).

42. D.O. Cowan, P. Shu, F.L. Hedberg, M. Rossi and T.J. Kistenmacher, J. Amer. Chem. Soc., 101, 1304 (1979); R.W. Callahan, F.R. Keene, T.J. Meyer and D.J. Salmon, J. Amer. Chem. Soc., 99, 1064 (1977).

43. Pyrazine bridged Ru(bipy)$_2$ oligimers have been described (S.A. Adeyemi, E.C. Johnson, F.J. Miller and T.J. Meyer, Inorg. Chem., 12, 2371 (1973)); however these involve only up to 3-4 monomer units; no solid state conductivity data were reported in this case.

44. S.W. Wright, C.J. Schramm, T.E. Phillips, D.M. Scholler and B.M. Hoffman, Syn. Metals, 1, 43 (1979/80).

45. A.J. Heeger, Comments Solid State Phys., 9, 65 (1979); R. Comés, G. Shirane, A.F. Garito, S.M. Shapiro and A.J. Heeger, Phys Rev., 14B, 2376 (1976); J.C. Scott, A.F. Garito and A.J. Heeger, Phys Rev., 10B, 3131 (1974); T.J. Kistenmacher, T.E. Phillips and D.O. Cowan, Acta Cryst., B30, 763 (1974).

46. J.B. Torrance, Acc. Chem. Res., 12, 79 (1979); S. Barišić, A. Bjelis, J.R. Cooper and B. Leontić, editors, Lecture Notes in Physics, Springer Verlag, Berlin, Vol. 96 on "Quasi One-Dimensional Conductors" (1979); W.E. Hatfield, editor, NATO Conf. Series VI. Mats. Sci., Vol. 1 on "Molecular Metals", Plenum Press, NY (1979); C.S. Jacobson, K. Mortensen, J.R. Anderson and K. Bechgaard, Phys. Rev. 18B, 905 (1978); R.H. Friend, D. Jerome, J. Fabre, L. Giral and K. Bechgaard, J. Phys. C., 11, 263 (1978).

47. D. Jerome, A. Mazaud, M. Ribault, and K. Bechgaard, J. Phys. Letters, 41, L-95 (1980).

48. L.V. Interrante, Adv. in Chem. Series, 150, 1 (1976); L.V. Interrante, K.W. Browall, H.R. Hart, Jr., I.S. Jacobs, G.D. Watkins and S.H. Wee, J. Amer. Chem. Soc., 97, 889 (1975); J.S. Kasper, L.V. Interrante and C.A. Secaur, J. Amer. Chem. Soc., 97, 890 (1975).

49. D. Salahub, R. Messmer, and R. Herman, Phys. Rev. 13B, 4252 (1976).

50. S.J. LaPlaca, P.W.R. Corfield, R. Thomas, and B.A. Scott, Solid State Commun., 17, 635 (1975).

51. J.S. Kasper and L.V. Interrante, AIP Conf. Proc., No. 53; Modulated Structs.-1979, J. M. Cowley, et al, editors (1979) p. 205.

NOVEL ASPECTS IN THE ELECTRO-CHEMISTRY OF REDOX SERIES

A. A. Vlček

The J. Heyrovský Institute of Physical Chemistry and Electrochemistry, Czechoslovak Academy of Sciences, Prague, Czechoslovakia

Abstract - Complexes of transition metals with redox active ligands, ML_m, form redox series the general pattern of which can be deduced by considering mutual interaction of redox orbitals in the ligand-cluster, L_m. Rules for maximum size of redox series are derived. Complexes with i.m electrons in the redox orbitals of the ligand-cluster posses relative electron stability.

INTRODUCTION

A redox series is a set of compounds with identical composition differing only in the overall number of electrons (n), e.g. for a complex ML_m^z (m - number of identical ligands, z - charge of the complex) the set

ML_m^z - ML_m^{z-1} - ML_m^{z-2} - ML_m^{z-3} represents a redox series.

Each redox series is characterized by the number of redox steps within the set (N, only sets with $N > 2$ are regarded as redox series), by the corresponding differencies in n ($\Delta z = \Delta n$, in most cases $\Delta z = 1$) between neighbouring members of the series and by the values of standard redox potentials (E_i^o) between neighbouring members of the set. Furthermore, rate constant of the interconversion between members z - (z+1), and intrinsic stability of individual members are important for general description and understanding of the series.

Redox series were firstly obtained chemically, however, the generality of the concept of redox series emerged fully only after they had been characterized by electrochemical techniques. Recently new redox series were discovered mostly using polarographic or voltammetric techniques. Electrochemical methods, when used properly, provide most of the characteristics mentioned above.

Redox series are being studied very intensely, mainly in relation with biologically important systems, or their models, or with the aim to cover gaps in the systematics of coordination compounds. However, their importance is much broader: Well defined redox series make it possible to investigate the influence of n upon the behaviour of a given atomic set or, by comparing redox series, differing in the nature of substituents on the ligands, the effect of substitution upon various orbitals in the complex can be studied. Recently the importance of redox series for tailoring specific redox agents and for the understanding of multielectron redox processes has been stressed (Ref.1). Furthermore, transitions between numbers of redox series play a decisive role in the homogeneous catalysis of redox reactions and compounds forming redox series seem to be potential catalysts of electrode processes (in soluble or anchored form).

All this points to the necessity of systematic investigation of redox series, mainly those formed by transition metal complexes. Problems to be solved concern mainly the mechanism of stabilization of individual members of the sets, localization of the charge change (closely related to the question of the definition of the oxidation state), the change of electronic and atomic structure with n and the mode of redox interaction of individual members of the redox series, i.e. the dependence of the mechanism of a redox process upon n. Experimental techniques are to be developed - or made more sophisticated - to make it possible to prepare and isolate those members of redox series which are formed at extreme potentials. Furthermore, the decomposition pattern is to be followed in more detail for those members of redox series the life time of which is very short.

Redox series are formed by most transition metals with suitable ligands. Among the redox series most interesting from the theoretical point of view and most promissing in application in redox reactions are those formed by complexes of the type ML_m where L is a redox active ligand, i.e. a ligand capable to undergo a reduction (or oxidation) in the free, uncomplexed form. It has to be noted at this point that not in all cases a reduction of the free ligand has been actually observed, mainly due to rather negative potentials required, or to the fact that the free ligand differs in its form from that present in the complex. Among these redox active (or potentially redox active) ligands are compounds with two donor atoms at the ends of a conjugated system (e.g. β - diketones) or directly involved in the cyclic conjugated system (e.g. dipyridyl) or molecules of the o-quinone type. Previously we have shown (Ref.2) that one of the structural factors governing the stability of redox series of complexes formed by these ligands is the direct or metal mediated ligand-ligand interaction, so that complexes of this type can be regarded in limiting cases as being formed by the metal atom and a cluster (or "supermolecule") of ligands, L_m. Further investigations from this Laboratory or published in the literature have confirmed this general conclusion and the experimental material which has been accumulated in last years made it possible to analyze the properties of the redox series of this type in more detail. In this contribution some new generalizations within the concept of redox series will be discussed with the emphasis on series formed by redox active ligands.

SIZE OF REDOX SERIES ML_m^z

The redox processes observed with the type of complexes under discussion can be, basically, looked at as metal and ligand based (see Note a) processes and the general conditions for their appearance might thus be derived by considering the ionization potentials or electron affinities of the central metal and ligands. In principle, all occupied or vacant "valence" orbitals can be taken into account. However, limits are set by the accessibility of the process under given experimental condition. In solution, the energy limit (i.e. +2V to -3V) for removing an electron is given by $(I - \Delta H_C - \Delta H_S)$, where I is the ionization potential of the metal atom or of the ligand in the gas phase, ΔH_C is the difference of the stabilization energy of reduced and oxidized form due to complex formation and ΔH_S that due to the solvation. For transition metal ions, ionization from d-orbitals is usually that which has to be taken into account; for the ligands of the type discussed, ionization from σ-orbitals is not observed and only rarely that from occupied π-orbitals. The energy limit for accepting the electron is similarly given by the balance between the electron affinity and stabilizing effect of complex formation and solvation. For central metal atoms the filling up of d-orbitals is energetically accessible. For ligands the filling up of π-antibonding orbitals is the most usual process, σ-antibonding orbitals being involved in redox processes in solution only very rarely. The redox series is usually terminated by the energy gap for that step the ionization energy of which cannot be balanced off by complex formation. In many cases this termination corresponds to the "normally" observed oxidation state of the metal or ligand, however, the specific interaction between redox active ligands and metal atom might overcome this gap and "unusual" oxidation states of the complex are reached. In this connection it has to be noted that the accessibility of a given level in the complex is in most cases different from that in the free ligand. The incorporation of the ligand into a complex, forming a redox series of the type discussed, results usually in the stabilization of the reduced form, i.e. ligand based redox processes are in many cases observed at more positive potentials as compared with those of free ligands. In terms of ionization potentials this reflects the increase of I due to the decrease of the overall negative charge caused by the interaction with the metal ion. As will be seen later, in some cases ligand based reductions are observed in the complex which are not observable in the free ligand. However, as n becomes very high the opposite effect, i.e. the relative shift of E^o towards more negative potentials, is observed (vide infra).

The maximum number of redox steps in a redox series, N_{max}, is given by the following expression :

$$N_{max} = N_M + mN_L \qquad (1)$$

Note a. The term "metal or ligand based" does not mean a process being metal or ligand localized - it reflects the fact that the electron or electron hole involved in the process was "brought" into the complex by the given component.

N_L is the number of electrons free ligand can exchange. It might seem arbitrary which form of the ligand is chosen as the reference state, however, regularities in the sequencies of redox steps, to be discussed later, show that the neutral (most oxidized) form of the ligand or the corresponding anionic form resulting from dissociation of hydrogen ions is to be chosen as the reference state. This means that N_L is the number of electrons by which the ligand can be reduced. In exceptional cases the neutral form of the ligand might be oxidized as well as reduced. In this case electrons exchanged both in oxidation and reduction steps are to be added to give N_L.

The estimation of N_M, i.e. of metal based redox steps, is not as unambiguous as that of N_L. Even if theoretical derivation, based on the analysis of ionization potentials could lead to N_M values, some empirical rules, based mainly on the knowledge of electrochemistry of the particular metal, seem at present to be more useful. For transition metal complexes only those metal based processes are taken into consideration in which d-electrons are exchanged. Electron exchange is, in dependence upon the nature of the metal, usually confined to intervals between some configurations, especially $d^0 - d^3$, $d^3 - d^6$, $d^6 - d^{10}$ (in the latter interval subgroups $d^6 - d^8$ and $d^8 - d^{10}$ appear, however, not as distinct as the main groups). Usually the number of metal based electrons does not exceed that corresponding to the metal atom.

As to which of these groups a given metal atom would belong can be judged from the preponderant configuration of the most frequent oxidation state of the metal in complexes with redox inactive ligands. This is, of course, very closely connected with the values of I of the free metal ion - most frequently those oxidation states are reached for which I_i is of the order 30 to 40 eV. This criterion would place titanium into the $d^0 - d^3$ group, chromium into the $d^3 - d^6$ group, cobalt into the $d^6 - d^8$ (d^{10}) group etc. The above specified groups are of course not absolute limits of configurations of metal atom from which members of redox series can be derived. However, the inspection of I values of gaseous metals and the splitting of the d-levels due to complex formation support this general pattern according to which metal from Ti to Fe would mostly reach the d^6 configuration as the upper limit, metals from Co to Cu the d^{10} configuration. Second and third row transition metal complexes exhibit usually a tendency to reach higher oxidation states - this is due to the fact that the values of higher ionization potentials of these metals are lower than those of the first row elements.

In estimating the N_M value the criterion of ΔE^o (see Note a on the next page) might also be used as can be demonstrated on iron series : The process $d^5 \longrightarrow d^6$ appears in many complexes at about +1V. The gap between d^6 (spin paired) and d^7 (spin paired) for iron (case 2 of ΔE^o criterion) is rather big and the process $d^6 \longrightarrow d^7$ would be expected to appear at potentials more negative than -2V. This confines the iron complexes into the group of $d^3 - d^6$ configurations. The process $d^4 \longrightarrow d^5$ would be by about 1V more positive than the $d^5 \longrightarrow d^6$, placing thus the corresponding value of E^o out of reach of the experiment and leading to most probable value of $N_M = 1$. Analogous arguments can be used in estimating N_M values for iridium complexes : $d^5 \longrightarrow d^6$ transition is at about +2V for trisdipyridyl complex (Ref.4). For iridium the $d^6 — d^7$ gap is extremely large so that again $N_M = 1$. Unlike iridium, cobalt shows an energy gap between d^5 and d^6 and a much smaller one between d^6 and d^7. This confines cobalt into the $d^6 - d^{10}$ group, with $N_M = 2$ or possibly even 4 (experimental data available at present support the lower value). Chromium, with the most frequent configuration d^3, is confined fully into the $d^3 - d^6$ group, i.e. $N_M = 3$. However, with ligands capable to compensate large positive charge even configuration d^2 could be expected (I for $d^3 \longrightarrow d^2$ is about 49eV).

N_{max} as defined by (1) is based on considerations of electron configuration only, factors governing the intrinsic stability of individual members being not taken into account. The redox series seems to be terminated also by the overall charge on the complex : If N_M is large and all corresponding steps accessible within the available range of potential then for N_{max} (with m = 3 and $N_L = 2$, as is the most usual case) the charge for the most reduced species would be too negative for overall intrinsic stability. Furthermore, with the high overall negative charge the $E^{o\prime}$s of ligand based processes would tend to move towards more negative potentials, i.e. out of the accessible range of potentials (i.e. more negative than about -3V). Thus e.g. for the series $Crdipy_3^z$ $N_M = 3$, $N_L = 2$, giving $N_{max} = 9$. The experiment shows N = 6, the most negative standard redox potential, E_6^o being at about -2,5V (Ref.5,6), i.e. about 0,3V more negative than the E_1^o of free dipyridyl (Ref.6,7). The analysis of the sequence of E^o-values for $Crdipy_3^z$ (vide infra, Fig.1) indicates that not all the possible ligand based steps are reached. The high overall negative charge and almost complete reduction of central metal atom shift the E_6^o to very negative potentials, and the next step, if intrinsicly possible at all, could be predicted to occur at -3V or even more negative potentials.

Note a. The experimental evidence, supported by MO-calculations shows (Ref.3) that the difference in subsequent E^o-values (ΔE^o) depends upon the nature of the process. Three limiting cases can be specified (a, b denote general redox orbitals in the complex) :

1) $a \longrightarrow a^1$, E_1^o $\qquad$ $a^1 \longrightarrow a^2$, E_2^o

$\Delta E^o \sim 0,3 - 0,9V$

2) $a^1 \longrightarrow a^2$, E_1^o $\qquad$ $a^2 \longrightarrow a^2b^1$, E_2^o

$\Delta E^o \sim 1,5 - 3V$

3) ionizations from closely spaced orbitals or from a nearly degenerate set of orbitals in the course of which changes in orbital and spin pairing energies are comparable (breakdown of redox orbital concept) lead to

$$\Delta E^o \sim 0,2 - 0,5V$$

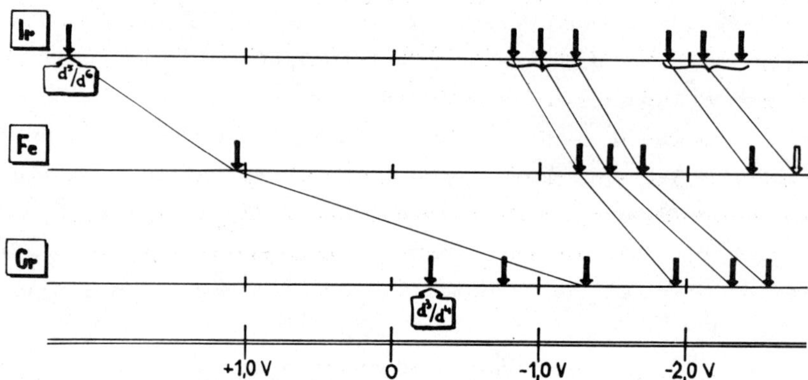

Fig. 1. Comparison of $E_{1/2}$ values for $Mdipy_3^z$ complexes (data (see Note a) taken from Ref.4, 6,8, 9). Open arrow denotes a not fully defined electrode process.

On the other hand the $Irdipy_3^z$ series (see Fig. 1, Ref.4) seems to be complete: $N_M = 1$ (vide ante), $N_L = 2$ so that $N_{max} = 7$. As is seen from Fig. 1 seven redox steps are observed in accordance with the prediction. For iron-dipyridyl series N = 7 should be observed. Experiments show only 6 redox steps, the ${}_6E_{1/2}$ value and the spacing of $E_{1/2}$'s indicate, however, that the missing step could be found around -3V.

Eq. (1) specifying the size of the redox series, together with ΔE^o criterion, can thus serve as a guide in looking for the missing members of a redox series, as in most experimentally studied redox series $N_{exp} < N_{max}$. Fig. 2 shows some more examples of redox series (with the most positive, $d^5 - d^6$ step ommitted). From these the $Mterpy_2^z$ series are of interest as both with iron and ruthenium two redox steps are missing ($N_M = 1$, $N_L = 2$, $m = 2$, $N_{max} = 5$) even if E_3^o is not at very negative potentials (vide infra).

SEQUENCE OF REDOX POTENTIALS

The inspection of Fig. 1 and 2 shows some regularities in the sequence of E^o values within the redox series. These regularities are in limiting cases, like e.g. in the iridium dipyridyl series, unambiguously clear cut, in other cases, like in the analogous chromium series, they can be traced only by comparison

---

Note a. Most of the data presented in the figures in this paper are based on references quoted, they have been, however, remeasured in this Laboratory, whenever possible, to ensure identical scaling.

with other series. The regularities we have deduced from the analysis of vast experimental material can be formulated as follows :

A redox series ML_m^z gives, in the limiting case, N_{max} redox steps. These are divided into N_M separated steps and into N_L sets of 1 electron steps each containing m individual steps.

Saji and Aoyagui in a most recent paper (Ref.10) noticed the regularity occuring within one set, however, without knowledge of N_{max} and analysis of complete series they were unable to deduce the general pattern given above.

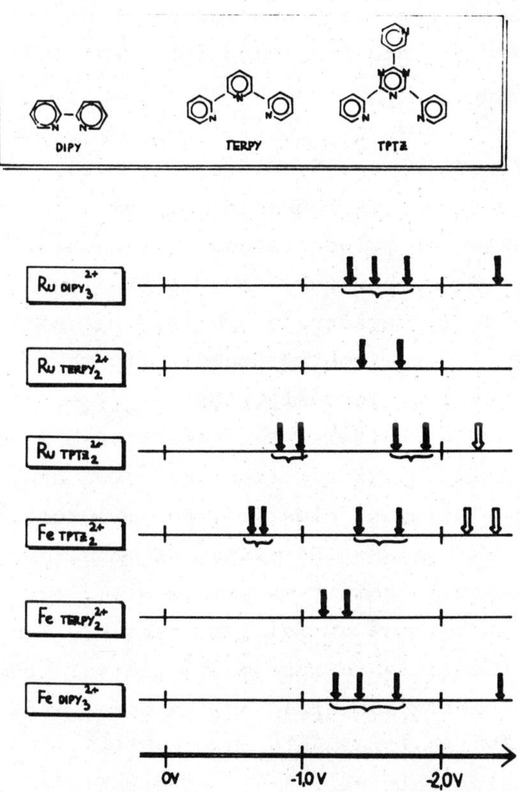

Fig. 2. Comparison of half-wave potentials of some RuL_m^z and FeL_m^z series (Ref.10, 17, 18). Open arrows indicate not fully identified processes.

$Irdipy_3^z$ series with $N_M = 1$, $m = 3$ and $N_L = 2$ shows (see Fig. 1) one isolated step at about +2V, and two ($N_L = 2$) "triplets" (m = 3). The steps within each triplet are closely spaced (ΔE^o corresponding to limiting case 3), both triplets being separated by ΔE^o value which is of the order of those for case 1, but does not, in this case, necessarily originate from the same mechanism (vide infra).

This general pattern of spacing of E^o values is seen in Fig. 1 as well as in Fig. 2 and can be traced for many other series (Ref.11). In the case of iron series (Fig. 1) the first triplet is fully developed, whereas the second one not (vide ante). The series with TPTZ ligand ($m = 2$, $N_L = 4$ (Ref.10)) should show four doublets. However, only three are seen for the iron series, the missing one being obscured at extremely negative potentials by the decomposition of the ground electrolyte.

Comparing the iridium and chromium series it is seen that for the latter case the pattern of E^o sequence is not so well developed as in the case of iridium, even if the "ligand triplet" could be traced by comparison with isoelectronic iridium or iron complexes. The "well behaved" iridium, iron and ruthenium series (to quote those series data for which are presented here) represent a limiting type of behaviour.

The MO-calculations (for dipy series see (Ref.12 & 13)) reflect the observed behaviour : The complex $Mdipy_3^z$ is looked at as being composed of the central metal atom and the cluster of three ligands, L_3. Each of the ligands has one vacant redox orbital (π-antibonding). Due to the ligand-ligand interaction this set of three originally degenerate orbitals is split (in D_{3d} symmetry) into a_2 and e orbitals (lower symmetry could split the e set further), separated by about 0,2 - 0,3eV. Analogously, the $d(t_{2g})$ set of the central metal atom is split into a_1 and e orbitals. The e sets of ligand cluster and metal ion do interact, the extent of interaction depending upon the energy difference between e(metal) - e(ligand cluster). For iridium, ion and ruthenium this difference is rather big and the mixing of metal and ligand orbitals is relatively small, at least in complexes with $z = +4, +3, +2$ (e.g. for $Fedipy_3^{2+}$ the lower e set has 83% of metal character). In complexes of Ir, Fe, Ru derived from d^5 configuration of the central metal atom the redox orbital is the a_1 orbital, dominantly localized on the metal atom. The most positive redox process gets fully localized into this orbital, the resulting decrease of positive charge causing only very small electronic relaxation, i.e. the general mode of interaction metal-ligands is not changed considerably. The next electron exchange is then fully localized into the $(e + a_2)$ set of mainly ligand based orbitals. The energy differencies of these orbitals or, as we are concerned with case 3 mentioned above, between states arising from stepwise filling up of these levels with electrons, are rather small and thus the above mentioned triplet of redox states results. The increasing negative charge does not, in this case, cause any considerable change in mixing of d- and π-antibonding orbitals. The second triplet of redox steps (see Fig. 1) corresponds to complete occupation of the $(e + a_2)$ set. As the comparison of spacing of E^o values in the first and second triplet indicates, there is not a substantial change in the mixing of d- and ligand orbitals with increasing n, especially in the second triplet. These conclusions are fully reflected by MO-calculations of the iron series.

These "well behaved" series are thus characterized by large energy separation of metal and ligand based orbitals and thus by weaker mixing of metal d- and ligand π - antibonding orbitals and, as a result of this, by rather small electronic relaxation effects.

The situation differs in systems in which the metal ion acquires a larger number of electrons : In the case of chromium dipyridyl series, the complex with $z = +3$ is derived from d^3 configuration of chromium. The lower set $(e + a_1)$ is mainly metal localized and is semioccupied. The first three reduction steps are localized into this set of orbitals (as follows, among other, from magnetic moments of the complexes). However, as n, in the first steps mainly metal localized, increases, the energy difference between metal and ligand based orbitals decreases resulting thus in the increase of mixing between these two sets of orbitals. This electronic relaxation accompanying actually each redox step obscures to a great extent the "well behaved" pattern of the redox series, i.e. the localization of redox change becomes continuously less pronounced even if in all three first steps only the $(e + a_1)$ set of orbitals is involved. The next three reduction steps resemble the first triplet in, e.g., iron series, however, due to a greater admixture of metal orbitals their separation from the metal-based redox steps is less pronounced. In 1960 (Ref.14) a relationship between half-wave potential of the complex and that of the free ligand was derived

$$ {}_{C}E_{1/2} = a \cdot {}_{L}E_{1/2} + \text{const} \qquad (2) $$

on the basis of which the admixture of ligand based orbital into the redox orbital of the complex could be deduced as a is directly proportional to the square of mixing coefficient of the ligand orbital. The implications of this equation were later (Ref.2) discussed for the type of redox series under discussion. When eq. (2) is applied to the chromium dipyridyl series deviations are seen for the first three steps, whereas the steps forming the triplet more or less obey this equation (Ref.6). This finding supports the above conclusion.

Chromium complexes with o-quinones represent another type of behaviour. Even if the observed redox series (Ref.15 & 16) are not complete their behaviour shows striking differences (see Fig. 3) when compared with that of dipyridyl series.

For Cr-o-quinone$_3^z$ series N_{max} should be the same as for the dipyridyl series, i.e. $N_{max} = 9$. With o-phenanthrenequinone two triplets are observed which, in analogy with other series, could be ascribed to predominantly ligand localized processes. With o-tetrachloroquinone, only the more negative triplet is seen. In this latter case the positive triplet would be expected in the region of +1,8V or at even more positive potentials. The striking feature of these

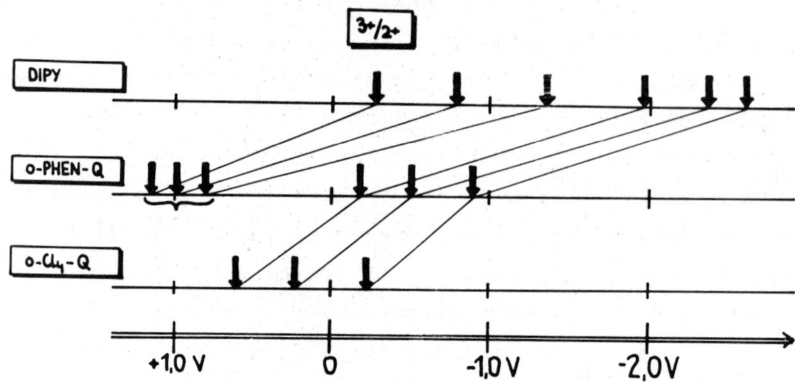

Fig. 3. Comparison of CrL_3^z redox series (data from Ref.6,15 & 16). Lines connect identical overall charge-change processes

series is the missing of metal-based processes. Preliminary investigation of this Laboratory indicates, however, a negative redox process with these complexes, the nature of which is to be still investigated in more detail. The o--quinones are reduced by > 1,5V more positive than the corresponding dipyridyls. This would place the ligand based redox steps in the o-quinone series into the region more positive than about -0,5V where actually the triplets of redox states are found. This observation together with preliminary MO-calculations indicate that in the case of o-quinone series the ligand based set of orbitals ($e + a_2$) is energetically equal or more stable than that of chromium and that the ligand based reductions might take place at more positive potentials than the metal based ones. It has to be noted, however, that in any case substantial metal and ligand orbital mixing is to be expected which in this particular case does not seem to obscure the triplet pattern. With increasing negative charge on the ligands rather extensive electronic relaxation is to be expected, leading to more pronounced metal character of LUMO in the most reduced member of the series (z = -3).

The same arguments used above for ML_3^z (N_L = 2) series hold for series with other values of m and N_L : For m = 2, N_L = 2 each ligand contributes one redox orbital. Ligand-ligand interaction results in the formation of a closely spaced set of two orbitals, the filling up of which gives up the two doublets of redox steps observed. For N_L = 4 each ligand contributes two redox orbitals, the ligand-ligand interaction gives, e.g. for m = 3, two sets of closely spaced orbitals (each set containing three orbitals) the consecutive filling up of which results in six triplets of redox steps. In an analogous way it is possible to predict the general pattern of the sequence of E^o values for a given redox series from the knowledge of the redox behaviour of free ligands. However, limitations mentioned above and the mixing with metal orbitals has to be taken into account in deducing the actual behaviour of the redox series.

This discussion points also to the possibility of making conclusions on the localization of the redox change : In the "well behaved" redox series the predominantly metal- and ligand-cluster localized steps are clearly distinguished. The more does the behaviour of a redox series deviate from the "well behaved" pattern, the less pronounced is the localization of the redox change till a situation is reached when it is not possible to distinguish between metal- and ligand-cluster localization and the redox change is to be ascribed to the complex as a whole.

STABLE CONFIGURATIONS

According to basic electrochemical principles equilibria are established between various redox states of the same compound in solution. For a redox series

$$A \xrightarrow{E_1^o} B \xrightarrow{E_2^o} C$$

the equilibrium constant

$$K = \frac{[B]^2}{[A]\ [C]}$$

depends upon the difference $(E_1^o - E_2^o)$. If this difference is < 180 mV, B species always disproportionates considerably into A and C. For $(E_1^o - E_2^o) > 300$mV this disproportionation can be essentially neglected and all three forms can be regarded as stable with respect to disproportionation or reproportionation.

Inspection of E^o sequencies for "well behaved" redox series shows that the ΔE^o within the individual ligand-based multiplets of redox steps (triplets or doublets, see Fig. 1, 2, 3) are usually smaller than 300mV, i.e. interconversion between the redox forms within each multiplet can be expected. On the other hand, the potential difference between subsequent multiplets is usually large enough to prevent the interconversion of redox forms belonging to different multiplets. The metal based redox steps are mostly well separated from the ligand-cluster localized processes.

Generalizing this observation - which holds for all redox series of the type discussed - shows that within a given redox series certain stable configurations exist which, due to the stabilization are well separated in $E^{o\prime}$s from the next more reduced configuration, do not undergo redox interconversion with these higher members of the series.

In every redox series there are

$$N_M + N_L$$

such stable configurations.

Stable configurations in a "well behaved" series are those resulting from a metal based process or that in which the ligand-cluster set of orbitals gets semi- or fully occupied. The stable configurations of a redox series, N_k, result from redox steps for which the following equality is fulfilled :

$$N_k = j + i \cdot m \quad (3)$$

where j runs from 0 to N_M and i from zero to N_L. Usually $i > 0$ only after j reaches the limiting value.

For the "well behaved" iridium-dipyridyl series we get stable configurations for

$$j = 1 \, , \quad i = 0$$
$$j = 1 \, , \quad i = 1$$
$$j = 1 \, , \quad i = 2$$

i.e. maximum value of $k = 3 = N_M + N_L$.

This further regularity within the redox series serves as an additional diagnostic criterion for the completeness of the series and for the localization of redox changes in the individual steps.

The simple MO picture, given above to explain the general pattern of the sequence of $E^{o\prime}$s, easily accounts for the existence of stable configurations resulting from predominantly metal-based redox changes. However, the separation of predominantly ligand-based redox processes into separated multiplets reflects another, up to now not recognized or discussed feature of the redox processes :

Each electronic configuration resulting from half or full occupation of the set of orbitals resulting from the interaction of ligand redox orbitals is characterized by an extra stabilization energy.

In a series ML_m^z the extra stabilization is achieved for compounds formally describable as $M(L^-)_m^z$ or $M(L^{2-})_m^z$ (or even for members derived from $(L^{3-})_m$ and $(L^{4-})_m$ for $N_L = 4$).

In term of electronic relaxation energy this observation means that the ionization of a species in which the ligand cluster caries formally a charge

$$-(i \cdot m + 1) \; (i = 1, \ldots N_L)$$

is accompanied by an electronic relaxation energy, stabilizing the configuration with formal charge -i . m on the ligand-cluster.

In terms of ligand-ligand interaction this finding indicates that the ligand--clusters L_m with half-filled or fully occupied redox orbitals are most stable. This is an analogy with the extra stability reached for semioccupied or fully occupied levels in free metal ions (e.g. d^5 and d^{10}) or to a certain extent, the analogy can be sought with aromatic systems. This extra stabilization of i.m-configurations confirms the importance of ligand-ligand interaction in forming the redox series and supports the view that the systems under consideration behave, at least when these stable configurations are reached, as being formed of the metal ion in interaction with ligand-cluster L_m.

As to the intermediate configurations, i.e. those in which the L_m-cluster is reduced by less than i.m electrons, the question remains open of the localization of the charge within the ligand-cluster. If all the ligands in the cluster are identical, as is the case of the unreduced cluster, and remain identical throughout all the reduction steps up to m . N_L, the redox change is to be delocalized equally throughout the ligand-cluster (ommitting for the moment the metal-ligand mixing). However, there is some experimental evidence (Ref. 15, 16, 19) that the redox change might be localized on one of the ligands only. This of course means that the ligands cannot after the reduction remain identical (otherwise the Jahn-Teller theorem would be violated). Even if a rapid intramolecular redox exchange between the ligands is assumed (see e.g. Ref. 16) this non-identity of the ligands would lead to a decrease in the stability of the ligand-cluster. The reduction steps leading to occupation numbers i.m in the ligand orbitals would make the ligands identical and would thus restore the stability of the ligand cluster. However, more experimental evidence is needed to establish this non-identity of ligands in partly reduced ligand--clusters. Theoretical work is in progress to establish the factors governing the stability and structural changes within partly reduced ligand clusters.

CONCLUSION

The analysis of the number and relative positions of redox steps occuring within a redox series formed by transition metal complexes with redox active ligands leads to the formulation of rules describing the general pattern of behaviour of the redox series. These rules are rationalized using the MO description of the complex. The theoretical as well as experimental evidence shows that the behaviour of a redox series is closely related to the redox behaviour of free ligands and to the ionization potentials of the central metal atom. The overall behaviour of a redox series, when compared with the limiting, "well behaved", series, is an important criterion of the localization of the individual redox changes and gives a deeper insight into the electronic structure of the complexes and its change with the change of the overall number of electrons.

Based on this picture, effects of substitution on the ligands upon the $E^{o\prime}$s values or even upon the rate of electron exchange process (Ref. 21) or on the mode of operation of the charge change compensation principle (cf. Ref. 20 & 21) can be rationalized.

The general idea, connecting the formation of extensive redox series with ligand-ligand interaction has been fully supported by the new experimental material.

The rules deduced proved their usefulness in the search for missing members of a redox series or for selecting suitable members of the series as specific redox agents or catalysts of redox reactions (Ref. 1).

REFERENCES

1. A.A.Vlček, Proceedings Döbereiner Symposium, Jena, 1980 - in press.
2. A.A.Vlček and S.Záliš, Proc.XVII.ICCC, p.6, Hamburg (1976).
3. A.A.Vlček, Proc.XIV.ICCC, p.220, Toronto (1972).
4. J.L.Kahl, K.W.Hauck and K.DeArmond, J.Phys.Chem. 82, 540 (1978).
5. A.A.Vlček, Nature 189, 393 (1961).
6. T.Saji and S.Aoyagui, J.Electroanal.Chem. 63, 405 (1975).
7. A.Rusina, A.A.Vlček and S.Záliš, Z.Chem. 19, 27 (1979).
8. T.Saji and S.Aoyagui, J.Electroanal.Chem. 60, 1 (1975).
9. J.M.Rao, M.C.Hughes and D.J.Macero, Inorg.Chim.Acta 35, L369 (1979).
10. T.Saji and S.Aoyagui, J.Electroanal.Chem. 110, 329 (1980).
11. A.A.Vlček, Coord.Chem.Rev. - to be published.
12. S.Záliš and A.A.Vlček, Proc.XIX.ICCC, Vol.II., p.133, Prague (1978).
13. S.Záliš and A.A.Vlček, Inorg.Chim.Acta - in press.
14. A.A.Vlček, Z.Anorg.Allg.Chem. 304, 109 (1960).
15. S.R.Sofen, D.C.Ware, S.R.Cooper and K.N.Raymond, Inorg.Chem. 18, 234 (1979).
16. H.H.Downs, R.M.Buchanan and C.G.Pierpont, Inorg.Chem. 18, 1736 (1979).
17. T.Saji and S.Aoyagui, J.Electroanal.Chem. 58, 401 (1975).
18. N.E.Tokel-Takvoryan, R.E.Hemingway and A.J.Bard, J.Am.Chem.Soc. 95, 6582 (1973).
19. A.Bensasson, C.Salet and V.Balzani, J.Am.Chem.Soc. 98, 3722 (1976).
20. A.A.Vlček, Rev.Chim.Minérale 5, 297 (1968).
21. A.A.Vlček, Structure and Dynamics in Chemistry, Acta Universitatis Uppsaliensis, p.258, Uppsala 1958.

ELECTRONIC STRUCTURES OF SIMPLE AND BIMETALLIC ALKOXIDES OF LATER '3d' TRANSITION ELEMENTS

R. C. Mehrotra

Chemical Laboratories, University of Rajasthan, Jaipur, India

Abstract - The alkoxo group (-OR) functions as a bridging ligand between similar as well as different metal atoms giving rise to coordination oligomers and bimetallic alkoxides respectively. The syntheses of a large number of simple alkoxides of Cr(III & IV), Mn(II), Fe(II & III), Co(II), Ni(II) and Cu(II) have been described. Most of these are non-volatile and insoluble in organic solvents, except chromium tetra-tertiary-butoxide, $Cr(OBu^t)_4$ and alkoxides of iron(III), $Fe(OR)_3$, in general. These polymeric new alkoxides of later '3d' metals differ from the alkoxides of earlier transition and main group elements in the comparatively much lesser lability of their alkoxy groups in general. The sharp differences in the alcoholysis reactions of these alkoxides with ramification of the alkyl group have been correlated with the changes in the stereochemistry of the alkoxide derivatives as revealed by physico-chemical studies. Further, a large number of monomeric volatile bimetallic isopropoxides of the above elements with aluminium, having the general formula, $M[Al(OPr^i)_4]_n$, have been described for the first time. Structures of all these derivatives have been suggested on the basis of spectroscopic (visible, ultraviolet, infra-red and electron spin resonance) and magneto-chemical studies, with tetraalkoxy aluminate moieties functioning as univalent bidentate and in some cases as tridentate ligands.

INTRODUCTION

As a ligand, the alkoxo group(-OR) has been of considerable interest to the coordination chemist for the past 2-3 decades, due to its ability to form strong covalent bonds with almost all elements and also its tendency to act as a bridging group between similar as well as different metal atoms. Bridging in the former type of metal alkoxides gives rise to coordination oligomers $[M(OR)_n]_x$(Ref.1). Bimetallic alkoxides, which were described about fifty years ago by Meerwein and Bersin(Ref.2) as 'alkoxo salts' formed by the neutralisation of basic with acidic(amphoteric) alkoxides, have also been recently shown to be coordination compounds in which alkoxo groups act as bridging ligands between different metal atoms. For example, a large number of volatile and apparently covalent compounds with the general formula,

$$M\left[\begin{matrix} & R & & \\ & O & & OR \\ \swarrow & & \searrow Al & \\ & O & & OR \\ & R & & \end{matrix}\right]_n$$

(where R = Pr^i or some other alkyl group and M = Li, Na, K, Rb, Cs, Be, Mg, Ca, Sr, Ba, Zn, Al, Ga, In, Ln, Th or Sn) and $(RO)_{n-2}M[Al(OR)_4]_2$ (where M = Zr, Hf, Nb or Ta) have been synthesized and characterised as coordination compounds with tetraalkoxyaluminate $[Al(OR)_4]^-$ group functioning as a monovalent bidentate (and in some cases, tridentate) ligand (Ref.3). Many other types of such bimetallic alkoxides, e.g., $M[Zr_2(OPr^i)_9]_n$(Ref.4); $M[Ta(OR)_6]_n$(Ref.5)

and $(Pr^iO)_4Nb \leftarrow$ [bridged by two OPr^i groups] $\rightarrow Ta(OPr^i)_4$(Ref.6) have also been described.

In spite of extensive work (Ref.7) carried out during the last three decades on alkoxides (simple as well as bimetallic) of main group and earlier transition metals (mostly in their d° states), much less attention has been paid to similar derivatives of later transition metals, although physico-chemical studies (such as, electronic absorption and spin resonance spectroscopy as well as magnetic including ferromagnetic behaviour) of these could be of more revealing interest to the coordination chemist. The literature on later '3d' transition elements upto 1977 is limited to a few publications on iron(III) (Ref.8) and chromium (III & IV) (Ref.9 & 10) alkoxides and mainly magnetochemical studies on methoxides of bivalent chromium, manganese, iron, cobalt, nickel and copper (Ref.9). This has been summarised in a recent book (Ref.7) and since then, two other publications have appeared on chromium(II) (Ref.11) and manganese(II) (Ref.12) alkoxides. In addition, detailed investigations (spectroscopic, magnetic and chemical) carried out during the last 2-3 years on the alkoxides of chromium(III & IV) (Ref.13 & 14), cobalt(II) (Ref.15), nickel(II) (Ref.16 & 17) and copper(II) (Ref.15) have revealed novel features in this area of alkoxide chemistry. The purpose of this presentation is to concentrate mainly on the unpublished results obtained in the author's laboratories on the alkoxy (simple as well as bimetallic) derivatives of some later '3d' metals.

In contrast to the soluble and volatile alkoxides of earlier transition metals, almost all the alkoxides of later '3d' elements (with the exception of iron(III) alkoxides, chromium(IV) tertiary butoxide and a few derivatives of bivalent chromium(Ref.11) and manganese(Ref.12) with highly hindered moieties, e.g., 2,6-ditertiarybutyl-phenolates) are non-volatile and insoluble in organic solvents. Another distinguishing feature of these new alkoxides is their selective reactivity towards other alcohols. Notwithstanding the strength of metal-oxygen bonds, one of the most characteristic features of alkoxides of main group and earlier transition metals, known so far, has been their lability due to facile exchange of alkoxo groups (both intra- as well as inter-molecular) ; this property has, in fact, been exploited extensively in our laboratories for the synthesis of a wide variety of higher alkoxides and other interesting derivatives by treating lower alkoxides of these metals with higher alcohols and other hydroxy ligands like silanols (Ref.18), glycols (Ref.19), B-diketones (Ref.20-22), B-ketoesters (Ref.21), alkanolamines (Ref.23), oximes, hydroxylamines(Ref.24) and Schiff bases (Ref.25) as well as other reagents like organic esters (Ref.26), silyl esters (Ref.27), B-ketoamines, thiols, thio-B-diketones (Ref.21 & 28), acyl halides (Ref.29), acid amides (Ref.30) and acid anhydrides (Ref.31). For the first time, sharp variations have been noticed in the alcoholysis tendencies of Cr(III)(Ref.14), Co(II) (Ref.15) and Ni(II) (Ref.17) alkoxides and these have been correlated with their distinct stereochemical geometries with varying thermodynamic stabilities, depending on the nature of alkyl or aryl group involved. The reactions of these new alkoxides have also been investigated with a number of hydroxy reagents (alkanolamines, B-diketones and carboxylic acids).

ALKOXIDES OF CHROMIUM

Methoxide and ethoxide of the most common oxidation state(III) of chromium were obtained by a novel method involving ultraviolet irradiation of tricarbonylarenechromium (Ref.9). Primary alkoxides of chromium(III) have been synthesised recently in our laboratories by the simple reactions of $CrCl_3.3THF$ adduct (which is soluble in organic solvents) with lithium alkoxides:

$$CrCl_3.3THF + 3LiOR \xrightarrow[C_6H_6]{ROH} Cr(OR)_3\downarrow + 3LiCl$$

$$(R = Me, Et\ or\ Bu^n)$$

$Cr(OPr^i)_3$ and $Cr(OBu^t)_3$ could not be prepared by this method ; instead, some hydrolysed products were obtained.

All the primary alkoxides of chromium are pale green polymeric solids insoluble in organic solvents. These do not undergo alcoholysis or trans-esterification reactions even under forcing conditions and hence, $Cr(OPr^i)_3$ or $Cr(OBu^t)_3$ could not be synthesised even through these routes. Chromium(III) phenoxide could, however, be obtained by refluxing $Cr(OEt)_3$ with excess phenol in benzene, removing the ethanol produced azeotropically with the solvent. This $Cr(OPh)_3$ was found to undergo reaction with excess isopropanol (but not with tertiary butanol) and on repeating the treatment a number of times, almost pure $Cr(OPr^i)_3$ could be obtained as a green insoluble solid. It may be of some interest that we were finally successful in synthesising $Cr(OBu^t)_3$ by an alternative simpler route, i.e., the reaction of $CrCl_3.3THF$ with three moles of $LiOBu^t$ (in the absence of excess Bu^tOH) in THF itself:

$$CrCl_3.3THF + 3LiOBu^t \xrightarrow{THF} Cr(OBu^t)_3\downarrow + 3LiCl$$

$Cr(OBu^t)_3$, obtained as a soluble blue product in the above reaction, gave volatile $Cr(OBu^t)_4$, which could be distilled as a blue liquid under reduced pressure. The spectrum of this liquid shows bands at 15,700 cm^{-1} , 13,870 cm^{-1} and a shoulder at 25,300 cm^{-1}, which can be understood on the basis of a tetrahedral environment for chromium in this compound (Ref.10). The special stability of the oxidation state(IV) for chromium in $Cr(OBu^t)_4$ also appears to be due to two singly occupied lower e_g shells.

Electronic spectra of chromium(III) alkoxides have been measured in the visible range in nujol mulls. The spectra are very similar and may be interpreted (Table 1) on the basis of an octahedral environment (Ref.9) for chromium(III):

TABLE 1. Electronic visible spectra of chromium(III) alkoxides

Product	$^4A_{2g} \longrightarrow {}^4T_{2g}$ (10Dq)	$^4A_{2g} \longrightarrow {}^4T_{1g}$	B
$Cr(OMe)_3^a$	17,610 cm^{-1}	24,150 cm^{-1}	612 cm^{-1}
$Cr(OEt)_3^a$	17,000 cm^{-1}	23,470 cm^{-1}	600 cm^{-1}
$Cr(OBu^n)_3^a$	17,060 cm^{-1}	23,700 cm^{-1}	610 cm^{-1}
$Cr(OPh)_3$	16,900 cm^{-1}	23,920 cm^{-1}	615 cm^{-1}
$Cr(OMe)_3^b$	17,240 cm^{-1}	23,800 cm^{-1}	609 cm^{-1}
$Cr(OEt)_3^b$	16,370 cm^{-1}	23,470 cm^{-1}	654 cm^{-1}
$Cr(OPr^i)_3^b$	15,880 cm^{-1}	22,940 cm^{-1}	720 cm^{-1}
$Cr(OMe)_3^c$	17,180 cm^{-1}	24,150 cm^{-1}	613 cm^{-1}
$Cr(OPr^i)_3^c$	16,180 cm^{-1}	23,280 cm^{-1}	728 cm^{-1}

a) Prepared from LiOR method ; b) Prepared from $Cr(OPh)_3$;
c) Prepared from $Cr(OBu^t)_4$.

The special inertness of Cr(III) alkoxides to alcoholysis reactions can be understood in the light of the stability of octahedral chromium(III), in which each of the three low energy t_{2g} orbitals are occupied singly ; the

Jahn-Teller effect does not appear to be effectively operative in disturbing the regularity of this octahedral species. Cr(III) derivatives in octahedral environment, therefore, do not tend to undergo substitution reactions both by the dissociative (S_N1) as well as associative (S_N2) mechanisms.

Although Cr(III) primary alkoxides do not undergo alcoholysis reactions, $Cr(OPr^i)_3$ could be converted into $Cr(OMe)_3$ or $Cr(OEt)_3$ by refluxing with excess MeOH or EtOH. $Cr(OPr^i)_3$ does not, however, undergo alcoholysis reactions with tertiary or other secondary alcohols even under forcing conditions. $Cr(OBu^t)_4$ on treatment with MeOH, EtOH or Pr^iOH readily gave the corresponding Cr(III) alkoxides, which is easily understood on the basis of greater stability of the octahedral species.

In view of the general inertness of primary alkoxides of chromium(III), a more detailed study of their substitution reactions was carried out. Although these are inert to other alcohols, yet they undergo interchange with chelating ligands like ethanolamine, B-diketones and carboxylic acids. A very wide variety of derivatives synthesised, in such reactions, have been characterised by their detailed spectral and magnetochemical studies (Ref.14):

$$Cr(OEt)_3 + x\ HOCH_2CH_2NH_2 \xrightarrow{\text{benzene}} Cr(OEt)_{3-x}(OCH_2CH_2NH_2)_x + x\ EtOH\uparrow$$

(where x = 1, 2 or 3)

(N.B. The above reactions are slow and yield products which are insoluble in organic solvents).

$$Cr(OR)_3 + x\ \text{B-dkh} \xrightarrow{\text{benzene}} Cr(OR)_{3-x}(\text{B-dk})_x + x\ ROH\uparrow$$

(where R = Me or Et ; B-dkH = acetylacetone(acacH), benzoylacetone(bzacH), or 2-theonyltrifluoroacetone(ttaH) and x = 1, 2 or 3).

(N.B. These reactions with B-diketones are slow in the first stage, but become more facile with the formation of soluble derivatives. Products $Cr(OR)_2$(B-dk) are polymeric and Cr(OR)$(\text{B-dk})_2$ are dimeric with chromium atoms in octahedral environment).

$$Cr(OR)_{3-x}(\text{B-dk})_x + (3-x)\ \text{B-dk'H} \longrightarrow Cr(\text{B-dk'})_{3-x}(\text{B-dk})_x + (3-x)ROH$$

(N.B. In spite of their solubility, these mixed ethoxide B-diketonates also do not undergo alcoholysis with higher alcohols, but react readily with other chelating B-diketone ligands).

Reactions of chromium alkoxides with carboxylic acids can be represented by the following equation:

$$Cr(OR)_3 + x\ R'COOH \longrightarrow Cr(OR)_{3-x}(OOCR')_x + x\ ROH\uparrow$$

(where R = CH_3 or C_2H_5 and R' = C_7H_{15}, $C_{13}H_{27}$, $C_{15}H_{31}$ or $C_{21}H_{43}$)

(N.B. Reactions and products are similar to those with B-diketones ; carboxylate moieties behave as bidentate ligands. Products can be recrystallized from benzene).

Highly oxygen sensitive (pyrophoric) alkoxides of chromium(II) have been recently reported (Ref.11) by alcoholysis of $Cr[N(SiMe_3)_2]_2.2LL'$, where L,L' = Ether, THF, or Py. All the normal Cr(II) alkoxides (ethoxide to pentyloxide) are yellow/orange except the methoxide which is purple ; all secondary alkoxides are purple/violet and all the tertiary alkoxides are blue derivatives. Solubility of these alkoxides is influenced strongly by drying conditions. Sterically hindered alkoxides, e.g., chromium(II)2,6-di-tertiary-butylphenoxide, $Cr(OC_6H_3Bu^t_2)_2.(THF)_2$, are less associated, depict higher solubility in general and tend to form crystalline adducts with donor ligands.

ALKOXIDES OF COBALT(II), NICKEL(II) AND COPPER(II)

Alkoxides of these metals have been prepared by the following reactions:

$$CoCl_2 + 2LiOR \xrightarrow[C_6H_6]{ROH} \underset{\text{(purple)}}{Co(OR)_2} \downarrow + 2LiCl$$

(where R = Me, Et, or Pr^i).

(N.B. $Co(OBu^t)_2$ could not be prepared by this method).

$$NiCl_2 + 2LiOR \xrightarrow[\text{1,4-dioxane}]{\text{ROH or}} Ni(OR)_2 \downarrow + 2LiCl$$

(where R = Me, Et, Pr^n, Bu^n, Hx^n, Pr^i, Bu^s, Bu^t, Am^t or Hex^t)

(N.B. Adducts $NiCl_2.ROH$ formed by adding $NiCl_2$ to ROH are soluble in cases of primary alcohols, but insoluble in secondary or tertiary alcohols. The reactions with LiOR in the latter two cases are facilitated by addition of a little pyridine due to its solubilising effect).

$$CuCl_2 + 2LiOR \xrightarrow{ROH} Cu(OR)_2 \downarrow + 2LiCl$$

(where R = Me, Et, Pr^i or Bu^t)

Out of the alkoxides of the above three metals, only Cu(II) alkoxides undergo facile alcohol interchange reactions similar to alkoxides of earlier transition metals:

$$Cu(OR)_2 + \underset{\text{(excess)}}{2R'OH} \xrightarrow{\text{benzene}} Cu(OR')_2\downarrow + 2ROH$$

(where R = Me, Et or Bu^n and R' = Pr^i, Bu^s, Bu^t or Am^t)

Primary alkoxides of Co(II) and Ni(II), on the other hand, resemble those of Cr(III) in not undergoing interchange even under forcing conditions. Branched alkoxides of these metals, however, undergo facile interchange with primary alcohols even at the room temperature. Extensive work (Ref.16 & 17) has been carried out in our laboratories since 1977 on the exchange reactions of nickel alkoxides with alkanolamines, B-diketones and carboxylic acids, with results similar to those described above for chromium(III) alkoxides.

Visible spectra of all the above alkoxides have been recorded in Nujol mulls and throw light on their stereochemistry. Co(II) alkoxides(purple in colour) show a multiple band in the range, $18235 \pm 285\ cm^{-1}$ and a shoulder on the higher frequency side in the range, $20170 \pm 450\ cm^{-1}$. These can be explained on the basis of the ν_3 transition, $^4T_{1g} \longrightarrow {}^4T_{1g}(P)$ which is characteristic for octahedral geometry of Co(II) ; these spectra are similar to those reported for $Co(OMe)_2$ by Adams and coworkers (Ref.8).

Spectra of Ni(II) primary alkoxides (light green in colour) are characteristic of octahedral derivatives, which exhibit three well defined spin-allowed bands at $8750 \pm 250\ cm^{-1}$ $[\nu_1\ ;\ ^3A_{2g} \longrightarrow {}^3T_{2g}]$; $14810 \pm 115\ cm^{-1}$ $[\nu_2\ ;\ ^3A_{2g} \longrightarrow {}^3T_{1g}(F)]$ & $24980 \pm 125\ cm^{-1}$ $[\nu_3\ ;\ ^3A_{2g} \longrightarrow {}^3T_{1g}(P)]$. The spectra of secondary and tertiary alkoxides (blue in colour) of Ni(II) clearly indicate a tetrahedral geometry with well defined spin-allowed transitions at $7580 \pm 100\ cm^{-1}$ $[\nu_2\ ;\ ^3T_1 \longrightarrow {}^3A_2]$ and $15850 \pm 70\ cm^{-1}$ $[\nu_3\ ;\ ^3T_1 \longrightarrow {}^3T_1(P)]$.

The magnetic moments of the primary alkoxides of nickel(II) fall in the range of 3.45 ± 0.04 B.M. and those secondary as well as tertiary alkoxides are found in the range of 3.65 ± 0.05 B.M. at the room temperature ; these observations are in accord with their octahedral and tetrahedral configurations respectively.

TABLE 2. Electronic spectra*, g values (e.s.r.) and magnetic moments of primary alkoxides of nickel(II).

Product	$^3A_{2g} \rightarrow {}^3T_{2g}$ ($10D_q$)	$^3A_{2g} \rightarrow {}^3T_{1g}(F)$ (ν_2)	$^3A_{2g} \rightarrow {}^3T_{1g}(P)$ (ν_3)	B	β	μ_{eff} (B.M.)	g
$Ni(OMe)_2$	8500	14700	25100	900	0.86	3.49	2.22
$Ni(OEt)_2$	8770	14490	25280	897	0.86	3.43	2.13
$Ni(OPr^n)_2$	9010	14600	24245	788	0.76	-	2.24
$Ni(OBu^n)_2$	9250	14750	23855	724	0.70	3.43	2.24
$Ni(OHex^n)_2$	9250	14925	24585	784	0.75	-	2.14
$Ni(OOct^n)_2$	9100	14815	24845	824	0.79	-	2.27

* Transitions and B in cm^{-1}

TABLE 3. Electronic spectra*, g values (e.s.r.) and magnetic moments of secondary and tertiary alkoxides of nickel(II).

Product	^1G	$^3T_1 \rightarrow {}^3T_1(P)$ (ν_3)	$^3T \rightarrow {}^3A_2$ (ν_2)	D_q	B	β	μ_{eff} (B.M.)	g
$Ni(OPr^i)_2$	22420 sh, 18657, 17065	15900	7550	409	870	0.84	3.65	2.22
$Ni(OBu^s)_2$	22472 sh, 18657, 17033	15790	7480	384	823	0.79	3.70	2.25
$Ni(OBu^t)_2$	22625 sh, 18618, 17007	15920	7680	395	827	0.79	3.61	2.23
$Ni(OAm^t)_2$	22522 sh, 18485, 16950	15850	7520	390	833	0.80	3.67	2.23

* Transitions, D_q and B in cm^{-1}

The ligand field(D_q) and Racah (B) parameters for the tetrahedral secondary and tertiary alkoxides of nickel (Table 3) were calculated by the method of Underhill and Billing (Ref.32). As expected, the magnitude of 10 D_q values obtained in all the cases of tetrahedral complexes are about four-ninth of the 10 D_q values observed (Table 2) for the corresponding octahedral compounds. The values of B in both octahedral and tetrahedral derivatives are found to be reduced below the free ion value (1041 cm^{-1}) showing an appreciable covalent character of metal-ligand bonds in these alkoxide derivatives.

At the room temperature, all octahedral as well as tetrahedral nickel(II) alkoxides give one signal in their electron spin resonance spectra in the polycrystalline state from which Lande splitting factors (g values) have been calculated to lie in the range, 2.13-2.27 (Table 2 & 3), indicating again a strong covalent character of the metal-ligand bonds in these complexes.

It may be interesting to record that the electronic spectra (Table 4) of a large number of allied derivatives of nickel(II), prepared by reactions represented for sake of brevity by the following equations, indicate an octahedral environment for nickel in all these cases (including those with ramified alkoxy ligands):

$$NiCl_2 + x\ ROH \xrightarrow{reflux} NiCl_2.x\ ROH \xrightarrow{Heat} NiCl_2.ROH$$

(where R = CH_3, C_2H_5, $C_3H_7^n$, $C_4H_9^n$, $C_6H_{13}^n$ and $C_8H_{17}^n$ and x = 1-4 at room temperature).

$$NiCl_2.MeOH + R'OH \longrightarrow NiCl_2.R'OH + MeOH\uparrow$$

(where R' = $C_3H_7^i$, $C_4H_9^t$ and $C_5H_{11}^t$; $NiCl_2$ does not dissolve or react with secondary and tertiary alcohols and the adducts could be prepared in these cases by alcohol interchange reactions only).

$$NiCl_2 + NaOR \xrightarrow{ROH} Ni(OR)Cl + NaCl\downarrow$$

$$Ni(OR)Cl + R'OH \xrightarrow{C_6H_6} Ni(OR')Cl + ROH\uparrow$$

(where R and R' = CH_3, C_2H_5, $C_3H_7^i$, $C_4H_9^n$ and $C_6H_{13}^n$).

$$Ni(OR)_2 + HOCH_2CH_2NH_2 \longrightarrow Ni(OR)(OCH_2CH_2NH_2) + ROH\uparrow$$

$$Ni(OR)_2 + 2HOCH_2CH_2NH_2 \longrightarrow Ni(OCH_2CH_2NH_2)_2 + 2ROH\uparrow$$

(where R = CH_3 and $C_3H_7^i$)

$$Ni(OR)_2 + HO\underset{\substack{|\\R'}}{C} = CHCOR'' \longrightarrow (RO)Ni(O\underset{\substack{|\\R'}}{C} = CHCOR'') + ROH\uparrow$$

$$(RO)Ni(O\underset{\substack{|\\R'}}{C}=CHCOR'') + HO\underset{\substack{|\\R'}}{C}=CHCOR'' \longrightarrow Ni(O\underset{\substack{|\\R'}}{C}=CHCOR'')_2 + ROH\uparrow$$

(where R = CH_3 and $C_3H_7^i$; R', R" = CH_3, C_6H_5, CF_3 and C_4H_3S).

$$Ni(OR)_2 + R'COOH \longrightarrow Ni(OR)(OOCR') + ROH\uparrow$$

$$Ni(OR)_2 + 2R'COOH \longrightarrow Ni(OOCR')_2 + 2ROH\uparrow$$

(where R = CH_3 and $C_3H_7^i$; R' = $C_{13}H_{27}$, $C_{15}H_{31}$ and $C_{17}H_{35}$).

A few mixed B-diketonates and carboxylates of nickel(II) could also be synthesised by the following types of reactions:

$$Ni(OMe)(B\text{-}dk) + H\ B'\text{-}dk \xrightarrow{Benzene} Ni(B\text{-}dk)(B'\text{-}dk) + MeOH\uparrow$$

$$Ni(OOC.CH_3)_2 + RCOOH \xrightarrow{Toluene} Ni(OOC.CH_3)(OOC.R) + CH_3COOH\uparrow$$

TABLE 4. Electronic spectra of a few other typical nickel(II) derivatives.

Derivative	${}^3A_{2g} \rightarrow {}^3T_{2g}$ (ν_1; $10D_q$)	${}^3A_{2g} \rightarrow {}^3T_{1g}(F)$ (ν_2)	${}^3A_{2g} \rightarrow {}^3T_{1g}(P)$ (ν_3)	B	β
$NiCl_2.MeOH$	7937	13333	22400	795	0.74
$NiCl_2.Pr^iOH$	7924	12903	21978	740	0.68
$NiCl_2.Am^tOH$	7520	12195	21740	758	0.70
Ni(OMe)Cl*	7900	12900	22100	753	0.72
Ni(OMe)Cl.MeOH*	8100	13300	24000	866	0.83
Ni(OEt)Cl*	8000	13200	23610	854	0.82
$Ni(OPr^i)Cl$*	8200	13100	22500	733	0.70
$Ni(OMe)(OCH_2CH_2NH_2)$@	9090	14390	23065	680	0.63
$Ni(OPr^i)(OCH_2CH_2NH_2)$@	9090	14925	25562	881	0.82
$Ni(OCH_2CH_2NH_2)_2$@	9615	14925	23516	640	0.59
Ni(OMe)(acac)°	8930	15528	24904	909	0.84
$Ni(OPr^i)(acac)$°°	8970	14706	23098	726	0.67
$Ni(OBu^t)(acac)$°°	9260	14860	24155	749	0.69
$Ni(acac)_2$°°	8800	15267	25210	938	0.87
$Ni(OMe)(OOC.C_{13}H_{27})$$	8585	14620	24272	876	0.84
$Ni(OPr^i)(OOC.C_{13}H_{27})$$	8695	14663	24155	849	0.81
$Ni(OBu^t)(OOC.C_{13}H_{27})$$	8695	14577	23923	828	0.79
$Ni(OOC.C_{13}H_{27})_2$$	8930	15015	23520	784	0.75

* Soluble in parent alcohols and undergo alcoholysis reactions

@ Insoluble in organic solvents and do not undergo alcoholysis reactions

° Soluble in organic solvents in which it shows tetrameric association

°° Soluble in organic solvents in which they show trimeric association

$ Soluble in organic solvents ; primary alkoxy derivatives do not undergo alcoholysis but secondary and tertiary alkoxy derivatives undergo alcoholysis.

Nickel alkoxides undergo insertion reactions (Ref.16) also with substrates like isocyanates and these reactions can be represented as :

$$Ni(OR)_2 + n\ R'NCO \longrightarrow (RO)_{2-n}\ Ni[N(R')COOR]_n$$

(where R = Me or Pr^i ; R' = Ph or Naph ; n = 1 or 2).

All these reactions are exothermic in benzene and their completion was indicated by the disappearance of band at ~2250 cm^{-1} (due to -N=C=O). The appearance of an intense band ~1700 cm^{-1} (due to C=O) in the addition products suggests that the insertion has occurred at the C=N site.

The spectra of the branched green alkoxides of copper, viz., $Cu(OPr^i)_2$, $Cu(OBu^s)_2$, $Cu(OBu^t)_2$ and $Cu(OAm^t)_2$ are characterised by broad absorptions in the visible range around 15200 ± 635 cm^{-1} which generally tail deep into the near infra-red region. This band can be assigned as a $^2E_g \longrightarrow {}^2T_{2g}$ transition, which is characteristic of Cu^{2+} in six coordinate tetragonal geometry. In addition to a sharper absorption in this region at 15500 ± 70 cm^{-1}, another band appears around 19100 ± 300 cm^{-1} in the spectra of blue primary alkoxides, $Cu(OMe)_2$, $Cu(OEt)_2$ and $Cu(OBu^n)_2$ which indicates a distorted octahedral environment around copper(II) in these derivatives.

Magnetic susceptibilities of copper alkoxides show a lowering in the value with decrease in temperature [$Cu(OAm^t)_2$: 1.83 at 297° to 1.37 at 87°K ; $Cu(OPr^i)_2$: 1.50 at 297° to 0.98 at 88°K and $Cu(OBu^n)_2$: 1.18 at 299° to 0.64 at 88°K], which suggests antiferromagnetic exchange interaction between copper pairs in all these alkoxides, based on infinite chains (Ref.33) of methoxy bridged copper atoms rather than a layer type structure suggested earlier (Ref.34). The values of exchange coupling constants(j) in these alkoxides have been calculated on the basis of Ising theory(Ref.35) as 129, 81 and 43 cm^{-1} respectively for $Cu(OBu^n)_2$, $Cu(OPr^i)_2$ and $Cu(OAm^t)_2$.

BIMETALLIC ALKOXIDES OF CHROMIUM(III), MANGANESE(II), IRON(II & III), COBALT(II), NICKEL(II) & COPPER(II) WITH ALUMINIUM.

Bimetallic isopropoxides of the above elements with aluminium have been prepared (Ref.15 & 36) by the following reactions:

$$MCl_n + n[KAl(OPr^i)_4] \xrightarrow{Pr^iOH} M[Al(OPr^i)_4]_n + n\ KCl\downarrow$$

(where n = 3 for Fe(III) and n = 2 for Mn(II), Fe(II), Co(II) Ni(II) and Cu(II) .

In view of the insolubility of $CrCl_3$ in organic solvents, its adduct $CrCl_3.3THF$ was used as a starting material for a similar preparation of $Cr[Al(OPr^i)_4]_3$. All these reactions are exothermic. The products are coloured liquids/solids which are miscible/soluble in organic solvents and can be purified by distillation under reduced pressure. All of these depict monomeric behaviour in refluxing benzene.

These bimetallic isopropoxides react quantitatively with excess of ethanol, 2,2,2-trifluoroethanol and normal butanol to give the corresponding derivatives which are also volatile and soluble in organic solvents:

$$M[Al(OPr^i)_4]_n + 4n\ ROH \xrightarrow[benzene]{} M[Al(OR)_4]_n + 4n\ Pr^iOH\uparrow$$

The products $M[Al(OMe)_4]_n$, obtained with excess methanol, however, are insoluble and non-volatile. The reactions with methanol were carried out in the case of $Cr[Al(OPr^i)_4]_3$ in 3:1 and 6:1 molar ratios also, yielding respectively $Cr[Al(OPr^i)_3(OMe)]_3$ and $Cr[Al(OPr^i)_2(OMe)_2]_3$; the former is soluble whereas the latter is only sparingly soluble in benzene.

Exchange reactionswith excess tertiary alcohols, however, yielded interesting end products of the following types, $M[Al(OPr^i)(OBu^t)_3]_2$, $M[Al(OPr^i)_2(OAm^t)_2]_2$, $M[Al(OPr^i)_2(OBu^t)_2]_3$ and $M[Al(OPr^i)_2(OAm^t)_2]_3$. All these bimetallic derivatives could also be purified, unchanged by distillation under reduced pressure and showed monomeric behaviour in refluxing benzene.

Isopropoxide acetylacetonate products, $M[Al(OPr^i)_{4-x}(acac)_x]_{3 \text{ or } 2}$ (where x=1 or 2), obtained by treating the bimetallic isopropoxide with stoichiometric quantities of acetylacetone have again been shown to be volatile monomeric products. Products of the types, $M[Al(OPr^i)_{4-x}(acac)_x]_{3 \text{ or } 2}$ (where x = 3 or 4) tended to dissociate into metal isopropoxide or acetylacetonate and aluminium acetylacetonate.

The chemical reactions as well as spectroscopic and magnetic properties of the above interesting derivatives appear to indicate that most of these derivatives have structure(I) similar to those suggested earlier (Ref.3, 15, 37 & 38), but the data for a few cobalt, nickel and copper derivatives appear to be more easily understood on the basis of a structure of the type II :

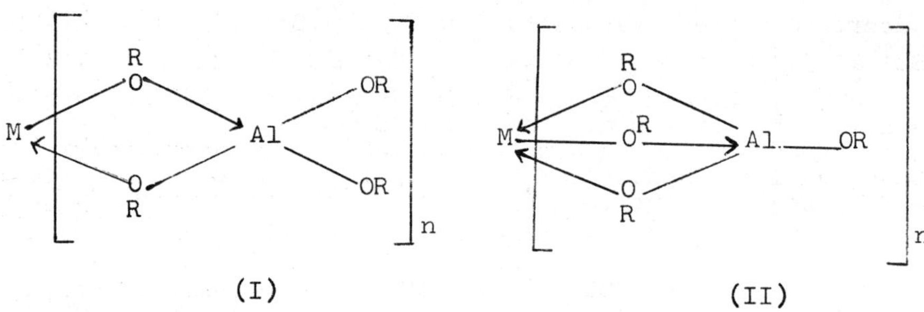

(I) (II)

A similar conclusion has been reported by Stumpp and Hillerbrand for products, $M[Al(OR)_4]_2$ (M = Co, Ni or Cu ; R = CH_3, C_2H_5, $C_3H_7{}^n$ or $C_4H_9{}^n$) in a later publication (Ref.39).

The above tendency to attain octahedral geometry, for example, by $Ni[Al(OR)_4]_2$ derivatives, appears to increase (Ref.15) as the alkoxy groups become smaller and less ramified. According to detailed investigations carried out by Singh (Ref.15) in our laboratories, $Ni[Al(OMe)_4]_2$ shows an electronic spectrum fully characteristic of octahedral geometry for nickel. $Ni[Al(OEt)_4]_2$ and $Ni[Al(OPr^i)_4]_2$, on the other hand, show increasing proportions of tetrahedral nickel species in equilibrium with octahedral forms. The effects of steric factors on this type of equilibrium can be discerned in a finer difference, i.e., the spectrum of $Ni[Al(OEt)_4]_2$ in ethanol shows a complete shift to octahedral species whereas for $Ni[Al(OPr^i)_4]_2$ in isopropanol, this type of shift is only partial and a stronger donor molecule like pyridine only is able to shift the same fully to the octahedral form.

Detailed physico-chemical measurements(volatility, molecular association, electronic and e.s.r.spectra as well as magnetic moments at varying temperatures) have been carried out on all the bimetallic alkoxides and products derived from them. For brevity, only a few illustrative physical data for some typical bimetallic alkoxides of later '3d' transition metals with aluminium and their mixed derivatives are given in Table 5. Investigations are now being extended to the bimetallic systems consisting of the above transition elements with new ligands like $[Ga(OR)_4]^-$; $[Zr_2(OPr^i)_9]^-$; $[Hf_2(OPr^i)_9]^-$; $[Nb(OR)_6]^-$ and $[Ta(OR)_6]^-$.

TABLE 5. Bimetallic alkoxides and allied derivatives of later '3d' transition metals.

Compound	Nature	Volatility (-°C/.. mm)	M.W. Found (Calc.)	μ_{eff} (B.M./°K)	D_q (cm^{-1})
$Cr[Al(OPr^i)_4]_3$	Green viscous liquid	190/0.6	838 (842)	3.90/100 3.92/297	1527
$Mn[Al(OPr^i)_4]_2$	Brown viscous liquid	145/0.6	607 (582)	5.95/88 5.90/297	-
$Fe[Al(OPr^i)_4]_3$	Brown viscous liquid	130/0.8	1003 (846)	5.06/89 5.39/296	-
$Fe[Al(OPr^i)_4]_2$	Brown semi-solid	125/0.8	605 (582)	4.53/87 5.06/297	-
$Co[Al(OPr^i)_4]_2$	Purple liquid	140/0.6	629 (586)	4.62/92 4.39/297	873
$Ni[Al(OPr^i)_4]_2$	Pink liquid	120/0.6	570 (585)	3.29/90 3.39/294	823(film) 895(Pr^iOH) 912(pyridine)
$Cu[Al(OPr^i)_4]_2$	Greenish blue liquid	135/0.6	604 (593)	1.22/87 1.64/297	1380
$Cr[Al(OPr^i)_3(OMe)]_3$	Light green solid	215/0.8	-	3.84/300	1572
$Cr[Al(OPr^i)_2(OMe)_2]_3$	Green solid	255/0.8*	-	3.86/300	1582
$Cr[Al(OEt)_4]_3$	Green solid	235/0.8*	-	3.86/300	1577
$Cr[Al(OCH_2CF_3)_4]_3$	Brown viscous liquid	120/0.8*	1353 (1321)	3.86/300	1520
$Cr[Al(OPr^i)_3(acac)]_3$	Green pasty solid	140/0.8	967 (962)	3.82/300	1675
$Cr[Al(OPr^i)_2(acac)_2]_3$	Green solid	180/0.8*	1233 (1082)	3.83/300	1692
$Fe[Al(OPr^i)_2(OAm^t)_2]_3$	Brown solid	270/0.6*	976 (1014)	-	-
$Ni[Al(OPr^i)(OBu^t)_3]_2$	Purple solid	140/0.6*	691 (670)	3.14/88 3.47/300	736
$Ni[Al(OPr^i)_2(acac)_2]_2$	Brown pinkish solid	240/0.6*	708 (745)	3.28/300	769
$Cu[Al(OCH_2CF_3)_4]_2$	Blue semi-solid	115/0.5	-	1.72/300	1602
$Cu[Al(OPr^i)(OBu^t)_3]_2$	Green solid	150/0.5*	-	1.74/300	1230 (benzene) 1490 (Nujol)

* Sublimed

The author is grateful to a large number of colleagues, especially Drs.Mohini Arora, M.M.Agarwal, P.N.Kapoor, Sarla Govil, A.K.Rai, N.C.Jain, C.K.Sharma, B.P.Baranwal, K.N.Mahendra, G.K.Parashar and Jagvir Singh for their dedicated research efforts in our research schools at the University of Rajasthan, Jaipur and University of Delhi, Delhi.

REFERENCES

1. D.C.Bradley, Nature 182, 1211 (1958) ; Progress in Inorganic Chemistry, 2, 303-361, Interscience, New York (1960).

2. H.Meerwein and T.Bersin, Ann. 476, 113-150 (1929).

3. R.C.Mehrotra and coworkers, Chem. Comm. 469-470 (1968) ; Inorg. Chim. Acta (Reviews) 5, 127-136 (1972) ; Inorg. Chem. 11, 2170-2174 (1972) ; Chem. Comm. 189 (1972) ; Synth. Inorg. Metal-Org. Chem.3,407-414 (1973) ; 5, 267-277 (1975) ; Inorg. Chim. Acta 15, 43-46 (1975) ; 29, 131-136 (1978) ; J. Ind. Chem. Soc. 54, 109-116 (1977) ; J.Inorg.Nucl.Chem. 40, 349-351 (1978).

4. R.C.Mehrotra and coworkers, J. Chem. Soc. (A), 1026-1027 (1967) ; Dalton-Trans 1203-1204 (1972) ; Coord. Chem. Rev. 14, 1-27 (1974) ; Aust. J. Chem. 28, 2125-2128 (1975) ; Ind. J. Chem. 14A, 878-879 (1976).

5. R.C.Mehrotra and coworkers, J. Chem. Soc. (A), 2673-2676 (1968) ; Synth. React. Inorg. Metal-Org.Chem. 6, 251-263 (1976).

6. L.G.Hubert-Pfalzgrof and J.G.Reiss, Inorg. Chem. 14, 2854-2856 (1975).

7. D.C.Bradley, R.C.Mehrotra and D.P.Gaur, Metal Alkoxides, Academic Press, London(1978) and references therein.

8. D.C.Bradley and coworkers, J.Chem.Soc. 126-129 ; 4153-4155 & 4647-4651 (1958) ; R.W.Adams and coworkers ; Aust.J.Chem. 19, 363-371 (1966) ; R.C.Mehrotra and P.P.Sharma, Ind. J. Chem. 5, 456-457 (1967) ; J. Ind. Chem. Soc. 45, 736-738 (1968) ; 46, 123-129 (1969).

9. R.W.Adams, et.al. Aust. J. Chem. 19, 207-210 (1966) ; D.A.Brown, et.al. J. Chem. Soc. (A) 1563-1568 (1968).

10. D.C.Bradley, et.al. J. Chem. Soc. (A) 772-776 (1971).

11. B.Horvath and E.G.Horvath, private communication.

12. B.Horvath, R.Moseler and E.G.Horvath, Z.anorg.allg.chem. 449, 41-45 (1979).

13. R.C.Mehrotra and coworkers, Inorg.Chim.Acta Letters 25,L5-L6 (1977) ; Trans. Met. Chem. 2, 161-164 (1977) ; 3, 130-133 (1978) ; Synth.React. Inorg. Metal-Org. Chem. 9, 213-222 (1979).

14. K.N.Mahendra, Synthesis and Physico-chemical Studies of some Organic Derivatives of Chromium(III), Ph.D. Thesis, Univ. of Delhi, India (1979).

15. J.Singh, Synthesis and Physico-chemical Studies of Simple and Bimetallic Alkoxides of a few later '3d' Transition Metals, Ph.D. Thesis, Univ. of Delhi, India (1980).

16. R.C.Mehrotra and coworkers, Ind. J. Chem. 15A, 458-459 (1977) ; 17A 77-78 (1979) ; Trans. Met. Chem. 2, 204-207 (1977) ; 3, 220-224 (1978) ; Z.anorg. allg. chem. 443, 284-288 (1979) ; Z.Naturforsch 34B, 459-473 (1979).

17. B.P.Baranwal, Synthesis and Physico-chemical Studies of some Organic Derivatives of Nickel(II), Ph.D. Thesis, Univ. of Delhi, India (1979).

18. D.C.Bradley and coworkers, J.Chem.Soc. 3404-3411 (1959) ; 204-207 (1963).

19. R.C.Mehrotra and coworkers, J.Chem.Soc. 4045-4047 (1961) ; 1032-1034 & 3819-3821 (1962) ; J.Ind.Chem.Soc. 39, 203-207 ; 635-640 (1962) ; Indian J. Chem. 5, 444-447 (1967) ; J.Chem.Soc. 2804-2806 (1963) ; J.Organometal. Chem. 4, 145-150 (1965) ; 6, 425-427 (1966) & 47, 95-102 (1973).

20. R.C.Mehrotra, J. Ind. Chem. Soc. 55, 1-6 (1978).
21. R.C.Mehrotra, R.Bohra and D.P.Gaur, Metal B-Diketonates and Allied Derivatives, Academic Press, London (1978) and references therein.
22. V.K.Jain, R.Bohra and R.C.Mehrotra, Synth. React. Inorg. Metal-Org. Chem. 9, 491-502 (1979) ; J.Organometal.Chem. 184, 57-62 (1980).
23. R.C.Mehrotra and coworkers, J.Organometal.Chem. 65, 195-204 (1974) ; Z.anorg.allg.chem. 403, 337-339 (1974).
24. R.C.Mehrotra, A.Singh, A.K.Rai and R.Bohra, Inorg.Chim.Acta(Reviews) 13, 91-103 (1975).
25. R.C.Mehrotra, M.Agrawal and J.P.Tandon, Ind.J.Chem. 18A, 151-156 (1979).
26. R.C.Mehrotra, J.Amer.Chem.Soc. 76, 2266-2267 (1954).
27. J.M.Batwara and R.C.Mehrotra, J.Inorg.Nucl.Chem. 32, 411-415 (1970).
28. V.K.Jain, R.Bohra and R.C.Mehrotra, Inorg.Chim. Acta 44, L265-L267 (1980).
29. R.C.Mehrotra and P.N.Kapoor, J.Less Common Metals 10, 348-353 (1966).
30. K.K.Sharma, S.K.Mehrotra and R.C.Mehrotra, J.Organometal.Chem. 142, 166-169 (1977).
31. R.C.Mehrotra, J.Friedrich Schiller Univ. 14, 171-180 (1965).
32. A.E.Underhill and D.E.Billing, Nature 210, 834 (1966).
33. R.W.Adams, et.al. Aust.J.Chem. 20, 2351-2356 (1967).
34. C.H.Brubacker and M.Wicholas, J.Inorg.Nucl.Chem. 27, 59-62 (1965).
35. B.H.McCoy and T.T.Wu. The two Dimentional Ising Model, Harvard Univ. Press, Cambridge, Mass. (1973).
36. J.V.Singh, N.C.Jain and R.C.Mehrotra, Synth. React. Inorg. Metal-Org. Chem. 9, 79-88 (1979).
37. R.C.Mehrotra, P.N.Kapoor and J.M.Batwara, Coord. Chem. Rev. 31, 67-91 (1980).
38. A.I.Yanovskii, N.G.Bokii, Yu. T. Struchkov and B.L.Tarnopol'skii, J. Inorg. Nucl. Chem. 41, 5-11 (1978).
39. E.Stumpp and U.Hillebrand, Z. Naturforsch, 34b, 262-265 (1979).

THE REACTIVITY OF SOME SIMPLE HYDROCARBON LIGANDS ATTACHED TO TRANSITION METALS

M. L. H. Green

Inorganic Chemistry Department, Oxford University, South Parks Road, Oxford OX1 3QR, UK

Abstract - Evidence for 1,2-hydrogen shift processes in the chemistry of transition metal-alkyls is presented and reviewed. The possible occurrence of 1,2-hydrogen shift equilibria in simple reactions such as olefin insertion and related olefin polymerisation processes is discussed.

I. INTRODUCTION

The transition metal-methyl group may not decompose by the β-elimination route available to most of the higher transition metal-alkyls. Homolytic fission giving the methyl radical can occur but appears to be relatively rare and hence presumably energetically unfavourable compared to other processes (Ref. 1). There are four reactions commonly available to transition metal-methyl compounds which can occur as homogeneous intramolecular processes and which result in the breaking of the metal-methyl bond. These are:

(i) Reductive-elimination of methane from a methyl-hydride system; the formation of a carbon-hydrogen bond:-

$$[M](H)(CH_3) \longrightarrow \left[[M]\cdots H \cdots CH_3 \right] \longrightarrow [M] + CH_4 \quad (1)$$

where [M] represents a coordinated transition metal centre.

(ii) Reductive-elimination of higher alkanes; formation of a methyl-carbon bond, e.g.

$$[M](CH_3)(CHRR') \longrightarrow [M] + CH_3{-}CHRR' \quad (2)$$

(iii) Methyl migration to a *cis*-carbonyl group; formation of an acetyl group (the carbonylation reaction), e.g.

$$[M](C{=}O)(CH_3) \longrightarrow \left[[M](C{=}O)\cdots CH_3 \right] \longrightarrow [M]{-}C({=}O){-}CH_3 \quad (3)$$

This process is often reversible.

(iv) Methyl-migration to a coordinated olefin: the olefin insertion reaction, e.g.

$$[M](CH_2{=}CH_2)(CH_3) \longrightarrow \left[[M](CH_2{-}CH_2)\cdots CH_3 \right] \longrightarrow [M]{-}CH_2{-}CH_2{-}CH_3 \quad (4)$$

The reactions (1) to (4) have been illustrated using valence bond descriptions in order to show that all four reactions may be regarded as reductive-elimination processes. Also, they proceed with the loss of two electrons from the metal centre *and* the initial electron number is not increased in the transition states. Therefore there is no reason why these processes should not be available for 18-electron compounds.

Until recently few chemists would have disputed the claim that all these processes were typical and of general occurrence in transition metal-methyl chemistry.

However, in this article I wish to adopt a sceptical, and somewhat speculative, attitude and to suggest that the situation may not be as straightforward as previously held, especially for the reactions (2) and (4).

II. EVIDENCE FOR REVERSIBLE 1,2-HYDROGEN SHIFT IN A TUNGSTEN-METHYL SYSTEM

It was some unexpected reactions of the compound $[W(\eta\text{-}C_5H_5)_2CH_3(C_2H_4)]PF_6$ that led us first to re-examine some of the assumptions and evidence concerning the reactions (1) to (4), and I will summarise this work first (Refs. 2-5).

(a) Treatment of a variety of compounds $[W(\eta\text{-}C_5H_5)_2CH_3L]PF_6$, where L = C_2H_4, PPh_3, SMe_2 or I^- with PMe_2Ph gives the compound $[W(\eta\text{-}C_5H_5)_2H(CH_2PMe_2Ph)]PF_6$, often in >90% yield, *viz.*

$$[W(\eta\text{-}C_5H_5)_2(CH_3)L]^+PF_6^- \xrightarrow{PMe_2Ph} [W(\eta\text{-}C_5H_5)_2(CH_2\overset{+}{P}Me_2Ph)H]\ PF_6^- \qquad (5)$$

The same reaction is observed when PMe_2Ph is replaced by other tertiary phosphines PR_3, where R_3 = Me_3, $MePh_2$ (Refs. 5,6).

(b) Thermolysis of solutions of $[W(\eta\text{-}C_5H_5)_2H(CH_2PR_3)]PF_6$, where R_3 = Ph_2Me, $PhMe_2$ or Me_3, in acetone at 70° causes steady rearrangement to the tungsten-methyl compounds $[W(\eta\text{-}C_5H_5)_2CH_3(PR_3)]PF_6$. The rate of the rearrangement is R_3 = Ph_2Me > $PhMe_2$ > Me_3. When R_3 = Ph_2Me or $PhMe_2$ the methyl product is formed almost quantitatively. However when R_3 = Me_3 *equilibrium* is established in acetone between $[W(\eta\text{-}C_5H_5)_2H(CH_2PMe_3)]PF_6$ and $[W(\eta\text{-}C_5H_5)_2CH_3(PMe_3)]PF_6$ and the equilibrium ratio at 70° is 28:72 respectively:

$$[W(\eta\text{-}C_5H_5)_2(CH_3)(PMe_3)]^+PF_6^- \rightleftharpoons [W(\eta\text{-}C_5H_5)_2(CH_2\overset{+}{P}Me_3)H]\ PF_6^- \qquad (6)$$

28% 72%

(c) When the deuteriomethyl compound $[W(\eta\text{-}C_5H_5)_2CD_3(C_2H_4)]PF_6$ is treated with PMe_2Ph then the reaction proceeds without exchange of deuterium with the hydrogens of solvents such as wet undeuteriated acetone. However the deuterium migrates reversibly from the CD_3 group to the metal and returns *quantitatively*, e.g.

$$[[W](CD_3)(C_2H_4)]^+PF_6^- \xrightarrow[\text{3 days, >95\%, 70°C}]{PMe_2Ph} [W](CD_2\overset{+}{P}Me_2Ph)(D)\ PF_6^- \xrightarrow{\text{70°C, 14 days, >95\%}} [[W](PMe_2Ph)(CD_3)]^+PF_6^- \qquad (7)$$

$[W] \equiv W(\eta\text{-}C_5H_5)_2$

(d) Where the kinetics are favourable then the PR_3 group in the molecules $[W(\eta-C_5H_5)_2H(CH_2PR_3)]PF_6$ can be exchanged with a different uncoordinated PR_3 molecule (Ref. 5), i.e.

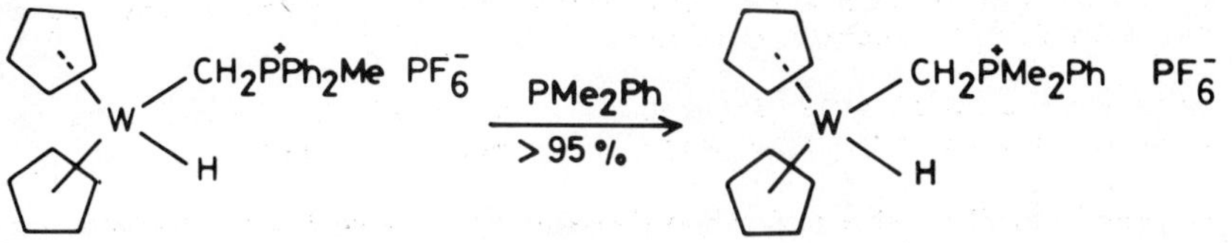

$$[W(\eta-C_5H_5)_2H(CH_2\overset{+}{P}Ph_2Me)]PF_6^- \xrightarrow[>95\%]{PMe_2Ph} [W(\eta-C_5H_5)_2H(CH_2\overset{+}{P}Me_2Ph)]PF_6^- \quad (8)$$

(e) Thermolysis of a mixture of $[W(\eta-C_5H_5)_2(\eta-C_2H_4)CH_3]PF_6$ and $[W(\eta-C_5H_5)_2(\eta-C_2H_4)CD_3]PF_6$ with PMe_2Ph in deuterioacetone gave the expected intermediates, and after fourteen days the ^1H n.m.r. of the reaction mixture showed the products to be $[W(\eta-C_5H_5)_2(PMe_2Ph)CH_3]PF_6$ and $[W(\eta-C_5H_5)_2(PMe_2Ph)CD_3]PF_6$. There was no evidence for the presence of CH_2D (or CD_2H) in the ^1H n.m.r. spectrum (typical values for J H/D for transition metal-deuteriomethyl compounds are 1.30 - 1.60 Hz (Ref. 7)). This shows that there is no intermolecular exchange of the methyl-hydrogens (Ref. 6).

In order to account for these observations we proposed an equilibrium between an intermediate 16-electron cation $[W(\eta-C_5H_5)_2CH_3]^+$ and the 18-electron carbene-hydride $[W(\eta-C_5H_5)_2H(=CH_2)]^+$ (Ref. 4). The role of these intermediates is shown in the reaction mechanism given in Fig. 1.

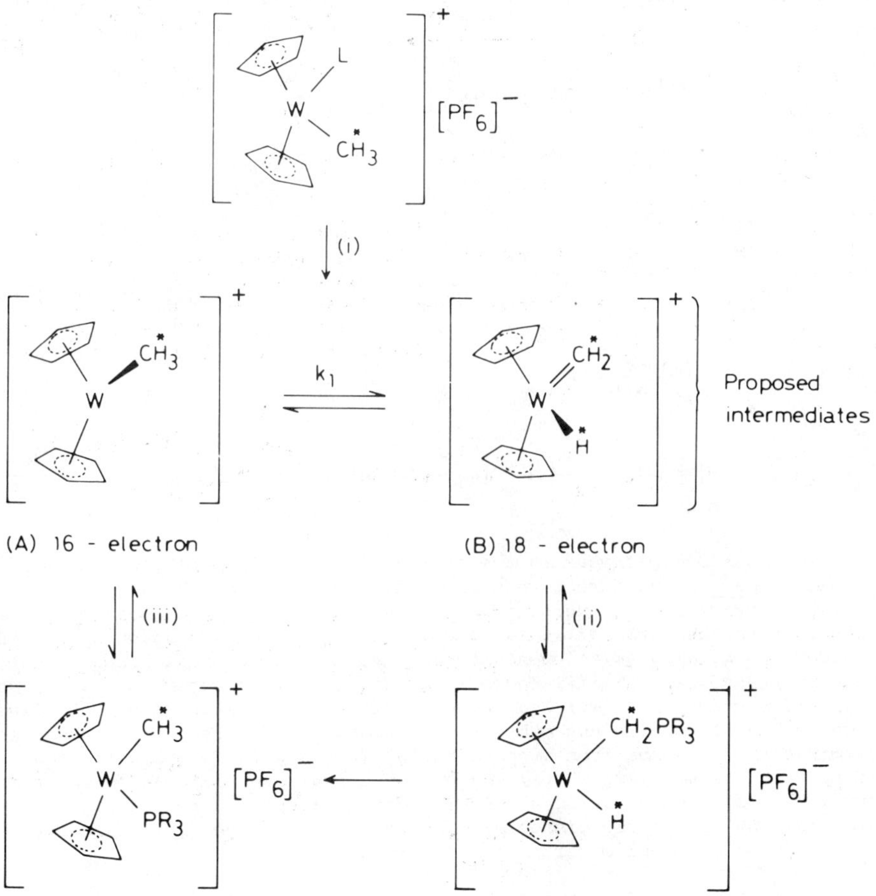

Fig. 1. (i) Dissociation of L. (ii) Reversible addition of tertiary phosphine, PR_3, to the carbenoid carbon. (iii) Reversible addition of tertiary phosphine to the tungsten atom.

The above observations comprise some of the strongest evidence for the occurrence of a reversible 1,2-hydrogen shift in a transition metal-methyl, i.e. the general equilibrium:-

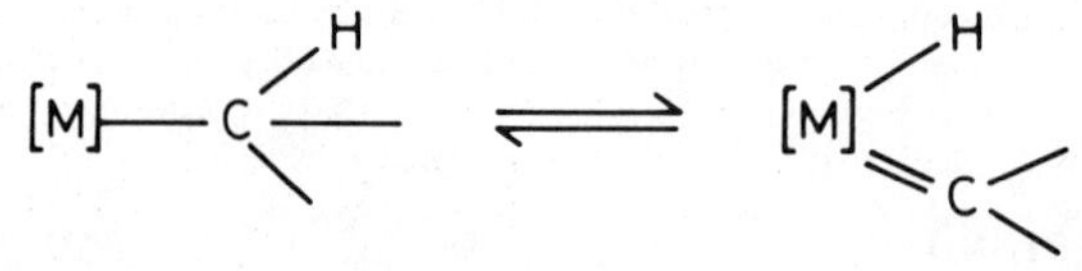

$$[M]-C(H)\ \rightleftharpoons\ [M](H)=C \qquad (9)$$

III. FURTHER EVIDENCE FOR 1,2-HYDROGEN SHIFT REACTIONS IN TRANSITION METAL-ALKYLS

(a) Thermolysis of transition metal alkyls

1,2-hydrogen shift (α-elimination) processes have been proposed to account for the products of thermal decomposition of transition metal-alkyls (Ref. 1). For example, the thermolysis of $FeMe_2(Ph_2PCH_2CH_2PPh_2)_2$ in the solid state yields methane, ethane and ethylene in the ratios 14:4:1. Thermolysis in CD_2Cl_2 yielded CH_4, C_2H_6, C_2H_4, CH_2CD_2 and CD_2CD_2 in the ratio 50:24:8:14:4; the deuteriated ethylenes were proposed to derive from reaction between CD_2Cl_2 and a $Fe{=}CH_2$ species (Ref. 8). Thermolysis of $CoMe(PPh_3)_3$ in the presence of dideuterium gives polydeuteriated methanes, possibly *via* 1,2-hydrogen shift equilibria (Ref. 9).

Figure 2 shows how use of the 1,2-hydrogen shift can give rise to all the products normally found in the thermolysis of *gem*-dimethyl transition metal compounds (Ref. 10). It is not necessary that the products of a particular reaction be a mixture of CH_4, C_2H_6, C_2H_4 and H_2; but if any one route is preferred then only one volatile product may be isolated.

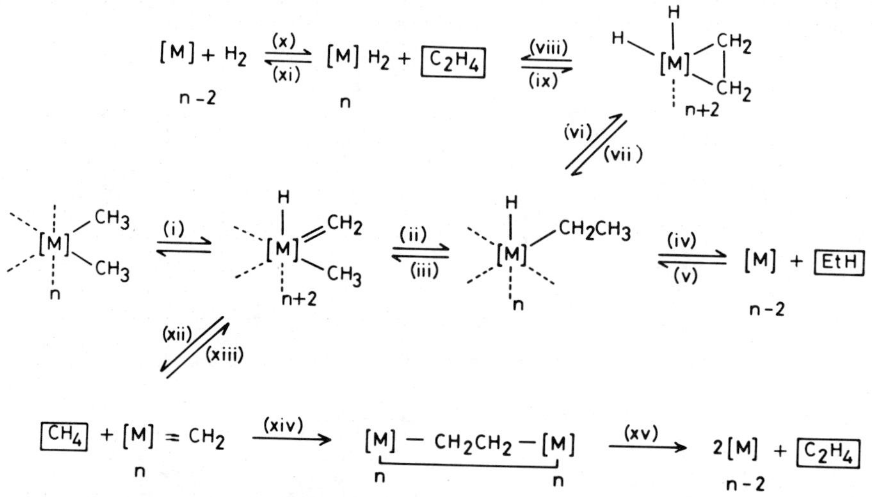

$[M]+H_2$ (n−2) ⇌(x)/(xi) $[M]H_2$ (n) + $\boxed{C_2H_4}$ ⇌(viii)/(ix) $H-[M](H)(CH_2CH_2)$ (n+2)

⇅ (vi)/(vii)

$[M](CH_3)_2$ (n) ⇌(i) $H-[M]{=}CH_2(CH_3)$ (n+2) ⇌(ii)/(iii) $H-[M]-CH_2CH_3$ (n) ⇌(iv)/(v) $[M]$ (n−2) + $\boxed{EtH}$

⇅ (xii)/(xiii)

$\boxed{CH_4}$ + $[M]{=}CH_2$ (n) →(xiv) $[M]-CH_2CH_2-[M]$ (n, n) →(xv) $2[M]$ (n−2) + $\boxed{C_2H_4}$

Fig. 2. Possible pathways in the thermal decomposition of gem-dimethyl compounds, excluding direct reductive elimination of ethane (Ref. 10). (i) The reversible 1,2-hydrogen shift equilibrium. (ii) Migration of the CH_3 *group to the carbene: this is comparable to acyl formation and should be stereochemically quite unencumbered. For circumstantial evidence for this step (Ref. 11). (iii) There is no direct evidence for this step; see, however, section VI. (iv) Reductive elimination of alkane from the alkyl-hydride. A sterically unencumbered reaction, in contrast to the reductive elimination of ethane from a gem-dimethyl (Ref. 10). (v) Oxidation addition of* sp^3 *C-H (Refs. 9,12). (vi) The common β-hydrogen elimination reaction. (vii) The well-known olefin to metal-hydrogen insertion reaction. (viii) and (ix) The reversible dissociation of olefin. (x) and (xi) Oxidative addition and reductive elimination of dihydrogen.*

Also it is proposed that the formation of alkenes or ylide complexes from platinacyclobutanes proceeds *via* a 1,2-hydrogen shift (Ref. 13). Further examples are also known (Refs. 1,14).

(b) α-Hydrogen abstraction giving metal alkylidene complexes

Further evidence for lability of α-hydrogens comes from the studies on niobium and tantalum compounds.

Unexpected lability of the α-hydrogen is shown by the abstraction by base of protons from compounds such as $[Ta(\eta\text{-}C_5H_5)_2Me_2]^+$ (Ref. 15), $[Ta(\eta\text{-}C_5H_5)_2Me(CH_2SiMe_3)]^+$ (Ref. 16) and $[Ta(\eta\text{-}C_5H_5)_2(CH_2SiMe_3)_2]^+$ (Ref. 17), giving the neutral alkylidene compounds $[Ta(\eta\text{-}C_5H_5)_2(CH_2)Me]$, $[Ta(\eta\text{-}C_5H_5)_2CH_3(CHSiMe_3)]$ and $[Ta(\eta\text{-}C_5H_5)_2(CHSiMe_3)(CH_2SiMe_3)]$ respectively. The bases used include Me_3PCH_2 (Ref. 16) and $Li[(N)SiMe_3)_2]$ (Ref. 17).

Whether the abstraction of the α-hydrogen proceeds by prior formation of the alkylidene-hydride system *via* 1,2-hydrogen shift or whether an alkyl group migration leads to a more direct abstraction of a proton is not known. Schrock has discussed steric and electronic factors concerning α-hydrogen abstraction from neopentyl complexes of niobium and tantalum (Ref. 18). Also, the migration of α-hydrogen of alkylidene and related alkyl compounds has been discussed in the light of a molecular orbital approach (Ref. 19).

In section V(b) we discuss the possibility that the decomposition of transition metal-alkyl MR_n induced by added tertiary phosphine giving the alkane RH may proceed *via* prior attack of the tertiary phosphine at the α-carbon.

(c) Miscellaneous

(1) Studies on a molybdenum(η-benzene)(η-ethylene)methyl cation. In an attempt to provide further evidence for 1,2-hydrogen shift equilibria it was decided to attempt to synthesise the compound $[Mo(\eta\text{-}C_6H_6)(dmpe)(\eta\text{-}C_2H_4)Me]PF_6$, 1, where dmpe = *bis*-1,2-(dimethylphosphino)-ethane. This compound is a d^4 analogue of the d^2 compound $[W(\eta\text{-}C_5H_5)_2(\eta\text{-}C_2H_4)Me]^+PF_6$.

The synthetic route to the compound 1 is given in Fig. 3. However, as shown in Fig. 3, treatment of the compound 1 with tertiary phosphines causes addition to the η-benzene ring rather than either addition to the η-ethylene or subsequent displacement of the ethylene. The resulting hexadienyl compound 2 is thermally stable in acetone for several days at 70° and when R_3P is Me_3P the *exo*-PR_3 group does not exchange with excess of free tertiary phosphine (6h at 70°) (Ref. 6).

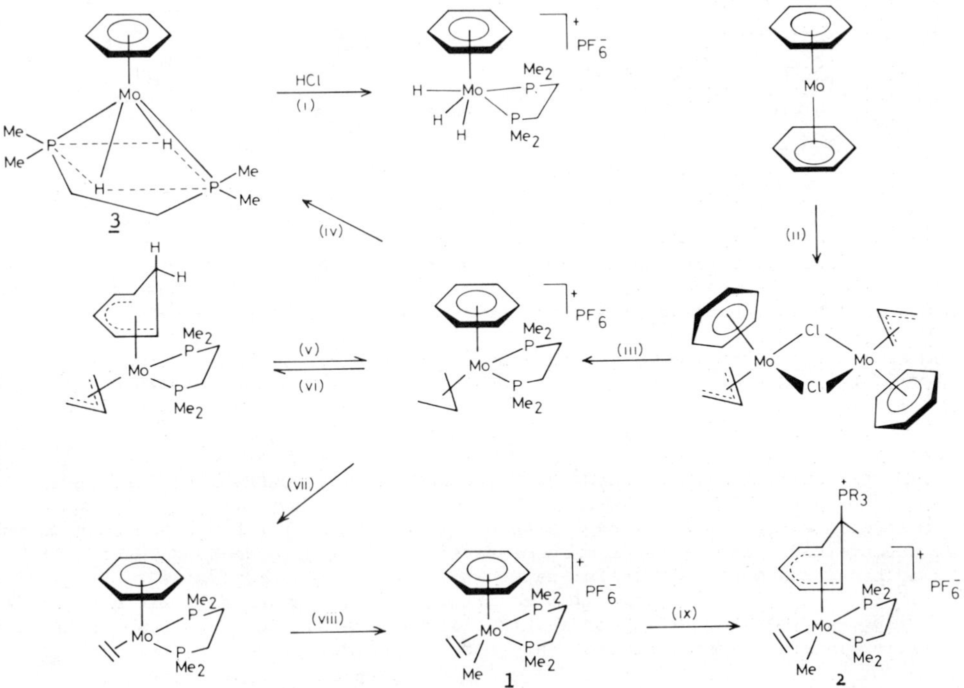

Fig. 3. (i) HCl aq. then NH_4PF_6. (ii) Allyl chloride, r.t., 70%. (iii) Dmpe in toluene, >90%. (iv) Na/Hg in dihydrogen, 1 atm. 80%. (v) Methyl iodide, 90%. (vi) $NaAlH_2(OCH_2CH_2OMe)_2$, 80%. (vii) Na/Hg in thf at r.t. and C_2H_4, 1 atm. 80%. (viii) MeI in thf at r.t., 30%. (ix) PR_3, R_3 = Me_3, Me_2Ph in acetone at r.t., >90%.

An unexpected observation arose in this study. The ^1H n.m.r. spectrum of the dihydrido compound 3 (Fig. 3) shows the four P-methyl groups to be equivalent as are the two Mo-hydrogens. On this basis the transoid structure is proposed. A similar structure has been found from X-ray diffraction on $Mo(\eta\text{-}C_6H_6)(PMe_3)_2Me_2$ (Ref. 20). It is interesting to contrast the reactivity of the previously described dihydrido compound $Mo(\eta\text{-}C_6H_5Me)_2(PPh_2Me)H_2$, 4, towards dinitrogen (Ref. 21) with that of 3. The former reacts very rapidly, giving dinitrogen compounds (Fig. 4), whilst the latter is inert to substitution even though close analogues to the expected product, i.e. $[(\eta\text{-}C_6H_6)Mo(dmpe)]_2(\mu\text{-}N_2)$ have been prepared by a different route (Ref.

22). It is tempting to suggest that the compound 4 is labile by virtue of the ability of the two hydrogens to move towards one another and meet up underneath the metal-ring axis in the manner indicated by the arrows in Fig. 4. Such a reductive elimination pathway is not possible for 3 as the CH_2CH_2 system interferes and this may account for the difference in reactivity between 3 and 4.

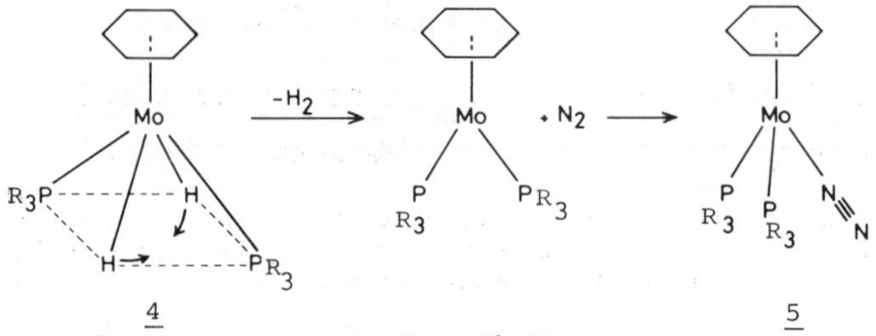

R_3 = Ph_2Me

Fig. 4. Formation of the dinitrogen compound 5 from the dihydride 4 showing the proposed movement of the two hydrogens which results in the reductive elimination of dihydrogen.

(2) Synthesis of transition metal-alkylidenes from phosphoranes. Phosphoranes $R_3P{=}CR'H$ will react with transition metals giving either metal-ylide complexes $[M]{-}CHR'PR_3$ (Ref. 23) or, *via* dissociation of the PR_3 group, the metal-alkylidene compounds $[M]{=}CHR'$ (Refs. 11, 24).

Treatment of $[W(\eta\text{-}C_5H_5)_2(\eta\text{-}C_2H_4)Me]PF_6$ with the ylide $Ph_3P{=}CH_2$ results in addition of the ylide to the ethylene ligand, as shown in Eqn. (10) (Ref. 6).

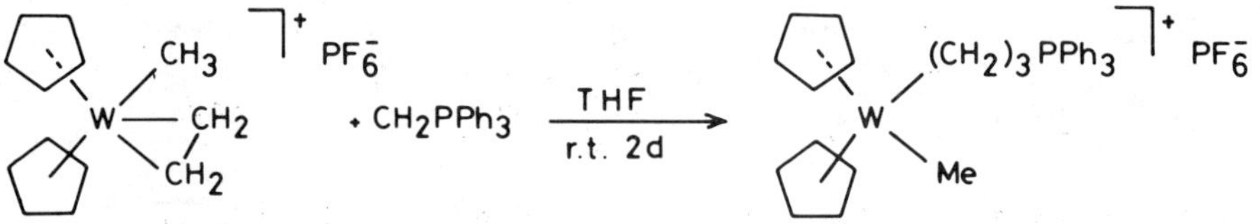

(10)

We had hoped to prepare the compound $[W(\eta\text{-}C_5H_5)(=CH_2)Me]PF_6$ by this reaction.

(3) 1,2-Shift processes on heterogeneous metal surfaces. The exchange between dideuterium and methane, catalysed by heterogeneous metal catalysts e.g. tungsten films, are thought to involve $M{=}CH_2$ species which may derive from 1,2-hydrogen shift processes (Ref. 25).

(4) Osmium cluster chemistry. The compound $HOs_3(CO)_{10}CH_3$ readily loses a C-H hydrogen forming $H_2Os_3(CO)_{10}CH_2$. However, this reaction may proceed *via* (an essentially) β-elimination mechanism (Ref. 26).

IV. ELECTRONIC AND STEREOCHEMICAL ASPECTS OF 1,2-HYDROGEN SHIFT EQUILIBRIA

(a) The rotational energy barrier about a transition metal double bond, M=C, can be substantial. For example, ^1H n.m.r. studies on some tantalum alkylidene derivatives show the rotational energy barrier about the tantalum-carbon bond to be 16-20 kcal $mole^{-1}$ (Refs. 16,18). It follows that the reversible 1,2-hydrogen shift equilibria will not *necessarily* lead to racemisation of a chiral alpha carbon, that is, if the other ligands on the metal retain their stereochemical integrity during the process, i.e.

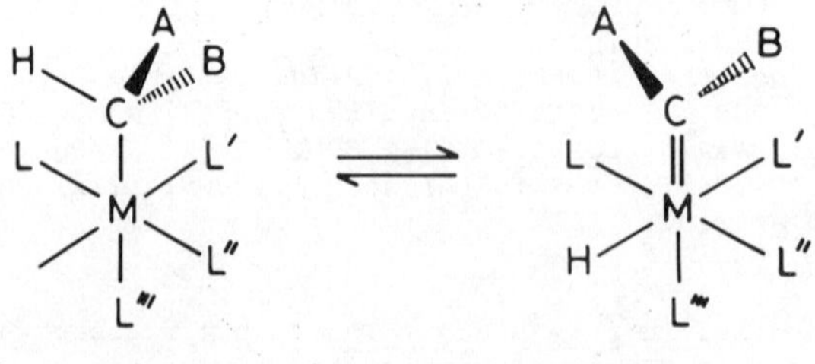

If the same hydrogen which leaves the alpha carbon returns to the identical position on the carbon then it will not be possible to obtain evidence for the intermediacy of carbene-hydride intermediates by either isotopic exchange or racemisation. Of course if the hydrogen leaves the *metal* or scrambles with other metal hydrogens in a reversible manner then isotopic scrambling may ensue.

(b) When the 1,2-hydrogen shift is written as follows

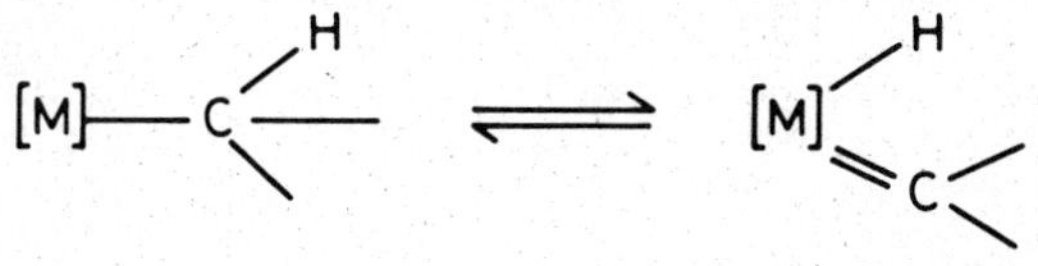

(11)

Electron No. = n Electron No. = n+2

Valency = x Valency = x+2

that is, as an internal oxidative-addition reaction, then the electron number of the metal centre is increased by two and the formal valency state will also increase by two. However, if a 1,2-hydride ion shift occurs then the valency state of the metal remains the same, e.g.

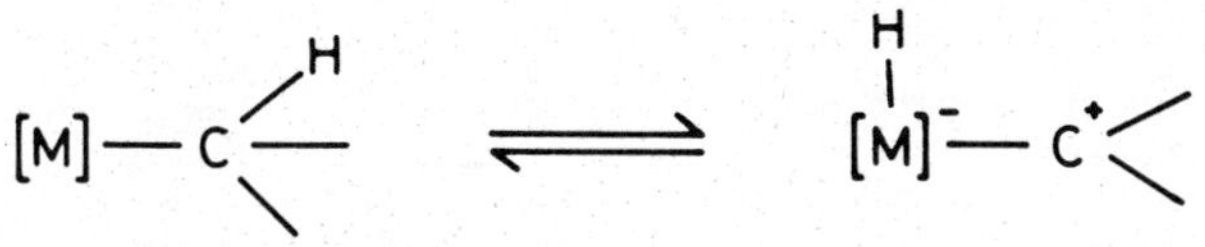

(12)

Electron No. = n Electron No. = n+2

Valency = x Valency = x

although the electron number still increases by two units. Such a hydride ion shift will be expected to be encouraged if the metal centre is unusually short of electrons, as in d^0 compounds and, also, if the intermediate carbonium ion can be stabilised, for example by a nucleophile, *viz.*

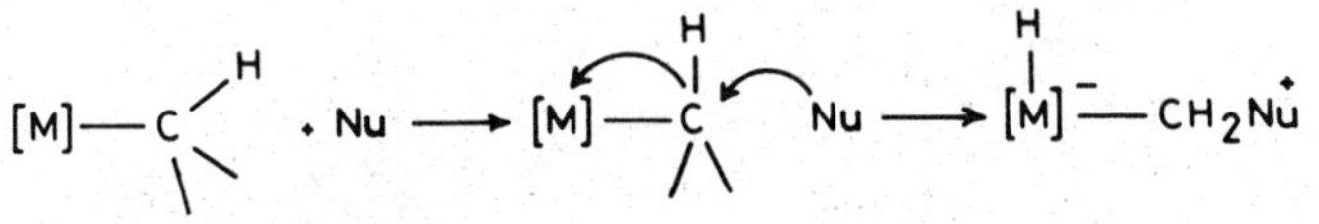

[M]—C(H) + Nu ⟶ [M]—C(H) Nu ⟶ [M]$^-$(H)—CH_2Nu^+ (13)

We note that, unlike the simple olefin insertion process, Eqn. (4) (section I(iv)), the 1,2-hydrogen shift equilibrium always involves an increase of the electron number of the metal centre by two and, therefore, should *not* be readily available to eighteen electron compounds.

V. THE POSSIBLE OCCURRENCE OF 1,2-HYDROGEN SHIFT PROCESSES IN COMMON REACTIONS

Where else do 1,2-hydrogen shift equilibria occur? We have seen from the comments in section IV(a) that it may be possible for 1,2-hydrogen shift equilibria to occur and yet not provide any obvious means to demonstrate the fact. The intermediacy of 1,2-hydrogen shift steps can be invoked to occur in the mechanisms of a number of well-known reactions, as is illustrated below.

(a) A possible mechanism for the insertion of olefin into metal-alkyl bonds

A 1,2-hydrogen shift mechanism can be written as follows (Ref. 27):-

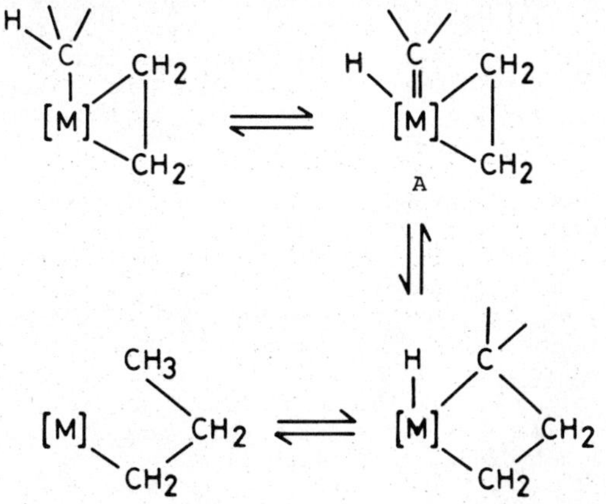

A

(14)

We note that if the intermediate A does not have a suitable high symmetry then the hydrogen can return uniquely to the carbon from which it originated. Elsewhere it is proposed that this step may occur in the stereospecific polymerisation of olefins catalysed by Ziegler-Natta catalysts (Ref. 28). Infra-red studies on supported chromia catalysts used for olefin polymerisation (Phillips catalysts) suggest that chromium-alkylidene species are present (Ref. 29).

Instead of a separate 1,2-hydrogen shift followed by the metallacycle formation one can envisage that there is a concerted 1,2-hydrogen shift with concomitant metallacycle formation *viz.*

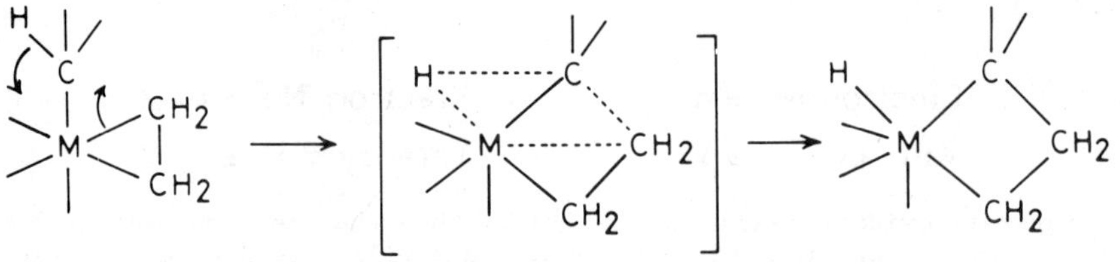

(15)

In this reaction the ethylene can be envisaged as acting as an intramolecular nucleophile, see Eqn. (13).

It may seem, at first, impertinent to query the long-accepted insertion mechanism for the reaction between an olefin and a transition metal σ-alkyl bond (Eqn. (4)). There is, however, very little direct evidence for such a step. We have made 18-electron compounds which contain *cis*-orientated methyl-olefin systems, e.g. compounds such as $[W(\eta\text{-}C_5H_5)_2(\eta\text{-}C_2H_4)Me]PF_6$ and, as shown in Eqn. (5), have been unable to cause them to react so as to give the expected insertion product, i.e. the propyl compound $[W(\eta\text{-}C_5H_5)_2(PMe_2Ph)Pr^n]PF_6$, even though the propyl compound itself is stable and may be prepared by phosphine-induced insertion of propene into the transition metal-hydrogen bond of the compound $[W(\eta\text{-}C_5H_5)_2(\eta\text{-}MeCH{=}CH_2)H]PF_6$ (Ref. 30).

We note that the insertion of carbonmonoxide into the metal-methyl bond in the compound 6 (Eqn. (16)) proceeds smoothly and quantitatively (Ref. 31).

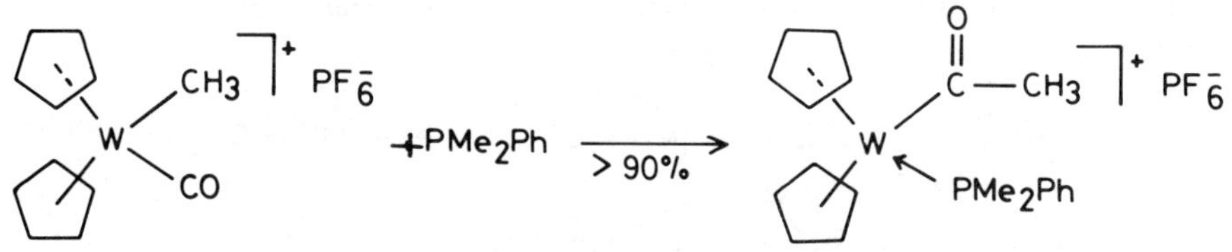

(16)

Similarly, the insertion of ethylene into the metal-hydrogen bond in the analogous compound 7 also proceeds readily and in very high yield (Ref. 31).

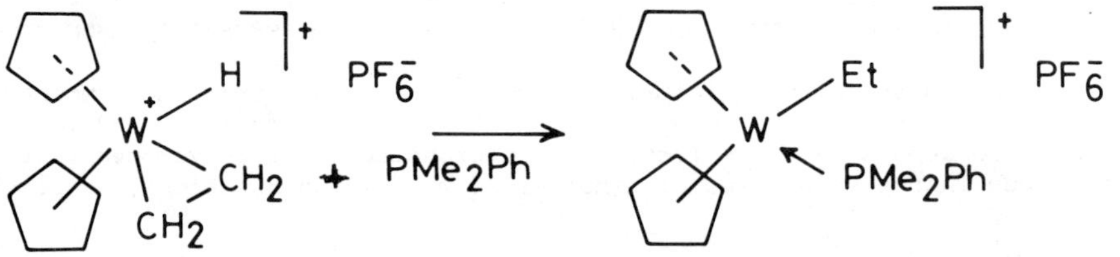

(17)

As noted in section I, the ethylene insertion reaction does not result in an increase in the electron number whereas the mechanism written in Eqn. (14) requires the metal to increase its electron number by two units, and therefore would be unfavourable for an 18-electron compound, such as $[W(\eta\text{-}C_5H_5)_2(\eta\text{-}C_2H_4)Me]PF_6$. A related observation is that the compound $Nb(\eta\text{-}C_5H_5)_2(\eta\text{-}C_2H_4)H$ reacts readily with ethylene *via* ethylene insertion forming the compound $Nb(\eta\text{-}C_5H_5)_2(\eta\text{-}C_2H_4)Et$, but that further reaction with ethylene causing insertion of ethylene into the Nb-ethyl bond does not occur (Ref. 32).

There are many examples of reactions between transition metal-alkyls and free,(initially uncoordinated) olefins which give rise to hydrocarbon products consistent with an olefin insertion (or 1,2-hydrogen shift) mechanism but for which the former mechanism has hitherto been assumed. Metal-containing products or intermediates are rarely isolated in these reactions (Ref. 33). A recent and elegant study by Bergman (Ref. 33) of the reaction between ethylene and $Co(\eta\text{-}C_5H_5)(PPh_3)(CD_3)_2$ gives as an initial product $CD_3CH{=}CH_2$ (>80%) and CD_3H (essentially 100%). The mechanism proposed is shown in Fig. 5. It has the conventional insertion step for formation of the carbon-carbon bond. The mechanism is entirely consistent with the data. However, alternative mechanisms may also be written which are also apparently consistent with the data. Figure 6 shows a 1,2-hydrogen shift mechanism.

A more unusual mechanism could proceed *via* the key sequence $[Co]C_2H_4(CD_3)_2 \rightarrow [Co](CH{=}CH_2)H(CD_3)_2$.

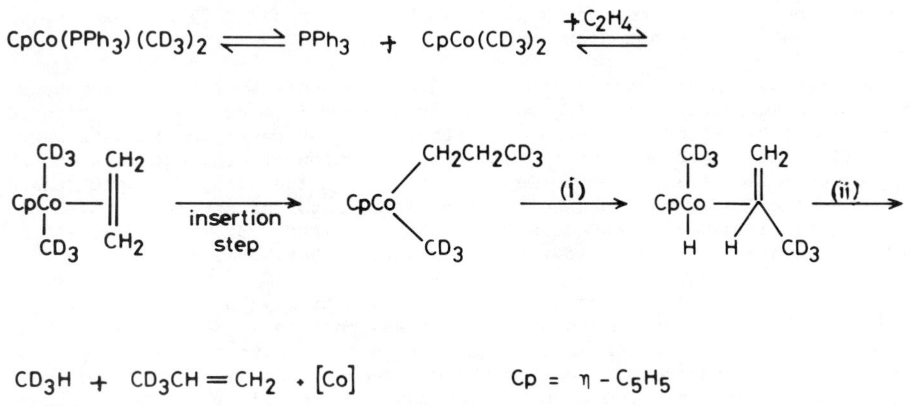
CpCo(PPh3)(CD3)2
PPh3 + CpCo(CD3)2
+C2H4
CD3 CH2
CpCo
CD3 CH2
insertion step
CH2CH2CD3
CpCo
CD3
(i)
CD3 CH2
CpCo
H H CD3
(ii)
CD3H + CD3CH=CH2 + [Co]
Cp = η-C5H5

Fig. 5. Mechanism proceeding via olefin insertion step.

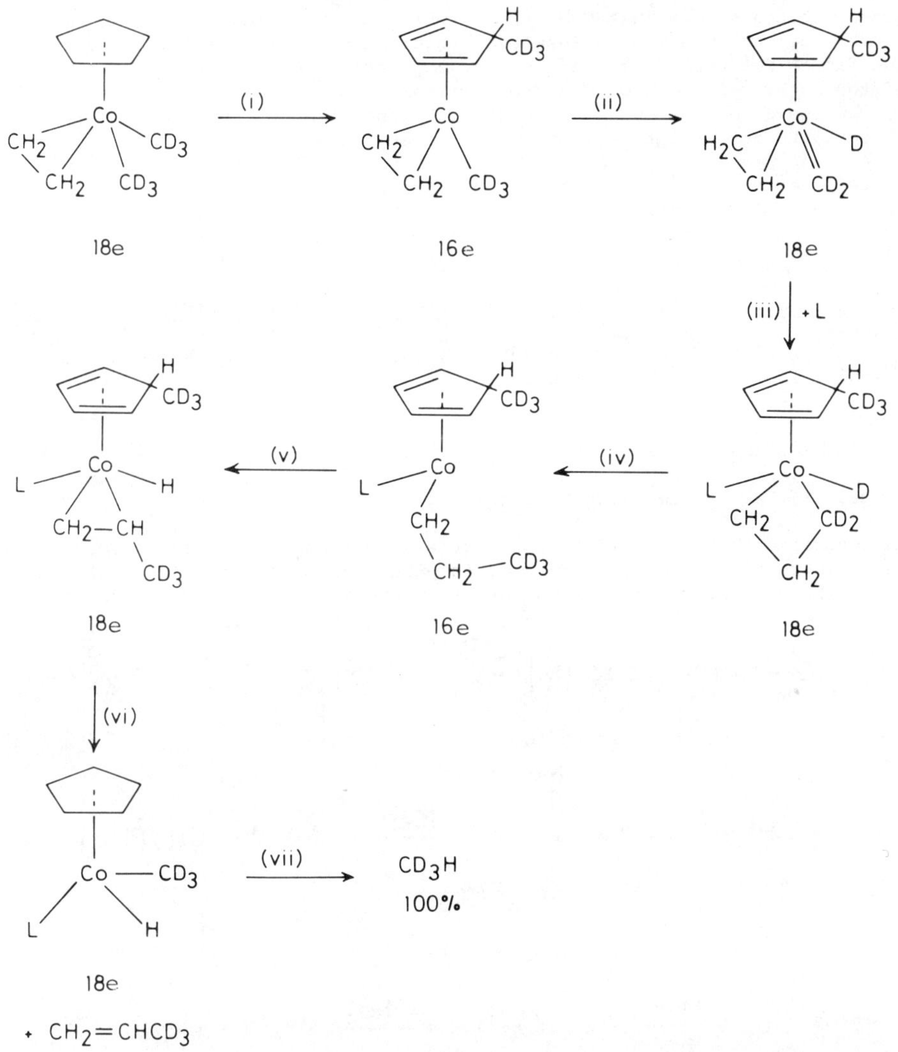
Co
CH2 CD3
CH2 CD3
18e
(i)
H
CD3
16e
(ii)
H2C D
CH2 CD2
18e
(iii) +L
L
CH2 CD2
CH2
18e
(iv)
CH2
CH2—CD3
16e
(v)
L H
CH2—CH
CD3
18e
(vi)
Co—CD3
L H
18e
(vii)
CD3H
100%
+ CH2=CHCD3

Fig. 6. (i) Migration of methyl group to η-C_5H_5 ring, see section VI and reference (Ref. 27). (ii) 1,2-Deuterium shift. (iii) Metallacyclobutane formation induced by stereospecific approach of L = solvent or tertiary-phosphine. The requirement for stereospecificity at this stage is a limitation of this mechanism. (iv) Reductive elimination. (v) β-elimination. (vi) Propene dissociation followed by migration of the endo-CD_3 to the metal (see section VI). (vii) Reductive elimination of CD_3H. The reaction proceeds via alternate gain and loss of two electrons, i.e. 16e ⇌ 18e.

We conclude that the insertion mechanism proposed by Bergman (Fig. 5) is the simplest explanation but the alternatives are not disproven.

The catalytic *dimerisation* of ethylene to a mixture of butenes by rhodium compounds was originally studied by Cramer (Ref. 34). The carbon-carbon bond-forming step was proposed to proceed *via* insertion of ethylene into a rhodium-ethyl bond. However, no hexenes were observed in the products. These might well be expected for insertion of ethylene into the rhodium-butyl bond. Another mechanism which seems consistent with the data, for which there was no precedent at the time Cramer put forward his mechanism, involves as the carbon-carbon bond-forming step the formation of a rhodametallacyclopentane (Ref. 35). However, a 1,2-hydrogen shift mechanism has also been proposed for this reaction (Ref. 36).

The products resulting from insertion of acetylenes into transition metal-alkyl bonds are also observed and a simple insertion mechanism has been assumed (Ref. 33). Finally, there is no doubt that the alkyl to acyl carbonylation equilibrium and the reversible insertion of ethylene into the metal-hydrogen bond occur. One of the most convincing pieces of evidence for these mechanisms is that in some examples both components of the equilibrium can be observed simultaneously, e.g. see Ref. 49. No system where both components of the equilibrium between alkyl-olefin and the higher alkyl derivatives can be observed is yet known.

As noted above, in the series $[W(\eta\text{-}C_5H_5)_2RL]^+$, where RL = (CO)Me, $(\eta\text{-}C_2H_4)H$, or $(\eta\text{-}C_2H_4)Me$, only the latter does not undergo an insertion reaction upon treatment with tertiaryphosphine. The dominant factor for this difference may be a greater steric obstruction to the approach of the methyl to the olefin carbon, compared to the migration of the methyl group to the carbonyl carbon or of the hydrogen to the ethylene carbon. Both the last two reactions would be expected to have relatively small steric barriers.

It may be noted that on steric grounds we would expect insertion of coordinated acetylene into metal-alkyl to be easier than for an olefin, and that aryl or alkynyl groups would normally present a reduced steric barrier to olefin insertion compared to alkyl.

(b) A possible rôle for tertiary phosphines in the alkane elimination reactions of transition metal alkyls

It is well established that tertiary phosphines, in particular the basic trimethylphosphine, cause the reductive elimination of alkanes from transition metal polyalkyl compounds. Examples are (Refs. 18, 37):-

$$M(CH_2CMe_3)_2X_3 + PMe_3 \longrightarrow M(CHCMe_3)X_3(PMe_3)_2 \qquad (18)$$

$$WMe_6 + PMe_3 \longrightarrow trans\text{-}WMe_2(PMe_3)_4 \qquad (19)$$

It has been suggested that the rôle of the tertiary phosphine might be to coordinate to the metal and thus increase steric pressure towards alkane dissociation (Ref. 37). Another possibility is that the PMe_3 group attacks the α-carbon and induces a hydride ion shift, *viz.*

$$[M]-C(H)< + PMe_3 \rightleftharpoons [M]-C(H)<\cdots PMe_3 \rightleftharpoons [M](H)^- - CH_2\overset{+}{P}Me_3 \qquad (20)$$

Thus the mechanism (21) can be written for the reaction (19).

$$WMe_6 + PMe_3 \longrightarrow Me_4W^-(Me)(H)(CH_2\overset{+}{P}Me_3) \xrightarrow{-MeH} Me_4W^- - CH_2\overset{+}{P}Me_3$$

$$Me_4W^- - CH_2\overset{+}{P}Me_3 \rightleftharpoons Me_4W + Me_3P{=}CH_2$$

$$Me_4W + Me_3P{=}CH_2 \xrightarrow{+PMe_3} Me_2W^-(Me)(H)(CH_2\overset{+}{P}Me_3) \xrightarrow{-MeH} Me_2W^- - CH_2\overset{+}{P}Me_3 \qquad (21)$$

$$Me_2W^- - CH_2\overset{+}{P}Me_3 \longrightarrow Me_3P{=}CH_2 + Me_2W \xrightarrow{+4Me_3P} \underline{trans}\text{-}WMe_2(PMe_3)_4$$

In support of this observation, the proposed intermediate $Me_3P{=}CH_2$ has been detected in the products of reaction (21) (Ref. 38).

VI. REVERSIBLE 1,2-ALKYL SHIFT

If reversible 1,2-hydrogen shift processes may occur readily then is the same true for 1,2-alkyl shifts? - i.e. the equilibrium

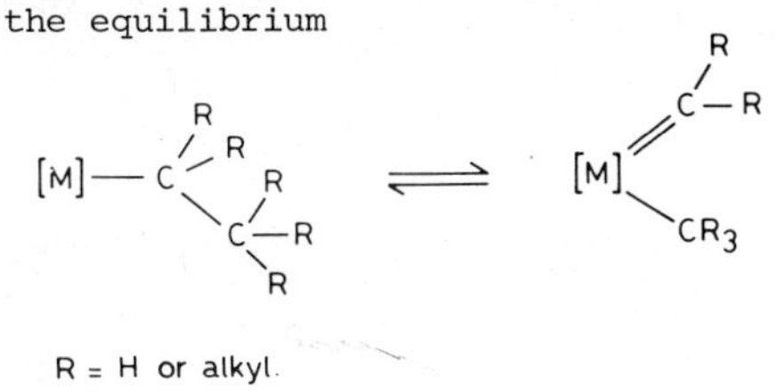

(22)

R = H or alkyl.

where R = H or alkyl.

There is at present no simple example of this reaction. However, related systems include the reversible decarbonylation of metal-acyls [M]COMe = [M]C(O)Me (Ref. 1) and the well established ring opening equilibrium of metallacyclobutane compounds, Eqn. (23) (Ref. 39), *viz.*

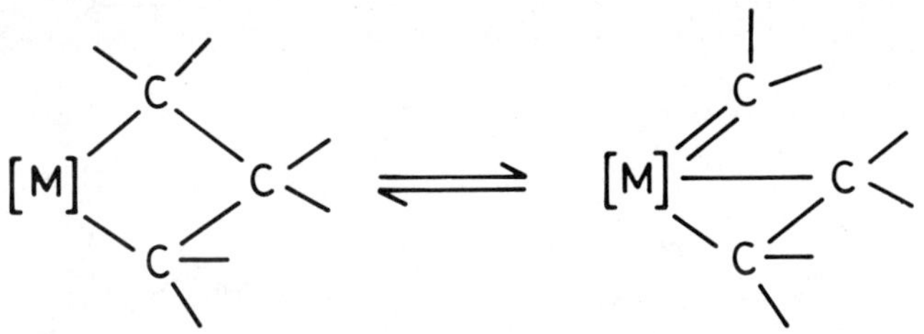

(23)

One problem is that β-hydrogen elimination is normally very facile and therefore would compete with 1,2-alkyl migration.

Under special circumstances, reversible carbon-carbon bond cleavage does occur. This was clearly demonstrated by the reactions of the molybdenum-ethyl compound (Ref. 40) shown in Fig. 7.

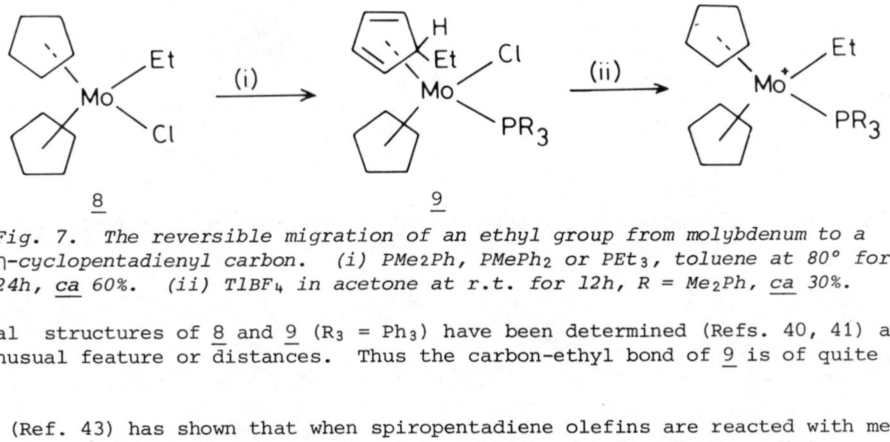

8 9

Fig. 7. The reversible migration of an ethyl group from molybdenum to a η-cyclopentadienyl carbon. (i) PMe_2Ph, $PMePh_2$ or PEt_3, toluene at 80° for 24h, ca 60%. (ii) $TlBF_4$ in acetone at r.t. for 12h, R = Me_2Ph, ca 30%.

The crystal structures of 8 and 9 (R_3 = Ph_3) have been determined (Refs. 40, 41) and they show no unusual feature or distances. Thus the carbon-ethyl bond of 9 is of quite normal length.

Eilbracht (Ref. 43) has shown that when spiropentadiene olefins are reacted with metal carbonyls then mono-σ-alkyl-η-cyclopentadienyl derivatives are formed, Eqn. (24).

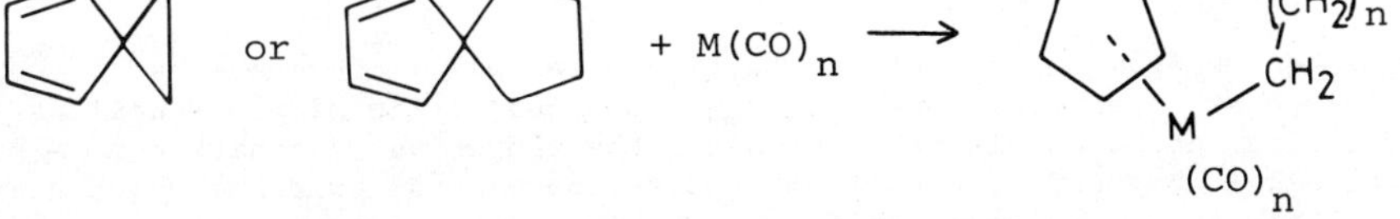

(24)

n = 1 or 3

We have found that cocondensation of the same spiropentadiene with metal vapours, e.g. of Ti, Mo or W, gives bis-σ-alkyl-η-cyclopentadienyl compounds (Ref. 44), as shown in Fig. 8. The spiro system is not essential; thus treatment of hexamethylcyclopentadiene with molybdenum atoms gives the bis-(η-pentamethylcyclopentadienyl)dimethylmolybdenum compound 10 (Ref. 45).

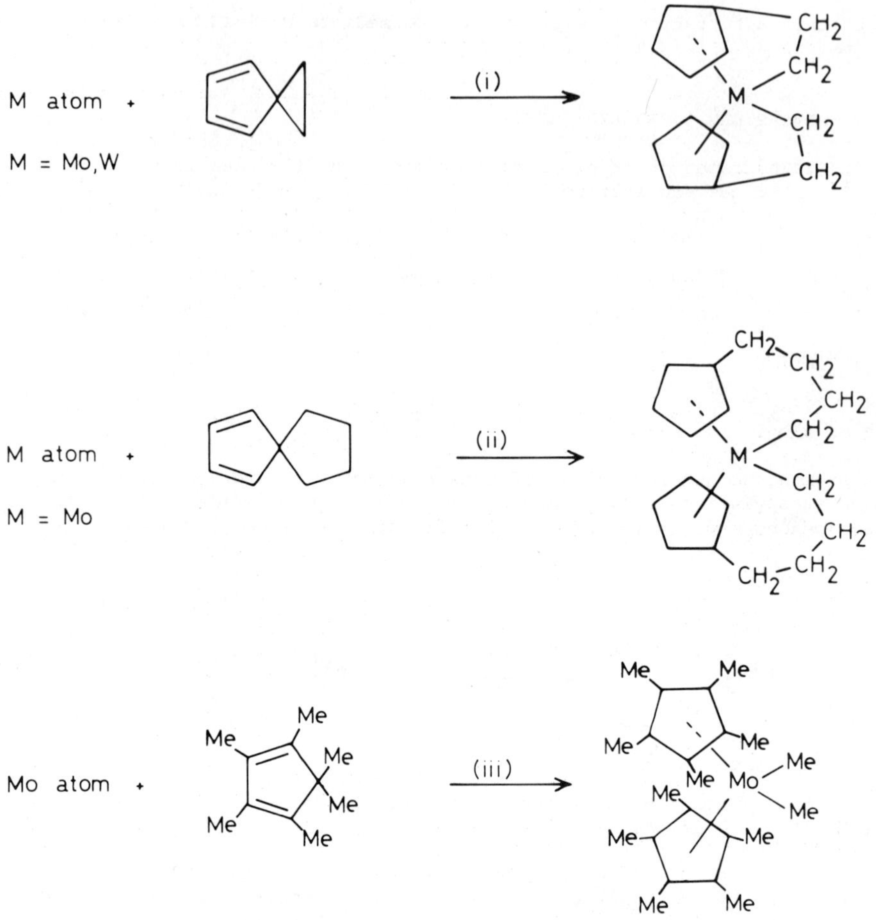

M atom + (spiro[2.4]hepta-4,6-diene) —(i)→ Mo(η-C5H4-σ-CH2CH2)2

M = Mo,W

M atom + (spiro[4.4]nona-1,3-diene) —(ii)→

M = Mo

Mo atom + (hexamethylcyclopentadiene) —(iii)→ 10

Fig. 8. Migration of alkyl groups from cyclopentadiene derivatives induced by transition metal atoms. (i) Typically, for Mo, 1.5g metal vapour was evaporated from a molten ingot (7g) over a period of 4h. The metal vapour was cocondensed with an excess of the diene ($50cm^3$) on a glass wall at -196°. The yields were ca 30%. The crystal structure of the compound $Mo(\eta\text{-}C_5H_4\text{-}\sigma\text{-}CH_2CH_2)_2$ has been determined (Ref. 46). (ii) Yield ca. 30%. (iii) Yield 20%.

A rather different alkyl bond shift mechanism has recently been proposed (Refs. 47,48), *viz.*

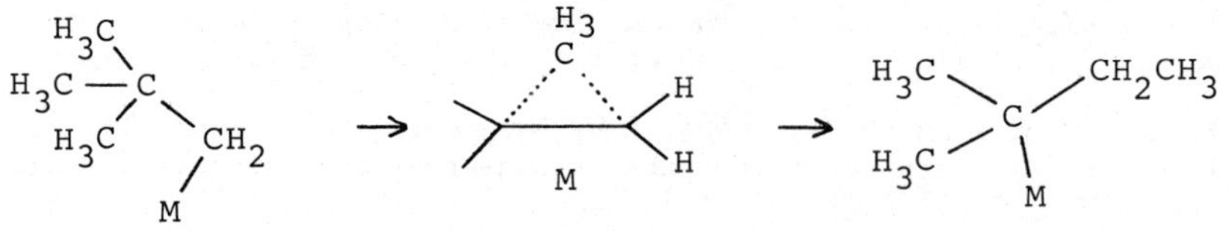

$$(H_3C)_3C-CH_2-M \rightarrow \text{[M-bridged } CH_3 \text{ intermediate]} \rightarrow (H_3C)_2C(CH_2CH_3)-M \qquad (25)$$

CONCLUSION

Evidence for 1,2-hydrogen shift equilibria in transition metal-alkyl compounds has been presented. It is possible that these equilibria occur quite generally in simple reactions such as the insertion of olefin into a metal-carbon bond and the reductive elimination of alkanes from transition metal-alkyl compounds. For the most part there is no evidence which unambiguously distinguishes between 1,2-hydrogen shift mechanisms and the more familiar mechanisms. Reasons why it can be difficult to obtain evidence for or against 1,2-hydrogen shift processes are also outlined.

In Oxford we will continue to seek evidence in the hope of answering questions raised above.

ACKNOWLEDGEMENTS

I wish to acknowledge those of my collaborators and colleagues who have assisted in the development of the experimental work and ideas:
Dr. N.J. Cooper, Dr. R. Mahtab and M. Canestrari (tungsten-methyl chemistry);
Dr. R. Barone (rhodium dimerisation of ethylene);
Dr. F.G.N. Cloke, Dr. A. Feigenbaum, P.R. Brown and Dr. R.A. Baretta (metal atom chemistry);
Dr. C.K. Prout (X-ray studies).
I also thank Dr. J.C. Green and Dr. D.M.P. Mingos for helpful discussions.

Finally I wish to thank the Science Research Council for financial support and the Petroleum Research Fund, administered by the American Chemical Society, for partial support.

REFERENCES

1. J.K. Kochi, *Organometallic Mechanisms and Catalysis,* Academic Press, New York (1978).
2. N.J. Cooper and M.L.H. Green, *J.C.S. Chem. Comm.* 208 (1974).
3. N.J. Cooper and M.L.H. Green, *J.C.S. Chem. Comm.* 761 (1974).
4. N.J. Cooper and M.L.H. Green, *J. Chem. Soc. Dalton,* 1121 (1979).
5. M. Canestrari and M.L.H. Green, *J.C.S. Chem. Comm.* 913 (1979).
6. M. Canestrari and M.L.H. Green, to be published.
7. J.D. Duncan, J.C. Green, M.L.H. Green and K.A. McLauchlan, *Diss. Farad. Soc.* 47, 178 (1969).
8. T. Ikariya and A. Yamamoto, *J. Organometallic Chem.* 118, 65 (1976).
9. E.L. Muetterties and P.L. Watson, *J. Amer. Chem. Soc.* 98, 4465 (1976).
10. N.J. Cooper, M.L.H. Green and R. Mahtab, *J.C.S. Dalton,* 1557 (1979).
11. P.R. Sharp and R.R. Schrock, *J. Organometallic Chem.* 171, 43 (1979).
12. R.H. Crabtree, J.M. Mihelcic and J.M. Quirk, *J. Amer. Chem. Soc.* 101, 7738 (1979).
13. R.J. Al-essa and R.J. Puddephatt, *J.C.S. Chem. Comm.* 45 (1980).
14. B. Akermark and A. Ljungquist, *J. Organometallic Chem.* 182, 47 (1979) and references therein; and P.S. Braterman and R.J. Cross, *Chem. Soc. Reviews* 2, 271 (1973).
15. R.R. Schrock and P.R. Sharp, *J. Amer. Chem. Soc.* 100, 2389 (1978).
16. R.R. Schrock, L.W. Messerle, C.D. Wood and L.J. Guggenberger, *J. Amer. Chem. Soc.* 100, 3793 (1978).
17. M.F. Lappert and C.R.C. Milne, *J.C.S. Chem. Comm.* 925 (1978).
18. R.R. Schrock, *Acc. Chem. Res.* 12, 98 (1979).
19. R.J. Goddard, R. Hoffman and E.D. Jemmis, *J. Amer. Chem. Soc.* (1980) in press.
20. J.L. Atwood, W.E. Hunter, R.D. Rogers, E. Carmona and G. Wilkinson, *J.C.S. Dalton,* 519 (1979).
21. M.L.H. Green and W.E. Silverthorn, *J.C.S. Dalton,* 301 (1973).
22. M.L.H. Green and W.E. Silverthorn, *J.C.S. Dalton,* 2164 (1974).
23. H. Schmidbauer, *Pure Appl. Chem.* 50, 19 (1979).
24. J. Schwartz and K.I. Gell, *J. Organometallic Chem.* 184, C1 (1980).
25. C. Kemball, *Catalysis Reviews* 5, 33 (1972).
26. R.B. Calvert and J.R. Shapley, *J. Amer. Chem. Soc.* 100, 7726 (1978).
27. M.L.H. Green, *Pure Appl. Chem.* 50, 27 (1978).
28. K.J. Ivin, J.J. Rooney, C.D. Stewart, M.L.H. Green and R. Mahtab, *J.C.S. Chem. Comm.* 604 (1978).
29. G. Ghiotti, E. Garrone, S. Coluccia, C. Mortenna and A. Zecchina, *J.C.S. Chem. Comm.* 1032 (1979).
30. F.W.S. Benfield, B.R. Francis and M.L.H. Green, *J. Organometallic Chem.* 44, C13 (1972).
31. M.L.H. Green and R. Mahtab, *J.C.S. Dalton,* 262 (1979).
32. F.N.Tebbe and G.W. Parshall, *J. Amer. Chem. Soc.* 93, 3793 (1971).
33. E.R. Evitt and R.G. Bergman, *J. Amer. Chem. Soc.* 101, 3973 (1979).
34. R. Cramer, *J. Amer. Chem. Soc.* 87, 4717 (1965).
35. R. Barone, M. Chanon and M.L.H. Green, *J. Organometallic Chem.* 185, 85 (1980).
36. F.A. Cotton and G. Wilkinson, *Advanced Inorganic Chemistry,* 4th ed., p. 1284, Wiley, New York (1980).
37. R.A. Jones, G. Wilkinson, A.M.R. Gales and M.B. Hursthouse, *J.C.S. Chem. Comm.* 926 (1979).
38. G. Wilkinson and R.A. Jones, personal communication.
39. N Calderon, J.P. Lawrence and E.A. Ofstead, *Adv. Organometallic Chem.* 17, 449 (1979).
40. F.W.S. Benfield and M.L.H. Green, *J.C.S. Dalton,* 1324 (1974).
41. C.K. Prout, T.S. Cameron, R.A. Forder, S.R. Critchley, B. Benton and G.V. Rees, *Acta Cryst.* B30, 2290 (1974).
42. E. Cannillo and K. Prout, *Acta Cryst.* B33, 3916 (1977).
43. S. Braun, P. Dahler and P. Elbracht, *J. Organometallic Chem.* 146, 135 (1978) and references therein.
44. A. Baretta, F.G.N. Cloke, A. Feigenbaum, K.A. Ford and M.L.H. Green, unpublished observations.
45. F.G.N. Cloke, J.C. Green, M.L.H. Green and C.J. Morley, unpublished observations.
46. C.K. Prout, A. Gourdon and M.J. Woolcock, personal communication.
47. M. Bartok and F. Notheisz, *J.C.S. Chem. Comm.* 744 (1979).
48. R. Hamilton, T.R.B. Mitchell, J.J. Rooney and M.A. McKervey, *J.C.S. Chem. Comm.* 731 (1979).
49. H. Werner and R. Faiser, *Angew. Chem. Int. Edit.* 18 157 (1979).

INTERACTIONS OF SOME NEUTRAL DIAZO MOLECULES AND CARBONYL SULFIDE WITH TRANSITION-METAL SYSTEMS

J. A. Ibers, T. R. Gaffney and K. Dahl Schramm

Department of Chemistry, Northwestern University, Evanston, Illinois 60201, USA

Abstract - A series of M-N_2R complexes has been prepared and characterized, where M is a transition-metal system containing Ir(I), Rh(I), Ni(0), Pt(0), or Ru(0), and N_2R is either a tetrahalide of diazocyclopentadiene or is 9-diazofluorene. The structures and reaction chemistry of these complexes are contrasted with one another and with those of the corresponding diazonium complexes. The reactions of COS with some of the same transition-metal systems has also been studied. Carbonyl sulfide complexes of transition metals have proved to be very reactive, and three reaction pathways have been identified: (i) decomposition to give a metal carbonyl; (ii) reaction with another molecule of COS to give a dithiocarbonate; (iii) rearrangement to give a metal sulfide or a metal thiol.

INTRODUCTION

The interactions of small molecules with transition metals has been a major area of research in our laboratories for the past fifteen years. In this paper we will discuss some recent, unpublished results on the interactions with rather similar transition-metal systems of two very different molecular species, neutral diazo molecules, RN_2, and carbonyl sulfide, COS.

It was our initial discovery (Ref. 1) of the bent M-N-O linkage, 1 (see Note a), that revealed the amphoteric nature of the nitrosyl ligand. Previously, only the linear

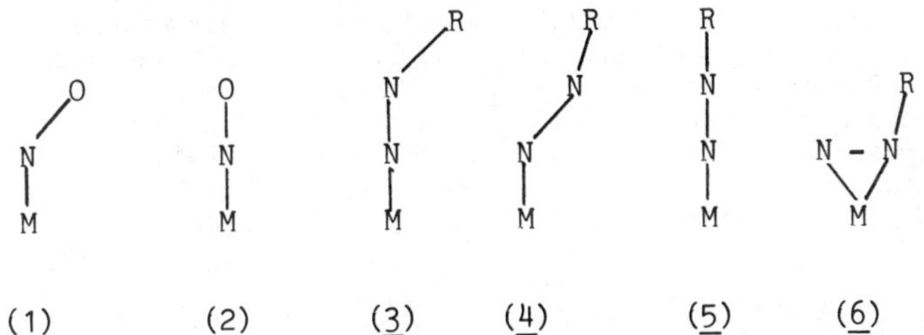

(1) (2) (3) (4) (5) (6)

linkage, 2, was known among transition-metal complexes. The study of amphoteric ligands, ligands capable of adopting two or more bonding geometries, is extremely important in transition-metal chemistry because it affords an opportunity to build a sensitive electronic probe directly into the complex. The correlation of bonding geometry with the electronic properties of the rest of the metal-ligand system is an important theoretical task; the correlation of reaction chemistry with bonding geometry has major implications beyond the specifics of a given ligand. Our research in this area has evolved over the past decade from the nitrosyl ligand to the diazonium ligand, N_2R^+, to neutral diazo molecules, N_2R. It has run the gamut from empirical structural studies to determine geometries, to the extensive development of spectroscopic techniques for rapid determination of most geometries and the flagging of possibly unusual geometries, to the probing of the reaction chemistry of the bound ligand.

As a result of an extensive interest in nitrosyl chemistry, engendered by the discovery (Ref. 1) of the bent M-N-O linkage, bonding modes 1 and 2 are probably about equally common (Ref. 2) and there is reasonable understanding of the differences in reaction chemistry of NO in these two bonding modes. Moreover, empirical rules have been developed (Ref. 3) which have proved effective in predicting M-N-O geometries from the NO stretching

Note a. In the sketches of bonding modes the lines are meant to display connectivity, not bond order.

frequency. Thus the need to carry out extensive structural studies on nitrosyl complexes has diminished. Our research evolved very naturally into studies of the corresponding diazonium chemistry, as the N_2R^+ ligand is in a sense isoelectronic with NO, and the R group "replaces" the lone-pair electrons on the oxygen atom and thus provides a more discernible probe of the bonding. Moreover, the diazonium ligand is closely related to the dinitrogen ligand; indeed it has been suggested (Ref. 4) that aryldiazonium complexes may be useful models for studying the reduction of dinitrogen in synthetic and biological systems. In addition, one could envision a number of bonding modes for the RN_2^+ ligand, 3-6. Although geometry 3 was known from earlier work (Ref. 5), we (Ref. 6) provided the first example of the doubly-bent geometry, 4. We suspected on the basis of spectroscopic screening techniques and we confirmed by diffraction methods the first example of a "half doubly-bent" geometry for the ligand, intermediate between idealized geometries 3 and 4 (Ref. 7). At present geometries 5 and 6 remain unknown for the RN_2^+ ligand. Despite the interest in diazonium chemistry and structures in the past five years, there are some difficulties which limit the area. The number of starting materials that can be safely handled is limited to aryl compounds or to alkyl complexes of large bulk. There is a lack of generally useful synthetic routes to diazonium complexes of transition metals. Part of the problem arises from the charged nature of the ligand; one is limited to reactions with anionic and neutral metal systems.

NEUTRAL DIAZO MOLECULES

The obvious extension of this type of chemistry is to organic diazo molecules, N_2R. In spite of the fact that a number of neutral diazo molecules are found in the literature (Ref. 8), the coordination and reaction chemistry of these ligands with transition metals is in its infancy. The use of neutral diazo molecules as ligands to form transition-metal diazo complexes presents a special synthetic challenge, since loss of dinitrogen from these molecules is very facile. Indeed the interaction of neutral diazo molecules with organometallic complexes generally proceeds in one of two ways: (i) loss of dinitrogen to form a transient carbene species which may or may not be stabilized by the metal or (ii) coordination of the intact diazo molecule. A number of organometallic carbene species have been strongly implicated in the polymerization of olefins (Ref. 9) and in the formation of cyclopropanes (Ref. 10). It clearly is of interest to investigate the conditions under which, on the one hand, reactive carbenes are formed from RN_2 molecules in the presence of transition metals and, on the other hand, stable transition-metal complexes of RN_2 molecules are formed. This, coupled with the wider range of starting molecules and the obvious ability to react such molecules with cationic as well as anionic and neutral transition-metal species, was our original motivation for extending our studies into this area. In quick succession (Ref. 10a and 11) we studied the structures of two RN_2-transition metal complexes and found geometries 5 and 6, neither of which has yet been found for RN_2^+ complexes. Coordination geometry 5, the totally linear arrangement, was found in the structure of $RuH_2(N_2B_{10}H_8SMe_2)(PPh_3)_3$ (Ref. 11); the η^2-linkage, 6, was found in the structure of Ni(t-BuNC)$_2$(9-diazofluorene) (Ref. 10a), (Ph = phenyl; t-BuNC = tert-butylisocyanide). It was thus immediately apparent that the structural chemistry of RN_2^+ and RN_2 complexes shows some exciting differences.

Complexes derived from $N_2C_5X_4$, X = Cl, Br

Thus far we have concentrated our efforts on the reactions of 9-diazofluorene and derivatives and of tetrahalides of diazocyclopentadiene with transition-metal systems. The metal systems studied include those of Ir(I), Rh(I), Ni(0), Pt(0), and Ru(0). In the Ir(I) systems (Ref. 12 and 13) with $N_2C_5Cl_4$, the key compound is $IrCl(N_2C_5Cl_4)(PPh_3)_2$ prepared by reaction (1)

$$IrCl(CO)(PPh_3)_2 \xrightarrow[N_2C_5Cl_4,\ 0°C]{CHCl_3/EtOH,\ ArCON_3} IrCl(N_2C_5Cl_4)(PPh_3)_2 \quad (1)$$

This compound has been characterized by the usual analytical and spectroscopic methods and by a complete crystal structure (Ref. 13a). The $N_2C_5Cl_4$ molecule is bound to the Ir center in the singly-bent linkage 3. Although we have characterized spectroscopically a number of derivatives of $IrCl(N_2C_5Cl_4)(PPh_3)_2$ (see Table 1), more extensive spectroscopic and structural studies on a wider range of compounds are needed so that spectroscopic methods can be developed to screen for unusual coordination geometries.

To take but one example of the difficulty of spectroscopic characterization: t-BuNC reacts instantaneously with $IrCl(N_2C_5Cl_4)(PPh_3)_2$ at -78° to form a bright purple solution from which we isolate the five-coordinate complex $IrCl(N_2C_5Cl_4)$(t-BuNC)$(PPh_3)_2$. The high value of ν(IrCl) of 314 cm^{-1} suggests a square-pyramidal coordination geometry and is consistent with the single resonance at δ -10.22 in the ^{31}P nmr spectrum. But the close

TABLE 1. Comparison of the reactions of $IrCl(N_2R)(PPh_3)_2$ with L

L	$N_2C_5Cl_4$ [a]	N_2Ph^+ [b]
PR_3	$IrCl(N_2C_5Cl_4)(PR_3)(PPh_3)_2$	$IrCl(N_2Ph)(PR_3)(PPh_3)_2^+$
t-BuNC	$IrCl(N_2C_5Cl_4)$(t-BuNC)$(PPh_3)_2$	$IrCl(N_2Ph)$(t-BuNC)$(PPh_3)_2^+$
CO	$IrCl(CO)(PPh_3)_2$	$IrCl(N_2Ph)(CO)(PPh_3)_2^+$
SO_2	$IrCl(SO_2)(PPh_3)_2$	?
NO^+	$IrCl(N_2C_5Cl_4)(NO)(PPh_3)_2^+$	$IrCl(NO)(PPh_3)_2^+$
HCl	$IrCl_2H(N_2C_5Cl_4)(PPh_3)_2$	$IrCl_2(HN_2Ph)(PPh_3)_2^+$

a)Reference 13, b)Reference 14

correspondence of the value of ν(NN) to that in the corresponding NO^+ complex suggests a similar disposition of the $N_2C_5Cl_4$ ligand in the two systems. If this ligand is in the basal plane of a square-pyramid in the t-BuNC complex, this puts the t-BuNC in the apical position, not a likely possibility. Clearly more and better spectral and especially more definitive structural data on a wider range of these five-coordinate N_2R complexes are needed.

The structures of $IrCl(N_2C_5Cl_4)(PPh_3)_2$ and $IrCl(N_2Ph)(PPh_3)_2^+$ (Ref. 15) are very similar: both contain the singly-bent diazo linkage. But the reaction chemistry of $IrCl(N_2C_5Cl_4)(PPh_3)_2$ resembles only to a point the chemistry of the cationic aryldiazonium complex $[IrCl(N_2Ph)(PPh_3)_2][PF_6]$ (Ref. 14). The chemistries are compared in Table 1. Both compounds form five-coordinate complexes with phosphines and isocyanides and exhibit similar decreases in the values of ν(NN) upon coordination of these ligands. However, the reactions with CO, HCl, and NO^+ are very different. The coordination of the nitrosyl ligand to $IrCl(N_2C_5Cl_4)(PPh_3)_2$ is especially surprising since NO^+ displaces the phenyldiazonium ligand from $IrCl(N_2Ph)(PPh_3)_2^+$. Presumably the subtle electronic changes engendered in going from N_2Ph^+ to the presumably poorer π-acceptor $N_2C_5Cl_4$ are sufficient to alter the chemistry even though the structures are very similar. Electronic changes manifest themselves in other ways. Our attempts to isolate discrete rhodium complexes $RhCl(N_2C_5Cl_4)L_2$ (L = phosphine) were unsuccessful, although these complexes were observed as transient species in solution. Evidently the much decreased basicity of the rhodium center does not provide the proper electronic balance for the isolation of stable diazo complexes. Similarly, the basicity (Ref. 16) of the phosphine ligand is critical. When "$IrCl(PPh_2(OMe))_2$", generated in situ from the μ-chloro-iridium cyclooctene dimer and $PPh_2(OMe)$, was allowed to react with $N_2C_5Cl_4$ no isolable diazo complex was obtained. It is apparent that these neutral diazo molecules as well as the diazonium cations are capable of coordinating only to those metal systems which display rather specific electronic properties.

The reactions of $N_2C_5X_4$ with other metal systems provide interesting contrasts with the Ir(I) systems above. Thus the complexes Ni(t-BuNC)$_2$($N_2C_5Cl_4$), $Pt(N_2C_5Cl_4)(PPh_3)_2$, and $Ru(CO)_2(N_2C_5Cl_4)(PPh_3)_2$ and a series of related complexes have been prepared (Ref. 17). Only the latter complex has been characterized crystallographically (Fig. 1). Again we have an example of the η^2-coordination, 6, of an RN_2 molecule, the second such example. On the basis of comparative spectroscopic data it appears as though all of these complexes have η^2-coordination of $N_2C_5Cl_4$.

Complexes derived from 9-diazofluorene

Since 9-diazofluorene forms a stable complex with Ni(0) (Ref. 10a), we have investigated other possible complexes of 9-diazofluorene. We find (Ref. 17) that it readily forms stable complexes with Ru(0) and Pt(0) in which the molecule is again η^2-coordinated. But the reaction of diazofluorene with $IrCl(N_2)(PPh_3)_2$ yields fluorenone ketazine and no complex containing diazofluorene (Ref. 13). We believe that the instability of the hypothetical IrCl(diazofluorene)$(PPh_3)_2$ molecule is electronic in origin, since space-filling models indicate that there are no serious steric constraints. A rough indication of the electronic nature of a given N_2R molecule may be obtained from the pK_a value of the parent R molecule, as the ability to stabilize negative charge within the carbon framework is certainly related to the stability of the possible N_2R complex. The pK_a value of $C_5Cl_4H_2$ we estimate to be 10-13 on the basis of the known pK_a of cyclopentadiene

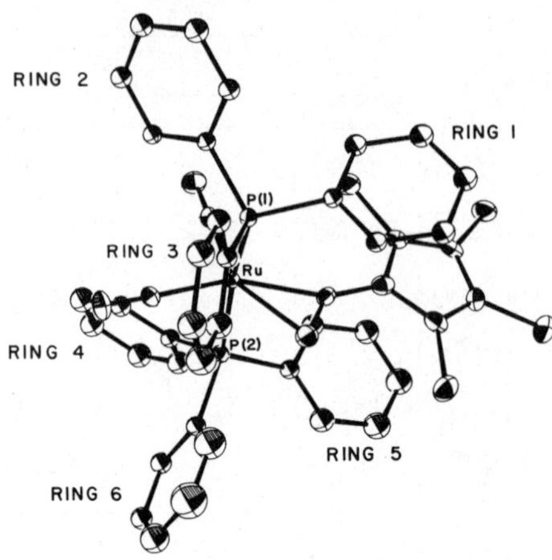

Fig. 1. The $Ru(CO)_2(N_2C_5Cl_4)(PPh_3)_2$ molecule (from Ref. 17).

(18.0) (Ref. 18). The pK_a of fluorene is 22.6 (Ref. 19). This suggests that if we select a derivative of 9-diazofluorene with a lower pK_a we might obtain a stable complex with "$IrCl(PPh_3)_2$". Candidates are 2,7-dibromo-9-diazofluorene, 2,2',7,7'-tetranitro-9-diazofluorene, and 2,7-dicyano-9-diazofluorene. If a stable complex is obtained how will the N_2R molecule be coordinated? Can we obtain a stable Rh(I) system by suitable modification of the electronic nature of the diazofluorene? These aspects are currently under study.

Comparisons of reaction chemistry

Let us provide one illustration of the varied reaction chemistry of these systems. Diazomethane and diazofluorene are catalytically decomposed by various nickel(0) or palladium(0) complexes in the presence of an excess of diethyl maleate to give cyclopropanation products. These products are derived from the direct reaction of Ni(0)-carbene complexes with the olefin (Ref. 20). However, when diazocyclopentadienes ($N_2C_5X_4$) are used as potential carbene precursors with Ni(0), no cyclopropane products are obtained. Instead, we (Ref. 17) obtain triphenylphosphonium cyclopentadienylidene (10) (Ref. 21). Diazo molecules such as diazocyclopentadiene and diphenyldiazomethane are known (Ref. 22) to react with triphenylphosphine to form the corresponding "phosphazine" compounds (7) and (8). When (8) is heated to 185° *in vacuo*, triphenylphosphine diphenylmethylene (9) is obtained (Ref. 22). All attempts to effect thermal decomposition of (7) to (10) have

$$C_5H_4{=}N_2 + PPh_3 \longrightarrow \underset{(7)}{C_5H_4{=}N{-}N{=}PPh_3} \nrightarrow \underset{(10)}{C_5H_4{=}PPh_3} \qquad (2)$$

$$Ph_2C{=}N_2 + PPh_3 \longrightarrow \underset{(8)}{Ph_2C{=}N{-}N{=}PPh_3} \xrightarrow{185^{\circ}} N_2 + \underset{(9)}{Ph_3P{=}CPh_2} \qquad (3)$$

failed. However, thermal decomposition of "$Ni(N_2C_5H_4)(PPh_3)_2$", generated *in situ* from $Ni(C_2H_4)(PPh_3)_2$ and $N_2C_5H_4$, yields the triphenylphosphonium cyclopentadienylidene product (10). One can envision two means of ylide formation: (i) the diazo ligand may attack the nickel-phosphine complex to form the "phosphazine" (7) which decomposes in the presence of the metal to the ylide (10), or (ii) the nickel-diazo complex decomposes to form a carbene species $(PPh_3)_2Ni{=}C_5H_4$ which preferentially attacks triphenylphosphine rather than diethyl maleate to form (10).

The reaction chemistry of diazocyclopentadienes coordinated to Ni(0) is thus very different from that observed for diazomethane or diazofluorene Ni systems. Perhaps the ability of the cyclopentadienyl carbene species $:C_5H_4$ to stabilize electron density on the "carbenoid" carbon atom by delocalization into a C_5 aromatic system is one reason for the differing reaction chemistry. Such stabilization would tend to diminish the carbenoid character of the C(1) carbon atom, and thus inhibit its reaction as a carbene with olefins to produce cyclopropane products. In fact the stabilization of the carbene by aromatization would tend to make the C(1) carbon atom more positive in character and thus facilitate its reaction with electron donor species, such as triphenylphosphine, to give ylide products.

REACTIONS OF CARBONYL SULFIDE, COS, WITH TRANSITION METALS

For a number of years we have been interested in complexes formed between heterocumulenes X=C=Y and transition metals. A recent example is the rhodium carbene complex formed by the reaction of $RhClP_3$ with benzoyl isothiocyanate (Ref. 23). Recently we embarked on a study of the reactions of carbonyl sulfide, O=C=S, with transition-metal systems (Ref. 24). The rationale for this work is (i) the paucity of information on the coordination chemistry of this interesting molecule, (ii) its obvious relationship to CO_2, a molecule which apparently forms few stable complexes, and to CS_2, whose coordination chemistry is well explored.

In 1967 Baird and Wilkinson (Ref. 25) reported that carbonyl sulfide reacts with $Pt(PPh_3)_3$ to give $Pt(COS)(PPh_3)_2$. The product appears to be similar to the structurally characterized carbon disulfide compound $Pt(CS_2)(PPh_3)_2$ (Ref. 26) in which the CS_2 molecule is bound to the platinum atom through an η^2(C-S) linkage. The compound is very labile; for example, the sulfur-bridged dimer, $Pt_2S(CO)(PPh_3)_3$, is produced when $Pt(COS)(PPh_3)_2$ is refluxed in chloroform (Ref. 25 and 27). Several other compounds containing carbonyl sulfide as a ligand have been reported. The complex $RhClH_2(PCy_3)_2$ (Cy = cyclohexyl) reacts with COS in benzene to give $RhCl(COS)(PCy_3)_2$ and H_2 (Ref. 28). Bonding through the C-S linkage has been proposed. This compound is unstable in solution, decomposing to yield $RhCl(CO)(PCy_3)_2$. The nature of the product, which contains sulfur, is not known. Carbonyl sulfide has been shown to bind to the coordinatively unsaturated compound $Pd(PR_3)_2$ (R = isopropyl) to give $Pd(COS)(PR_3)_2$ (Ref. 29). Although attempts to prepare the related nickel compound (R = Cy) were unsuccessful, Ni(COS)(bipy) (bipy = bipyridyl) was prepared (Ref. 30) by replacement of cyclooctadiene from Ni(COD)(bipy).

A common reaction of COS is insertion into a metal-ligand bond. Thus insertion into a M-H bond is known (Ref. 31). The compound $[Ru(OSCH)(PMe_2Ph)_4][PF_6]$ is formed when $[RuH(PMe_2Ph)_5][PF_6]$ is allowed to react with COS. If excess dimethylamine is present, $[Ru(OSCNMe_2)(PMe_2Ph)_4][PF_6]$ is formed and H_2 is liberated. Infrared and nmr data are consistent with the thiocarbamato ligand being bound through both oxygen and sulfur in a bidentate manner. These compounds are similar to the structurally characterized CO_2 insertion product $[Ru(O_2CNMe_2)(PMe_2Ph)_4][PF_6]$ (Ref. 31) which contains a bidentate carbamato ligand. Carbon dioxide, carbonyl sulfide, and carbon disulfide also insert directly into metal-nitrogen bonds. Chisholm and Extine (Ref. 32) have prepared $M(OCSNMe_2)_4$ (M = Ti,Zr) and $Ta(OCSNMe_2)_5$ by direct reaction of carbonyl sulfide with the respective metal amine. Thorium and uranium thiocarbamates, $Th(OCSNR_2)_4$ and $U(OCSNR_2)_4$, (R = Me, Et, i-Bu) are also prepared similarly (Ref. 33).

We have investigated reactions of carbonyl sulfide with group VIII metal complexes (Ref. 24). Three reaction types have been observed: (i) carbonylation of a metal complex; (ii) coordination of carbonyl sulfide; and (iii) abstraction of sulfur.

Carbonylation reactions

The general equation for carbonylation of a metal complex by carbonyl sulfide is shown in (4).

$$M(CO)_nL_m + COS \longrightarrow M(CO)_{n+1}L_{m-1} + SL \qquad (4)$$

Reactions of this type which we have studied are shown in (5)-(7).

$$RuClH(CO)(PPh_3)_3 + COS \longrightarrow RuClH(CO)_2(PPh_3)_2 + SPPh_3 \qquad (5)$$

$$(RhCl(PPh_3)_2)_2 + COS \longrightarrow RhCl(CO)(PPh_3)_2 + ? \qquad (6)$$

$$Fe(CO)_2(PPh_3)_3 + COS \longrightarrow Fe(CO)_3(PPh_3)_2 + Fe(CO)_4(PPh_3) + SPPh_3 \qquad (7)$$

The formation of triphenylphosphine sulfide is not necessary for carbonylation to occur. Thus, the ethylene-substituted iron compound $Fe(CO)_2(C_2H_4)(PPh_3)_2$ forms $Fe(CO)_3(PPh_3)_2$ upon exposure to COS (Ref. 24), but the fate of the sulfur has not been determined. It is significant that reactions (5) and (7) produce stable metal-CS_2 products, $RuCl(S_2CH)$-$(CO)(PPh_3)_2$ and $Fe(CO)_2(CS_2)(PPh_3)_2$, when CS_2 is substituted for COS (Ref. 34 and 24).

That the carbon-sulfur bond in COS is much more susceptible to cleavage than in CS_2 is apparent from these reactions and from the thermochemistry. We calculate that to break the CS bond in COS requires about 20 kcal/mole less energy than to break the CS bond in CS_2 (Ref. 35).

Coordination of carbonyl sulfide

We have prepared several carbonyl sulfide complexes. The general reaction is given in equation (8).

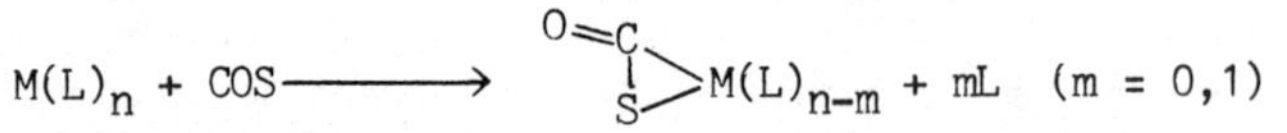

$$M(L)_n + COS \longrightarrow (\eta^2\text{-}OC{=}S)M(L)_{n-m} + mL \quad (m = 0,1) \qquad (8)$$

The compound $Ru(CO)_2(PPh_3)_3$ readily reacts with carbonyl sulfide to give the complex shown in equation (9).

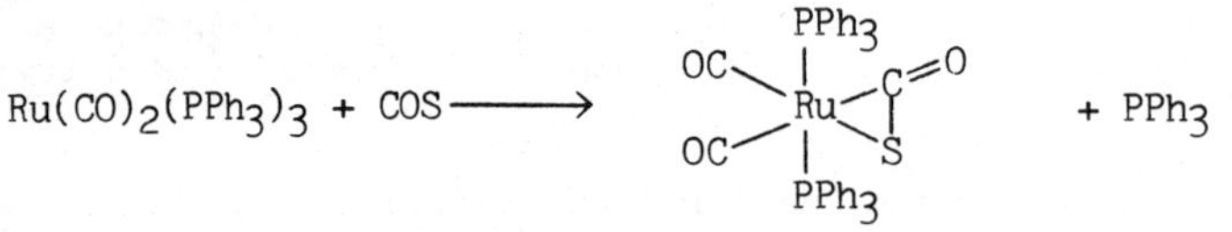

$$Ru(CO)_2(PPh_3)_3 + COS \longrightarrow Ru(CO)_2(\eta^2\text{-}C(O)S)(PPh_3)_2 + PPh_3 \qquad (9)$$

The product may be precipitated quantitatively from the reaction mixture, but it readily decomposes if allowed to stand in solution (equation 10).

$$Ru(CO)_2(COS)(PPh_3)_2 + PPh_3 \longrightarrow Ru(CO)_3(PPh_3)_2 + SPPh_3 \qquad (10)$$

Reactions of type (4) may initially form π-bound carbonyl sulfide complexes which then decompose to give the carbonylation products:

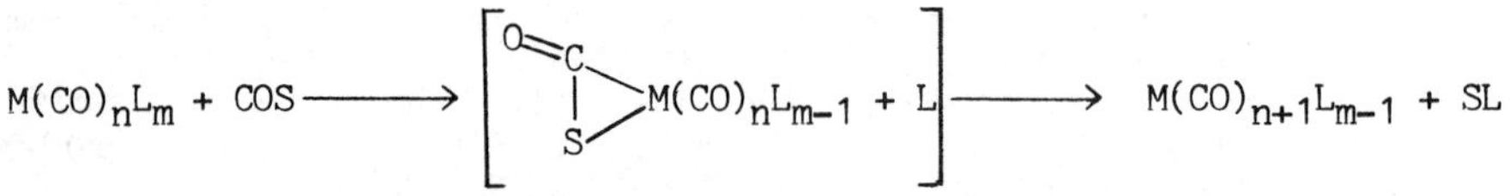

$$M(CO)_nL_m + COS \longrightarrow \left[(\eta^2\text{-}OC{=}S)M(CO)_nL_{m-1} + L \right] \longrightarrow M(CO)_{n+1}L_{m-1} + SL \qquad (11)$$

This reaction sequence is supported by reactions (9) and (10), in which the intermediates can be isolated.

A more basic metal complex may be required to bind COS than is needed to bind CS_2. The equilibrium shown in equation (12) lies to the left for X = Cl, Y = S, L = PPh_3 and is to the right when X =I, Y = S, L = PPh_3 (Ref. 25).

$$IrX(CO)L_2 + YCS \longrightarrow IrX(CO)(YCS)L_2 \qquad (12)$$

Attempts to form the corresponding carbonyl sulfide complexes (Y = O) failed (Ref. 24). However, when the basicity of the metal complex was increased by a change in L, activation of COS was achieved. For X = Cl; Y = O, L = PPh_3,$PMePh_2$ no reaction occurs (see Note b), but for L = PMe_2Ph or PMe_3 the carbonyl sulfide complexes are rapidly formed. Although several isomers are possible, ir and ^{31}P nmr data are consistent with the formation of a single isomer with trans-phosphine ligands. We favor isomer (11) over (12) although structural evidence is lacking.

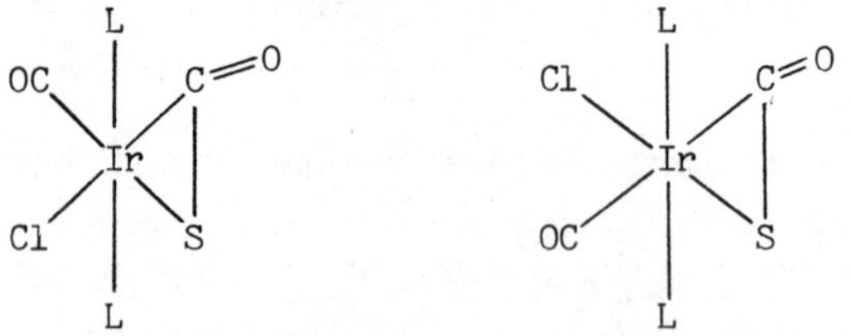

(11): trans-L, Ir with OC, Cl, and η²-C(=O)S

(12): trans-L, Ir with Cl, OC, and η²-C(=O)S

The effect of metal basicity has also been observed in the reactions of PdL_3 with COS and CS_2. The compound $Pd(PPh_3)_4$ reacts readily with CS_2 to form $Pd(CS_2)(PPh_3)_2$ (Ref. 25). We have prepared the analogous carbonyl sulfide complex from $Pd(PPh_3)_3$, but in this case the reaction is slow and the product is contaminated with unreacted starting material (Ref. 24). If a slightly more basic phosphine is used (L = $P(p\text{-}C_6H_4CH_3)_3$), the reaction proceeds rapidly and to completion.

Note b. After prolonged reaction times, compounds which are different from the simple metal-YCS adducts may be isolated. The nature of these products is under investigation.

$$Pd(P(p\text{-}C_6H_4CH_3)_3)_3 + COS \longrightarrow Pd(COS)(P(p\text{-}C_6H_4CH_3)_3)_2 + P(p\text{-}C_6H_4CH_3)_3 \quad (13)$$

Sulfur abstraction reactions

Metal complexes may abstract sulfur from carbonyl sulfide. The complex $Ru(CO)_2(COS)(PPh_3)_2$ reacts with carbonyl sulfide to give a dithiocarbonate.

$$Ru(CO)_2(COS)(PPh_3)_2 + COS \longrightarrow (OC)_2Ru(PPh_3)_2(S_2C{=}O) + CO \quad (14)$$

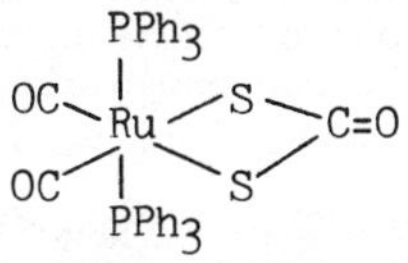

The compound $Pt(COS)(PPh_3)_2$ also reacts with carbonyl sulfide to form a compound which was formulated as the bis(carbonyl sulfide) adduct, $Pt(COS)_2(PPh_3)_2$ (Ref. 36). We believe the original formulation to be incorrect; rather a dithiocarbonate is formed by sulfur abstraction.

$$Pt(COS)(PPh_3)_2 + COS \longrightarrow Pt(S_2CO)(PPh_3)_2 + CO \quad (15)$$

The dithiocarbonate has been identified by spectral comparison with an authentic sample prepared by a literature method (Ref. 37). Both dithiocarbonates (equations (14) and (15)) may be prepared in one step by allowing the parent metal phosphine ($Ru(CO)_2(PPh_3)_3$ or $Pt(PPh_3)_3$) to react with an excess of carbonyl sulfide.

The complex $RhH(CO)(PPh_3)_3$ also abstracts sulfur from COS to give a rhodium thiol, as established by spectroscopic and diffraction studies (Ref. 24). The structure is shown in Fig. 2.

$$RhH(CO)(PPh_3)_3 + COS \longrightarrow Rh(SH)(CO)(PPh_3)_2 + CO + PPh_3 \quad (16)$$

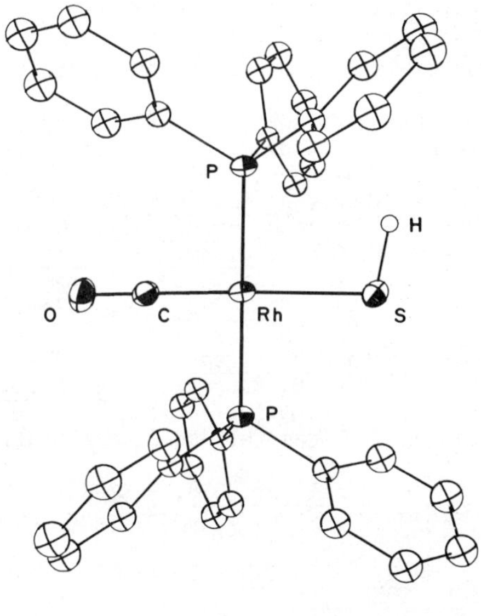

Fig. 2. A sketch of the structure of $Rh(SH)(CO)(PPh_3)_2$.

Unlike the other sulfur abstractions, this reaction does not involve coupling of two COS molecules, and no formal oxidation of the metal has occurred. The reaction could proceed through a metal-COS complex by hydride transfer to sulfur. We are investigating the analogous iridium reaction in an attempt to detect the proposed intermediate.

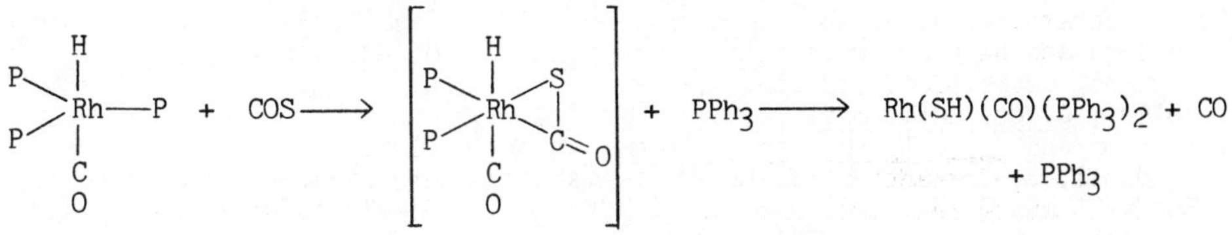

$$RhH(CO)P_3 + COS \longrightarrow [RhH(CO)P_2(SC{=}O)] + PPh_3 \longrightarrow Rh(SH)(CO)(PPh_3)_2 + CO + PPh_3 \quad (17)$$

CONCLUSIONS

We have shown that the synthesis, characterization, and reaction chemistry of complexes formed between neutral diazo molecules and transition metals offer many very exciting possibilities. We and others (Ref. 38) have thus far barely touched this rich chemistry. Even so, we have observed three different bonding modes of N_2R to transition metals, two of which have not been observed in the closely related N_2R^+ complexes, and we have demonstrated important differences between the reactions of $N_2C_5Cl_4$ and 9-diazofluorene. Comparison of the structures and reactions of these complexes with those of the related complexes of N_2R^+ will ultimately prove to be especially useful in understanding this chemistry.

Similarly, we feel that the reactions of COS with transition-metal systems lead to a very rich and diverse chemistry. A more basic metal center is needed to bind the C-S linkage of COS than is needed to bind CS_2. But once formed, such metal complexes are very reactive and three reaction pathways have been identified: (i) decomposition to give a metal carbonyl; (ii) reaction with another molecule of COS to give a dithiocarbonate; (iii) rearrangement to give a metal sulfide (Ref. 25 and 27) or metal thiol (Ref. 24).

Acknowledgments - This work was kindly supported by the U.S. National Science Foundation (CHE76-10335). We are indebted to Johnson Matthey, Inc. of Malvern, Pennsylvania for the loan of the precious metals used in this work.

REFERENCES

1. D. J. Hodgson, N. C. Payne, J. A. McGinnety, R. G. Pearson, and J. A. Ibers, J. Am. Chem. Soc. 90, 4486-4488 (1968).
2. B. A. Frenz and J. A. Ibers in M.T.P. International Review of Science, Physical Chemistry, Series One, 11, 33-72 (1972).
3. B. L. Haymore and J. A. Ibers, Inorg. Chem. 14, 3060-3070 (1975).
4. (a) G. W. Parshall, J. Am. Chem. Soc. 89, 1822-1826 (1967).
   (b) D. J. Sutton, J. Chem. Soc. Rev. 4, 443-470 (1975).
   (c) A. B. Gilchrist, G. W. Rayner-Canham, and D. Sutton, Nature 235, 42-44 (1972).
5. G. Avitabile, P. Ganis, and M. Nemiroff, Acta Crystallogr. B27, 725-731 (1971).
6. A. P. Gaughan, Jr., B. L. Haymore, J. A. Ibers, W. H. Myers, T. E. Nappier, Jr., and D. W. Meek, J. Am. Chem. Soc. 95, 6859-6861 (1973).
7. M. Cowie, B. L. Haymore, and J. A. Ibers, J. Am. Chem. Soc. 98, 7608-7617 (1976).
8. (a) A. P. Cox, L. F. Thomas, and J. Sheridan, Nature 181, 1000-1001 (1958).
   (b) D. M. Lemal, F. Menger, and G. W. Clark, J. Am. Chem. Soc. 85, 2529-2530 (1963).
   (c) H. E. Zimmerman and D. H. Paskovick, J. Am. Chem. Soc. 86, 2149-2160 (1964).
   (d) N. Obata and I. Moritani, Bull. Chem. Soc. Japan 39, 1975-1980 (1966).
   (e) G. B. Ansell, J. Chem. Soc. (B), 729-732 (1969).
   (f) C. T. Presley and R. L. Sass, Acta Crystallogr. B26, 1195-1198 (1970).
   (g) D. J. Abraham, T. G. Cochran, and R. D. Rosenstein, J. Am. Chem. Soc. 93, 6279-6281 (1971).
   (h) S. I. Murahashi, Y. Yoshimura, Y. Yamamoto, and I. Moritani, Tetrahedron 28, 1485-1496 (1972).
   (i) H. Hope and K. T. Black, Acta Crystallogr. B28, 3632-3634 (1972).
9. (a) B. A. Dolgoplosk, K. L. Makovetsky, T. G. Golenko, Y. V. Korshak, and E. I. Tinyakova, Eur. Polym. J. 10, 901-904 (1974).
   (b) B. A. Dolgoplosk, T. G. Golenko, K. L. Makovetskii, I. A. Oreshkin, and E. I. Tinyakova, Dokl. Akad. Nauk. SSSR, Ser. Khim. 216, 807-809 (1974).
10. (a) A. Nakamura, T. Yoshida, M. Cowie., S. Otsuka, and J. A. Ibers, J. Am. Chem. Soc. 99, 2108-2117 (1977).
   (b) H. Bonnemann, B. Bogdanovic, D. Uvalic, G. Schromburg, and G. Wilke, Proc. Int. Conf. Organometal. Chem 4th, Abstract J4 (1969).
   (c) P. W. Jolly and G. Wilke, The Organic Chemistry of Nickel, Academic Press, New York, Vol. 1, 340-342 (1974).
11. K. D. Schramm and J. A. Ibers, Inorg. Chem. 16, 3287-3293 (1977).
12. K. D. Schramm and J. A. Ibers, J. Am. Chem. Soc. 100, 2932-2933 (1978).
13. (a) K. D. Schramm and J. A. Ibers, Inorg. Chem. 19, 1231-1236 (1980).
   (b) K. D. Schramm and J. A. Ibers, Inorg. Chem., in press (1980).
14. B. L. Haymore and J. A. Ibers, J. Am. Chem. Soc. 95, 3052-3054 (1973).
15. B. L. Haymore, unpublished results.
16. C. A. Tolman, J. Am. Chem. Soc. 92 2953-2956 (1970).
17. K. D. Schramm and J. A. Ibers, Inorg. Chem., in press (1980).
18. F. G. Bordwell, J. Branca, and H. Fried, private communication.
19. F. G. Bordwell and G. J. McCollum, J. Org. Chem. 41 2391-2395 (1976).
20. G. Wilke, Angew. Chem. 72 581-582 (1960).

21. E. Lord, M. P. Naan and C. D. Hall, J. Chem. Soc. (B), 1401-1410 (1970).
22. F. Ramirez and S. Levy, J. Org. Chem. 23, 2036-2037 (1958).
23. K. Itoh, I. Matsuda, F. Ueda, Y. Ishii, and J. A. Ibers, J. Am. Chem. Soc. 99, 2118-2126 (1977).
24. T. R. Gaffney and J. A. Ibers, unpublished results.
25. M. C. Baird and G. Wilkinson, J. Chem. Soc. (A), 865-872 (1967).
26. R. Mason and A. I. M. Rae, J. Chem. Soc. (A), 1767-1770 (1970).
27. A. C. Skapski and P. G. H. Troughton, J. Chem. Soc. (A), 2772-2781 (1969).
28. H. L. M. van Gaal and J. P. J. Verlaan, J. Organometal. Chem. 133, 93-105 (1977).
29. H. Werner, W. Bertleff, O. Kolb, and K. Leonhard, IX International Conference on Organometallic Chemistry, Abstracts, B25.
30. E. Uhlig and W. Poppitz, Z. Chem. 19, 191-192 (1979).
31. T. V. Ashworth, M. Nolte, and E. Singleton, J. Organometal. Chem. 121, C57-C60 (1976).
32. M. H. Chisholm and M. W. Extine, J. Am. Chem. Soc. 99, 782-792 (1977).
33. K. W. Bagnall and E. Yanir, J. Inorg. Nucl. Chem. 36, 777-779 (1974).
34. S. D. Robinson and A. Sahajpal, Inorg. Chem. 11, 2718-2722 (1977).
35. JANAF Thermochemical Tables, 2nd edition, 1971, Natl. Bur. Stand., NSRDS-NBS 37.
36. R. K. Poddar and U. Agarwala, J. Coord. Chem. 6, 207-209 (1977).
37. P. J. Hayward, D. M. Blake, G. Wilkinson, and C. J. Nyman, J. Am. Chem. Soc. 92, 5873-5878 (1970).
38. W. A. Herrmann, Ang. Chem. Int. Ed. Eng. 17, 800-812 (1978), and references therein.

TRANSITION METAL HYDRIDES AS INTERMEDIATES IN ORGANOMETALLIC REACTIONS

L. M. Venanzi

Laboratorium für Anorganische Chemie, ETH-Zentrum, CH-8092 Zürich, Switzerland

Abstract - The insertion reaction of EtC≡CEt, CH_2=CH_2 and CH_2=$CHCO_2Me$ into the Pt-H bond of trans-$[PtH(CH_3CN)(Ph_3P)_2]^+$ is described. It is shown that the pathway of this reaction is strongly influenced by the presence of the ester group on the unsaturated hydrocarbon.
The regioselectivity of the insertion reaction of CH_2=$CHCO_2Me$ into the Pt-H bond of trans-$[PtH(NO_3)(Et_3P)_2]^+$ is strongly solvent-dependent. This reaction, when carried out in methanol, produces only the straight-chained alkyl derivative while the same reaction, when carried out in acetone, produces 20 % of the straight-chained derivative and 80 % of the branched isomer.

The insertion reactions of unsaturated hydrocarbons with binuclear hydrido-bridged species $[Pt_2H(\mu_2\text{-}H)(Ph)(Et_3P)_4]^+$, $[Pt_2(\mu_2\text{-}H)_2(Ph)(Et_3P)_4]^+$ and $[ItPtH_2(\mu_2\text{-}H)_2(Et_3P)_3]^+$ are also briefly described.

INTRODUCTION

Transition metal hydride complexes play a major role in organometallic reactions, both stoicheiometric and catalytic. Species containing metal-hydrogen bonds have been either identified or postulated as intermediates in many reactions of actual or potential synthetic interest (Ref. 1).

This wide range of applications of hydrido-complexes is largely due to their very varied reactivity. Thus, most 'unsaturated' organic and inorganic molecules react with many hydrido-complexes to give less 'unsaturated' coordinated moieties. Some typical reactions of this type are shown in Scheme 1.

SCHEME 1

Some "Insertion" Reactions into Metal Hydrogen Bonds

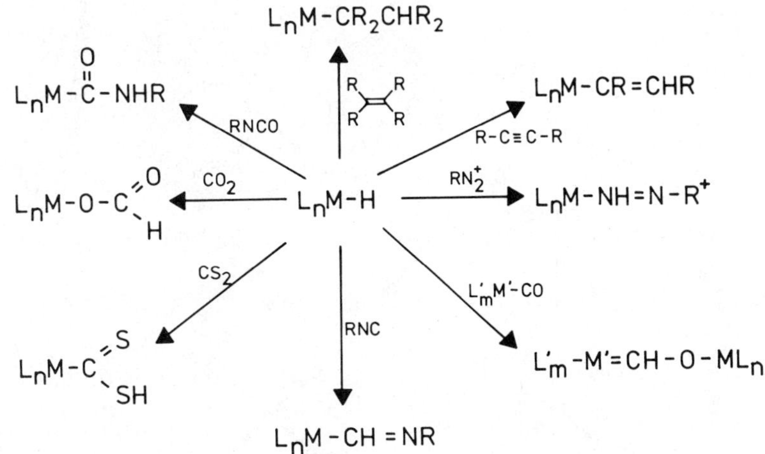

The insertion of alkenes and alkynes into metal-hydrogen bonds (Ref. 2) is, undoubtedly, among the most important reactions in organometallic chemistry. They also appear to be the most complex. Recent investigations (Ref. 3) of the reaction:

$$\underline{\text{trans}}\text{-}[PtH(CH_3CN)(Ph_3P)_2][BF_4] \quad + \quad MeO_2C\text{-}C{\equiv}C\text{-}CO_2Me$$

have shown that, in $CDCl_3$, traces of moisture in the solvent react very rapidly, and apparently quantitatively, with the hydrido-complex according to:

$$\underset{\text{(I)}}{\underline{\text{trans}}\text{-}[PtH(CH_3CN)(Ph_3P)_2]^+} \quad + \quad \underset{\text{(II)}}{MeO_2C\text{-}C{\equiv}C\text{-}CO_2Me} \quad + \quad H_2O$$

$$\rightarrow \quad \underset{\text{(III)}}{[Pt(MeO_2C\text{-}C{\equiv}C\text{-}CO_2Me)(Ph_3P)_2]} \quad + \quad CH_3CN \quad + \quad H_3O^+$$

The platinum(0) complex (III) thus formed reacts further to give the vinyl complex (IV) shown below:

$$\text{(III)} \quad + \quad CH_3CN \quad + \quad H_3O^+ \quad \rightarrow \quad \underset{\text{(IV)}}{\underline{\text{cis}}\text{-}[Pt\{C(CO_2Me)C{=}CH\text{-}CO_2Me\}(CH_3CN)(Ph_3P)_2]^+} + H_2O$$

It was also established (Ref. 3) that, under the experimental conditions used, the rate for the production of (IV) from (III) is much slower than that for the direct alkyne insertion reaction. This direct insertion reaction, when carried out under pseudo-first order condition, was found to follow the well-established two-term rate law characteristic of nucleophilic substitution reactions of platinum(II) complexes, i.e., $k_{obs} = k_1 + k_2[L]$ (Ref. 4). Approximate values of these rate constants for the formation of (IV) were obtained and the slower rearrangement of (IV) to the corresponding trans-isomer was also noted.

It was proposed (a) that the alkyne-independent pathway arose from the slow formation of a hydrido-carboxylate complex which, subsequently, underwent rapid alkyne insertion and (b) that the alkyne-dependent pathway involved a five-coordinate intermediate containing the alkene bound through the triple bond.

In order to test whether this reactivity pattern was generally applicable, the insertion reaction of other alkynes and of some alkenes was studied.

THE INSERTION REACTION OF HEX-3-YNE

The results of the reaction of hex-3-yne with trans-$[PtH(CH_3CN)(Ph_3P)_2]^+$ (I) are summarized in Scheme 2 (Ref. 5).

SCHEME 2
The Insertion Reaction of 2-Hexyne into trans-$[PtH(CH_3CN)(Ph_3P)_2][BF_4]$

P. Boron, 1980

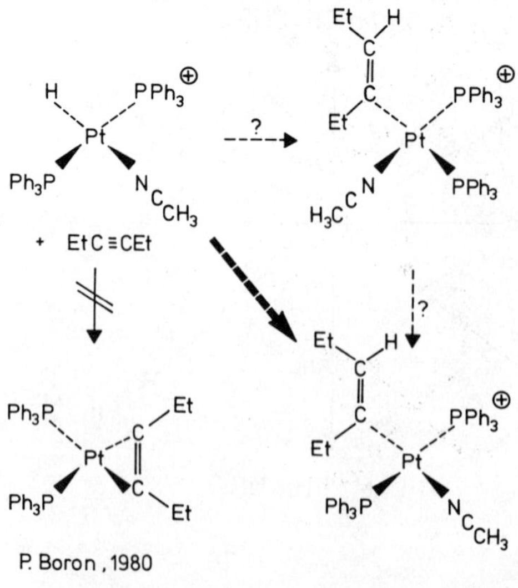

It was found that, under our experimental conditions (Ref. 3), the only complexes present in detectable quantities during the reaction were the initial hydride and the final product trans-$[Pt\{C(Et)C{=}CHEt\}(CH_3CN)(Ph_3P)_2]^+$. Furthermore, the observed insertion rate depended only on the concentration of the hydrido-complex as can be seen on Fig. 1.

FIGURE 1
Rate of Alkyne Insertion, under Pseudo First Order Conditions, of EtC≡CEt into trans-$[PtH(CH_3CN)(Ph_3P)_2][BF_4]$ in $CDCl_3$ at 251°K

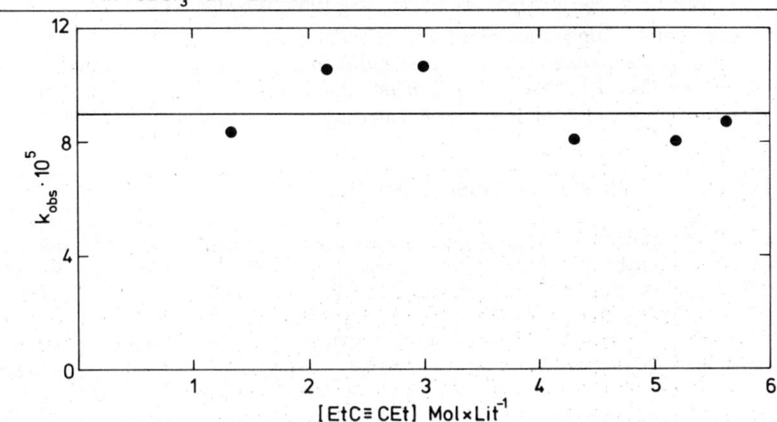

THE INSERTION REACTION OF ETHENE

The reaction pattern observed for hex-3-yne was also observed for ethene (Ref. 6). The failure to observe the formation of platinum(0) and of cis-species both here and in the hex-3-yne reation suggests that, in these cases, insertion may occur by a pathway which is different from that operative in the case of MeO_2C-C≡C-CO_2Me, a suggestion which is supported by the experiments described in the next section.

THE INSERTION REACTION OF METHYL ACRYLATE

The results of the reaction of CH_2=CH-CO_2Me with trans-$[PtH(CH_3CN)(Ph_3P)_2]^+$ (I) are summarized in Scheme 3. As can be seen, the observed pattern is similar to that found for

SCHEME 3
The Insertion Reaction of Methyl Acrylate into trans-$[PtH(CH_3CN)(Ph_3P)_2][BF_4]$

H, PPh_3, ⊕, Pt, Ph_3P, $NCCH_3$ + CH_2=CH—CO_2Me → CO_2Me–CH_2–CH_2, PPh_3, ⊕, Pt, H_3CCN, PPh_3

↓ CO_2Me–CH_2–CH_2, PPh_3, ⊕, Pt, Ph_3P, $NCCH_3$

(not observed) Ph_3P, Ph_3P, Pt, CH_2–CH–CO_2Me + $H^{\oplus}$ + CH_3CN

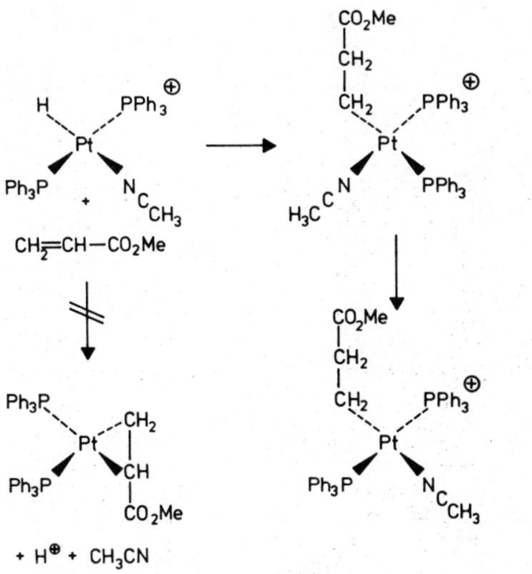

MeO_2C-C≡C-CO_2Me, i.e., a cis-organometallic intermediate can be detected prior to its isomerization to the trans final product and the latter reaction can be prevented by carrying out the insertion reaction at low temperatures (Ref. 5). Under these reaction conditions no [Pt(CH_2=CH-CO_2Me)(Ph_3P)$_2$] could be detected although this compound could be obtained in a separate preparative experiment (Ref. 6).

At the present stage of this study the following pattern is emerging:

1. the formation of detectable quantities of cis-organometallic intermediates appear to be characteristic of functionalised alkenes and alkynes and it appears likely that this behaviour is associated with the formation of chelate rings of the type 'Pt-CH_2-CH_2-C(O)OMe' somewhere along the reaction coordinate;
2. the formation of platinum(0) complexes is a side-reaction which becomes significant in insertion processes only in special cases e.g., when the alkene or alkyne carries electron-attracting substituents and the solvent can act as a proton acceptor.

REGIO-SELECTIVITY EFFECTS IN ALKENE INSERTION REACTIONS

The insertion reaction of unsymmetrical alkenes (or alkynes) into metal-hydrogen bonds normally gives rise to mixtures of products. Thus, when a terminal olefin is used both n- and iso-alkyl derivatives can be formed as shown schematically below.

L_nM-H ⋮ ⋮ RHC=CH_2 → L_nM-CH(R)CH_3 L_nM-H ⋮ ⋮ H_2C=CHR → L_nM-CH_2-CH_2R

Most of the insertion reactions produce more of the branched chain isomer and this has been rationalized in terms of the bond polarities of the alkene and of the metal-hydrogen bond (Ref. 8).

The study of the insertion reaction of methyl acrylate with trans-[PtH(NO_3)(Et_3P)$_2$] has shown that the regio-selectivity of this reaction is strongly solvent-dependent (Ref. 6). Some of the data are summarized in Scheme 4.

SCHEME 4

The Influence of Solvent on the Regioselectivity of the Methyl Acrylate Insertion into trans-[PtH(NO_3)(Et_3P)$_2$]

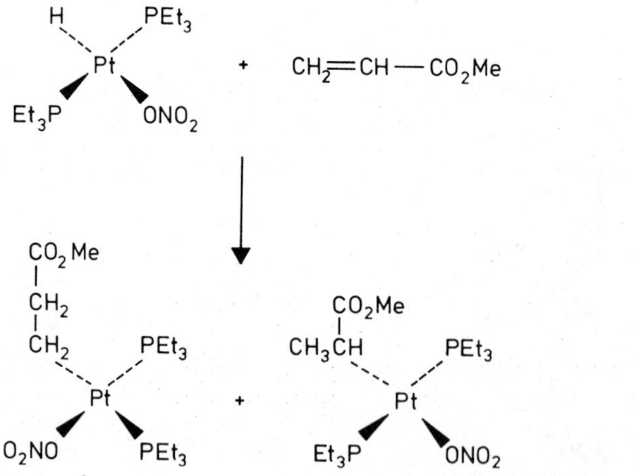

[Pt(H)(PEt_3)(Et_3P)(ONO_2)] + CH_2=CH—CO_2Me ↓

[Pt($CH_2CH_2CO_2Me$)(PEt_3)(O_2NO)(PEt_3)] + [Pt($CH_3CH(CO_2Me)$)(PEt_3)(Et_3P)(ONO_2)]

Solvent		
MeOH	100 %	-
Acetone	20%	80%
CH_2Cl_2	50%	50%

The cis-isomers above slowly isomerize to the corresponding trans-species.

These observation can be rationalized on the basis of the study of this reaction carried out by D. L. Thorn and R. Hoffmann (7). These authors conclude that: "The necessary final way-point of ethylene and hydride *cis* seems in the calculation to be best achieved by a sequence of associative and, preferably, dissociative steps".

Some of the possible low-energy five-coordinate intermediates (Ref. 7) in the insertion reaction of unsymmetrical alkenes are shown in Scheme 5.

SCHEME 5

Some Possible Intermediates in the Insertion Reaction of Unsymmetrical Alkenes

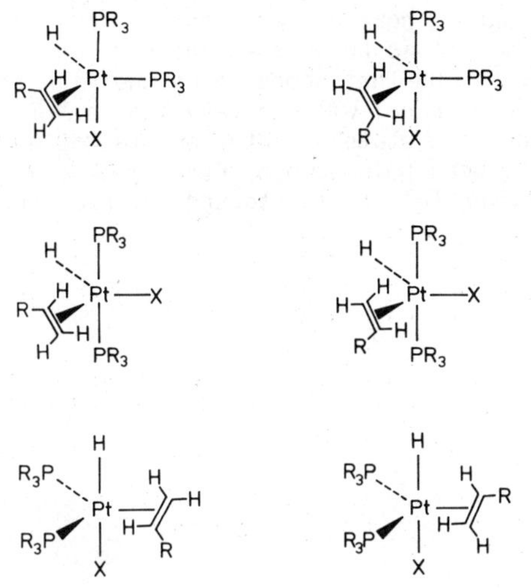

As can be seen, steric effects could play a significant role as to whether the alkene (or alkyne) is oriented with its substituent towards the hydride ligand or on the opposite side. The anionic ligand and the carboxylate group, however, would be solvated and, thus, would not exert significant mutual repulsions. One of the possible pairs of intermediates showing the different orientations of the coordinated alkyne is illustrated in Scheme 6.

SCHEME 6

A Possible Pathway for the Insertion of $CH_2{=}CH{-}CO_2Me$ into *trans*-$[PtH(NO_3)(Et_3P)_2]$ in CH_2Cl_2 and Acetone

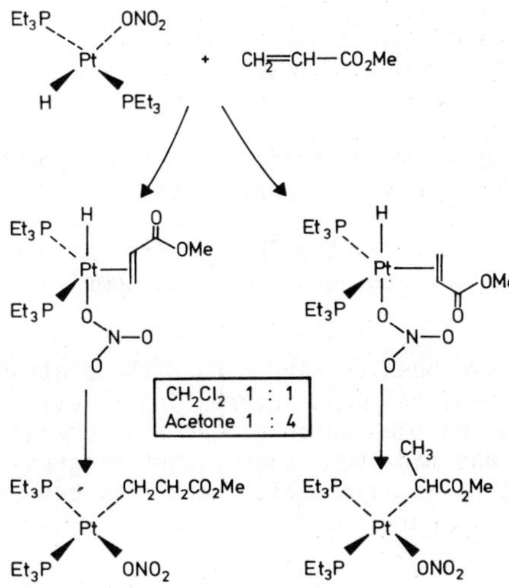

CH_2Cl_2	1 : 1
Acetone	1 : 4

When the insertion reaction is carried out in acetone it is likely that this process is associative as it is found that there is no significant nitrate dissociation in this solvent (Ref. 6).

The experimental results show that, when the reaction is carried out in acetone the straight-chained/branched isome ratio is 1:4, i.e., in the range observed for most 'normal' insertion reactions and it can be assumed that this distribution is controlled by the electronic factors mentioned earlier (Ref. 8).

When this reaction is carried out in dichloromethane an associative pathway is also likely to be favoured. In this medium, however, there will be no significant solvation of the nitrate and carboxylate groups which will, therefore, exert a mutual repelling effect favouring the alkene orientation which leads to the formation of the straight-chained isomer.

The results of the reaction carried out in methanol, however, are best rationalized by invoking a three-coordinate intermediate (Ref. 7). It is known that the hydrido-nitrate complex is extensively solvated in methanol (Ref. 6) and that, because of the high trans-effect of the hydride ligand (Ref. 9), the coordinated methanol will be very labile. Thus, in this case, the formation of a three-coordinate transition state or intermediate would be a low activation energy process. Furthermore, it has been pointed out (Ref. 7) that a three coordinate platinum(II) species is subject to Jahn-Teller effects and the rearrangement shown in Scheme 7 is of low energy.

SCHEME 7

A Possible Pathway for the Insertion Reaction of $CH_2{=}CH{-}CO_2Me$ into *trans*-$[PtH(NO_3)(Et_3P)_2]$ in Methanol

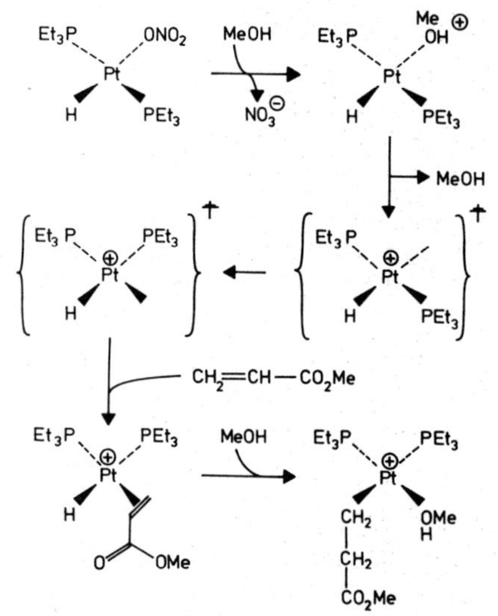

The regio-selectivity, in this case, would arise from the preferred orientation of the double bond relative to the two cis-ligands which are of very different sizes.

It may have become apparent by now that there is ample justification for the earlier statement that the alkene and alkyne insertion reactions are among the most complex in organometallic chemistry.

Although most of the work on these reactions have been carried out on the platinum system discussed above, from the catalytic point of view, the most interesting reactions are those involving dihydrides, i.e., those occurring during the course of the rhodium-catalyzed homogeneous alkene hydrogenation. This study has made very significant progress in recent years (Ref. 10), particularly the aspects concerning asymmetric induction, but its discussion would go beyond the scope of this paper.

INSERTION REACTIONS OF COMPLEXES WITH BRIDGING HYDRIDE LIGANDS

In recent years the study of the catalytic properties of polynuclear and cluster complexes has been actively pursued. Bi- and polynuclear complexes have been used as hydrogenation catalysts in the search for better and more selective synthetic routes. The complexes $[Ir_2Cl_2(\mu_2\text{-}H)(\mu_2\text{-}Cl)(\eta^5\text{-}C_5Me_5)_2]$ and $[Ir_2Cl_2(\mu_2\text{-}H)_2(\eta^5\text{-}C_5Me_5)_2]$, studied by P. M. Maitlis and co-workers, are examples of catalyst precursors containing bridging hydride ligands.

It has recently become apparent that binuclear hydrido-bridged complexes can be considered as being composed of a mononuclear hydrido-complex acting as a Lewis base and of a coordinatively unsaturated complex acting as a Lewis acid as shown in Scheme 8.

SCHEME 8

A Schematic Formulation of Hydrido-Bridged Complexes

"Lewis Acid" + "Lewis Base" → "Bridged Complex"

Schematic examples:

ACCEPTORS		DONORS		PRODUCTS
L_mM (coordinatively unsaturated species) OR $L\ M(S)_x$ (S=labile ligand)	+	$L'_mM'H$	→	$L_mMHM'L'_m$
	+	$L''_pM''H_2$	→	$L_mMH_2M''L''_p$
	+	$L'''_qM'''H_3$	→	$L_mMH_3M'''L'''_q$

Many compounds of this type have been reported in the literature (Ref. 1) and the insertion reactions of three types of compound recently prepared in our laboratories will be discussed here.

The first example to be discussed is that of the compound $[Pt_2H(\mu_2\text{-}H)(Ph)(Et_3P)_4][BPh_4]$ (V) (Ref. 12). This compound reacts at room temperature, with methyl acrylate as shown in Scheme 9 (Ref. 6).

SCHEME 9

Reaction of $[Pt_2H(\mu_2\text{-}H)(Ph)(Et_3P)_4]$ with $CH_2{=}CH{-}CO_2Me$

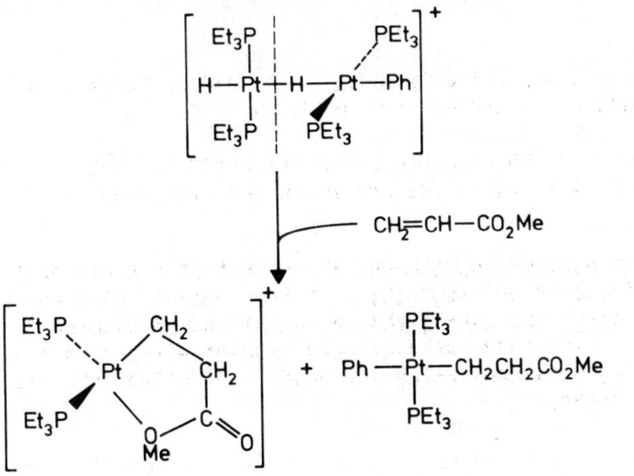

$$[H{-}Pt(PEt_3)_2{-}H{-}Pt(PEt_3)_2{-}Ph]^+ \xrightarrow{CH_2=CH-CO_2Me} [(Et_3P)_2Pt(CH_2CH_2C(=O)OMe)]^+ + Ph{-}Pt(PEt_3)_2{-}CH_2CH_2CO_2Me$$

The rapid stoicheiometric reaction shown above is followed by a slower reaction which, eventually leads to the formation of decomposition products. As can be seen, bridging hydrido-complexes of this type can easily undergo the alkene insertion reaction.

The second example is provided by a complex containing two bridging hydride ligands, i.e., $[Pt_2(Ph)(\mu_2\text{-}H)_2(Et_3P)_4][BF_4]$ (VI) (Ref. 13). This compound also reacts with methyl acrylate giving insertion products analogous to those given by (V). This reaction is still under investigation.

The last example describes the reactions of the bimetallic complex (VII) [Ref. 14).

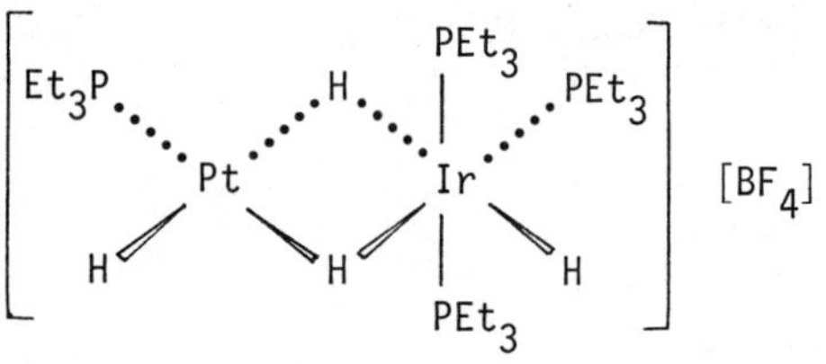

$[BF_4]$

(VII)

$[BF_4]$

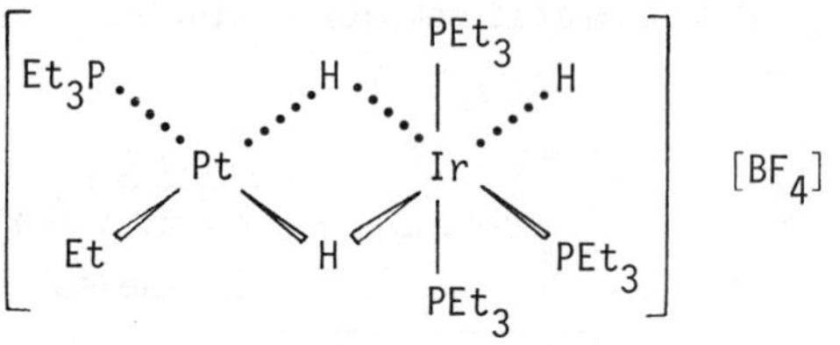

(VIII)

This compound reacts readily with ethene to give the ethyl derivative (VIII) which, on treatment with molecular hydrogen, gives ethane and the hydrido-complex (IX) (Ref. 15).

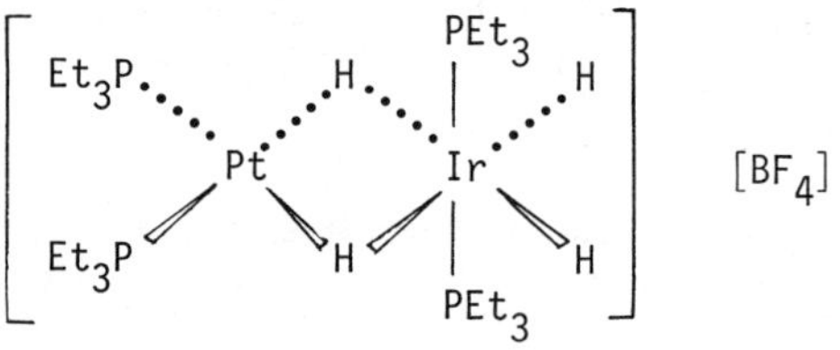

$[BF_4]$

(IX)

Compound (VII) reacts with hex-l-ene and hydrogen giving hexane. This catalytic reaction is, at present, under investigation. It can be presumed that, after the first initial stoicheiometric reaction, the actual catalyst is compound (IX).

The ease of formation of hetero-bimetallic hydrido-complexes opens up new and interesting areas of potential interest for homogeneous catalysis. Further work will show to what extent this potential can be realized.

REFERENCES

1. "Transition Metal Hydrides", R. Bau Ed., Adv. in Chem. Series 167, Am. Chem. Soc.(1978), and references quoted therein.
2. G. Henrici-Olivé and S. Olivé, Topics in Current Chemistry, 67, 107 (1976).
3. L. M. Venanzi, Pure & Appl. Chem., (1980) Lectures presented at the XX. International Conference on Coordination Chemistry, Calcutta, 10-14 December 1979, and references quoted therein.
4. C. H. Langford and H. B. Gray, "Ligand Substitution Processes", Benjamin, New York 1965.
5. P. Boron and L. M. Venanzi, unpublished observations.
6. G. Bracher, ETH Disseration, 1978.
7. D. L. Thorn and R. Hoffmann, J. Am. Chem. Soc., 100, 2079 (1978).
8. G. Henrici-Olivé and S. Olivé, Topics in Current Chemistry, 67, 107 (1976).
9. J. K. Burdett, Inorg. Chem., 16, 3013 (1977) and references quoted therein.
10. J. M. Brown and P. A. Chaloner, J. Chem. Soc. Chem. Comm., 345 (1980) and references quoted therein.
11. P. M. Maitlis, Accts. Chem. Res., 11, 301 (1978) and references quoted therein.
12. G. Bracher, D. M. Grove, L. M. Venanzi, F. Bachechi, P. Mura and L. Zambonelli, Angew. Chem., 90, 826 (1978); Angew. Chem. Int. Ed. Engl., 17, 778 (1978).
13. G. Bracher, D. M. Grove, P. S. Pregosin and L. M. Venanzi, Angew. Chem., 91, 169 (1979); Angew. Chem. Int. Ed. Engl., 18, 155 (1979).
14. A. Immirzi, A. Musco, P. S. Pregosin and L. M. Venanzi, Angew. Chem. in press.
15. A. Musco and L. M. Venanzi, unpublished observations.

TRANSITION METAL COMPLEXES AS CATALYSTS IN BIOCHEMICAL SYSTEMS

M. E. Vol'pin

Institute of Organoelement Compounds, Academy of Sciences of the USSR, Moscow, USSR

Abstract - It was suggested that synthetic metal complexes can be used as catalysts for regulation of certain processes in living cell. The complexes have been selected on the basis of their catalytic activity in model chemical reactions such as autooxidation of coenzyme Q_{10} and cytochrome c. Cobalt (II) complexes with 1,2,3,7,8,12,13,17,18,19 - decamethyloctadehydrocorrin, N,N'-bis-(salyciliden) ethylenediamine, o-phenanthroline and other chelates proved to be active catalysts. Possible mechanism of those catalytic action is considered. A possibility of creating catalytic processes competing with the enzymatic ones has been tested experimentally by examples of this complexes interaction with the mitochondrial respiratory chain and with the photosynthetic electron transfer system of purple bacteria. It has been shown that some of above-mentioned chemical catalysts of the respiratory chain components autooxidation can be integrated in electron transport at subcellular level and can carry out catalytic electron transfer from coenzyme Q to oxygen in mitochondria. Such process competes with the enzymatic one and is comparable with it in rate. Cobalt (II) tris - o - - phenanthroline perchlorate was shown to interact with photosynthetic electron transfer system of purple bacteria, stimulating membrane energization in chromatophores.

INTRODUCTION

It is generally accepted that the activity and selectivity of enzymes are much superior to those of synthetic chemical catalysts. Nevertheless, we suppose the modern coordination chemistry and homogenous catalysis to open the possibilities to create some abiotic transition metal catalysts capable to take part effectively in metabolism of some biological substrates in the living cell. This could open new ways to regulate some biochemical processes. Respiratory chain components may serve as appropriate objects in the investigation of such a problem. The cell respiration is a fundamental living process, being the source of energy for living organisms. The main part of the energy is formed in the respiratory chain, as a result of the stepwise oxidation of organic substrates and is utilized for formation of ATP. In the course of the respiratory chain electrons are gradually transferred from substrates to oxygen through the chain of components:

$$\text{substrate} \longrightarrow \text{NADH} \longrightarrow \text{FAD} \longrightarrow \text{coenzyme Q} \longrightarrow \text{cytochrome b} \longrightarrow \text{cyt. c} \longrightarrow \text{cyt. } a_1, a_3 \longrightarrow O_2$$

We have attempted to catalyse the electron transfer from some components of the cellular respiratory chain directly to the molecular oxygen, making a by-pass for enzymatic process. Transition metals complexes with cobjugated ligands capable of oxygen activation and fast electron transfer could be active catalysts of such processes (see Note a).

Note a. This investigation was accomplished in collaboration with G.N. Novodarova, E.M. Kolosova (Institute Organoelement Compounds), Y.N. Lejkin, N.V. Guzhova, A.A. Kononenko (Moscow State University),

CHEMICAL SYSTEMS

At the first stage of this work we undertook a search of homogeneous catalysts which would stimulate the autooxidation of certain respiratory chain components such as NADH, ubiquinol (a synthetic model compound Q_4H_2 was used) and ferrocytochrome c by the air in aqueous or methanolic media at pH 7 and 25° (in order to approach physiological conditions as close as possible).

$$\text{NADH} + O_2 \xrightarrow{cat} \text{NAD} + H_2O_2$$

$$Q_4H_2 + O_2 \xrightarrow{cat} Q_4 + H_2O$$

$$\text{Ferricytochrome c } (Fe^{II}) + O_2 \xrightarrow{cat} \text{Ferrocytochrome c } (Fe^{III})$$

The direct oxidation of NADH by molecular oxygen is known to be rather slow probably due to direct two-electron transfer to non-excited oxygen molecule being forbidden.

It could be supposed that transition metal complexes capable to change the spin state of O_2 molecule upon coordination should stimulate NADH autooxidation. Indeed, we have found that various complexes of vanadium, chromium, manganese, iron, cobalt, copper etc. to catalyse autooxidation of NADH in aqueous or alcoholic solutions at room temperature (Ref. 1-4). Thus, catehole complexes of copper and vanadium or o-phenanthroline complexes of cobalt and copper as well as some cobaltous complexes with chelating ligands proved to be active catalysts.

The catalytic action of the following types of complexes was studied in more detail: (i) transition metal complexes with chelate ligands, in the main with Shiff bases, (ii) corrine and octadehydrocorrine complexes, (iii) porphyrine complexes [4] and (iv) o-phenanthroline complexes (Fig. 1). Among these complexes that of Co(II) with N,N'-bis (salicyliden) ethylendiamine Co(salen) and 1,2,3,7,8,12,13,17,18,19 - decamethyloctadehydrocorrin Co(dmodc) were extremely active (Table 1).

In order to elucidate the mechanism of NADH catalytic autooxidation we have studied the kinetic of this reaction in the presence of Co(salen) and Co(dmodc) (Ref. 2,3). In both cases the reaction was found to be close to first-order with catalyst and 0,5-order with NADH. The catalytic reaction can be described as following:

$$[Co^{II}] + \text{NADH} + O_2 \overset{K}{\rightleftharpoons} [Co^{II}]\cdot\text{NADH}\cdot O_2$$

$$[Co^{II}]\cdot\text{NADH}\cdot O_2 \xrightarrow{k_1} [Co^{II}] + \text{NAD}^+ + HO_2^-$$

where the reaction rate is expressed by an equation

$$W = \frac{k_1 K[\text{NADH}][O_2][Co]}{1 + K[\text{NADH}][O_2]}$$

The data obtained indicate the step of oxygen coordination to be essential for catalytic activity of cobalt complexes. Thus, the complex of nickel with the same ligand which is unable to coordinate oxygen lacked the catalytic activity (Table 1). The addition of imidazole and pyridine which compete in coordination to cobalt were found to impede the reaction markedly.

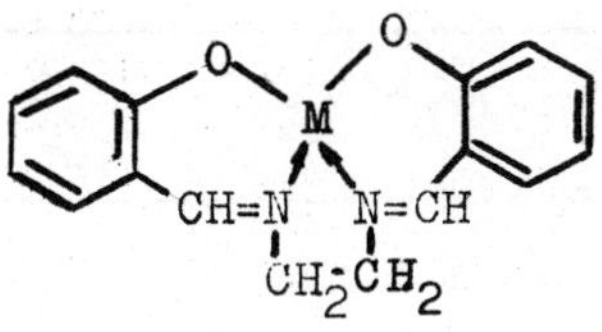

M·N,N -bis-salicyliden-ethylendiamine(salen) /M=Co,Ni,Cu,Mn/

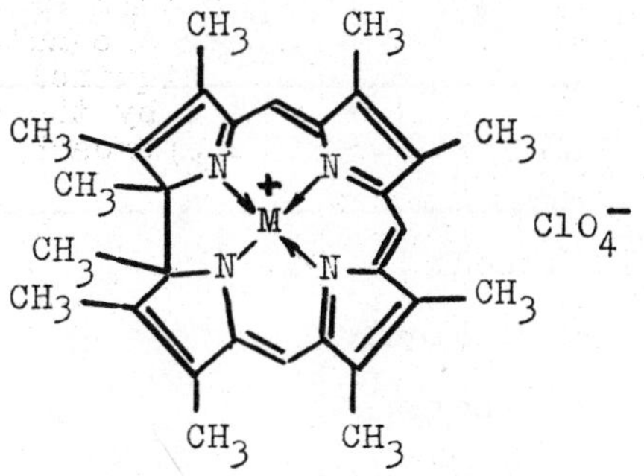

M·decamethyloctadehydrocorrin(dmodc) /M=Co,Ni/

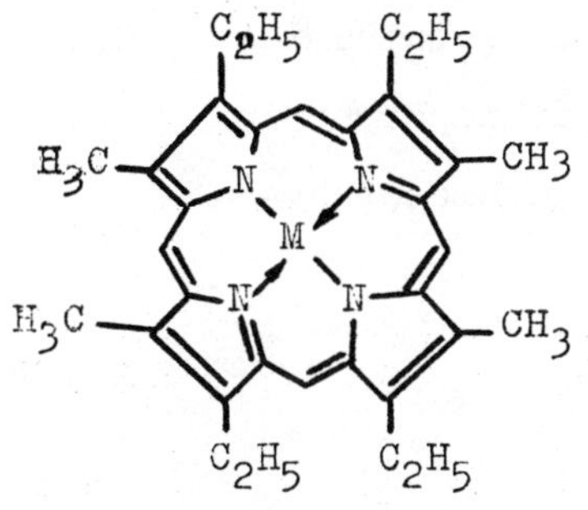

M·ethioporphyrin II /M=Cu,Ni,Mn,VO,Co,Fe/

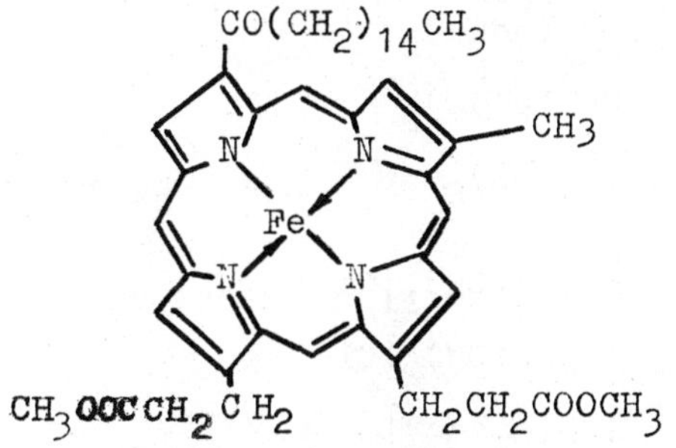

Fe· 2-methyl-4-palmitoyl-deiteroporphyrin IX (dp)

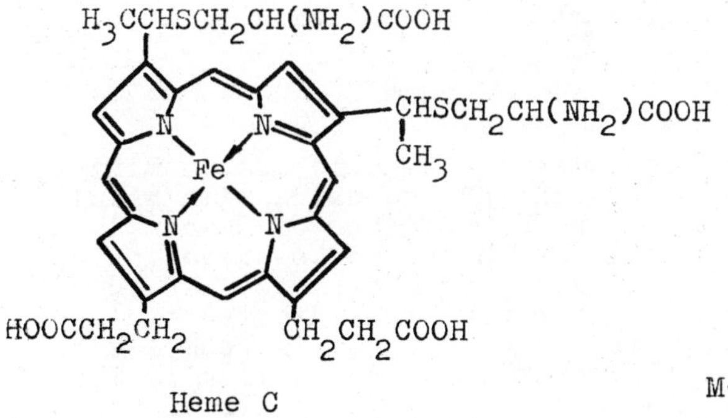

Heme C

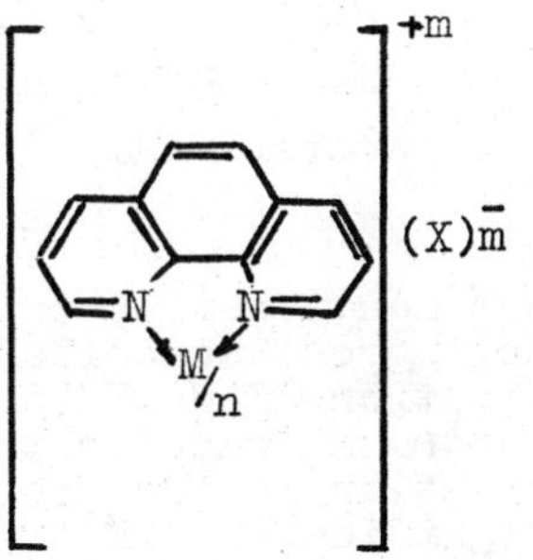

M·phen /M=Co, Cu,X=Cl,ClO_4/

Fig. 1. The investigated transition metal complexes.

TABLE I. Catalytic activity of the transition metal complexes (Note a) in NADH autooxidation (10^{-4}M NADH, 10^{-5}M complex, 25°)

Catalyst	V x 10^7 M·min^{-1}	Catalyst	V x 10^7 M·min^{-1}
Without	0.1	Aquacobalamine	3.4
Mn (salen)	0.8	Cyancobalamine	0.1
Ni (salen)	0.5	Methylcobalamine	0.1
Cu (salen)	1.3	Adenosylcobalamine	0.1
Co (salen)	8.0	Aquacobinamide	2.5
Cu $(acac)_2$	0.4	Cyancobinamide	0.1
Vo $(acac)_2$	0.9	Adenosinecobinamide	0.1
Co $(acac)_2$	3.5	Co^{II} ethioporphyrin II	0.1
Cu $(DH)_2$	0.2	Fe^{III} ethioporphyrin II	0.1
$[PyCo(DH)_2]Cl$	4.0	Fe^{III}dp	0.1
$[PyRh(DH)_2]Cl$	0.5	Fe^{II}dp + $NaBH_4$	12.0
$[Co(dmodc)]^+ (ClO_4)^-$	27.8	Heme c (Fe^{III})	0.1
$[PyCo(dmodc)]^+ (ClO_4)^-$	10.2	Heme c (Fe^{II}) + $NaBH_4$	18.0
$[Ni(dmodc)]^+ (ClO_4)^-$	0.1	Cytochrome c	0.1
		Cytochrome c + $NaBH_4$	0.1

Note a: The experiments with cobalamine and cobinamide derivatives were carried out in the darkness in order to prevent the decomposition of cobalt-carbon bond inducing by light in water media.

All the above mentioned factors together with the kinetic measurements enable us to suggest so-called "the inner-sphere" mechanism with simultaneous coordination of NADH and O_2 to 5- and 6 positions of Co-complex and with two electrons transfer to O_2 without the change of Co oxidation state. The NADH oxidation in the presence of Co(salen) and Co(dmodc) was found to slow down significantly in time. A set of experiments indicated that H_2O_2 produced in the course of the reaction is involved in Co(II) complex catalyst oxidation. The resulting Co(III) complex is catalytically inactive. Addition of catalase or Ni-complex with monoethanolamine destroying H_2O_2 abolished the inhibition (Ref. 5). In general Co(III) complexes are much less active, which can be due to their inability to coordinate and activate the molecular oxygen. Thus, a number of Co(III) complexes belonging to a group of vitamin B_{12} had revealed an activity significantly lower than that of Co(II) complex with related octadehydrocorrin ligand.

Metalloporphyrins appeared to be inactive in NADH autooxidation due to rapid and irreversible oxidation of Co(II) and Fe(II) in protic solvents. Having used the reduced Fe(II)-2-methyl-4-palmetoildeitero-porphyrin IX (Fe^{II}dp) (with an excess of a reductant $NaBH_4$), stabilized by lipid environment (so-called "vesicles") and also reduced heme c we succeeded in obtaining metalloporphyrin systems with significant catalytic activity (Ref. 6). Nevertheless, cytochrome c in reduced form was inactive as catalyst in NADH autooxidation probably due to the protein surrounding of the heme, preventing coordination of NADH and O_2.

Further on we turned to o-phenanthroline complexes of cobalt and copper. Such complexes are known to be widely used in redox catalysis. Our data on the catalytic activity of the cobalt and copper o-phenanthroline complexes in NADH, hexahydroubiquinol Q_4H_2 and ferrocytochrome c autooxidation are listed in Table 2. The highest activity in NADH oxidation was displayed by

TABLE 2. Catalytic activity of copper and cobalt complexes in autooxidation of some components of the respiratory chain (10^{-4}M NADH in water, 10^{-4}M Q_4H_2 in isooctane-water, 10^{-4} cytochrome c in water, 10^{-5}M complex).

Catalyst	$V \times 10^7 M\ min^{-1}$		
	NADH	Q_4H_2	cyt.c
Without	0.1	1.0	0.2
$[Co(phen)_3]\ (ClO_4)_3$	0.1	33.0	95.0
$[Co(phen)_3]\ (ClO_4)_2$	7.5	50.0	20.6
$[Co(phen)_2Cl_2]$	87.0	40.0	90.0
$[Co(4,7\text{-}Ph_2\text{-}phen)_3]\ Cl_2$	0	129.0	0
$[Cu(phen)Cl_2]$	25.0	23.0	80.0
$[Cu(4,7\text{-}Ph_2\text{-}phen)]\ Cl_2$	20.0	306.0	0
$[Co(dmodc)]^+\ ClO_4^-$	26.0	23.7	-
Co(salen)	8.0	1.6	-
Aquacobalamine	3.4	7.5	-

$Co^{II}(phen)_2Cl_2$. The related cobalt (III) complexes did not show any appreciable activity.

NADH usually is considered to be a two-electrons donor, while the other two substrates - Q_4H_2 and cytochrome c can function mainly as one-electron donors.

Most of the complexes studied including Co(dmodc) are rather active in Q_4H_2 autooxidation. As regards to the oxidation of ferrocytochrome c in the presence of p-phenanthroline complexes the essential feature of the mechanism, is, probably, a contact between heme peripheral regions and o-phenanthroline nucleus as it had been found for the similar stoichiometric reaction [7]. Introduction of the balky phenyl substituents into positions 4 and 7 of phenanthroline nucleus markly reduces the rate of cytochrome c oxidation (Table 2).

BIOCHEMICAL SYSTEMS

In the next part of the work we attempted to test whether it is possible to use the investigated metal complexes for creating catalytic processes in biological systems. As such latter we have chosen (a) the mitochondrial electron transfer chain and (b) the system of photoinduced electron transfer of purple bacterial chromatophores.

a. The mitochondrial respiratory chain

The compounds, found to be the most active in the chemical experiments, have been investigated in these studies [8].

The action of some compounds on succinate and glutamate + malate oxidation in rat liver mitochondria is shown in Table 3. The addition of Co(dmodc)

TABLE 3. The rate of oxygen consumption (V nmol O_2/min per I mg of protein) by rat liver mitochondria in the presence of some cobalt complexes.
The medium of incubation contains 0.15 M sucrose, 0.075 M KCl, 0.005 M KH_2PO_4 (pH 7.4), 0.0028 M $MgCl_2$, 3-4 mg/ml of protein, 0.006 M succinate or 0.005 M glutamate + 0.005 M malate, 10^{-5}M complex

Complex	Substrate	
	glutamate + malate	succinate
Without	2.4	2.8
$[Co(dmodc)]^+ClO_4^-$	7.4 (Note a)	17.6
$[Ni(dmodc)]^+ClO_4^-$	-	7.8
Co(salen)	1.8	2.6
Aquacobalamine	2.0	2.8

which is an effective catalyst of NADH and coenzyme Q oxidation was found to stimulate succinate oxidation by the mitochondrial suspension more than 6-fold. In the presence of NADH-dependent substrates (glutamate + malate) there was 3-fold stimulation of respiration by Co(dmodc) but, upon subsequent incubation, the rate of respiration returned back to its original level. The corresponding nickel complex Ni(dmodc) being inactive in model chemical systems was no more active with respect to mitochondrial redox systems.

In our further studies we concerned with the problem which of the respiratory chain components donates electrons Co(dmodc) in mitochondrial electron transfer chain. Specific respiratory chain inhibitors were used as a tool (see scheme below). The Co(dmodc) catalysed oxidation of succinate and NADH by intact mitochondria was found to be insensitive to antimycin A which inhibits electron transfer in the cytochrome b region of the respiratory chain (Table 4). This observation exclude the terminal respiratory chain carriers as possible electron donors in Co(dmodc) catalysis. It has been also shown that mitochondria being osmotically shocked with a subsequent removal of cytochrome c by salt extraction did not decrease the Co(dmodc)-dependent succinate oxidase activity of mitochondria. The rate of oxygen consumption by mitochondria oxidizing succinate in the presence of Co(dmodc) was found to be not affected by rotenone which inhibits the reversed electron transfer from succinate to NAD. On the other hand the addition of α-thenoyltrifluoroacetone which is known to block electron transfer at the succinate dehydrogenase - CoQ step brought about virtually 100% inhibition of respiration in the presence of both succinate and Co(dmodc). Similar results were obtained for the submitochondrial particles (Keilin-Hartree preparation) which are devoid of endogenous pyridine nucleotides and do not catalyse the reversed electron transfer and other endergonic functions characteristic of intact mitochondria.

All these data indicate Co(dmodc) to catalyse electron transfer to oxygen from a respiratory chain component localized between flavoproteins and cytochrome b. Coenzyme Q seems to be the most probable electron donor under the conditions studied.

Note a: The starting rate.

TABLE 4. The rate of oxygen consumption (V nmol O_2/min per 1 mg of protein) by rat liver mitochondria in the presence of Co(dmodc) (10^{-5}M) and respiratory chain inhibitors.

Compound added	Substrate	
	glutamate + malate	succinate
Without	2.4	2.8
$[Co(dmodc)]^+ClO_4^-$	7.4	17.6
Rotenone	1.4	3.0
Rotenone + $[Co(dmodc)]^+ClO_4^-$	1.4	18.5
Antimycin A	-	0
Antimycin A + $[Co(dmodc)]^+ClO_4^-$	-	17.6
Thenoyltrifluoracetone	-	0
Thenoyltrifluoracetone + + $[Co(dmodc)]^+ClO_4^-$	-	0

In order to test this possibility we have prepared submitochondrial particles deficient in endogenous CoQ by treatment of the liophylized Keilin-Hartree preparation with pentane resulted in CoQ extraction. The submitochondrial particles thus obtained was practically devoid of the NADH and succinate oxidase activities. The addition of Co(dmodc) did not effect in this case on the rate of oxidation. But the addition of exogenous Q_6 restored the catalytic activity of Co(dmodc) and its sensitivity to inhibition by α-thenoyltrifluoroacetone.

Thus in this part of the work we have been demonstrated the ability of cobalt octadehydrocorrin complex which is an active catalyst of a chemical autooxidation to interfere with biological electron transfer at subcellular level, so that this compound maintains a catalytic process of electron transfer from coenzyme Q to oxygen competing with an enzymatic one and comparable to the latter in rate. It also turnes out that Co(dmodc) takes electrons from coenzyme Q as it is shown in the scheme below:

$$
\begin{array}{l}
\text{Glu+mal} \xrightarrow{\bar{e}} \text{NADH} \rightarrow \text{FAD-I} \searrow \\
\qquad\qquad\qquad\qquad\qquad\qquad \text{CoQ}_{10} \rightarrow \text{cyt b} \rightarrow \text{cyt c} \rightarrow \text{cyt a,a}_3 \rightarrow \text{O}_2 \\
\text{Succinate} \xrightarrow{\bar{e}} \text{FAD-II} \nearrow \quad \downarrow \bar{e} \text{ - - - Co(dmodc) - - - } \uparrow \\
\qquad\qquad\qquad\qquad\qquad\qquad\qquad \text{"by pass"}
\end{array}
$$

It was shown analogously that some o-phenanthroline complexes of cobalt being the catalysts of chemical autooxidation manifest their activity also in submitochondrial particles and intact plant mitochondria respiration (Ref. 9).

b. The systems of bacterial photoinduced electron transfer

These systems with cyclic photoinduced electron flow have been explored in considerable detail (Ref. 10). The photoinduced electron transfer can be studied conveniently with the intracellular closed membranous structures which can be isolated from purple bacteria. These particles retain the photosynthetic electron transfer chain and the energy-coupling system which are involved in the transduction of the light-energy into the energy of electrochemical ionic gradients. The primary photosynthetic processes are known to occur in the so-called reaction centres (RC) that are molecular complexes of porphyrin pigments with certain redox cofactors bound to specific proteins and which are integral constituents of the photosynthetic membranes. These structures are the minimal fragments possessing the specific photochemical activity.

We have studied the effect of cobalt and copper complexes with o-phenanthroline and its derivatives on the photoinduced electron transfer and related functions in RC and chromatophores from purple bacteria (Ref. 11).

The o-phenanthroline complexes studied have been found to fall into two groups: (i) cobalt complexes which possess an electron donor-acceptor activity and enhance membrane energization and (ii) copper complexes which de-energize the membrane, presumably by a penetrating ion mechanism (Tables 5,6).

TABLE 5. Stimulation of electron transfer in RC by cobalt and copper o-phenanthroline complexes. The medium of incubation contains 4 mcM $(BChl)_2$, 0.05% LDAO, 10^{-4}M complex, phosphate buffer, pH 7.5, 25°. (Note a).

Cobalt complexes	Relative activity	Copper complexes	Relative activity
$[Co(phen)_3](ClO_4)_2$	0.11	$[Cu(phen)_2](ClO_4)_2$	0.68
$[Co(phen)_3](ClO_4)_3$	0.31	$[Cu(phen)]Cl_2$	1.0
$[Co(phen)_3]Cl_2$	0.36	$[Cu(5\text{-}NO_2\text{-}phen)]Cl_2$	1.0
$[Co(phen)_2Cl_2]$	0.57	$[Cu(4,7\text{-}Ph_2\text{-}phen)]Cl_2$	1.0
$[Co(4,7\text{-}Ph_2\text{-}phen)_3]Cl_2$	0.75	$[Cu(4,7\text{-}Ph_2\text{-}phen)_2](ClO_4)_2$	1.0
$[Co(5\text{-}NO_2\text{-}phen)_3]Cl_2$	1.0	$[Cu(5\text{-}NH_2\text{-}phen)_2](ClO_4)_2$	1.0

Let us concern with the effect observed by an example of the cobalt (II) tris-o-phenanthroline complex perchlorate that proved the most active in the experiment with RC.

In the absence of exogenous cofactors, there is only a photoinduced electron exchange between the bacteriochlorophyll dimer $(BChl)_2$ and the quinone acceptors (the primary $[X_1Fe]$, and the secondary one X_2) that occurs in RC. (see scheme below). In the actinic continuous saturating light RC are largely in the $(BChl_2)^+[X_1Fe]\ X_2^-$ state. In the presence of the most active cobalt complex $[Co(phen)_3](ClO_4)_2$ (10^{-4}M) an induction splash in the $(BChl)_2$ photoinduced kinetics can be observed. A virtually complete oxidation is brought about initially by the actinic illumination, followed by a rapid re-reduction of the pigment. Special experiments with a flash photoactivation showed the rate of $(BChl)_2$ re-reduction in the dark to be much higher in the presence of complex as compared to the control. The decrease in the steady-state $(BChl)_2$ photooxidation is accompanied by a steady-state reduction of the quinone acceptors somewhat increased and the rate of their dark reoxidation slowed down marked. These data can be easily explained since the cobalt complex undergoing consecutive oxidation and reduction can by-pass the segment of the electron transfer chain between the oxidized pigment and the reduced quinones as it is presented the scheme:

Note a. The value of relative activity is calculated from the ratio: $A_{870\ exp}/A_{870\ cont}$, taken from $(BChl)_2$ differential absorbance spectra in the presence of complex (exp), and without complex (cont). The smaller is the value of the relative activity - the greather is the effect of complex; when the value is equal to 1.0, it means that complex has no effect.

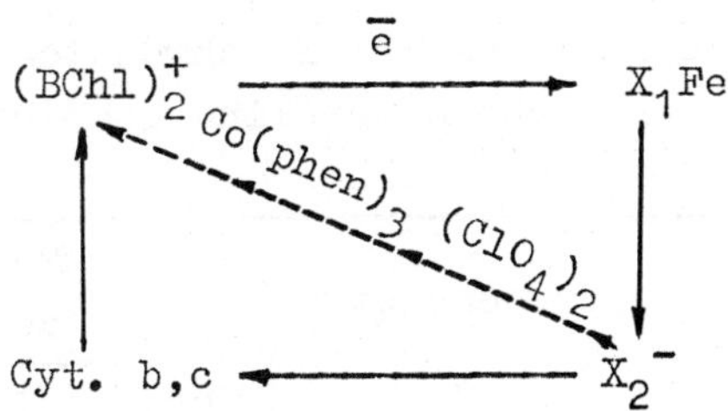

The fact that multiple and fully reversible turnovers can be observed in RC in the presence of this complex, confirms the conclusion that the cyclic electron flow is being generated involving this cofactor.

Rapid oxidation of cobalt complex ($Co^{II} \longrightarrow Co^{III}$) by the RC pigment (100 ms) and relatively slow reduction of one ($Co^{III} \longrightarrow Co^{II}$) by the quinones (5 s) should displace the steady-state in the functioning RC + cobalt complex system towards accumulation of the $(BChl)_2$ $[X_1^- Fe]$ X_2^- state.

The differential spectra of RC "light minus dark" also indicate that in the presence of cobalt complex there are the bands of the reduced quinols dominating in the 300-460 nm interval (the range of semiquinone anion radicals absorption) and a long-wavelength shift of the bacteriopheophytin absorption band in the 700-800 nm interval characteristic of a local electrostatic field shift in the RC protein upon a photomobilized electron captured by the quinone acceptors.

The ability of the cobalt-phenanthroline complexes to stimulate cyclic electron flow is of particular interest in view of o-phenanthroline being inhibitory to electron transfer from $[X_1Fe]$ to X_2 [39]. $CoCl_2 \cdot 6H_2O$ and $NaClO_4$ did not affect the kinetics of the RC photoinduced transitions. Hence the functional effects found should be attributed to the complexes themselves (see Table 5).

Having characterized behaviour of the complex compounds in the system of functioning RC we evaluate then the action of those compounds on the integral photosynthetic membranes. The cobalt complexes capable of supporting the photoinduced cyclic electron flow from the reduced quinone acceptors to the oxidized pigment were, naturally, of the primary interest (Table 6).

The addition of complexes to bacterial chromatophores stimulated long-wavelength shifts of the BChl and carotenoid absorption bands, which indicated the protonic electrochemical potential gradient generation in the membrane enhanced.

It should be emphasized that redox transitions of the (Co^{II}/Co^{III}) complexes are pure electronic and do not involve proton binding or release as it occurs with many other redox cofactors (dichlorophenolindophenol, diaminodurene, phenazine methosulfate).

Being lipophylic, cobalt complexes can be incorporated in the electron-transport chain at the inner face of the chromatophore membrane, providing electron transfer from the quinone acceptor to $(BChl)_2$.

The complexes studied ranged with respect to their energizing activity in chromatophores are listed in Table 6 .

All the copper compounds shown above to lack donor-acceptor activity with RC system revealed uncoupling action with chromatophores decreasing membrane potential. The mechanism of the copper complexes uncoupling action may be similar to that of other penetrating ions. The copper compounds studied given in a series according to their decreasing uncoupling activity in Table 6.

In order to explain such a significant difference between copper and cobaltous o-phenanthroline complexes with respect to their activity in mediating cyclic electron flow in RC and in affecting membrane energization in chromatophores one would consider redox potentials of two groups of complexes. Redox potentials of cobalt complexes (E = 0.3 + 0.4 V) appear to be just in that narrow range of oxidation-reduction potentials where an "optimal" catalyst is both an active acceptor and donor with respect to substrate. This

TABLE 6. The level of the membrane energization in chromatophores by cobalt and copper o-phenanthroline complexes (Note a)

Cobalt complex	Relative activity		Copper complex	Relative activity	
	I	II		I	II
$Co(phen)_3\ (ClO_4)_2$	1.58	1.8	$Cu(4,7\text{-}Ph_2\text{-}phen)\ Cl_2$	0.25	0.03
$Co(phen)_3\ (ClO_4)_3$	1.42	1.6	$Cu(4,7\text{-}Ph_2\text{-}phen)_2\ ClO_4$	0.5	0.21
$Co(phen)_2Cl_2$	1.12	1.35	$Cu(5,6\text{-}Me\text{-}phen)\ Cl_2$	0.54	0.36
$Co(phen)_3\ Cl_2$	1.1	1.3	$Cu(5\text{-}NH_2phen)_2\ (ClO)_2$	0.62	0.5
$Co(5\text{-}NO_2phen)_3\ Cl_2$	1.0	1.0	$Cu(5\text{-}NO_2phen)\ Cl_2$	0.78	0.48
$Co(4,7\text{-}Ph_2phen)_3\ Cl_2$	0.2	0.01	$Cu(phen)_2\ (ClO_4)_2$	0.80	0.70
			$Cu(phen)\ Cl_2$	0.95	0.76

Note a: The value of relative activity is calculated from differencial absorbance spectra: I - from the ratio $A_{850\ exp}/\ A_{850\ cont}$ for $(BChl)_2$ and II - from the ratio $A_{530\ exp}/\ A_{530\ cont}$ for carotenoides. The greater the value of the relative activity correspondes to the greater of the energize effect of complex in chromatophores.

enable cobalt o-phenanthroline complexes to operative efficiently in electron transfer between the reduced quinone (E = 0.10 v) and the oxidized pigment (E = 0.46 v) both in RC and in chromatophores. At the same time this transfer of an electron from the quinones to the oxidized pigment may be hindered in the case of copper o-phenanthroline complexes (E = 0.100 - 0.120 v).

Obviously, it is also the structure of complexes that should be of importance their ability to interfere with electron transfer in RC and chromatophores. In particular, the low activity of the cobalt complex with 4,7-diphenyl-o-phenanthroline may be explained in terms of an outer sphere mechanism of electron transfer between the o-phenanthroline cobalt complex and $(BChl)_2$. The bulky substituents in o-phenanthroline could hinder a contact of the catalyst molecule peripheral regions with the RC pigment and thus decrease a rate of electron transfer.

Thus the data obtained prove a possibility to catalyse the metabolism of biological substrates, including at the level of biological systems, with the use of synthetic metal complexes. To our opinion this approach provides new facilities for regulation of biochemical processes and should promote revealing new compounds with high biological activity.

REFERENCES

1. M.E. Vol'pin, and G.N. Novodarova, Dokl. Akad. Nauk SSSR 216, 558-560 (1974).
2. M.E. Vol'pin, G.N. Novodarova, E.M. Kolosova and A.V. Savitskij, Izv. Akad. Nauk SSSR, Ser. Khim. 1498-1503 (1976).
3. M.E. Vol'pin, G.N. Novodarova, E.M. Kolosova, V.M. Beresovskij, T.A. Melentyeva and N.S. Genokhova, Izv. Akad. Nauk SSSR, Ser. Khim. 2231-2235 (1977).
4. M.E. Vol'pin, G.N. Novodarova and E.M. Kolosova, Izv. Akad. Nauk SSSR, Ser. Khim. 175-178 (1980).
5. P. Stopka, E.M. Kolosova, M.E. Vol'pin and G.N. Novodarova, Izv. Akad. Nauk SSSR, Ser. Khim. 2793-2795 (1977).

6. M.E. Vol'pin, A.F. Mironov, G.N. Novodarova, E.M. Kolosova and V.A. Ioffe, Izv. Akad. Nauk SSSR, Ser. Khim., 175-178 (1980).
7. V.Y. Mc Ardle, K., Yocom, H. Gray, J. Amer. Chem. Soc. 98, 4141-4145 (1977).
8. Yu.N. Leikin, G.N. Novodarova, E.M. Kolosova and M.E. Vol'pin, Biokhimiya 44, 97-103 (1979).
9. N.V. Guzhova, G.N. Novodarova, E.M. Kolosova and M.E. Vol'pin, Biokhimiya 44, 1369-1376 (1979).
10. R.K. Clayton, The Photosynthetic Bacteria, Plenum Press, New York - London (1978).
11. E.P. Lukashev, A.A. Kononenko, N.I. Zaharova, A.B. Rubin, G.N. Novodarova, E.M. Kolosova and M.E. Vol'pin, Biokhimiya 45, 273-285 (1980).

BIOLOGICAL COORDINATION CHEMISTRY OF NICKEL

B. Sarkar

Research Institute of the Hospital for Sick Children, Toronto M5G 1X8, and Department of Biochemistry, University of Toronto, Toronto M5S 1A8, Ontario, Canada

Abstract - The incidence of carcinogenesis among workers in nickel mining and the high levels of serum nickel in the neighboring populations have prompted our research into the biological chemistry of this metal. The low molecular weight nickel-binding component in human blood was identified as L-histidine. In the macromolecular fraction albumin was shown to be the main nickel-binding component. Equilibrium dialysis experiments suggested albumin to possess a specific nickel-binding site. Nickel and copper were shown to share the same NH_2-terminal site of albumin. A tripeptide model for this site, L-aspartyl-L-alanyl-L-histidine-N-methyl amide has been synthesized and its nickel-binding properties have been studied. Species distribution analysis shows the main species to be an $MH_{-2}A$ complex ($\log \beta_{1-21} = -5.95$) at physiological pH, an observation which is supported by spectroscopic results (λ_{max} = 420 nm). Minor species MA, MA_2 and $MH_{-1}A_2$ are also present. Nickel-albumin visible spectra are very similar to the nickel-peptide absorption. Further structural elucidation of the site was made by ^{13}C- and ^{1}H-NMR investigation of the nickel-peptide system. The aspartic carboxyl carbon was the most affected one by nickel binding. The shifts provided strong supportive evidence that the α-amino group is a metal ligating group. The imidazole ring also showed a large variation. In DMSO-d_6 solution, there is a complete disappearance of Ala-NH and His-NH protons as shown by ^{1}H-NMR spectra, which confirms the coordination of these two peptide nitrogens. Thus, it appears that nickel-transport site of human albumin is a pentacoordinated structure involving α-NH_2 nitrogen, two intervening peptide nitrogens, imidazole nitrogen and the carboxyl side chain of the aspartic residue. Studies of organ distribution of nickel in rats revealed that nickel was primarily accumulated in kidney. Subsequent fractionation of kidney homogenate provided the evidence for nickel-binding proteins. In studying the removal of nickel in toxic accumulation, a detailed investigation was carried out with nickel-binding to triethylenetetramine (Trien) and D-penicillamine (Pen). These two compounds were administered to rats by *im* injection to investigate their effectiveness in prevention of death after parenteral injection of $NiCl_2$. These compounds were shown to be most efficient antidotal agents against nickel toxicity. The results suggest that the efficiency of Trien as a therapeutic agent is dependent upon its flexibility in being able to adopt a number of configuration forming several complex species with high stability constants. In contrast, Pen forms the species MA and MA_2 only. The latter species is the only species from pH 5.8 to 10.0. This complex gains additional stability by adopting a square planar configuration via coordination of the N, S atoms of the ligand molecules. Complexes of nickel involving Pen are also more stable than those formed with the related, naturally occurring amino acid, L-cysteine.

INTRODUCTION

Nickel is widely distributed in nature. It appears that nickel is an essential trace element. For certain plants and animals there is an absolute requirement of nickel. But little is known about its biological function in animals or in man. A number of nickel compounds have been shown to induce malignant tumors in experimental animals. Lung and nasal cancers have been documented with enhanced frequency among workers in nickel mines. There is a great deal of concern around the world regarding the health hazards caused by excessive intake of metals due to occupational exposure or environmental pollution. In our program of studying the biological transport of metals and its removal, we have been investigating the biological coordination chemistry of nickel. In this lecture, I shall summarize some of our results and discuss its relevance in relation to the health problems caused by nickel.

NICKEL IN THE ENVIRONMENT

Nickel is one of the more abundant trace elements which finds its way in plants, animal tissues and in foods. Since nickel is present in rocks, soils and sea water, it is estimated that significant amounts of airborne particulates containing nickel have natural sources. Furthermore, there are anthropogenic sources which account for a significantly higher atmospheric nickel particulates concentration in urban and urban-industrial complexes compared to more rural areas. McNeely et al. (1) compared the environmental related data on nickel between the inhabitants of Sudbury, Ontario, the site of the largest open-pit nickel mine in North America and those of Hartford, Connecticut, a city with relatively low environmental concentration of nickel. These data suggest that residents of Sudbury probably inhale much more nickel in the air than do the residents of Hartford. Studies also revealed that the mean concentration of nickel in the samples of municipal tap water from Sudbury (200 μg/liter) was 182 times greater than that in the samples of municipal tap water from Hartford (1.1 μg/liter). The mean concentration of serum nickel found in the Sudbury population was 1.8 times greater than that in the Hartford population (2.6 μg/liter). Nickel in urine of Sudbury population was 3.2 times greater than that in the Hartford population. The above comparison is an example of the importance and significance of environment-related nickel. However, it should be emphasized that there is no evidence that the environmental exposures to nickel in Sudbury, Ontario, are associated with adverse effects in man or animals or that they are deleterious in any way to the health of the inhabitants. The serum nickel levels of nickel workers often exceed 10 - 20 μg/liter. The determination of nickel in urine provides a useful indication of the severity of exposure to nickel and also serves as a guide to the treatment which should be given.

NICKEL CARCINOGENESIS

Increased risk of occupational cancer has been demonstrated in nickel refinery workers from Great Britain, Canada, Norway, Germany, New Caledonia and the Soviet Union. Sunderman (2) has compiled cases of respiratory cancers among workers who were exposed to inhalation of nickel compounds. There are cases of both lung cancer and nasal cancer. The work of Pedersen et al. (3, 4) demonstrated that among employees of nickel refinery in Norway there was a high incidence of not only lung and nasal sinus cancer, but also laryngeal cancer. The highest cancer risk was observed for men involved in roasting, smelting and electrolysis. Nelems and coworkers (5) investigated cytologic abnormalities in the sputum of asymptomatic men exposed to nickel sulfide. Figure 1 shows opening of bronchus and

Fig. 1. The patient had left upper lobe tumor diagnosed by selective brushing. This picture shows opening of bronchus and carcinoma (photograph by courtesy of Dr. J.M. Bill Nelems).

carcinoma in a patient who worked in a nickel mine. Figure 2 shows the cytological signs of malignancy in the bronchus.

NICKEL-BINDING FRACTIONS OF HUMAN BLOOD SERUM

Nickel-binding constituents of human serum were obtained by fractionating the whole serum containing nickel on Sephadex G-150 (6). A solution of serum with $^{63}NiCl_2$ added to an albumin/nickel ratio of 1 produced the fractionation pattern shown in Fig. 3. Four distinct peaks with absorbance at 280 nm were observed. Three of these peaks are associated with fractions containing ^{63}Ni. From the average of 3 experiments, 95.7% of the total nickel was associated with the nickel-binding peaks eluted in fractions 50 - 90 and 4.2% with a peak eluted in fraction 115 - 130. A third peak of radioactivity was associated with fractions 40 - 48; the fractions under this peak always contained less than 0.1% of the total activity. When the serum was dialyzed before addition of $^{63}NiCl_2$ and fractionation on Sephadex G-150, the nickel peak in fractions 120 - 140 was not observed. This nickel fraction must therefore involve nickel bound to low-molecular weight dialyzable compounds.

In view of the findings in the literature (7), the nickel in fractions 50 - 90 was assumed

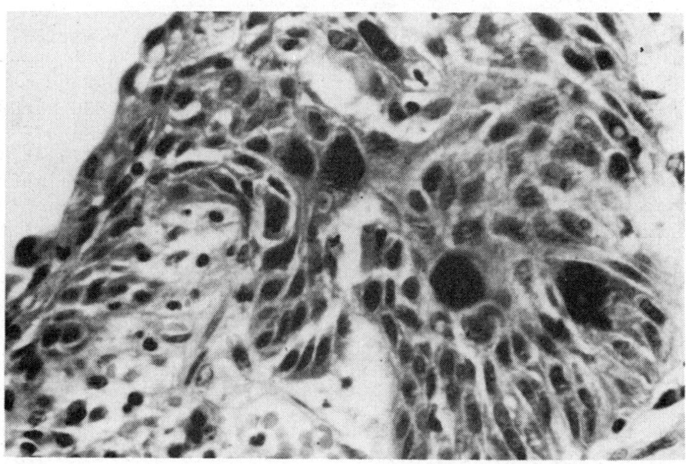

Fig. 2. A microscopic picture of the bronchus region showing cytological signs of malignancy (photograph by courtesy of Dr. J.M. Bill Nelems).

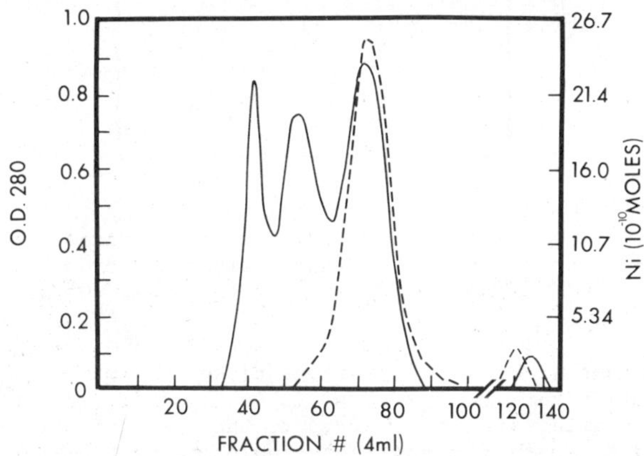

Fig. 3. Fractionation of native human serum with nickel on Sephadex G-150 at pH 7.4 in 0.05 M Tris-HCl buffer. Solid curve absorbance at 280 nm; dashed curve, nickel concentration (6).

to represent albumin-bound nickel. This was proved correct by comparing the fractionation profile obtained when a solution of albumin with 22 amino acids and $^{63}NiCl_2$ was fractionated on the same column. This protein was further identified by gel electrophoresis on 7% acrylamide gels. Its relative mobility from Sephadex G-150 fractionation was identical to that of pure albumin. To determine the location of the ^{63}Ni on the gel, the gel was sliced into sections and each section was individually counted after treatment with hyamine hydroxide. The radioactive profiles from the Sephadex G-150 fractionation of the native serum and nickel as well as albumin-nickel are represented in Fig. 4 a and b respectively.

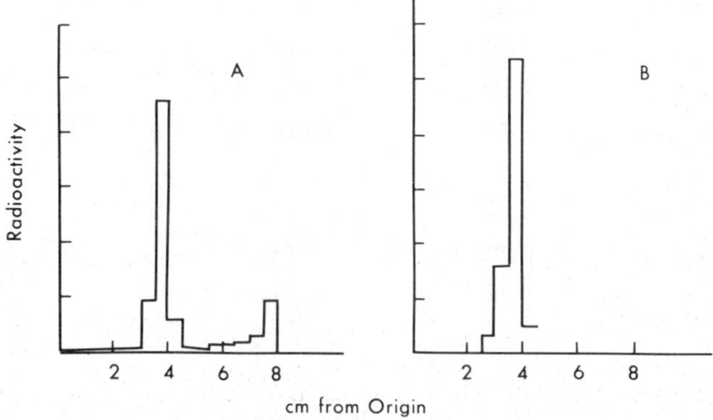

Fig. 4. Acrylamide gel electrophoresis at pH 8.3 in Tris-glycine buffer to detect nickel-binding protein using $^{63}NiCl_2$, (a) native human serum with nickel, (b) nickel added to human serum albumin (6).

In both cases, a radioactive nickel peak was observed at the same position as that of albumin.

LOW MOLECULAR WEIGHT NICKEL-BINDING SUBSTANCES IN HUMAN BLOOD SERUM

The low molecular weight nickel fraction was separated by ultracentrifugation at 183,400 x g for 19 h. Under these conditions the supernatant was found to be protein-free. The percentage of the added nickel remaining in the supernatant after ultracentrifugation was determined. Four different systems were used: (a) albumin (5.8 x 10^{-4} M) with 22 amino acids, (b) native human serum, (c) dialyzed serum, and (d) dialyzed serum reconstituted with amino acids. The ratio of ^{63}Ni to albumin was varied from 0.25 to 2.5. Figure 5 shows

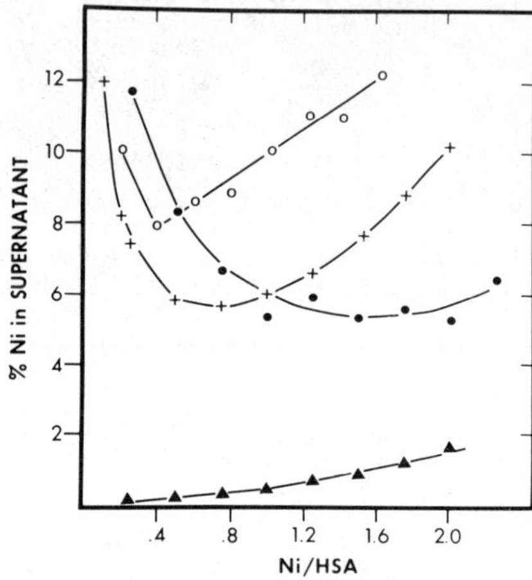

Fig. 5. Distribution of supernatant nickel as a percentage of total nickel after ultracentrifugation at various nickel/human albumin ratios. (▲) Dialyzed serum; (+) dialyzed serum with amino acids; (●) native serum; (O) albumin with amino acids (6).

the percentage of supernatant nickel at the various nickel/albumin ratios for the four systems. Already the profile for dialyzed serum is vastly different from those for the other three systems. When amino acids were added to the dialyzed serum the profile was restored to that observed for native serum. This indicated that amino acids are the low molecular weight nickel-binding constituents of serum.

To determine the amino acid(s) responsible for nickel binding, the same ultracentrifugation experiments were performed using pure albumin with an albumin/amino acid ratio of 1.0 and a nickel/albumin ratio of 0.2. The data given as the percentage of total nickel in the supernatant for each amino acid are shown in Table 1. The only amino acid that picked up

TABLE 1. Effect of the L-amino acids on the percentage distribution of Ni in the supernatant after ultracentrifugation[a] (6)

Amino acid	Ni in supernatant (%)	Amino acid	Ni in supernatant (%)
Alanine	0.93	Leucine	1.00
Arginine	0.90	Lysine	1.05
Asparagine	1.55	Methionine	0.93
Aspartic acid	1.93	Ornithine	1.03
Citruline	0.90	Phenylalanine	0.88
Cysteine-HCl	1.60	Proline	0.93
Glutamic acid	0.98	Serine	0.88
Glutamine	0.95	Threonine	1.08
Glycine	1.05	Tryptophan	1.13
Histidine	71.75	Tyrosine	0.88
Isoleucine	0.85	Valine	0.90
		Blank	0.90

[a] Ni/HSA = 0.2; HSA/L-amino acids = 1.0

a substantial amount of nickel was L-histidine (71.75%).

The nickel-binding ability of L-histidine was further tested by variations in the ultracentrifugation experiment, using dialyzed serum supplemented with physiological concentrations of amino acids. In one case, nickel binding to the supernatant at varying nickel/albumin ratios was studied in a system containing all of the amino acids except L-histidine (Fig. 6).

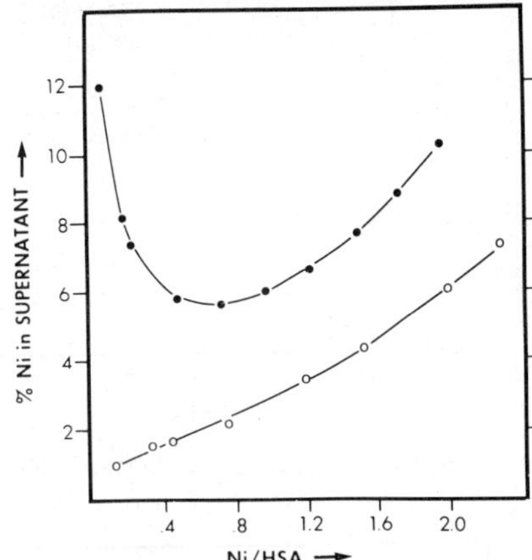

Fig. 6. Distribution of supernatant nickel concentration after ultracentrifugation of dialyzed serum with amino acids at various nickel/albumin ratios. (●) Dialyzed serum with all amino acids; (O) dialyzed serum with all amino acids except L-histidine (6).

In the absence of L-histidine, the typical U-shaped profile found with all of the amino acids was replaced by the profile observed with dialyzed serum alone. In other variation, L-histidine alone was added to the dialyzed serum (Fig. 7). This resulted in restoration of the binding profile of native serum.

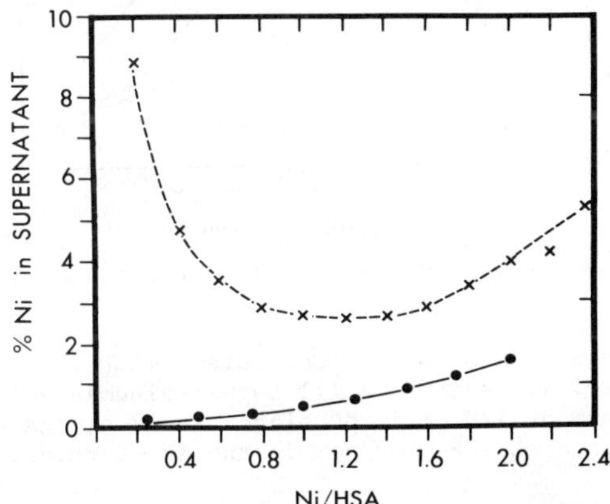

Fig. 7. Effect of L-histidine on supernatant distribution of nickel in dialyzed serum after ultracentrifugation at various nickel/albumin ratios. (X) Dialyzed serum with L-histidine, (●) dialyzed serum (6).

NICKEL TRANSPORT SITE OF HUMAN ALBUMIN

Studies with human albumin

The specific interaction of nickel with albumin was studied by equilibrium dialysis experiment (7). In this experiment increasing molar equivalents of $^{63}NiCl_2$ were added to a solution of albumin in N-ethylmorpholine buffer, pH 7.5. It is shown in Fig. 8 that there is a 1:1 correspondence between the number of moles of nickel bound per mole of albumin. It is clear that there is a stronger, preferential binding site for nickel on albumin. The effect of pH on the visible absorption spectrum of 1:1 nickel-albumin solution is shown in Fig. 9. At neutral pH the absorption maximum at 420 nm was observed.

The NH_2-terminal binding of nickel to albumin was demonstrated by competition studies with copper. Copper is known to bind albumin at the NH_2-terminal (8). When the nickel-albumin dialysis described above is performed in the presence of one molar equivalent of copper, the specific nickel binding is essentially abolished indicating the exclusion of nickel by copper. This finding confirms that the specific nickel-binding site involves the NH_2-

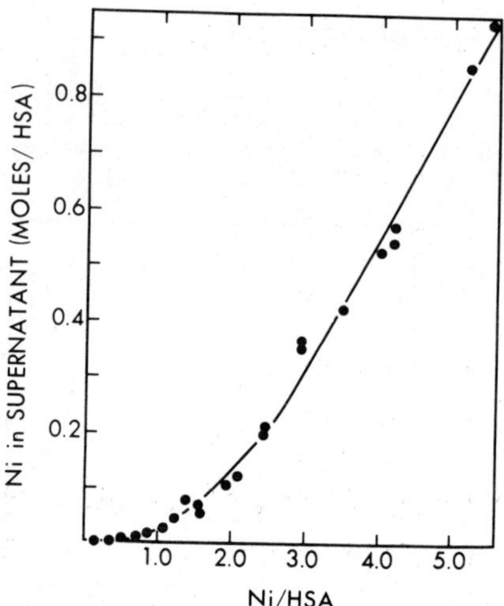

Fig. 8. Stoichiometry of nickel-binding to human albumin as a function of nickel/albumin molar ratio.

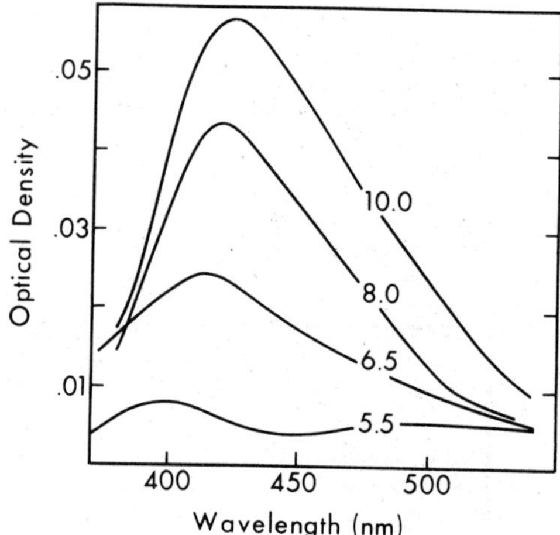

Fig. 9. Visible absorption spectra of 1:1 nickel/albumin complex at various pH values.

terminal region of the protein. This is also consistent with the spectral results. When one molar equivalent of nickel is added to a 1:1 copper-albumin solution at pH 7.5, no absorption peak with a maximum at 420 nm is developed in 12 h, again demonstrating that the primary binding site for both nickel and copper is the NH_2-terminal region of albumin.

Studies with NH_2-terminal peptide segment of human serum albumin

The nickel-binding to Asp-Ala-His-$NHCH_3$ was studied by Analytical Potentiometry (9-11). The initially predominating MA complex (log β = 5.50) is quickly overtaken by the formation of the major species $MH_{-2}A$ (log β = -5.95). Minor species MA_2 (log β = 11.56) and $MH_{-1}A_2$ (log β = 4.76) were also shown to be present in the system. The visible spectra of the main species $MH_{-2}A$ show a λ_{max} = 420 nm.

The structure of nickel-complex of the peptide was further studied by ^{13}C- and ^{1}H-NMR spectroscopy (12). The ^{13}C spectrum (Fig. 10) shows that the nickel complex is in slow exchange on the NMR time scale, and resonances for bound and unbound complexes are observed clearly in the pH range 6.4 to 9.1. Since the system is in slow exchange, it is possible to unequivovally assign the carbon resonances for the nickel complex. The individual chemical shifts ($\Delta = \delta_{1/1\ complex} - \delta_{free\ peptide}$) for all carbons are shown in Fig. 11. All the carbons are shifted downfield except the C(5) imidazole which is shifted upfield. The Asp C_β shows a downfield shift at low pH but at pH 9.1 it is shifted upfield. The Asp COO^- carbon is affected most of all by nickel binding (Δ = 8.22 ppm at pH 9.1), which is consistent with carboxylate-nickel coordination. The imidazole system also shows a large variation. Similar effects have been observed upon protonation of imidazole. The amino titration (pK = 7.73) affects the Asp CO more strongly than Asp COO^- and β carbon more strongly than the nearest α carbon. But upon complexation, nickel-binding to the NH_2-terminal and COO^- group affects the α carbon (4.69 ppm) more strongly while in the case of the β carbon, we observe

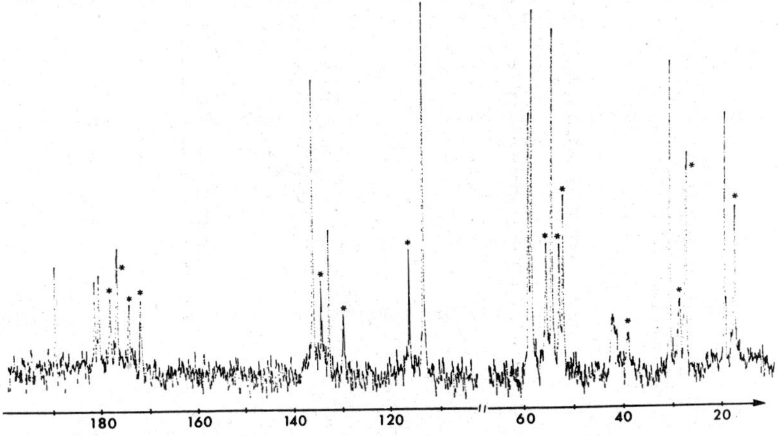

Fig. 10. 25.16 MHz ^{13}C-NMR spectrum of peptide:nickel (3/2) in D_2O at pH 7.0. Peak with * is free peptide; peak without * is nickel-peptide complex (12).

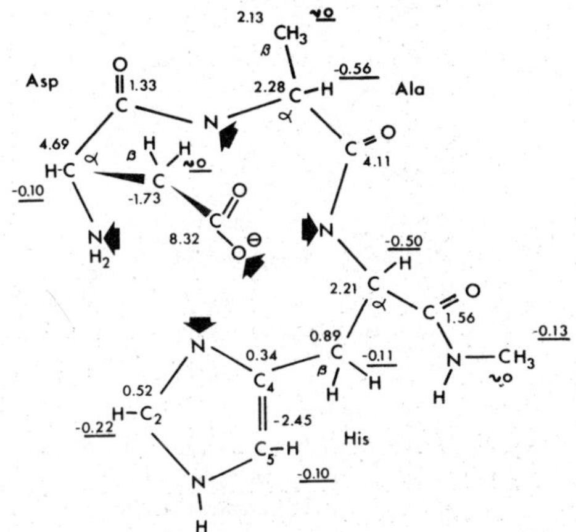

Fig. 11. Chemical shift ($\Delta = \delta_{1/1\ complex} - \delta_{free\ peptide}$) for the 1/1 peptide-nickel complex in D O at pH 9.0. Underlined numbers represent ^{1}H values and numbers without underline shows ^{13}C values in ppm. Arrows are directing to the proposed site of nickel-binding to the peptide (12).

a shielding effect (-1.73 ppm) at pH 9.1. The shielding effect could be explained in terms of spin transmission by the through-space polarization mechanism.

The introduction of nickel ion into the solution containing peptide causes profound changes in the ^{1}H-NMR spectra in the pH range 6.4 to 9.1 in 1/1 nickel:peptide solution. There are overall upfield chemical shifts for all protons. The same phenomenon has been observed for different nickel complexes with peptides (13). Many upfield chemical shifts are observed for imidazole residues C(2)H (0.22 ppm), C(5)H (0.10 ppm) and also the CH_α protons (Asp α (0.10 ppm), Ala α (0.56 ppm), His α (0.50 ppm)) all at pH 9.1. For all groups which are affected by titration, the upfield chemical shifts are more pronounced in case of complexation (Asp $CH_2\beta$, Asp CH_α, C(2)H and C(5)H) than deprotonation at pH 9.1. It appears that the pronounced upfield shifts induced by diamagnetic nickel ion result from the diamagnetic metal ion and not from the ligand involved. Most significantly, in DMSO-d_6 solution containing nickel-peptide, there is a complete disappearance of Ala and His NH protons, which confirm the coordination of these two peptide nitrogens.

Studies of spin-lattice relaxation times suggest that complexation results in a rigidification and restriction of segmental motion. The T_1 measurement shows that (1/1) nickel-peptide complex moiety is more rigid than the free peptide. Assuming that the (1/1) nickel-peptide complex tumbles isotropically, the overall results provide confirmatory evidence for the existence of a definite complex. The above results suggest that nickel forms complex with the NH_2 terminal peptide of human albumin involving the α-NH_2, N(3) imidazole and two deprotonated peptide nitrogens and the Asp COO^- group in a pentacoordinated structure as shown by the arrows in Fig. 11. Nickel complexes are commonly found to be square-planar or octahedral. However, Sacconi and coworkers (14) first reported a pentacoordinated nickel complex and since then several such complexes have been found.

The identity of the nickel-binding site of human albumin
The results show a considerable similarity in the binding properties of nickel-peptide and those of nickel-albumin. Nickel-binding to dog albumin determined by equilibrium dialysis in 0.1 M N-ethylmorpholine-HCl buffer at pH 7.5, 6°C and ionic strength 0.16 show the lack of a specific nickel-binding site apparent in human albumin. The visible spectra as a function of pH of nickel-human albumin and nickel-dog albumin are also different. It is known that the histidine in the third position of dog albumin is replaced by a tyrosine residue (15). Taking these all into account it appears that the nickel-binding site of human albumin is located at the NH_2-terminal of the protein and involves the α-amino group, two intervening peptide nitrogens, imidazole nitrogen of the third position histidine residue, and the β-carboxyl side chain of the aspartyl residue in a pentacoordinated structure as shown in Fig. 12.

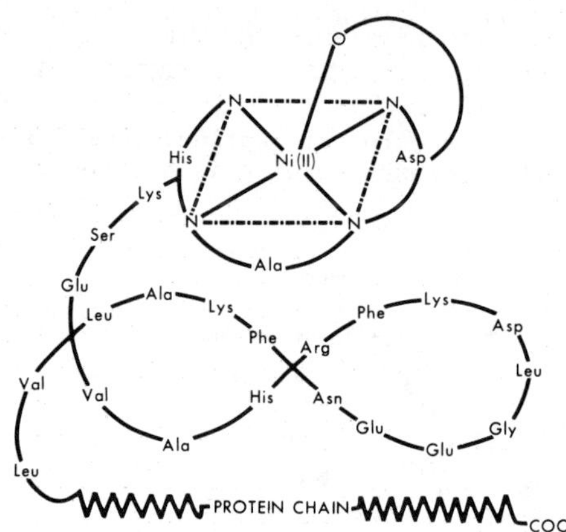

Fig. 12. Proposed structure of the nickel-binding site of human albumin.

ORGAN DISTRIBUTION OF NICKEL IN RAT

Sprague Dawley rats with an average weight of 240 g were used for these experiments. Average dose per rat was 82 μg nickel per kg body weight. Radioactive nickel ($^{63}NiCl_2$) was used as a tracer and the dose was administered intraperitoneally. After different time intervals, the rats were sacrificed and the organs were collected. Similarly, blood and urine samples were collected from each rat after the end of the specified time. For the determination of nickel, the samples were digested. It was first treated with conc. HNO_3 overnight and then conc. H_2SO_4 and 60% perchloric acid were added. The digestion was continued until a clear solution was obtained. After cooling, water and NH_4OH were added. It was then mixed with ammonium pyrrolidine-dithiocarbamate solution and shaken. The mixture was then extracted with methylisobutylketone. The extracted upper solvent layer was separated and placed into a scintillation counting vial and evaporated to dryness at 50°C under a stream of N_2 gas. The residue was decolorized with a few drops of H_2O_2 solution and acetone and was again evaporated to dryness. The residue was then dissolved in acetone and organic counting scintillation fluid. The radioactivity in the sample was measured by a Mark I Beta counter. The results are presented in Table 2. It shows clearly that the higher concentration of nickel was found in kidney and in urine.

FRACTIONATION OF NICKEL-BINDING PROTEINS FROM RAT KIDNEY HOMOGENATE

The above results suggested that there may be some proteins in kidney that bind nickel specifically. This was investigated by fractionation of rat kidney homogenate. Rats of average weight 250 g were given an intraperitoneal injection of 82 μg nickel containing $^{63}NiCl_2$/kg body weight. After six hours the animals were sacrificed and kidneys were collected. Kidneys of average weight 1.7 g were cut into small pieces and homogenized with 4 ml of solution containing 0.025 M sucrose, 0.02 M Tris-HCl buffer in a Potter-Elvehjem Teflon pellet homogenizer. The homogenate was centrifuged at 30,000 rpm for 30 min. The supernatant was then applied to a Sephadex G-50 column equilibrated with 0.02 M Tris-HCl buffer, pH 8.6. Fractions were collected at 4°C. An aliquot was taken from each fraction and mixed with 10 ml aquasol and radioactivity measured. The optical density of proteins in each fraction was determined at 280 nm. The radioactivity and the OD at 280 nm are plotted as a function of fraction numbers in Fig. 13. The results indicate there are several nickel-protein fractions; whether they are different proteins or aggregates of the same protein is not clear. The studies are continuing.

TABLE 2. Distribution of nickel in rats following intraperitoneal administration of $^{63}NiCl_2$

	Percentage dose/g wet weight of tissues		
	Time after injection		
	6 h	18 h	24 h
Heart	0.135	0.082	0.07
Kidney	3.55	1.04	1.54
Liver	0.06	-	0.04
Lung	0.20	0.132	0.09
Spleen	0.32	0.084	0.07
Muscle	0.045	0.034	0.02
	Percentage dose/ml		
Serum	0.76	0.457	0.29
Urine	5.57	4.28	-

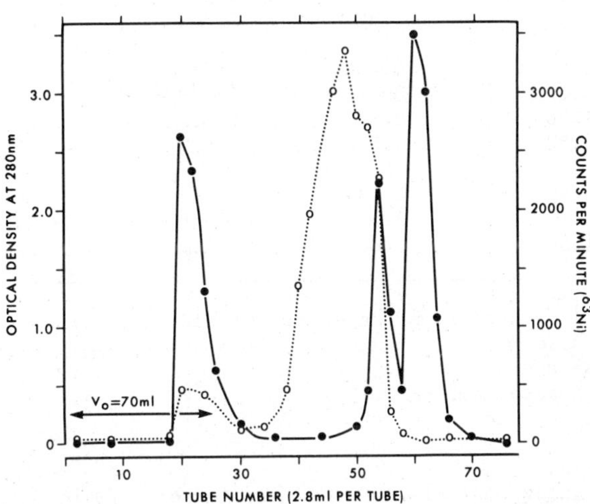

Fig. 13. Fractionation of nickel-binding protein from rat kidney homogenate by Sephadex G-50. —— OD; •••• ^{63}Ni at 280 nm.

ANTIDOTAL EFFICIENCY OF CHELATING DRUGS UPON ACUTE TOXICITY OF NICKEL IN RATS

We have studied six chelating agents for their relative effectiveness in prevention of death after a single parenteral injection of $NiCl_2$ in rats (16). Calcium disodium versenate and D-penicillamine (Pen) were included in this study since they are both used widely in clinical medicine for treatment of metal poisoning. Four other chelating drugs were examined: (a) sodium diethyldithiocarbamate, which is an antidote for nickel carbonyl poisoning in man and animals (17); (b) triethylenetetramine (Trien), an analytical reagent for nickel and copper, which has been employed as a drug for mobilization of copper in patients with Wilson's disease (18, 19); (c) reduced α-lipoic acid, a sulfhydry-containing metabolite, which has been identified as a target for metal toxicity and which has been suggested as a possible therapeutic agent in metal poisonings (20, 21); and (d) diglycyl-L-histidine-N-methylamide, a synthetic analogue of the specific binding site for nickel and copper (22, 23).

The experimental animals were female albino rats of the Fisher-344 strain with an average body weight of 175 g. In most experiments, the chelating drugs were administered by intramuscular injection in a vehicle volume of 4 ml/kg body weight. At 1 min after intramuscular injection of the chelating drugs, the rats were given an intraperitoneal or intramuscular injection of $NiCl_2$. All of the rats were observed for at least two weeks after the injection of $NiCl_2$ or chelating agent or both.

The results are summarized in Table 3. Following administration to rats by *im* injection in

TABLE 3. Effects of *im* injection of chelating drugs upon acute mortality of rats after *ip* injection of $NiCl_2$ (16)

Group	Drug	Drug Dosage[a] (mmole/kg)	NiCl Dosage (mmole/kg)	Deaths Within Two Weeks Mortality Ratio	Mortality %	Time of Deaths
A-1	None	0	0.136	62/90	69	<2h
A-2		0	0.41	69/70	99	<2h
A-3		0	0.82	20/20	100	<1h
B-1	α-LA[b]	0.68	0.136	20/30	67	<1h-1d
B-2		0.68	0.41	24/25	96	<1h-1d
C-1	Ca-EDTA[c]	0.68	0.136	8/25[h]	32	<1h
C-2		0.68	0.41	21/25	84	<1h
D-1	GGHMA[d]	0.68	0.136	0/10[h]	0	
D-2		0.68	0.41	4/10[h]	40	<1h
E-1	Na-DDC[e]	0.68	0.136	2/35[h]	6	3h-2d
E-2		0.68	0.41	25/35[h]	71	<1h-1d
E-3		1.36	0.82	20/20	100	<2h
E-4		2.72	0.82	20/20	100	<1h
E-5		4.08	0.82	20/20	100	<2h
F-1	d-Pen[f]	0.68	0.136	0/20[h]	0	
F-2		0.68	0.41	6/30[h]	20	<1h-1d
F-3		1.36	0.82	14/20[h]	70	3h-5d
F-4		6.80	0.82	0/20	0	
G-1	TETA[g]	0.68	0.136	0/25[h]	0	
G-2		0.68	0.41	0/25[h]	0	
G-3		1.36	0.82	5/20[h]	25	2h-4d

[a] Drugs injected *im* at 1 min before *ip* injection of $NiCl_2$
[b] α-Lipoic acid, reduced form
[c] Calcium disodium versenate
[d] Diglycyl-L-histidine-N-methylamide
[e] Sodium diethyldithiocarbamate
[f] d-Penicillamine-HCl
[g] Triethylenetetramine-4HCl
[h] $P < 0.001$ *vs* corresponding controls (*Groups A-1, A-2* or *A-3*) by χ^2 test

equimolar dosages, Trien and D-Pen were approximately equal in their effectiveness in preventing death from *im* injection of $NiCl_2$. Under similar experimental conditions, *im* injection of Trien was more effective than Pen in preventing death from *ip* injection of $NiCl_2$. However, this evidence of superior effectiveness of Trien over Pen was counterbalanced by the greater acute toxicity of Trien in comparison to Pen. In order of decreasing antidotal effectiveness, diglycyl-L-histidine-N-methyl amide, sodium diethyldithiocarbamate and calcium disodium versenate significantly reduced the acute mortality of rats following *ip* injection of nickel. α-Lipoic acid was not effective as an antidote for acute nickel toxicity.

STUDIES OF NICKEL-CHELATING AGENTS: TRIEN AND PEN

Trien

There is a general agreement on the formation of a 1:1 complex between nickel and Trien, but there have been some uncertainties over other species present, particularly above pH 7. The nickel-Trien system was investigated in detail by Analytical Potentiometry (24). The stability constants of the species are presented in Table 4 and the species distribution as a function of pH is shown in Fig. 14. Most of the earlier work has listed MA and MHA as being the major species. However, our species distribution shows that MA is only a major species in the pH 5.0 - 6.5 region. The species MHA is only evident in our studies as a possible species below pH 5, but must be insignificant since most of the nickel is in the form of the aquo complex below pH 5. The stability constant of the MA species is in good agreement with earlier determination. Reports of this species being the major one above pH 7 can be attributed to lack of consideration of species other than mononuclear ones.

TABLE 4. Log stability constant (β_{pqr}) of complex species $M_pH_qA_r$ (M = Ni(II), A = triethylenetetramine) in 0.15 M NaCl at 25°C (24)

Species			$\log \beta^{a}_{pqr}$
p	q	r	
1	0	1	14.34 (0.02)
1	1	1	b
1	2	1	b
1	0	2	20.64 (0.02)
1	1	2	b
1	2	2	37.28 (0.06)
2	0	3	40.05 (0.06)
2	1	3	49.20 (0.10)
2	2	3	55.02 (0.10)

^{a} Figures in parentheses are 'estimated' errors, standard deviations only ±5%.
^{b} Observed as an insignificant species.

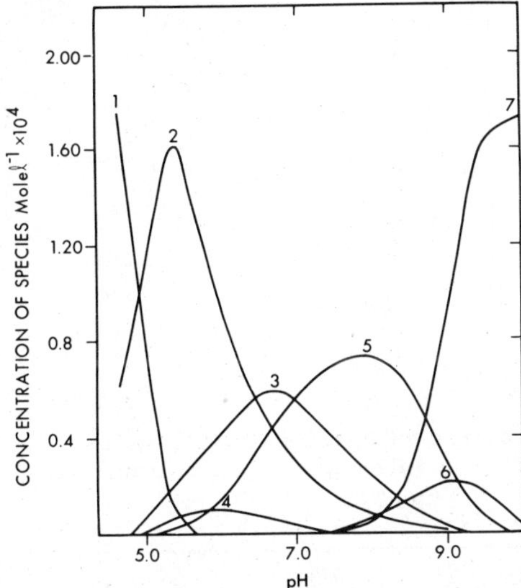

Fig. 14. Species distribution as a function of pH for nickel-triethylenetetramine solution of Ni, 2.00 x 10^{-4} M; Trien, 8.022 x 10^{-4} M; NaCl, 0.15; T = 25°C; 1, M^{2+}; 2, MA; 3, MH_2A_2; 4, $M_2H_2A_3$; 5, M_2HA_3; 6, M_2A_3; 7, MA_2 (24).

Intuitively, with nickel having six coordination sites and Trien having only four donor atoms, one would expect bis-chelated or bridged systems to form above pH 7 in the presence of excess Trien. Indeed, the formation of polymeric nickel species in which an octahedral environment is maintained is well known and is often referred to as one of the anomalies of nickel chemistry (25).

Solutions with nickel/Trien = 1:4 were used to obtain the spectra as a function of pH. The measurements were made using nickel concentrations of 1.2 - 25 x 10^{-3} M. Representative spectra showing the strong pH dependence are given in Fig. 15. Resolution of these spectra into contributions from different species was achieved using the Beer-Lambert law, eq. [1], as previously described (26):

$$A^{\lambda}_{\ell} = \sum^{i} \varepsilon_{\alpha,i}\,\ell\,[M_pH_qA_r]_i \qquad [1]$$

The ε value was determined for each species at 20 nm intervals. Spectra were resolved at pH 5.07, 7.55 and 9.52 for all species except $M_2H_2A_3$. At pH 5.07 account was taken of the substantial amount of free Ni^{2+}_{aq}. After obtaining ε values for all species except those for the species $M_2H_2A_3$ over the 300 - 800 nm range, the resolved spectrum of $M_2H_2A_3$ was then obtained from the observed spectrum at pH 6.70 using the ε values obtained for the other species. All six species gave an excellent fit to the observed spectra. The individual spectra are shown in Figs. 16 and 17.

For all the species two peaks were evident. These are as expected for octahedrally coordinated nickel ion. There is no evidence of any square-planar nickel ion. The peaks in

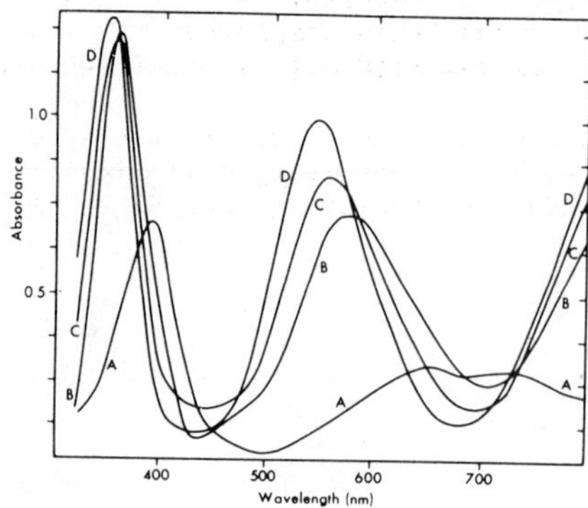

Fig. 15. Visible absorption spectra of nickel-triethylenetetramine solutions as a function of pH, Ni, 0.025 M; Trien, 0.101 M; NaCl, 0.15 M; T = 25°C, 5 cm path-length. A, pH 3.98_6; B, pH 5.07_1; C, pH 7.55_3; D, pH 9.52_3 (24).

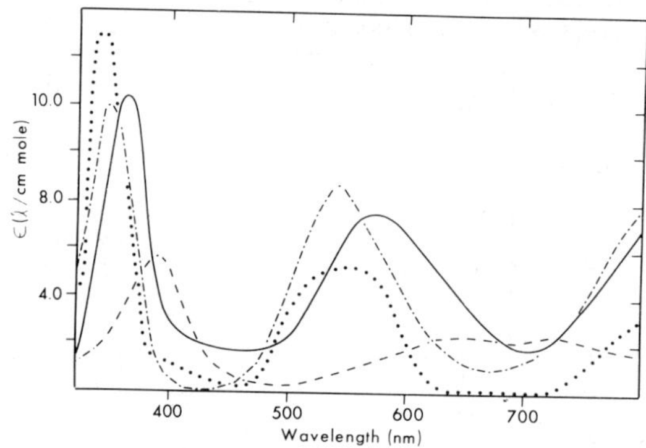

Fig. 16. Visible absorption spectra of Ni^{2+}_{aq} (observed), ----; and those of species MA, ——; MA_2 —·—·— and MH_2A_2, ···· (computed from the spectra given in Fig. 15); NaCl, 0.15 M; T = 25°C (24).

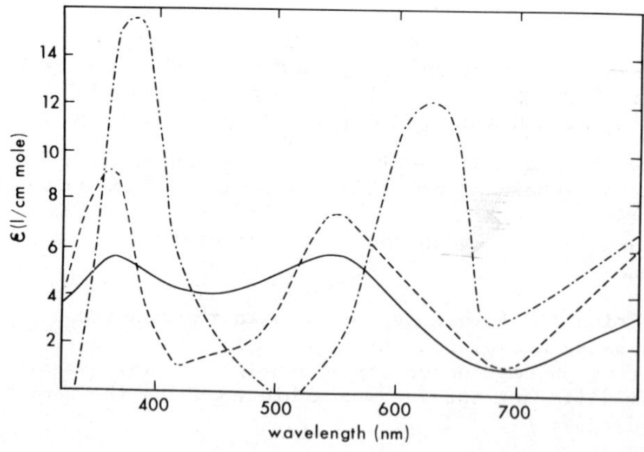

Fig. 17. Computed visible spectra of the dinuclear species M_2A_3, ——; M_2HA_3, ----; $M_2H_2A_3$, —·—·—; NaCl, 0.15 M; T = 25°C (molar extinction coefficients based on per M Ni) (24).

the 500 - 600 nm and the 340 - 360 nm regions can be assigned to $^3A_{2g} \rightarrow {}^3T_{1g}$ (F) and $^3A_{2g} \rightarrow {}^3T_{1g}$ (P) electronic transitions of octahedral symmetry. The corresponding transition for $Ni(H_2O)_6^{2+}$ are at 650 - 720 nm (doublet) and 935 nm, respectively. The occurrence of this doublet for the aquo ion and its disappearance upon replacement of H_2O with a nitrogen-donor ligand has been well documented, as also has the shift of λ_{max} to shorter wavelengths with increases in ε values as H_2O ligand are replaced by nitrogen-donor ligands. The resolved spectra show these expected features. A third d-d transition ($^3A_{2g} \rightarrow {}^3T_{2g}$) is expected above 800 nm (~900 nm for the Trien complexes). The beginning of this peak can be seen above 700 nm (the third peak for $Ni(H_2O)_6^{2+}$ is at 1,100 nm).

The resolved visible absorption spectra indicate all the species to be octahedral. The species MA must therefore have the stoichiometry $[Ni(Trien)(H_2O)_2]^{2+}$, with the possible structures shown in Fig. 18. The *cis* isomers (α and β) are likely to be the more important

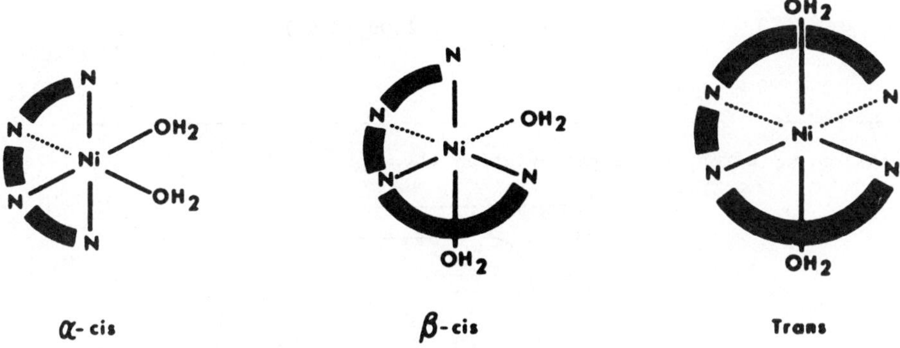

Fig. 18. Possible structures of $[Ni(Trien)(H_2O)_2]^{2+}$ (24).

structures: firstly, the Trien is less strained than in the planar configuration required for the *trans* isomer; secondly, two available *cis* coordination sites are necessary for the formation of the species MH_2A_2, MA_2 and M_2A_3 as depicted in Fig. 19. The species M_2A_3 makes

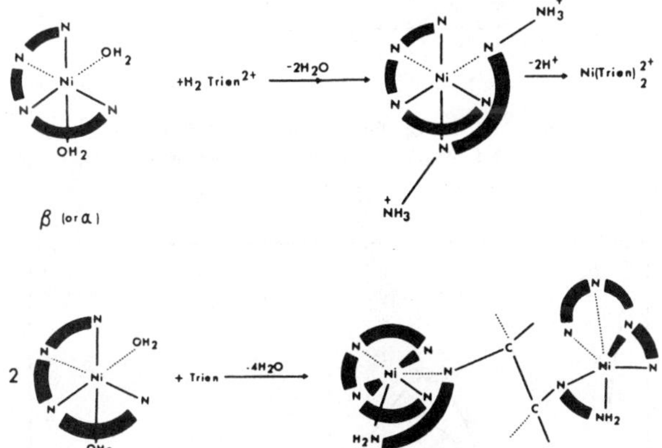

Fig. 19. Formation of MH_2A_2, MA_2, M_2A_3 (24).

maximum use of the available metal coordination sites and the available ligands donor atoms. Molecular models show that a Trien molecule can bridge the two pairs of *cis* site on adjacent $[Ni(Trien)(H_2O)_2]^{2+}$ ions, resulting in the central

$$\diagdown N{-}CH_2{-}CH_2{-}N \diagup$$

moiety being elongated and the two methylene groups having a staggered conformation with respect to each other. Formation of the species M_2HA_3 from M_2A_3 must involve protonation at a coordination site with consequent breaking of the Ni—N bond. This is consistent with the observed spectral differences between these species.

Pen

Nickel-Pen system showed the presence of just two species MA and MA_2 in the pH range 4.4 - 10.0. The stability constants obtained are shown in Table 5 and the species distribution in Fig. 20.

Consistent with the potentiometric results of a single species above pH 5.8, the visible absorption spectrum (300 - 800 nm) was found to be invariant over the range pH 5.8 - 10.0 (Fig. 21). The spectra were recorded with solutions containing a nickel:Pen ratio of 1:4 using nickel concentrations over the range 1.0×10^{-3} - 5.0×10^{-2} M. Resolution of spectra

TABLE 5. pK_a and log stability constants (β_{pqr}) of complex species $M_pH_qA_r$ (M = Ni, A = D-penicillamine) in 0.15 M NaCl at 25°C (24)

Species *p*	*q*	*r*	pK_a	log β_{pqr}
0	1	1	10.60 (0.02)[a]	
0	2	1	8.08 (0.02)	
0	3	1	1.99 (0.03)	
1	0	1		11.22 (0.02)
1	0	2		22.71 (0.01)

[a]'Estimated' error, standard deviation ±1%.

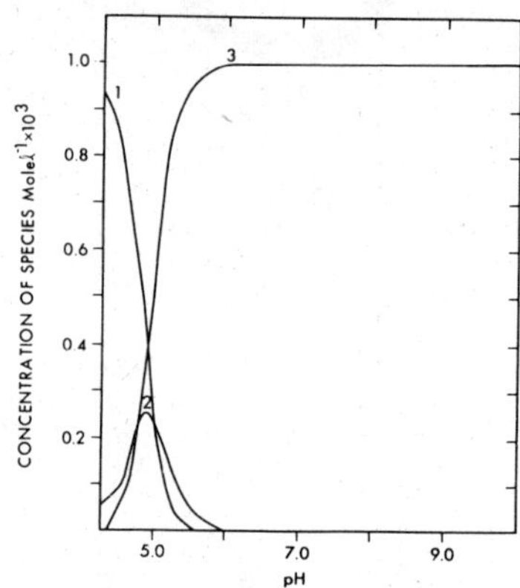

Fig. 20. Species distribution as a function of pH for nickel-D-penicillamine solution of Ni, 1.00 x 10^{-3} M; Pen, 4.00 x 10^{-3} M; NaCl, 0.15 M; T = 25°C. 1, M^{2+}; 2, MA; 3, MA_2 (24).

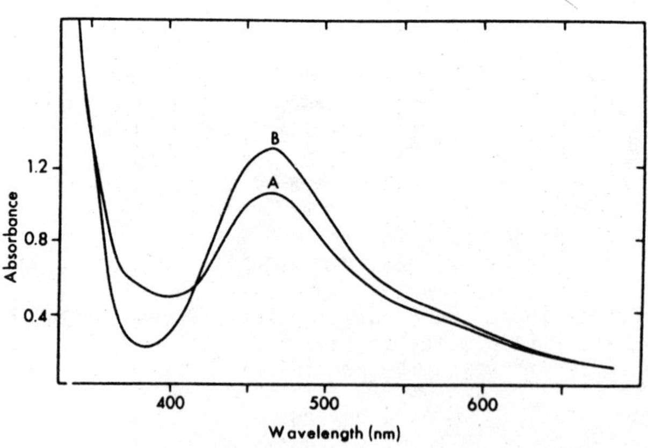

Fig. 21. Visible absorption spectra of nickel-D-penicillamine solutions as a function of pH. Ni, 0.010 M; Pen, 0.040 M; NaCl, 0.15 M; T = 25°C, 1 cm pathlength. A, pH 5.40; B, pH 5.8 - 10.0 (24).

at lower pH in order to obtain the spectrum of the 1:1 species was not attempted because this species is only formed to a minor extent. The red color of the nickel-Pen solutions and their spectra are in marked contrast to those of the blue nickel-Trien system, and suggest a square-planar configuration for $Ni(Pen)_2$. The electronic transitions are expected (27) for a square-planar nickel system: $^1A_{1g} \rightarrow {}^1A_{2g}$ in the region 660 - 430 nm (ε ~ 50 - 500 L cm^{-1} mol^{-1}), and $^1A_{1g} \rightarrow {}^1B_g$ in the region of 430 - 370 nm (ε variable). For $Ni(Pen)_2$ three transitions are evident, a very intense band below 300 nm (presumably a ligand → metal charge transfer transition), a band with a maximum absorbance at 463 ± 2 nm (ε 127), and from the asymmetry of the band at 463 nm, a further, weaker band is evident at approximately

560 nm. The latter band is tentatively assigned to the $^1A_{1g} \rightarrow {}^1A_{2g}$ transition and the band at 463 nm to the $^1A_{1g} \rightarrow {}^1B_{1g}$ transition.

L-Cysteine, which is closely related to penicillamine (penicillamine = β,β-dimethylcysteine), is a naturally occurring amino acid and an important metal-binding agent in blood serum. A comparison of the binding properties of D-penicillamine and L-cysteine with nickel is therefore important. Both form MA and MA_2 species in aqueous solution, the latter in both cases being a red, square-planar complex. The stability constants for the MA and MA_2 species are greater, by a factor of approximately 10 in each case for the Pen system, presumably reflecting the influence of the two methyl substituents adjacent to the thiol group in Pen. The methyl groups also exert a steric influence in that no polynuclear species are observed with D-Pen, in contrast to the finding of polynuclear species with L-cysteine.

EXPLANATION FOR THE ANTIDOTAL EFFICIENCY OF TRIETHYLENETETRAMINE AND D-PENICILLAMINE IN NICKEL TOXICITY

Both Pen and Trien have been found to be the most effective of a number of chelating agents in preventing nickel toxicity in rats. The results obtained so far show that these ligands are, as has been well known, very effective chelating agents for nickel, but a number of additional features are also shown to be of importance. At ratios of Trien/nickel > 1 and at the physiological pH of 7.4, Trien chelates nickel in a number of ways; i.e., as the species M_2HA_3, MA_2A_2, MA, plus the minor species M_2A_3, MA_2 and $M_2H_2A_3$. The efficiency of Trien as a therapeutic agent therefore lies in its flexibility in being able to adopt a number of configurations. In contrast, Pen, at high Pen/nickel ratios exclusively form $Ni(Pen)_2^{2-}$, this complex gains additional stability by adopting a square-planar configuration. Complexes of nickel involving Pen are also more stable than those formed with the related, naturally occurring amino acid, L-cysteine.

Acknowledgement - I wish to acknowledge the contributions made by V. Del Castillo, J. Glennon, E. Horak, S.H. Laurie, J.-P. Laussac, M. Lucassen, D.H. Prime, F.W. Sunderman, Jr., and J. O'C. Westerik. Special thanks are due to Miss Kitty Yue who patiently and carefully typed the manuscript. The research was supported by the Medical Research Council of Canada.

REFERENCES

1. M.D. McNeely, M.W. Nechay and F.W. Sunderman, Jr., Clin. Chem. 18, 992-995 (1972).
2. F.W. Sunderman, Jr., Ann. Clin. Lab. Sci. 3, 156-180 (1973).
3. E. Pedersen, A.C. Høgetveit and A. Andersen, Int. J. Cancer 12, 32-41 (1973).
4. E. Pedersen and A. Andersen, Ann. Clin. Lab. Sci. 8, 503-504 (1978).
5. J.M. Bill Nelems, J.C. McEwan, D.W. Thompson, G.R. Walker and F.G. Pearson, J. Thoracic Cardiovas. Surg. 77, 522-525 (1979).
6. M. Lucassen and B. Sarkar, J. Toxicol. & Environ. Health 5, 897-905 (1979).
7. J. O'Connor Westerik and B. Sarkar, Proc. Can. Fed. 18, 286 (1975).
8. T. Peters, Jr., and F.A. Blumenstock, J. Biol. Chem. 242, 1574-1578 (1967).
9. B. Sarkar and M.V.A. Blair, Proc. Can. Fed. 21, 29 (1978).
10. B. Sarkar, 62nd Canadian Chemical Conference, p. 39 (1979).
11. J. Glennon and B. Sarkar, 63rd Canadian Chemical Conference, p. 55 (1980).
12. J.-P. Laussac and B. Sarkar, Can. J. Chem. in press (1980).
13. M.K. Kim and A.E. Martell, J. Am. Chem. Soc. 91, 872-878 (1969).
14. L. Sacconi, P.L. Orioli and M. Di Vaira, J. Am. Chem. Soc. 87, 2059 (1965).
15. J.W. Dixon and B. Sarkar, J. Biol. Chem. 249, 5872-5877 (1974).
16. E. Horak, F.W. Sunderman, Jr., and B. Sarkar, Res. Commun. Chem. Path. & Pharmacol. 14, 153-165 (1976).
17. F.W. Sunderman, Jr., Ann. Clin. Res. 3, 182-185 (1971).
18. J.M. Walshe, Lancet 2, 1401-1402 (1969).
19. J.M. Walshe, Quart. J. Med. 42, 441-452 (1973).
20. R.R. Grunert, Arch. Biochem. Biophys. 86, 190-194 (1960).
21. M. Webb, Biochim. Biophys. Acta 89, 431-446 (1964).
22. S. Lau, T.P.A. Kruck and B. Sarkar, J. Biol. Chem. 249, 5878-5884 (1974).
23. S. Lau and B. Sarkar, Can. J. Chem. 53, 710-715 (1975).
24. S.H. Laurie, D.H. Prime and B. Sarkar, Can. J. Chem. 57, 1411-1417 (1979).
25. F.A. Cotton and R.G. Wilkinson, Advanced Inorganic Chemistry, 3rd ed., p. 894, J. Wiley and Sons (1972).
26. S.H. Laurie and B. Sarkar, J. Chem. Soc. Dalton Trans., 1822-1827 (1977).
27. A.B.P. Lever, Inorganic Spectroscopy, Elsevier (1968).

INDEX